LEGAL THRILLER

MARCUS MCGEE

PEGASUS BOOKS

ISBN 0-9673123-8-8

Comments about *Legal Thriller* and requests for additional copies, book club rates and author speaking appearances may be addressed to Marcus McGee or Pegasus Books c/o Ms. McGhee, P.O. Box 235, Neptune, New Jersey, 07754, or you can send your comments and requests via e-mail to marcus.media@yahoo.com

This is a work of fiction. The events described are imaginary, and the characters are fictitious and are not intended to represent specific living persons. Even when the settings are referred to by their true names, the incidents taking place there are entirely fictitious; the reader should not infer that the events set there ever happened.

For Bernadette, For Mark and For Natsumi

For their love
For their faith
For their goodness
For their patience

That made this work possible

DID JORDAN DO IT?

It's the story of a lurid murder in San Francisco. The case of Jordan Alexander, a socialite, would have never gone to trial if district attorney Peter Granucci hadn't been preparing to run for mayor. Granucci chooses Destiny Mitchell, a passionate young lawyer, to prosecute Jordan, the mayor's best friend, in this difficult and highly publicized case. Jordan is accused of brutally murdering his ex-wife in her Pacific Heights home. He denies any involvement and suggests his wife was murdered by black hoodlums. It is a case that no one, including Granucci, believes Destiny can win. The shocking conclusion comes 14 years later in a dramatic courtroom showdown. Disturbingly violent at times, sexy, racially-charged and full of intrigue, Legal Thriller will forever change the way readers evaluate trial and judgment.

For murder, though it have no tongue,
will speak with most miraculous organ...

William Shakespeare

LEGAL THRILLER

Marcus McGee

Legal Thriller

By
Marcus McGee

CHAPTER 1

"I hate these things! If Suzi wasn't my favorite little sister, I wouldn't be anywhere *near* this place today!"

Standing at the car, Bryan Osaka watched in admiration as the young couple bowed to proud friends and relatives. Ritual complete, they traversed a path winding through a manicured garden of low shrubbery, growth-stunted miniatures and coordinated ornamentals. Slowly, they made their way up to the elevated temple. Inside the aged redwood structure, he knew there would be a series of five 3'x 6' tightly woven tatami straw mats placed in a rectangular pattern.

There would be cushions on the far end designated for the bride and groom. An older male would be squatting off to one side, playing a traditional marriage melody on a hand-made bamboo flute.

Somewhere in the room, there would be a low table for gifts; and near the doorway, in a pit filled with glowing embers, there would be a pot with boiling water. Next to the pit, there would be a fanciful urn full of powdered tea, wooden serving utensils and cups prepared for one of the most important events of the day: the tea ceremony.

"At least they like you. You're family."

Destiny Mitchell hesitated, looking toward Bryan as she shut the steel-gray car door. Worry showed on his face as he hurried around the car and took her by the hand.

"You're family too... or you will be. Right?"

Destiny softened, smiling as she fingered the nearly two-carat radiant cut solitaire on her left ring finger.

"Sometimes I wonder. Let's just get in and out of there as soon as possible, okay?"

"You got it. In and out."

Even as Bryan and Destiny made their way up the tortuous

path, he could make out indistinct comments spoken in colloquial Japanese. He was certain one old family friend suggested he should have *left his prostitute in the street.* Another suggested he was *an embarrassment to his parents and his family.*

Bryan and Destiny weren't, after all, a couple in the traditional Japanese fashion. Bryan was handsome, and at five-nine, he was noticeably tall for an Asian-American. Although he was forty-four, his hair was still jet-black and styled. While he was *nisei,* or first-generation born in the United States, he was darker than most Japanese and Americanized.

Smiling, he took Destiny Mitchell's hand and led her out of the sun and heat to a corner of the rectangle in the box-shaped wooden structure. From the moment she knelt onto the cushion, a sea of eyes swelled in her direction. She was, after all, the only non-Japanese in the small assemblage.

Destiny Mitchell was African-American, but she insisted on being called black. She despised pomp and ceremony, though her lifestyle and career forced her to attend more than a dozen functions a month to maintain business and public relationships for the foundation.

Destiny's dark brown hair was styled short and simple. Permanently-straightened, the bangs curled to the left and hung high on her smooth brown forehead while the rest of the short hair on top was combed forward. The shorter sides were combed down. The back was a little longer, tapered and trimmed in a neat line just above her suit collars.

Her complexion and skin were creamy smooth, colored mocha brown. She wasn't tall, standing only about five foot six or seven in her highest pumps. While she looked all of twenty-two or twenty-three years old, she was actually forty-three.

She had always wanted to make a difference. It was why she became a lawyer in the first place. Yet while she considered herself practical and unimpressed by superficiality, she had a weakness for glamorous, expensive clothing. She had a weakness for fashion, her only vice, as she called it.

For Suziko's wedding and the tea party, she chose a red silk, gold-embroidered, kimono-style Halston purchased special for the occasion, with low red silk pumps and a small gold handbag. The shoes were left outside the door. Kneeling on a cushion in the gazebo, she figured she hadn't impressed many in the critical audience, yet she knew she had floored Bryan. He hadn't taken his eyes off her all afternoon.

The bride and groom knelt, the bride bowing before her mother-in-law, Hatsuki Yoshinaga of Yokohama, Japan. It would have been impossible for Hatsuki to hide signs of her immense wealth and she didn't try.

Throughout the nuptial arrangements, she treated Suziko with an air of silent contempt. Suziko, respectful of the new relationship, took the teapot from her new husband, continuing to bow while pouring first for Hatsuki, and then for father-in-law.

Hatsuki would not look at the nervous girl. Facing her husband, she studied her new daughter-in-law from the corner of her right eye. Bowing, he drank first and smiled, and Hatsuki followed, forcing a labored smile of her own. From her lap, she lifted a velvet case and presented it to Suziko. The audience sighed as Suziko opened the case and presented the necklace to guests, allowing her husband to attach the string of large pearls around her neck.

After bowing to her stern mother-in-law, she moved to the next guest.

"Oh great! After that, Suzi will think I'm a cheapskate," Bryan whispered as he squeezed Destiny's hand.

"Sssh!" she retorted. "They're staring enough as it is!"

Suziko, or Suzi, and her husband worked their way down the row of guests, first pouring tea and then accepting and presenting expensive gifts. While Suzi received jewelry and trinkets, guests presented her new husband with envelopes containing cash, documents and various other instruments that conveyed wealth or property.

Humbly, the couple stooped before cousin Mitsuko and her daughter Mary, before Bryan's parents, before Aunt Harumi from Tokyo and before Bryan and Destiny. With all the bowing going on in the room, Destiny found herself humbly bowing in kind.

Embarrassed and awkward at the tea ceremony, she gripped the sides of her dress, making a conscious effort to sit erect. She didn't want to be accused of bowing wrong or at the wrong time or to the wrong person or too little or too much. Sighing, she realized she always felt uncomfortable at ceremonies, regardless of the culture.

On the floor, Suzi bowed low and poured the tea. The tiny cup began to heat in Destiny's sweaty fingers as she watched fragments of tiny particles swirl in the golden brown liquid and the thin thread-like wisp of steam that spiraled toward her face. She recognized the aroma. Bringing the cup to her lips, she took a half sip, which confirmed the presence of lotus in the tea.

Bryan presented his gift, a thick shiny herringbone gold necklace to Suzi. She smiled, wanting to embrace him, but mindful of the ceremony, she struggled to restrain herself. Shooting a nervous sideward glance toward her trenchant mother-in-law, she smiled toward Destiny and squeezed her hand. Widening moist eyes, she mouthed silent words, which Destiny understood,

"Thank you so much for being here!"

Destiny smiled and winked before pressing the small black velvet pouch into the pretty bride's trembling hand. Suzi emptied the little sac into a ready palm and presented the gift to the other guests. Gleaming in one of the shafts of light, which filtered through the ceiling of the enclosure, it was a delicate gold pendant fashioned in intricate, stylized Japanese characters.

"Prosperity!" she announced happily.

With the last guests served tea and the final gifts presented, the bride and groom bowed to each guest again and excused themselves for a photo session over at the house. Eager to leave, Destiny tugged at Bryan's coat sleeve, motioning toward a path that would lead to a stealthy egress. Surely, she wouldn't feel so much pressure once she got to the reception in downtown San Francisco. However, Destiny wasn't the only woman in the crowd tugging for Bryan's attention.

Outside the wooden building, rows of chairs were arranged near a table with additional teapots and dishes filled with traditional Japanese snacks.

"Irasshai! Irasshai!"

Calling from a seat between two other Japanese women, Aunt Harumi from Tokyo gestured, insisting that Bryan should come over to her.

He hesitated before turning to Destiny.

"This won't take long. I promise."

Taking her hand, he started toward Harumi, but Destiny wasn't moving.

"Two minutes max. Come on," he almost begged.

Reluctantly, she followed.

If Harumi had been pretty as a young woman, any such beauty had faded from her mature form that sat there squat, dumpy and wheezing as she slurped from the ornate little teacup, a family heirloom. She had a gold ring on each short chubby finger and perhaps as many as ten gold necklaces around her sagging pock-infested neck. Her thick hair, dyed black and pulled back in a bun, was actually quite pretty.

On her left sat a younger woman who resembled her, while at her right sat a young, thin, undernourished woman who sucked at a Marlboro cigarette while tapping her left foot.

Harumi first took Bryan's hand and then pulled him close, crying on his shoulder and saying something to him in Japanese. Remembering herself, she allowed him to back away as she presented him to her daughter and daughter-in-law respectively.

After an exchange of greetings and small talk, Bryan dragged Destiny out in front of the group.

"*Destinyni aisatsushite hosii. Bokuno tsumani narunda*," he said before introducing Destiny to each of the women.

Looking over her glasses, Harumi examined Destiny in much the same manner that she inspected her farm animals at home.

"Kanojowa totemo kawii kedo, watashino oi niwa fujubunne," she said, with an air of contempt for the black woman.

Surprised by the comment, Bryan backed, saying nothing while Harumi and her cohorts, noting his displeasure, laughed to themselves.

"What did she *say*, Bryan?"

Destiny's voice had assumed her lawyerly tone. Because he knew she would insist on the truth, he decided to translate accurately.

"She says 'you are very pretty, but that you are not good enough for her nephew.'"

Destiny turned away, recomposing herself. That sow of a woman had some nerve!

Forcing an ambivalent smile, she responded to Bryan,

"Tell her that here in America we have a more *civilized* and *intelligent* way of regarding each other. Here we're all considered equals."

Pleased that Destiny had taken the insult so well, he turned to Harumi and translated the response in Japanese. Because Bryan translated the condemnatory tone of Destiny's reply so honestly, Harumi and the other two ladies seemed at once insulted.

Thus looking at Destiny, Harumi offered,

"Americano hanzairitsuno takasawa kokujinno seiyo dakara Nihonni otorunoyo."

The other ladies, seeming to express a sense of redemption

after the comment, nodded in agreement.

Destiny was quick to demand a translation.

"What did she say, Bryan?"

Backing, he hoped to diffuse the situation and suspend the inevitable conclusion.

"Uh, I don't think I want to do this. Let's just go on to the reception. Come on, please."

She hadn't budged.

"What did she *say*, Bryan?"

Looking toward smiling Harumi and then back at Destiny, he began,

"She says that, that the *blacks* are the reason for the high crime rate in America and that the *blacks* are the reason America falls behind Japan."

Once again, Destiny forced a strained smile and made a reply,

"Tell her that here in America, thinking like hers is considered small-minded and ignorant and that the only persons who speak such words are dullards and fools who don't know any better."

Hesitant, Bryan smiled, turned toward Harumi and seemed to translate Destiny's words with passion and great attention to detail. Perceiving innuendo in the response, Harumi gasped aloud and, wrinkling her brow, scowled at Destiny. Then she glowered at Bryan before shooting coarse, staccato, burning Japanese words in the audacious black woman's direction.

"Nantekoto o iuno! Antanante tadano kokujin-urionna yo!"

Bryan cringed at the sound of the words, knowing what would follow. Yet even before he could turn back to his fiancée and translate, Destiny had closed to a place directly before Harumi.

"Don't bother. I know *exactly* what she said!" And then, in louder speech, she spoke to Harumi in perfectly-intoned Japanese.

"Watashio okorasenaide! Antaga sonnani baka nanowa wakatteruwa. Sono okina oshirio ugokashite Nehonno sotono sekaio manade kurunone!"

Harumi just sat there, her mouth falling open in disbelief. She could not believe the words were coming from the mouth of a black person in America! Forgetting herself, her fingers loosened their grip on the delicate teacup just enough to let it slip, bound off her thick thigh and shatter on the cement foundation.

Other guests standing or sitting around in various locations heard Destiny's words and the tragic high-pitched crash. As all attention in the tea garden shifted to Harumi, she only raised her culpable hand to her mouth, still in shock.

The burning cigarette had dropped from her daughter-in-law's mouth, scorching the expensive red silk dress on its way to the ground. At left Harumi's daughter grunted aloud, widened eyes fixed on Destiny.

"Nihongo ga deki-masu ka?" she exclaimed. "You! You speak Japanese?"

Fixing an intense glare at Aunt Harumi from Tokyo, Destiny paused for effect and answered,

"Hai! Watashi wa Nihongo o hanashimasu!"

CHAPTER 2

Thirty minutes later, southbound traffic on the Golden Gate had slowed to a sluggish crawl across the bridge. Neither Bryan nor Destiny had spoken a word in the fifteen minutes since they hurried away from the tea ceremony. As the new Lexus idled behind a mid-size courier truck, Destiny broke the silence.

"Look, I'm sorry I lost my temper, but she called me a *black whore*!"

He only shrugged, laughing to himself as he re-lived the moment.

"Hey I don't blame you. I might have done the same thing."

He shrugged as he checked the car's mirror and then bit down on his bottom lip with his top teeth.

"Oh, on second thought, I don't think I would have told my Aunt Harumi from Tokyo she needed to get off her fat ass and see there was a world outside Japan. I might have thought it, but I wouldn't have said it."

As Destiny sat there, she found herself fighting back the tears swelling in her eyes.

"I'm sorry, Bryan, but I'm not like Suzi. I can't just bow my head and be silent. I can only put up with so much of your family's bullshit racist attitudes!"

She wanted to escape the car, to be alone for a moment, but she was in a car on a crowded bridge in traffic that was not moving. Solitude was unthinkable. She felt trapped.

"This is never going to work. 'You and I' are never going to work!"

He sighed, unemotional.

"We've been through this before. You're marrying me, not my family, so if you can't deal with it, that's up to you."

She sighed and rolled her eyes, saying nothing. The two sat in silence for another minute before Bryan laughed aloud.

"I can still see the shocked look on Aunt Harumi's face. It was actually kind of funny."

She struggled to keep from smiling.

"For you maybe, but I didn't think any of it was funny at all."

"I don't understand it. Why didn't you just tell my aunt when she first started on you that you speak Japanese?"

"It's simple. Something I learned in my years as a lawyer. It's impractical to answer a question unless..."

She had paused to build a degree of suspense. Bryan's natural curiosity, as always, provided the needed cue.

"Unless what?"

For the first time in a half-hour, she did smile. He was so predictable.

"Unless that question is asked."

Destiny began the study of Japanese when she was eleven years old. Kiyomi Yamakita, her best friend since the seventh grade, lived only two doors away. The Mitchells, like the majority of the city's blacks, lived in San Francisco's Western Addition on Divisadero between Geary Boulevard and Fulton Street.

The blacks, who came *en masse* during World War II, inherited the neighborhood from the Japanese, many of whom were ousted and sent to various detainment camps as prescribed by the State. Returning to find their neighborhoods overrun by blacks, many of the returning Japanese families decided to settle elsewhere in the city.

Hank Yamakita, Kiyomi's father, had been an exception. He loved living among the blacks, or the *kokujin*, as he called them. He liked the fried catfish, the black-eye peas, the chitlins, the sweet potato pies, the ham hocks and collard greens, the backyard barbecues, the gambling, the drinking and the *big butt black girls*. He liked it all.

He and Martin Mitchell, Destiny's father, weren't close friends, but they respected each other, and they encouraged the friendship that blossomed between their two daughters. During summers, Kiyomi would sometimes sleep over for three weeks in a row, but Destiny spent just as much time at the Yamakita's. In fact, during the summer of the girls' sophomore year, Destiny went with Kiyomi to Gifu in Japan for three months.

While Destiny never set out to learn Japanese, she just sort of picked up the language as a result of her close association with Kiyomi and her family. One of her favorite people in the world had been Kiyomi's grandmother, Reiko, whom both girls called *Obasan*. By the time she finished college, Destiny minored in the language, returned to Gifu twice and spent a month by herself in Tokyo. As Destiny spoke the language better than many of the *nisei* in San Francisco, Harumi was not the first to suffer the *kokujin*'s corresponding insults in Japanese.

After pulling into the parking lot at Tommy Toy's on Montgomery between Washington and Clay, Bryan killed the engine, sighed and turned to kiss his fiancée. He took her hand.

The hesitation, the lack of direct eye contact and general uneasiness indicated he wanted to talk about something that would be uncomfortable.

"Destiny, I've never been one to cushion anything, so I'll just say it outright."

His eyes waited for engagement.

"It's probably best that I tell you because I'm sure you'll hear about it before the day's over anyway."

Preparing herself for unfavorable news, she responded.

"What is it?"

"I have a reliable source who has indicated that there will be a press conference on Monday, and that at that press conference a woman named Karen Epps will come forward and claim she has information that will bring an end to an unsolved murder case from 1986."

Destiny understood the reference. That murder trial had been the most significant event in her forty-three years of life, an event she had never gotten over. It still haunted her dreams and her solitude. She lived and breathed that case. What could she have missed? What could this woman possibly know?

"Karen Epps? I've never even heard that name before. Who is she?"

He pulled a legal sized manila file from underneath the seat, commenting as he scanned a page inside.

"She's a nobody, really. Divorced, two kids, in jail twice for DUI. Oh, this is interesting. Somehow I didn't notice it before. Convicted of welfare fraud. Fine, no jail time. Evicted twice, moves a lot. Presently lives in a low-income housing project off Geneva and Mission Street."

Destiny spoke to herself, perplexed.

"What could she possibly know?"

Bryan answered while reading.

"Don't know, but she's got something going on. Seems pretty media savvy. I understand she's hired an agent, lawyers and even that Wilke woman's PR firm for this press conference. It's supposed to be something really big."

Elements of the episode thirteen years earlier returned to overwhelm Destiny. Epps. Karen Epps! Destiny knew more about the murder case than anyone, so why hadn't she ever heard the name? Her head reeled and ached as she re-visited the emotion and disturbing circumstances of that trial.

At once, her frustrations with a system more concerned about politics than justice returned. The disgusting hypocrisy of the mayor's office and the incestuous nature of politics in San Francisco loomed large in those memories. In the end, even Peter Granucci, the district attorney and a man she adopted as a mentor, had acquiesced to outside pressure and ambition only to abandon her.

She was lambasted daily by all the newspapers and she was criticized by colleagues on television and radio talk shows during that trial. In its aftermath, much of the blame and criticism leveled at the State and the court system in the much-publicized Alexander case was attributed to the unconventional trial strategies of lead prosecutor Destiny Mitchell.

Even the most generous among critics offered that her personal hatred for Jordan Alexander clouded her judgment and prevented her from being "the skilled and capable lawyer she could have been." They had one thing right. She hated Jordan Alexander and everything he stood for, but that wasn't the point.

She was convinced he murdered his wife in cold blood and that, because of his family's social, political and business status in the city, the system was just too beholden, cowardly and corrupt to do anything about it. They were fine with letting him walk away, unpunished.

"This Karen Epps woman, has she said anything about *how* she's going to solve the murder?"

Slipping the file between the seat and the console, Bryan answered.

"Nothing. Calls are being referred to her lawyers and press agents. No one's going to be able to talk to her until Monday. We're just going to have to wait."

Monday seemed an eternity away. Perhaps this woman really *had* stumbled onto something. Maybe she found the knife where Jordan hid it or maybe she was his secondary lover and he confessed the details of the murder to her in an unguarded moment. What did the woman know?

When Destiny felt herself getting woozy, she realized she was hyperventilating. She tried to slow her breathing, but her autonomic nervous system had taken over. She could feel one of Bryan's hands on her shoulder and the other wiping tears from her face, but she couldn't stop gasping for air.

Her vision grew blurry. Her thoughts became muddled and incoherent. She could feel her arms thrashing and extended, her hands reaching, groping for something just beyond her fingers, and then she could feel nothing more. As if dreaming, she remembered.

CHAPTER 3

August 17, 1986

The huge estate in Pacific Heights was cordoned off with yellow caution tape. It was 4 a.m., and few people in the city were aware of what would be one of the biggest news events of the decade. At 11:58 p.m. on Sunday, August 17, an unidentified man phoned the San Francisco Police Department with an anonymous tip.

"I'd like to report a murder," he said without emotion, "at the Alexander residence on Sacramento Street in Pacific Heights. There're kids in the house, so you better send someone over right away."

The dispatcher reported the call to Dennis Webber, the night commander. He told her to send a couple of patrol cars over to the house. Commander Webber was aware of the history of problems at the Alexander residence on Sacramento Street.

Over the past three years, he had dispatched units there on five or six separate occasions. As he poured another cup of coffee, he remembered the first incident, one in which Jordan allegedly tried to strangle Lynette with her own hair. And there was another time when he got mad about something and set her new Jaguar on fire.

Jordan had a temper, all right. Webber knew that. The first verbal exchange he ever had with Jordan Alexander hadn't been pleasant. Jordan was intoxicated and had just been arrested for bruising Lynette's face, apparently from slapping her. He took a swing at the arresting officer and wrestled with another before he was subdued, handcuffed and brought down to the station. But that was just the beginning.

Jordan Alexander was one of the most unpleasant detainees who had ever been at the station. It was a long and ugly night. Jordan called in his high-powered lawyers, who were rude assholes. He belittled the officers for being peons and "petty little flunkies." He even threatened to have Webber fired for being the one who made the call that authorized the patrol officers to arrest him. He was the worst, no doubt about it.

A pretty woman in uniform knocked on the open door.

"Commander Webber. Affirmative on the murder. Looks like it finally happened. Officers Walker and Price are at the Alexander house now. They say it's pretty gruesome. They want to know what they should do with the kids."

Webber flipped up the plastic cover of the Rolodex and sorted through the cards while answering.

"Well, I guess we better bring them down here until we make all the necessary notifications. Where are they now?"

"In a squadcar. Price said they were sleeping when he got there. I don't think they know."

Webber pulled the card and fumbled for his glasses.

"They'll know soon enough. Look, I want a criminologist out there right away. I want inspectors. I want a photographer. I want the collection people. On the double. No fuck-ups! We only have about six hours before this city becomes a goddamned zoo."

Satisfied that the investigation was underway, Webber picked up the receiver and dialed a number.

"Osaka? Bryan? This is Webber. I've got a special assignment for you."

Destiny counted four squad cars in front of the Eastlake-style Victorian house. The criminologist's van was also there, parked across the driveway. The property's outside lighting was off, casting the silent home in an eerie darkness. If this was a murder investigation, it was low key.

Kiyomi, who was then working as an investigative writer at the Chronicle, called Destiny an hour earlier and had asked for a special favor. Kiyomi got a tip about the murder from a source at central police headquarters and wanted an inside edge.

She hoped her friend Destiny, the brightest young lawyer in the San Francisco prosecutor's office, could gain access and provide her with the first details of the murder and the ensuing investigation.

Destiny resisted, but Kiyomi convinced her to go to the house and take a look around. She parked just beyond the corner of the next block, exited her car and walked toward the house.

The breeze from the bay was chilly that night. Clouds of vapor billowed from her face with each breath she took. Her heart pounded as she neared the dim walkway and turned the corner. Somewhere in that gigantic house looming in the gloomy darkness, was a poor dead woman, probably murdered by her husband.

But this husband was no ordinary man. He was one of the most prominent figures in San Francisco society. Rich, good-looking and charming in public, Jordan Alexander was one of the city's favorite sons.

His great, great grandfather, Thomas Alexander, amassed the family's fortunes through silver mines he owned in Nevada, and from a precious metals exchange during San Francisco's gold rush.

Through the family's diversified businesses and holdings, CEO Jordan was one of the largest contributors to citywide political campaigns, the Opera Society, various museums, foundations and business developments. The mayor was his best friend, but he was also seen out on the town with sports icons like Joe Montana, and he often named Frank Sinatra among his personal friends.

She approached the stairs.

"I'm sorry, Ma'am, but this area has been designated as a crime scene. I can't let you go any further."

The young officer was shining a large flashlight into her face. Instinctively, she opened her purse and withdrew the badge.

"Destiny Mitchell with the District Attorney's office."

The nervous rookie studied the badge in the trembling light.

"Can you wait here for just a minute, please. I've gotta clear this with the captain."

The same officer returned a few minutes later, accompanied by a tall, well-groomed man in his mid-forties who wore a long black jacket and a matching fedora. She recognized him, but she let him speak first.

"Destiny? It's four-fifteen. What are you doing here?"

Peter Granucci, the district attorney, was a guarded man who seldom ventured out in the field for any reason. Yet this matter was different. What he would do on that night and in the following few days was of extreme importance.

Young, practical and spirited, Destiny had been his favorite prosecutor since he met her six years earlier. She was at the Alexander residence for a specific purpose.

"How'd you know about this?"

He already knew the answer, and Destiny knew he knew.

"Kiyomi over at the Chronicle."

"How'd they know?"

"How else? Friends at the police department."

He shook his head, cutting a sidelong glance at the shaky officer.

"Yeah, best friends a DA ever had."

Pulling her by the hand, he draped his right arm over her shoulder and began walking with her toward the house.

"Ever seen a real-live murder close-up?"

"No."

"Eat a big dinner last night?"

"Chinese. Why?"

"You wasted your money."

Peter escorted her along a final forty-five degree bend in the walkway and up the stairs to the large double-doors in front of the house. Withdrawing two pairs of latex gloves from the left pocket of his jacket, he passed one to her and began to slip the other onto his hands. From the right pocket, he produced clear plastic bags, which he indicated were to protect the crime scene.

The last thing his office needed was two sets of misleading footprints to confuse the investigation. He gave her another bag to cover her hair.

"Now remember, don't touch anything. Don't even breathe on anything."

He reached for the over-sized brass door opener, depressed the thumb lever, pushed the door open and spoke to another edgy officer who stood guard just inside.

"This is Ms. Mitchell with my office. We'll be taking a cursory look around the place."

Standing in the white marble tiled foyer, he glanced up past the dimly lit crystal chandelier. An elaborate wooden staircase spiraled down to a large reception area.

"They through with the body up there?"

Nervous, the officer glanced toward the stairs.

"Addelberg's come down, but I think the photographer's still up there and a second medical examiner's on the way."

Peter smiled, winking at Destiny.

"You wanted to get a look at things, didn't you?"

She nodded in the affirmative. Granucci turned toward the staircase.

"Well come on. And watch your step."

Eyes fixed on her own careful footwork along the plush cream-colored carpet, Destiny noticed what seemed to be a faint bloody footprint facing in the opposite direction! And there was a second, more bloody than the first, then a third bloodier still. It seemed like so much blood, and they had only ascended halfway so far!

For a reason she could not understand, she thought of Lynette just then. She had never met Lynette formally, but she had seen her at functions around town and in interviews on television. Could this really be Lynette's blood? Lynette was such a beautiful, down-to-earth, affable woman who seemed to exude warmth and concern for others. Was this really that woman's blood smeared all along the stairs?

As Destiny slid her latex-covered hand along the lacquered white oak banister near the top, she wanted to turn and run back down the blood-soiled steps and out the house. She followed Peter nonetheless.

As a shaken, distraught photographer passed headed down the stairs, Peter pointed to a heavy, reddish-brown or rust-colored streak across the wall just outside the room. It was as if the killer had dragged his bloody hand along the wall on his way to the stairs.

There was a shoulder height asymmetrical spatter on the outside of the doorjamb, and Peter paused to examine it in better detail.

Terrified, Destiny watched Peter's face as he peered into the room. His sudden pained and distraught expression only confirmed the worst of her fears. He took her hand and pulled her through the doorway.

Nothing in her life, nothing in a hundred lifetimes could have prepared her for what she saw. Blood literally seemed to cover everything. It was spattered on the walls, on the carpet, on the nightstand with the telephone and even in places on the ceiling.

There was a bloody trail on the sheets from one side of the bed to the other and two discernible right handprints spaced about three feet apart. The orientation of the prints seemed to indicate the body rested on the other side of the bed. She cringed in horror on seeing what appeared to be a severed finger near the foot of the bed. It oozed blood onto the carpet.

Destiny tried to look away. She tried to think calming thoughts. This wasn't real, she thought. It was just a gory scene from some dreadful movie. There was no dead body, no murdered woman on the other side of the room. Yet traces of a heavy, sick odor assaulted her lungs.

Peter stepped over to the other side of the bed, dragging

her with him. Right away, she heard him groan before his body heaved and he doubled over, and suddenly she was alone in that chamber of torture.

Don't look! she thought, *Just get the hell out!* Yet even as she began to turn she was caught.

From the corner of her right eye she saw it. She tried to avert her eyes, but she saw it. From that moment on she could not look away. She felt compelled to turn toward the horror.

There it was, the poor, murdered, semi-nude bloody body of the person who had been Lynette Alexander. Lynette's state of repose resembled her earliest stage of life. She lay there in a fetal position, her terror-stricken eyes wide open. Her skin, where it was not stained with blood, was a ghastly white.

More horrific than perhaps anything else, her throat, which was slashed up to the ear on one side, had spilled and spurted blood all over the area around the body so that the carpet was reddish-brown. The puncture wounds were too numerous to assess.

She was stabbed in the cheek, in the neck and in her left breast. Her forehead was slashed, her arms had been sliced in several places and there seemed to be similar wounds on her right thigh. There were more puncture wounds in her thoracic area, probably a dozen or more. A bulge from her intestines protruded through one of the openings, spilling a dark green and brown stain onto the body and down to the carpet.

But then Destiny saw a single component of the scene she knew would haunt her contentment and solitude for the rest of her life, an image that threatened to steal the last traces of peace from her soul. One of Lynette's punctured hands, the hand missing the better parts of two fingers, seemed to rest in a position shielding her pelvic area. That's when Destiny's eyes locked on it. Lynette's pelvic/genital area had been punctured so many times that the flesh had turned to mush and the bone was exposed. A thick pool of blood had congealed on the carpet in the area just below it.

Destiny felt mildly nauseous until the smell of the punctured intestines reached her. Tears swelled into her eyes and her mouth became full of a distinctive, salty saliva. She could feel her face and neck covered with a light, unnatural perspiration. Deep down, her stomach churned and began a set of spasms that grew with each second that passed. Her body heaved, her stomach vigorously forcing its contents into her mouth, but she managed to hold it back as she rushed toward the bathroom door on the left.

Falling facedown into the toilet, she yielded to the next

violent action of her stomach, spilling what remained of last night's Kung Pao chicken on top of the curdled remnants of Peter's spinach tortellini and tenderloin of pork. Raising her head, she looked over at Peter who squatted in the corner, wiping his mouth with a segment of bathroom tissue. Her breathing was labored as she spoke.

"Jordan Alexander is one sick asshole! Whatever it takes, we've gotta nail that bastard."

CHAPTER 4

It was 4:17 when Bryan Osaka pulled up to the venerable Victorian home in the upper end of the Haight Ashbury district. He was certain of the time because it had been his habit for the past three years to reset his watch before going out on an assignment.

Taking a compact flashlight from the glove box, he double checked the address on the darkened facade and continued to drive down the street. He swung around 180 degrees and parked just beyond the corner, determining he would watch the house from there, sixty feet away.

He withdrew a ledger book and began writing notes.

No traffic, street abnormally dark due to failing lamp at mid-block, slight breeze, actually chilly, moon almost full, subject property quiet, windows dark, no cars in driveway, no cars in front of house, white convertible Jeep in front of home on left, California license plate JKZ 978, porch light and second level light on at house on right, large cream-colored BMW in driveway.

He wrote for twenty minutes before placing the ledger on the dashboard. Set-up complete, he settled into the seat and poured himself a steaming cup of cinnamon hazelnut coffee from the thermos. Some special assignment! And Webber roused him from his warm bed at 1:30 in the morning for this! The street was quiet, deserted.

Fortunately, Bryan had the *New York Times* crossword puzzle for the day, and he had just begun to fill in the boxes for 2 DOWN when he noticed the headlights in his rearview mirror.

He slid down in the seat, hoping to be clandestine as the white car rolled past him. He wasn't sure he could discern if there were one or two persons in the car. Peering over the dash, he watched the garage of the subject property open.

The white car, a 1986 Lincoln Towncar, California license plate 77 SNST, rolled up the driveway and into the garage as the door was still opening. The door closed before he could see anyone exit the car. Using a smaller flashlight for illumination, he wrote,

4:59— white Towncar approaches from intersection of Masonic, driver indiscernible, passenger(s), if any, indiscernible, driven into garage, 5:01— lights on downstairs, 5:23— tan Chevrolet from Masonic, two men exit car, knock on door, 5:27— door open, 5:35— men/detectives speak to man, do not enter.

Bryan picked up the radio and called the dispatcher,

whispering.

"Hey, did Webber send an unmarked car over here?"

The voice that answered was hard to understand through the static.

"Osaka? Maybe Webber didn't tell you, but you've been watching Jordan Alexander's house."

"I know that, but I still don't understand why I'm not over at the crime scene?"

The static grew worse. Bryan held his ear to speaker, struggling to make out the non-responsive words.

"Lynette Alexander was murdered on Sacramento Street last night and I think the commander wants to consider all the possibilities."

More static. He attempted to fine-tune the worn-out radio by increasing the gain. Bryan and some of the other inspectors had cellular phones for back up, but the technology was new, expensive and unreliable in many places around town.

He re-attached the mouthpiece to the radio unit and sipped at the lukewarm coffee again. Murder? he thought. *And Lynette Alexander of all people!* No matter what happened, this thing was going to be big.

The lights were off by the time the detectives knocked on the door. A light came on upstairs only after a second and third series of knocks. Inspectors Elliot Garner and Eddie Harris spotted the light and waited for someone to answer.

Three minutes later, a male voice called from the other side.

"Who is it?"

Garner and Harris exchanged expressions of uneasiness. At almost five thirty, it would have been better if he had just opened the door. Harris withdrew his badge, holding it up to the peephole.

"Inspectors with the San Francisco Police Department. Will you open the door, please, Sir?"

There was no answer, but after almost a minute they heard the sound of the deadbolt being released and then the sound of the door opening. A man's face appeared in the crack.

"It's five thirty in the morning. I must have called you guys seven hours ago!"

Both Garner and Harris recognized the face. It belonged to

Jordan Alexander, and it was obvious his left eye was bruised and swollen. Mindful of Jordan's well-known temper, Garner nodded and began the process.

"Mr. Alexander, would you mind if we came inside?"

Jordan seemed reluctant to open the door.

"Fellas look, it's late... or it's early. Either way, I called you at 11:30 and you finally come to wake me up in the middle of the night? Why don't you come back tomorrow?"

Harris placed a foot in the door and grabbed the handle.

"Now look, Mr. Alexander, we don't know who you called at 11:30, or why, but we're not here for that. We need you to open the door and let us in."

Jordan hated being told what to do.

"I'm afraid you're mistaken there. I don't *need* to do anything I don't want to do, especially at five thirty in the morning. Now whatever you have to say to me or ask me, you're going to do it from right where you stand."

Irritated, Harris shook his head and continued.

"Okay, if that's how you want it."

Harris was uncomfortable as he began.

"We're here to tell you that your wife was murdered earlier tonight."

Jordan's shocked expression seemed genuine.

"Lynette? You're lying. She can't be!"

As he raised his hand to his forehead and turned, Garner noticed what seemed like a scratch that ran across from a place just under his right eye to the right temple.

Jordan closed his eyes to control the sudden surge of emotion.

"You're lying! How? I just talked to her yesterday morning!"

Harris interrupted

"Your wife is dead, Mr. Alexander. We're very sorry."

"The girls!" Jordan blurted, "Are my girls okay? Where are my girls?"

"They're safe at the station. They've been asking for you."

Garner, who had worked with Harris for over eleven years, knew it was his turn to press the investigation.

"Uh, Mr. Alexander. We would really like to come in so we could sit down and ask you a few questions. The first forty-eight hours are the most crucial. If we're ever going to catch her killer, it's very important that you share as much as you can about your wife with us right away."

Jordan didn't even take the time to consider the request.

"Look, I want to help you, and I'll do whatever you ask, but right now the only thing I can think of is my poor daughters alone down there in that cold, dirty police station. If you have questions to ask, you can do it down there."

A woman's voice called out from a place in the house not far behind the door.

"Jordan? What's going on down there?"

He called over his shoulder.

"I'll tell you later. Get my clothes out. I've got to go down to the police station."

"Why?"

"Don't ask me why! Just *do* it!"

He turned back to the befuddled inspectors.

"Where'd you park? I'll follow you on over."

CHAPTER 5

Commander Webber continued to scribble on the page containing the text he would use as the basis for the official statement from the San Francisco Police Department. He wanted to take a no-nonsense approach, no false sympathy, no grandstanding, no second-guessing, and no promises of any arrest, just the facts.

Lynette Alexander was murdered, stabbed more than 40 times, the murder weapon, most likely a large single-edged knife, had not been found, there were no suspects so far, the County Medical Examiner and the District Attorney would issue separate statements.

The channel 7 News called at 5:45, and almost all the other stations and the newspapers followed within two minutes of that time. The chief scheduled a Police press conference at 8:00 a.m. and sent the public relations people over to brief Webber at thirty-minute intervals.

Rikki Thomas, who came to police public relations from the mayor's office, showed up at 6:00 sharp. Rikki was one of those women who had used her pretty face and shapely body to advance further and faster than more modest and less-endowed girls. Webber and many of the officers at SFPD knew her story from whispered rumors that flew around the department in the weeks after she was hired.

She was a UCLA graduate who arrived in San Francisco in 1983. She was married to a rich mortgage banker at the time, but she immediately became intimately involved with Mort Davies, a man who had netted over six hundred million dollars developing major shopping malls in the Bay Area. Within the year, her marriage to the banker was over and San Francisco became her permanent home.

Davies made the mistake of introducing Rikki to Anthony Martini, a friend on the County Board of Supervisors who was running for mayor in 1984. Not surprising, Rikki ran the campaign and Martini became mayor. Martini was married and a family man, so when the details of his two-year affair with his attractive campaign manager threatened to become public, he arranged for her to be transferred to another city assignment.

Rikki, confident of her ability and the mayor's vulnerability, negotiated for a high-profile job with a fat paycheck. The terms of the settlement made her head of public relations and spokesperson for the police department at an unprecedented salary.

Standing at his desk, Webber stole a look at Rikki's shapely legs as she sat and crossed them. She smiled, removed her glasses, withdrew a thin file from her soft leather briefcase and placed it on the table. She began after he sat.

"It's all right there. Apparently, Mr. Alexander called the police department last night at about 11:33 on a non-emergency line and reported he had been mugged. He also reported that his wallet, keys and his Silver Shadow Rolls Royce had been stolen."

Skeptical, Webber picked up the file and examined the first page.

"This is all a mighty big coincidence. A little funny, don't you think?"

Early on, Rikki had made her position clear.

"Not at all. Do you?"

Webber shut the file as he tried to hide growing frustration and anger.

"According to the detectives, Alexander has a bruised left eye and a scratch under his right. Another big coincidence."

"It's perfectly logical. Two guys mug him, they take his wallet and ID which still lists his old address, Lynette's address. But they don't know that. So they take his Rolls and go over to rob the house. Lynette's there, she surprises them and gets herself murdered in the process. End of story."

Webber tossed the file down and slid it in her direction.

"I don't buy it. I'll tell you how it really went down. He went over and fought with his wife, murdered her in a fit of rage, ditched the car, came home and called to say he had been mugged to cover his ass. Come on, the man has a history of beating his wife. He just went over the edge this time."

She sighed, annoyed.

"Commander, we have a press conference at eight. That's in two hours. The department and the city have a lot at stake here. I don't have to tell you, because you've been through this before. Reporters will be begging you to guess on a motive and about a suspect. Now if you even *think* to suggest such a far-fetched, irresponsible and damaging explanation like the one you just did, I'll personally serve you your balls for breakfast at nine. Just stick to the facts, Webber. Isn't that what you always say?"

Webber trembled in anger as he stood. He clinched his fists as it took all the discipline he had to refrain from launching the verbal invective he rehearsed after every other meeting he had with

Rikki. He had never hit a woman before, but one of his favorite fantasies involved slapping Rikki across the room.

He never intended to share his theory on the murder at the press conference. He knew better than that. He was sure that Rikki knew he knew better than that. Of course she did, but his suspicion about Jordan Alexander gave her just another opportunity to bust his balls, which she loved to do.

She stood and smiled, satisfied that she had unnerved the unflappable commander.

"And Dennis, get a shower and a shave before we go on. You look like shit."

"Your left eye is noticeably swollen Mr. Alexander. Would you mind explaining what happened?"

Jordan had already made necessary arrangements for the disposition of his three daughters, Caitlyn, Denver and Lyndsey, and they were already *en route* to his mother's home in Sausalito. Until they were settled and properly prepared, the girls would not be told specific facts about the murder of their mother. Jordan insisted he would provide the details to them himself when the appropriate time came.

Inspectors Garner and Harris approached him after the limousine carried the girls away, asking for an interview. Jordan hesitated, but under the circumstances, he could find no excuse for not answering their questions, so he consented, with some reluctance.

The detectives led him to a small room off a remote hallway and seated him on the other side of a well-worn table in cramped Spartan surroundings. With his right hand, he pressed on the area just below his left eye. He hadn't realized it was still so swollen and painful.

"It's like I said in the report. I was mugged last night as I was leaving the wharf after dinner. Two big black guys. I feel lucky to be alive."

Garner took careful notes while Harris asked the questions.

"You said in the report it happened at eight thirty? And no one saw it?"

He wasn't expecting an answer and moved to the next question.

"Where exactly did this mugging take place, Mr.

Alexander?"

"The wharf, in the covered parking lot next to the Vagabond Inn on Embarcadero."

Harris sat back in the chair in an attempt appear less confrontational. He forced himself to smile.

"Can you tell us what you remember about the mugging, Mr. Alexander? And try not to leave out anything no matter how insignificant it might seem. Sometimes the smallest details end up helping us the most."

Jordan was becoming apprehensive as he wondered if he should have insisted on his lawyer being present. Hesitating, he decided he would stop the proceeding if questions became too calculated and praetorian. Glancing at his watch, he began.

"I had dinner on the wharf at Alioto's with a friend of mine, Bernie Katz. You can check that with the restaurant. We finished at about eight, eight-fifteen. Had two bottles of Sangiovesse between us, a couple cognacs after dinner. He had to go pick up his daughter, but my girls were with Lynette. I had nothing to do, so I called Stephanie. She's the woman I've been dating, a model. Things have gotten pretty serious lately."

He stopped, surprised at how intently the detectives were listening and writing.

"I told Stephanie I was on my way over and left. My car was parked closer to Pier 41, so I had to walk about ten, fifteen minutes to get there. Anyway, when I got to my Rolls, there was this big black guy sitting in the back seat. When I tapped on the window, he opened the door and told me he was taking my car. I think the exact word he used was 'jacking.' Yeah, he said he was jacking my car and told me to give him my wallet, my keys and all my jewelry."

The scratch under Jordan's right eye had dried, becoming a little darker than the rest of his face. The shallow cut stung as tiny beads of sweat, popping out on his face in the stuffy room, seeped into it.

"I guess I didn't move fast enough because, unknown to me, he had a buddy who came up behind me. This guy threw me up against the car and started telling me how he was the kind of black person—*nigger* was the word he used. He said he was the kind of *nigger* who would kill me as easy as he could look at me. And then he started hitting me. That's all I remember until I woke up."

The room was silent as the inspectors, writing, caught up on the details of Jordan's narrative. Garner looked up.

"And what happened when you woke up?"

"It's in the report. I woke up in pitch darkness. I didn't know *where* I was. They threw me in a garbage bin, a big blue dumpster. I couldn't tell if I was shot or stabbed or just hurting, so I crawled out and just lied there. They took my watch, so I didn't know what time it was, but I found a quarter in the area where my car was parked and called Stephanie. It was about 11:30 by the time she picked me up and we got back to my house. That's when I called the police. I had no idea they would go over to Lynette's, but the address listed on my driver's license was hers, and I guess that's where they went."

Harris looked up.

"So your driver's license listed the address you had when you lived at *home* with your wife?"

"Yes. I hadn't changed it because I guess I thought there was still hope for us."

"Was there anything in the car listing your *present* address?"

Jordan thought for a moment and answered.

"The registration had my present address."

Tears swelled in his eyes.

"I still can't believe she's dead. We were supposed to be getting a divorce, but I still loved her, and I know she loved me."

He took a deep breath, sighed and wiped his eyes.

"I'm sorry. It's just that..."

He almost broke.

"I can't believe she's dead. We're all going to miss her so much."

Looking up from his notebook, Harris stuttered as he began.

"We're, we're sorry too, Mr. Alexander, but is that what you think? Do you think these same two black guys who stole your keys and your car then went over to Lynette's house and murdered her?"

Jordan was careful in his reply.

"Well, when you said she was murdered I just kind of put two and two together and really kind of assumed it was the same two black guys."

"Did anyone here at the police department tell you what actually might have happened? Did you discuss the murder with anyone?"

Jordan stood, glancing toward the door.

"Look, I've got a lot of things to do today. It looks like I'll have to make funeral arrangements for my wife among other things. We'll have to continue this discussion some other time."

Garner stood, insistent.

"Can you answer the question? Did you discuss it with anyone here at the police department?"

Jordan deliberated for a moment and answered.

"Rikki Thomas, briefly. Why?"

"Just wondering. One more question. What kind of clothing were you wearing at Alioto's and at your car last night?"

Jordan answered as he walked around the table and toward the door.

"Dark blue Hugo Boss, subtle pinstripe."

Inspector Eddie Harris stood as Jordan pulled open the door.

"I have one more question for you, too, Mr. Alexander."

Jordan stopped to listen to the inspector, though he did not turn around.

"Just for the record, Jordan. Did you murder your wife?"

Jordan turned, his blue eyes flashing with equal parts pain, contempt and anger, answering as best he could.

"Fuck you!"

The small room vibrated with the sound of the door being slammed. Garner and Harris just stood there, wondering what to think about the man who just left and the story he told.

Garner shrugged.

"Do you think it happened the way he said? Do you think he was telling us the truth?"

Harris, seeming perplexed, wagged his head and sighed.

"Either Jordan Alexander's telling the truth or he's the most convincing liar I've ever come across in all my life."

It was three minutes after seven when Bryan left his car and approached the Victorian -style home, sixty feet away. He had his apprehensions about the plan, but he was determined to go through with it. Walking in the brisk morning air, he hustled up the steps and knocked on the door. After a few moments, he knocked again. He waited a minute and knocked once more.

"Who is it?"

He held up the badge.

"Inspector Osaka with the San Francisco Police Department. Can you open the door please, ma'am?"

The door opened, though not very wide.

"Ma'am, I'm not sure if you've been informed, but Lynette Alexander was *murdered* last night, possibly by two black males who mugged Mr. Alexander and stole his keys and car."

The door opened wider and a very pretty face appeared.

"I heard about it."

"Ma'am, we found Jordan Alexander's car in Golden Gate Park at about six this morning, but we have reason to believe the men who murdered Lynette Alexander might be headed to this residence next. They know the address and, as far as we know, they still have the keys for access."

Stephanie Rodriguez stepped outside, nervous, glancing back over her shoulder. She wore only a long tee shirt, since Bryan's knocking had startled her up from bed. Stephanie was tall and thin, but she was shapely. She had come to San Francisco from nearby Modesto to work as a model and found more than enough work to pay the bills lately.

Stephanie wasn't imperceptive, though at 21 years old she was gullible. It hadn't taken much for Bryan to spook her about the possibility of danger.

"Is there much space behind the house? Maybe an area back there where a person might hide?"

By that time, she had ventured to the front of the porch, unsettled with the thought of the murder. At once noticing the nipples of her un-harnessed breasts were protruding through the shirt, she crossed her arms, embarrassed.

"There's a small backyard, but I've never been out there."

"Have you heard anything in the past couple of hours?"

She sat on the ledge, pulling down the shirt and crossing her legs to cover her naked crotch area.

"No, but I've been knocked out. It was a long night for me."

"Mind if I take a look back there?"

She smiled, grateful.

"It would make me feel better if you wouldn't mind."

Leaving her on the chilly porch, Bryan walked down the stairs and opened the gate that led to the backyard.

"You don't have to wait. I won't be long."

Stephanie eyed the open door and turned back toward the inspector.

"It's a big house and I'm a little scared about what

happened. I think I'll just wait out here till you come back."

"If that's what you want."

Bryan trotted back up the stairs and stopped next to her. He removed his soft brown leather jacket and draped it over Stephanie's shivering shoulders. She smiled in appreciation and pulled the body-warmed jacket around her raised knees.

"Thanks."

"Back in a few."

She stared at empty space at the open door after Bryan disappeared through the gate.

Sunday had been a weird, highly unusual and overall kind of creepy day all around. Jordan called her early that morning, telling her he was finally ready to move on, that he was finally ready to put his bad marriage behind him. But then, he stood her up for a promised brunch date at the Crown Plaza Restaurant in the Fairmont Hotel, calling to apologize only as she was passing the front desk on her way out.

The next time he called, he seemed sad and troubled as he canceled dinner plans at the Carnelian Room on the top floor of the Bank of America building. He said he and good friend Bernard Katz had important business to discuss. So while she was thrilled he had indicated he was ready to make more of a commitment to her, she couldn't help wondering about how honest he was being with himself.

And when Sunday night, Jordan phoned her and told her he was coming over but never showed, Stephanie was certain he had gone to see Lynette.

She discovered later she was wrong. He hadn't gone to Lynette's at all. When he called her at 10:45, wild and confused and begging her to come pick him up, he said he'd been mugged on the way to his car. He said two big black guys grabbed him, beat him up and hijacked the Rolls. Then they blindfolded him, tied him up and drove him to a remote location.

According to Jordan, the men stopped along a foggy road, leaving him in the car wondering when and how they were going to kill him. They even joked about it. He said it was so upsetting and stressful that he soiled his pants. Then they drove him to Golden Gate Park where they untied him, ditched him and drove off. They were real nasty criminals who warned him that if he said anything to anyone, they'd find his wife and daughters, rape them and kill them.

When Stephanie picked him up at the park, he begged her not to tell anyone. He told her that if anyone asked, she was to say she picked him up near the wharf. Once the men were caught and his daughters were safe, he promised, then he'd come out with the truth.

Until that time, he and Stephanie would stick to the story that he was mugged and thrown in the garbage bin. That night, after Stephanie picked him up and they got to his house, he showed her a heavy, bundled package that felt like some kind of cushion or padding wrapped around a brick. He told her he was over Lynette, that the parcel contained all the letters and personal effects she had given him.

Per instructions from his counselor, in order to move on with his life, he had to get rid of all the things that made him miss and long for his wife, all the vestiges of his life with her. That was why Stephanie drove that "bundle of failed promises and dreams" onto the Golden Gate and tossed it over the side.

She wasn't certain why he insisted, but he made her promise never to tell anyone about the package. She didn't hesitate to promise because she was happy to be rid of Lynette, but then the news came about her death. It was horrible. Lynette wasn't one of Stephanie's favorite people, but no one deserved to be murdered.

It was after 5:15 a.m. when Stephanie crawled into bed next to Jordan, only to have Jordan awakened minutes later by detectives and shocked by the news of the murder. She tried to sleep after he left and had just begun to doze off when Bryan Osaka started his insistent knocking downstairs.

Only then, as she sat on the porch with Bryan's jacket wrapped around her, did she wonder if Jordan could in any way be involved in the murder. It was a passing thought, but she dismissed it as she observed Bryan coming up the stairs.

"See anything back there?"

"No... I mean, actually there were a couple of broken bushes and some faint footprints, but those could have been made days ago. There's a meter back there."

He glanced toward the open front door.

"Hey, you mind if I get a look inside? From what I've been told, these guys have keys to the house. They could have gotten in through the back door."

While she tried to evince calmness, her face showed concern.

"Do you think that's possible?"

"You never know. Depends on if you want to take that chance. Anyway, my job's done here. If there's nothing else, I'll just be going."

When he attempted to ease the jacket from her shoulders, she resisted.

"Uh, Inspector?"

"What is it?"

"I'm not sure if I want to go back in there. Okay. You can go in and check, but please try to get in and out before Jordan gets back. Something tells me he wouldn't want you inside without his permission."

Bryan smiled as he adjusted leather jacket around her neck.

"Don't worry. Chances are Mr. Alexander will never even know I was here."

The interior of the home was elegant and immaculate, owing to the efforts of a zealous housekeeper. Standing at the entrance, Bryan scanned the floor area and the walls. Nothing suspicious so far. As Stephanie approached from behind, he spotted a doorway on the left and walked toward it.

"Is this the way to the back door?"

"Uh yeah, right through the kitchen there."

First he examined the door, opening and shutting it, and then, putting on his glasses, he checked for fingerprints and footprints. There was no sign of a forced entry.

"You have an excellent alarm system here. Make sure you set it after I leave."

Walking to the pantry door, he pulled it open, turned on the light and scanned the inside.

Coming out, he examined another doorway.

"Where does that lead to?"

"Dining room."

Within ten minutes, Bryan had inspected the entire downstairs area. Returning to the huge entranceway, he glanced toward the stairs.

"I should probably check up there just to be sure."

"Yeah, I think you should."

Smiling, he ascended the stairs on the right, with Stephanie following close behind.

"Where is Mr. Alexander's room?"

"To your left."

For the first time since he arrived, Bryan drew his gun. Flicking lights on before him, he approached the room and pushed open the door. A huge raised brass bed sat against the far wall, perhaps thirty feet away. It was covered with an elaborate colored comforter that matched the wallpaper and drapes. The plush carpet was eggshell white, and it seemed and smelled new.

A glossy mahogany desk sat on the right side of the room next to the window. On it sat four pictures: three studio-quality portraits of young girls ranging from perhaps eight to fourteen, and one of a beautiful seductive blonde wearing only a teddy and a mischievous smile. A delicately designed black and gold oriental screen stood along most of the opposite wall. Further left was the closet door.

Bryan moved toward the closet, scanning the carpet and walls as he moved. He opened the door and peered inside, sighing to himself. The space was almost as large as the bedroom in his apartment.

The three racks of expensive designer suits toward the end were more impressive than any three he had ever seen at Macy's. Equally impressive was the motor-driven rack of suits, slacks and shirts overhead. Touching a button, he watched a pair of tan snakeskin shoes on a lower rack rising toward him. He examined the carpet and walls, noticing nothing out of the ordinary.

He had almost given up when, coming out of the closet, he noticed distinct reddish-brown staining on the left side of the bed. Looking closer, he thought he could make out footprints that led toward the far side of the screen. Dropping to his knees in order to get a good look, he crawled along the screen and around the corner.

Finally, when he rose to his feet, he found himself looking at something of major significance, something that should not have been where it was on that morning in particular. He removed his glasses to get a better view. Bryan's heart pounded as he knew he had just discovered what would be perhaps the most important piece of evidence in what might be the biggest criminal case in San Francisco's recent history.

There, plastered against the screen wall, was a small lock of blond hair. It was pasted there, attached to the screen in a brownish substance that could have been partially dried blood! He gasped aloud upon seeing it.

Stephanie, on the other side of the room, screamed on hearing his reaction. She was certain some person behind the screen had stabbed him.

"Inspector?"

He staggered out into the open, nearly out of breath. He had never been so excited in his life.

"Inspector! Are you all right?"

"I'm fine. The phone! I need a phone!"

She rushed over to the telephone set, grabbed it and shoved it toward him. Slamming the receiver to his ear, he dialed the numbers. The response on the other end was immediate.

"Yeah, Commander Webber, I think I've got something!"

His excited voice continued after a brief pause.

"It's blonde hair and something that looks like blood. I'm *sure* it's blood! Call your judge! We need a warrant yesterday!"

CHAPTER 6

Destiny, along with eight other prosecutors, sat at the long, timeworn table in the conference room. She feigned nonchalance, but her clenched hands belied the stress and despair that had resulted from viewing Lynette's battered and ravaged body, blood trickling from so many wounds. At one time, Destiny's eyes swelled with tears she struggled to fight back by batting her eyes.

The other lawyers bantered about the murder and speculated about whom Jordan would hire for his defense. Most of them agreed. It would be the notorious Barry Alexander Divine, Jordan's own cousin, one of the best in the business. But who in the District Attorney's office would be given the task to prosecute the case?

Ted Waters, an older white male seated on the far right end, hinted that whoever was put on this case would be able to write his own ticket when it was over, not to mention inevitable offers he would get from book publishers. Ted, the most senior prosecutor at the table, had been with the District Attorney's office for 28 years. It became clear early on that he saw himself as the most logical choice.

It was evident Janice Prescott wanted the job. She was also older, in her fifties. The self-proclaimed grandmother of the squad had been with the office for 12 years. And while she was the shrewdest and most resourceful lawyer in the office, her inattention to what she called "the irrelevancies of clothing, shoes, styles and coordination" worked against her. Though she argued well, she came across to juries as old, out of touch and just plain frumpy.

Brett McPherson, seated across from Destiny, was no slouch either. Just a week earlier, he received an attractive job offer from the city's largest law firm. Gail Friedman, on Destiny's left, had lost only one case in fourteen. In fact, the nine lawyers assembled in the conference room that morning were the best nine murder case prosecutors the District Attorney's office had to offer. This was the elite team selected to handle the Lynette Alexander matter.

Peter Granucci convened the meeting for the purpose of determining a procedural strategy and for planning his press conference. Pursuant to the conference, he would assign two prosecutors from the nine to pursue the case. One would act as lead counsel, and another would be named co-counsel.

The rest of the group would contribute to the investigation and the substantial workload. They would be called upon to file and argue motions, to prepare briefs and written arguments and for other assistance during the trial as directed by the attorney in charge.

But who would Granucci name to handle this volatile political and high profile case? Ted Waters was the consensus choice, but over the years Peter Granucci hadn't garnered a reputation for making practical decisions. In fact, he was better known for occasional incidents of flippancy.

All second-guessing aside, Peter was late as usual. As the clock over the whiteboard neared eight, the attorneys made fewer and fewer comments, each awaiting the initial fact pattern that would come from the police press conference.

Brett pointed the remote control toward the television set resting on the tall cart and clicked. The shift of focus in the room was instantaneous. On the screen was reticent Commander Webber of the San Francisco Police Department, standing next to a pretty brunette who dominated the scene and who disseminated sketchy details surrounding the murder.

Lynette Alexander's death was the result of a vicious, brutal and intentional act, but there was no murder weapon and there seemed to be no recognizable motive. Lynette had no known enemies and had spent the years since the separation helping battered women and raising money for various charitable women's causes in the city.

Rikki Thomas, the attractive police spokesperson, made it a point to say the police were not considering anyone as a suspect at the present time. Nonetheless, she promised that the department would use its vast resources to solve the crime and bring the killer or killers to justice.

Dennis Webber stood, appearing vexed during the entire fifteen or so minutes Rikki dominated the microphone, and he came forward only after reporters began firing blunt, penetrating questions.

Kiyomi Yamakita was the first to press the issue.

"Commander Webber, you've been investigating murders for years. In the absence of any other, isn't the husband always the first and primary suspect?"

Webber shrugged before clearing his throat and answering.

"That is often the case, but it's too early to speculate on that now. I believe Ms. Thomas here said that we haven't as of yet considered any person a suspect. I think we need to add that we haven't eliminated anyone either. Next question."

A pale, thin, effeminate male from the *Examiner* rose and began in a weak, unsteady voice.

"Until this time, has anyone with the department interviewed Mr. Alexander? Has he established where he was and what he was doing at the time his wife Lynette was murdered?"

Rikki broke in before Webber could answer.

"We've found no reason to interview Mr. Alexander up to this point. The man loved his wife and is understandably upset and shaken. As for what he was doing—he was having dinner with a friend at Alioto's when his wife was killed. It's a terrible tragedy."

She sighed, her voice reproachful.

"Instead of this unfounded suspicion, which some of you might find expedient and sensational for the time being, Jordan and his three lovely daughters deserve our heartfelt prayers and condolences. By refraining from exploiting this tragic event, you might lose a convenient source of lurid fiction for your front pages and gossip columns. But stop for a moment and remember, Jordan and his daughters have lost a cherished wife and mother. Show some compassion for a change. Next question, please."

The man who rose seemed more a carnival ride operator than a reporter.

"Is there any truth to a story told by Alexander himself that he'd been robbed by black gang members who stole his car and may have murdered his wife?"

Rikki refused to yield the microphone.

"As we said before, our investigation is just getting underway. We're pursuing all possible leads, but we're not going to get all caught up in wild speculation and rumor at this point."

Another reporter rose uncalled, and clamored out.

"It's common knowledge that Jordan Alexander beat his wife on several occasions. Isn't this murder just the result of another one of those beating sessions gone berserk?"

She only glared and rolled her eyes.

"Next question."

Still another voice shouted,

"Do you expect a full confession from Mr. Alexander? Isn't that what you met with him about?"

Rikki looked toward Webber and turned back to the

reporters with a disapproving glance.

"Ladies and Gentlemen, it seems we're going nowhere with this line of questioning."

Kiyomi's voice interrupted hers.

"Ms. Thomas, as spokesperson for the department, aren't you aware that not more than ten minutes ago, a search warrant was issued for Jordan Alexander's residence and that detectives are over there right now?"

Rikki scowled at Webber, took a deep breath and addressed Kiyomi.

"Ms. Yamakita, you of all people ought to know better. There's been no warrant. You simply don't know what you're talking about."

She sneered at the reporter.

"Even if what you're suggesting was true, how would you possibly know?"

Confident, Kiyomi retorted.

"It's true. I've checked my facts and I have details of undisclosed discovery and a copy of the warrant from a close and reliable source. I'm just surprised you didn't know."

Rikki was beginning to turn red. She glanced toward the cameras and whispered to her partner on stage.

"Did you know about this?"

Webber feigned mild confusion.

"Not about the warrant. All I heard was that a detective found something in the house."

Turning back toward the reporters and cameras, Rikki recovered.

"As we told you earlier, this story is evolving fairly rapidly, and this happens to be one of those evident occasions in which a major development has taken place even during the few moments that we've been here briefing you."

She forced a stern smile as she sought a comfortable conclusion.

"The San Francisco Police Department will make every effort to keep you informed on future developments at other briefings throughout the day, but until we provide you with better detail, we strongly urge you not to speculate, make inferences or draw conclusions from information which may or may not be reliable."

She stopped, her eyes glimpsing toward Kiyomi as she

exited the room.

"The murder of Lynette Alexander is a horrible tragedy for all of us. The killer or killers must be brought to swift and certain justice commensurate with the crime, but none of us can afford a rush to judgment. The ongoing investigation into Lynette Alexander's murder would be compromised by a rush to judgment on *anyone*'s part."

She paused to take a breath. Looking toward the cameras, she pursed her lips and finished.

"So ladies and gentlemen, when you write your stories and broadcast your reports, I know it'll be difficult, but try to restrain yourselves a little so that you're not running ahead of and in the way of the investigation. Refrain from all the sensationalism, the wild plots, the sub-plots, the UFO involvement, the psychic connections. Leave those for the tabloid press. You have my promise that we'll give you all the facts in great detail as we ascertain them. There will be another briefing at one this afternoon. Thanks for coming."

Television coverage cut to the news desk where a reporter confirmed that a search warrant had indeed been issued for Jordan's Haight Ashbury residence. The details were sketchy, but it seemed a detective had discovered blood and blond hair attached to a wall during an unofficial survey of the premises. He added that Jordan's young girlfriend requested the inspection. The reporter's voice continued as cameras cut to the exterior of the home, partitioned off with the wide yellow *POLICE LINE DO NOT CROSS* tape.

By that time, it was close to eight-thirty. The street, all the way back up to Masonic, was lined with news vans and various cars on both sides. Traffic had come to a dead stop in the middle of the block, about thirty feet from the house. A large crowd, growing by the minute, had assembled on the sidewalk and street in front of the house.

Many of the people were neighbors, but countless others had come across town to witness all the excitement of the lurid story close-up. Yet if the commotion in front of Jordan's house seemed overwhelming, it appeared small compared to what was happening outside Lynette's residence.

There were at least seven or eight camera crews scurrying

up and down the sidewalk from one place to another. They were interviewing neighbors, domestic workers and even first graders. A throng of vigorous hard copy reporters stood outside the tape barrier, calling out pointed questions to the uniformed officers and detectives as they entered and exited the house.

There were hundreds of people scattered along the street. Helicopters and small engine airplanes flew overhead, capturing the larger images and the scope of the scene for viewers at homes all across the country.

The narrator's voice was hurried and excited as he described the reaction from horrified neighbors and the brutal nature of the murder. He and the local news anchor speculated about whether or not Jordan Alexander would be arrested before the day was over.

Though the newscast was riveting enough to engross the nine attorneys sitting at the table, the station found it necessary to cut away for a commercial break. That's when Brett, in control of the remote, killed the broadcast by turning off the television set.

Destiny, along with six other embarrassed lawyers sitting there, looked across the table to see that only Ted Waters and Janice Prescott had been taking notes. It was becoming clear that Ted and Janice were to be the chief prosecution team.

Egos aside, they were the most experienced lawyers in the office. Ted could be a blowhard know-it-all sometimes, and Janice was outright sloppy on occasion, but both were confident, competent and professional. Because both were older and had more knowledge than Peter, the district attorney, they often questioned his judgments and would often lend unrequested advice on policy and leadership.

Though Peter Granucci liked both, as he began to consider the possibilities of a higher office, he became concerned he'd be perceived as a subordinate rather than a leader in his own office. He knew some city officials and judges considered Ted Waters to be the de facto district attorney.

It was 9:15. After District Attorney Peter Granucci was ninety minutes late, the lawyers, one by one, began excusing themselves. Gail Friedman stepped out to take a phone call and never returned. Brett explained he had a meeting with the FBI at 9:45. Hector Aguirre had to be in court at 10:00, and so it went until two attorneys remained, Ted Waters and Destiny Mitchell.

Ted cleared his throat and began.

"Destiny, I heard you were out at Lynette Alexander's with Peter last night."

"You heard right. I was out there."

Subtlety had never been one of Ted's outstanding qualities.

"Look, I'm not saying it's going to happen, but if it does, I want you to know where I stand."

"What are you talking about, Ted?"

He was standing over her.

"If Peter chooses you as lead prosecutor in this case, tell him you don't feel qualified for the job. You're young, inexperienced and you wouldn't be credible to a jury. Just tell him the only person in the office capable of handling and winning a case like this one is me."

She smiled for the first time since leaving the murder scene. It wasn't because she thought Ted's suggestion was funny. Rather, it was because he had the shameless temerity to offer it. She smiled because she knew Ted, for all his affected invulnerability, for all his experience and confidence, had for the first time in the seven years she knew him, allowed an insecurity to betray his pride. For the last two years she suspected that Ted felt threatened by her growing success in the office. Now she knew it. Standing to assume equal ground with him, she answered.

"I don't care who gets the case, Ted. You, Janice, Hector. It doesn't matter. I just want to make sure Jordan Alexander pays for what he did to his wife."

CHAPTER 7

"You stupid little *bitch*! You have no idea what you've done to me! You've ruined my life!"

Though Jordan spoke in a hushed tone, the ire and violence in his voice was unmistakable. He was still at the police station when he saw detectives rummaging in and around his home on the television monitor.

So incensed then that he could barely breathe, he called up his cousin, Barry Divine, for immediate advice. From the looks of things, the detectives were in his house illegally. He had told them on two separate instances that morning he did not want them to come into the house. For some suspicious reason, they were insistent about getting inside, but he had denied them.

And not three hours later they had cordoned off the house and were involved in what amounted to a microscopic inspection of the place. It was a flagrant abridgment of his constitutional rights guaranteed by the Fourth Amendment! Some gung-ho cop was going to lose his job for this!

"We'll deal with that later," Barry advised, "But right now you need to get over there and demand that they pack up and leave. Don't let them take anything. I'll meet you there."

Jordan hung the phone and sprinted to his convertible Testarosa. Ignoring speed limits, lights and stop signs, he weaved through the waning morning commute with adrenaline-aided precision. He saw the sea of onlookers only after he whipped around the corner from Masonic onto his street.

On recognizing him, the masses out front focused on his approach. The crowd parted so Jordan could drive right up to his house, and he hopped over the driver's side door without opening it.

Walking up the walkway, he grabbed the yellow caution tape and pulled, stretching it to the point of tearing it. Balling up the tape in his hands, he deposited it next to the front door. The officer at the barrier let Jordan pass, never looking at him, but he told three bold observers to back up when they tried to follow.

Jordan was shouting as he slammed the front door shut behind him.

"Get the hell out of my house! All of you! Get the hell out! And I mean now!"

Desmond Collins, the intern criminologist, happened to be

in the wrong position at the wrong time. He was on his hands and knees testing a stain for the presence of blood when Jordan exploded into the house. Jordan walked over and kicked him in the rump so hard that Desmond was airborne before crashing into a wooden newspaper caddie. That action brought officers from all quarters of the house. They pinned Jordan to a wall, restraining him.

Face darkened by anger, Jordan shouted, choking.

"I want all of you out! You have no business here!"

He fought to free himself, but the two officers held him.

"Who's in charge here?"

A middle-aged, overweight, balding man stepped into Jordan's field of vision.

"I am, Mr. Alexander."

He spoke to the two officers.

"You can let him go. I'll take it from here."

At once released, Jordan closed on the stout man.

"Who are *you*, Fatboy?"

"Lieutenant Trevor Allenby, and if you do anything else to interfere with this investigation, I'll have you handcuffed and arrested. You got that, Asshole?"

Jordan eyed the pudgy-jawed man before remembering what Barry advised.

"Searching my home without my permission or a warrant is a violation of my Fourth Amendment rights. I'm ordering all of you out of my house, now!"

Allenby grunted, clearing his throat, and opened the metal legal file held in his left hand. He withdrew a crumpled sheet of paper, handing it to Jordan.

"Judge issued us a search warrant this morning."

Jordan studied the document in disbelief before coming to the purported cause:

> *...in an examination of the premises as requested by occupant, a police detective found what appeared to be blood stains on carpet and a dime-sized blood smear on the wall that appeared to be sticky. There was also a mass blond hairs that could have come from Mrs. Alexander.*

Jordan crumpled the warrant in his hands.

"As I'm sure you're aware, Mayor Martini and Chief McGuire are close personal friends, and you guys are going to pay for this! That whole warrant is based on a lie! I never requested any examination of my house. I specifically told your detectives they *couldn't* come in."

Lieutenant Allenby still stood there, unflinching.

"If you read further down, Mr. Alexander, you'll realize Inspector Osaka *was* requested to come in and inspect the place. I believe the woman's name there was Stephanie Rodriguez. Doesn't she live here?"

In that very moment Stephanie had come down the stairs and around the corner.

"You!"

She was terrified on seeing Jordan's reddened, enraged face.

"Jordan? Jordan, I'm sorry. I was scared. I didn't mean for any of this to happen!"

He turned to Allenby.

"Am I under arrest?"

"Not so far, but we'll need you to come down to the station for a more detailed interview."

Jordan tore the warrant in two, looking across the room at two officers, who were sifting through the kitchen garbage.

"Good. Stephanie, I want to talk to you in my office. Now!"

He went into a room on the right and slammed door behind him. Allenby caught Stephanie's arm as she scurried by, stopping her.

"You don't have to go in there if you don't want to."

She wrenched her shoulder away, sobbing as she spoke.

"Don't touch me! It's all your fault! You guys tricked your way inside in the first place! You tricked me! And now look what you're doing! I hate you!"

She rushed toward the door and tapped. It opened and Jordan's hand reached out, snatching her inside.

In the room, he clutched her shoulders, shaking her like a ragdoll.

"You are so stupid!"

He butted her face with his forehead.

"How could you be so dumb? Any moron would have known what they were up to!"

"I'm sorry, Jordan! I was scared! He said he was just going to check the house for—"

He pushed her away and swept a lamp from the table onto the floor where it shattered.

"Check? Is that what you think that fat fuck and the rest of them are doing out there? *Checking* the house? Come here!"

He grabbed her by the collar of her shirt.

"Come here!"

He pulled her face close to his and whispered.

"I trusted you. I was going to give it all up for you, and look what you do to me. You've ruined my life!"

He shoved her so hard into the china cabinet that a shelf collapsed, spilling its fragile and expensive contents onto the level below. Still pleading, she crawled toward him and clutched his leg.

"Jordan, please! Please don't be mad at me! Don't leave me! I'll die without you!"

He kicked her away. This time, her body crashed into a rack of brass fireplace tools.

"I have no room in my life for disloyal people like you."

Stephanie was hysterical. Rushing to him again, she clung to his neck.

"Please, Jordan!"

This time he wrested her loose and slapped her across the face.

"What is it that you don't understand, Stephanie? I want you out of my house! Get out! Get the fuck out now!"

Pulling her up by the hair, he twisted her left arm behind her back.

"I should have known better than to trust a fuckin Mexican!"

He opened the door and shoved her outside, following close behind. As she struggled to her feet, it was plain to see she was bleeding from her mouth.

Two younger officers in the immediate area, wondering about whether to arrest Jordan for battery, looked toward Allenby for direction, but the dispassionate lieutenant watched the weeping woman as she grabbed a jacket from the closet and hurried out the front door. Jordan looked toward the front door where a well-dressed man in sunglasses was entering.

He smiled toward the lieutenant.

"So what are you going to do, Fatboy? Arrest me?"

Allenby withdrew the handcuffs, staring at the arrogant murder suspect. He nodded to the two officers, indicating that they should follow Stephanie. Then he grabbed Jordan's right wrist, twisting it behind his back.

"Mr. Alexander, you are now under arrest. You have the right to remain silent. Anything you say or do from this point on can or will be used against you in a court of law."

He secured the handcuffs on both wrists.

"You have the right to an attorney. If you cannot afford an attorney, the court will appoint one for you."

The well-dressed man stepped forward, presenting a card. He removed the sunglasses.

"Lieutenant Allenby, my name is Barry Alexander Divine. I *am* Jordan's attorney. Would you mind telling us what he's being arrested for?"

The lieutenant became nervous on seeing his distinctive face and hearing his name. He was aware of Barry's reputation for beating up on and embarrassing the San Francisco Police Department. Divine was a manipulative defense lawyer who would exploit any error or omission to make the department seem either corrupt or inept.

Because Allenby didn't want to end up in a courtroom explaining or justifying probable cause for a murder arrest, he opted for the lesser charge.

"Assault and battery, assault and battery for now. We're taking him. You can talk to him down at the station."

Barry stood between the lieutenant and the door.

"Assault and battery? Where's the victim?"

Allenby glanced through the window at the area in front of the house.

"She's out there. She's making a report."

Barry didn't move.

"His hands are white, Lieutenant. I think someone put the cuffs on too tight. Would you be kind enough to loosen them, please?"

As Allenby checked the handcuffs, adjusting them, Barry continued.

"While you're at it, Lieutenant, why don't you just take them off? Lot of people out there. And cameras. No need to embarrass him in front of his neighbors and the rest of the world, unless of course that's what you *intend* to do?"

The lieutenant became defensive.

"Hey look Mr. Divine, I got nothing against you or your cousin. I'm just doing my job here. It's department policy. I gotta put handcuffs on him if I arrest him."

"Then do you have to arrest him? Can't you let him come to the station on his own? I'll escort him to make sure he gets there. You have my word on it."

Allenby was intimidated by Barry's deportment and was inclined to open the cuffs until his eyes fell on Jordan's mocking expression.

"That's not gonna happen, Mr. Divine. I'm sorry, but I've arrested him. There's nothing you can do now but meet us down at the station."

Barry, as usual, was relentless.

"Lieutenant, are you sure you have the authority to make a call like this with all its inherent liability to the city? Don't you think maybe you should check with someone downtown?"

Trevor Allenby was already on his way out the door, with Jordan in tow.

"I don't tell you how to do your job, Mr. Divine. Don't try'n tell me how to do mine!"

Peter Granucci was thirty minutes late for the scheduled two o'clock meeting in the conference room. The same nine attorneys from earlier were seated around the table, each anxious to know which two would be chosen to prosecute Jordan Alexander for the murder of his wife.

Ted Waters sat next to Chester Douglas, his closest ally in the office. Chester hadn't been in the DA's office as long as Ted, but he seemed as old. During the course of each day, Janice Prescott's hair would evolve from what was passable to *down-right unruly, in an embarrassing way.* At two o'clock that afternoon, her hair had reached a little beyond the mid-point. Gail Freidman tapped the back of her pen on the table, an annoying idiosyncrasy that caused Hector to glare in her direction a few times before asking her to stop.

Hosea Carter, the other black attorney in the office, sat there, entertaining no hope or desire of getting the case. If Ted told him he was too inexperienced and inadequate for the job, Hosea would have agreed, though he had been in the office for only one year less than Ted.

The receptionist's husky voice interrupted the moment of silence and introspection in the room.

"Just thought you'd all like to know. Grannucci's on his way up."

When Peter entered the room a little more than five minutes later, he seemed apprehensive, owing to the uncertainty that always accompanied such a major decision. He kept his eyes fixed forward and raised above the attorney's heads. He didn't sit in the empty seat usually reserved for him. Instead, he stood, pouring himself a glass of water.

After taking a long sip and a deep breath, he began.

"As you may or may not know, Jordan Alexander was arrested earlier today for assault and battery. But between now and the time of our press conference tomorrow, there's a good chance the charge will be changed to murder. Police found his Rolls Royce in Golden Gate Park this morning. The driver's seat and the floor had numerous bloodstains and smears.

"They also found a shred of torn material on a bush nearby. It was dark blue or black, probably from a suit, but there was blood there also. Earlier reports said he was eating at Alioto's when the murder occurred, but the medical examiner's office said the murder most likely happened at about 10:30, at least an hour after people remember seeing him leave the restaurant. Then there's the bloodstain on the wall at the house not to mention the numerous incidents of violence he directed toward his wife. We'll have more evidence against him as this office has four investigators working on the case."

He sipped the water again as he scanned the rapt expressions of the faces in the room.

"All in all, I think we've got enough to go on, but we have to be careful, because most people in San Francisco don't know Jordan Alexander the way we know him, and the way some over at the police department know him. To most of them, he's their favorite son, he can do no wrong."

He sipped from the water glass again.

"As we know, the Alexander family does more charity work than anyone in San Francisco, and that doesn't even begin to touch their involvement in state and city politics. They even donated money to my campaign."

Ted interrupted by clearing his throat.

"So what are you *saying*, Peter?"

"All I'm saying is there'll be a backlash as a result of the arrest, and this office won't be popular for pursuing murder charges."

Ted continued the questioning.

"A backlash by who?"

"I'm certain you know, Ted. By the Alexander family, by the

people in the city, by the mayor's office and some of them over at the police department. They're all going to want to sweep this one under the carpet."

Destiny spoke out.

"But you won't! Right?"

Peter's face was resolute.

"No Destiny. I won't. It'd be convenient to blame this thing on two black gang members. We'd never find them, of course, but Jordan would go free."

He opened his maroon leather briefcase, withdrew two files, and placed them on the table.

"I've planned a press conference for 5:00 p.m. tomorrow, where I'll announce my intention to charge Jordan for murder. I have chosen two from the nine of you to stand there with me as we begin what I'm sure will be one of the most publicized trials in the state's history."

He directed the next statement toward Ted.

"I know there are some in this office who think that, for their experience and record alone, I should automatically assign them to the case. It was my initial intention, but then as I considered this individual situation and the unique problems we'd be facing with a circumstantial case and the politics involved, I changed my mind."

Ted was beginning to turn red. Eyes fixed on Peter, he sparked.

"It's obvious you didn't choose me. Who did you choose?"

Peter's expression matched Ted's intensity.

"I chose Destiny Mitchell and Brett McPherson."

The room fell silent as shocked lawyers reached for words to express their surprise. Janice Prescott had, after all, been with the office for longer than Destiny and Brett combined. There were many combinations Peter could have chosen, but these two?

Ted was the first to offer an explanation.

"Let me guess, Peter. Because you want to run for *mayor*, you're forced into either pursuing the murder charges or being considered bought by the Alexanders. You're charging Jordan with murder, but you don't want to *win*. So you're putting two novice, clueless lawyers up against Barry Divine, a guy who's going to feed them their lunch and send em packin."

Offended, Peter interrupted.

"I'm warning you, Ted."

Ted continued.

"If you were half as smart as I thought you were, Peter, you'd put me and Chester on the case, we'd win it, and you'd get the credit for being honest and ethical enough to bring down Jordan in spite of his stature in this city."

"That's enough, Ted!"

Peter trembled in anger.

"In spite of what you think of yourself as a lawyer, I don't think you could win against Barry Divine, but I think Destiny here has a shot. You want this case for the publicity. You want to show off at press conferences and sign books, but you don't give a damn about what happens, and that's why you could never win against Barry Divine. This is no ordinary case for him. He'll be defending his cousin and the reputation of his family, something he feels passionately about—while you're posing for publicity shots and getting your sorry old ass kicked."

He slammed the briefcase shut.

"Destiny, on the other hand, was there. She only wants to bring Jordan to justice, to make him pay for killing his wife. She was deeply offended by the crime and feels for the victim! That's what I want in a lead prosecutor. I need someone who'll match Barry Divine, passion for passion."

It was Chester Douglas' turn to question Peter's decision.

"All passion and campaign strategy aside, Peter, there are a couple of really big disadvantages Destiny has working against her. No offense intended, but one, she's a woman. A woman lawyer, no matter how skilled she is, will never win a case against an attorney like Divine. It might not be fair, but juries reflect the biases of society as well as its sense of justice.

"And the second reason: she's black. Reasons are the same, but even more so. A black woman could never win a case against a white man who's as rich, powerful and popular as Jordan, especially if he has an adequate defense. And as we know, Jordan has the best."

Peter sat into his seat. Looking at Destiny, he sighed aloud, contemplating.

"You're probably right, Chester. I considered those factors before making my decision. Destiny has two inherent disadvantages through no fault of her own, but all the rest of you have one disadvantage or another. Janice is older and a woman, Ted's a pompous, establishment white male, Hector's a young Mexican, Gail's a rich Jew. I'm an asshole. The way I figure it, all those factors make a difference initially, but they become less significant as juries begin to consider the facts of the case."

He sighed, as he always did before a final summation.

"What we have to remember is that Destiny won't be the focus of this case. She'll just be the lead prosecutor. We'll never let them pit Destiny against Jordan Alexander or Barry Divine. Instead, she'll be the surrogate voice of a pitiable murdered white woman pleading for justice. This case will transcend race and gender."

Ted hadn't conceded. Rather, he had one more card to play.

"That's all well and good, Peter, but when you were busy doing your white-liberal good deed for affirmative action, you never considered that maybe Destiny doesn't *want* to be lead prosecutor. Maybe she doesn't feel adequately experienced to accept the job. She indicated as much to me earlier today. Why don't we ask her if she is up for the assignment? Destiny?"

"Of course I am."

Ted was certain she didn't understand the question.

"No. What I'm asking is if you think you're up to facing Cyclops in court."

She stood.

"I heard you, and I said of course I am. I think Peter's right. If anyone in this office has a chance of getting a conviction against Jordan Alexander, it'll be me. I was at that house. I saw Lynette. I saw her blood all over the room. I saw the mutilation, I smelled it. She'll never be able speak out against the man who murdered her, a man she once loved. She wanted to tell the world what a monster he is, I saw it in her eyes."

By this time, Destiny didn't even try to hide the fact that tears were streaming down her face.

"I owe that to her. I'm going to speak for her, and even if I lose, I'm going to say what she'd want me to say, and that'll be enough."

Ted Waters, untouched by the young woman's emotion, sighed in disgust before getting in the last word.

"She's going to lose. Believe it. And mark my words, Peter. This whole thing is going to blow up in your face, and when it does, I'm going to have your job."

CHAPTER 8

It was her favorite spot to sit in solitude, a private place she had never shared with anyone. At six-thirty that morning as she watched the foam-capped waves cascading onto the glimmering rocky shoreline near her feet, the scene had never been more beautiful. The ocean, eternal and ever steady, always calmed her and made her consider the more spiritual elements of life.

This is where she came to cry when, at nineteen, she lost her father to a heart attack. Her father invested for his entire life in real estate and died leaving a little over ninety-five thousand dollars to each of his three children. This was the place where she went to sort things out when Darryl, her first boyfriend and the love of her life, dumped her a year before that for a girl who *would.*

But it wasn't always tragedy that drew her to the weather and water-worn rocky site not three hundred yards south of Point Lobo. She was sitting below that faithful crag when she determined that the University of California at Berkeley was her college choice, and she was there two years later when she made up her mind to pursue a career in law.

Today, she was in that exact place as she struggled for mental calmness in the face of what loomed as the biggest challenge of her life, the ultimate test of her mettle. Over the years, Destiny had gone through many changes, but the rock and the sea had remained the same.

When she was fifteen, Destiny went with her Uncle Lester to the restaurant that stood in place of Sutro's castle on the cliff. Walking along the hill, she viewed what was left of the baths—the foundation, the outlines of the huge pools. Scanning south, her eyes fixed on a single massive rock that stood in stark defiance between the bluff and the sea.

Later, as she and Lester walked along the beach, she went up to the rock, touched and inspected it, claiming it has hers. Lester died in a train crash two weeks later. While Destiny was devastated by his death, the tragedy made her only more resolved to accomplish something meaningful in her life, something that would have made her uncle Lester proud.

She determined at fifteen years old that she was a survivor. Like the rock that sat alone out there on the beach, an unassuming mass of stony material whose weathered face had witnessed Sutro's vain quest for immortality, a rock whose scarred arms and shoulders had never yielded to the never-ending assaults of the eternal sea. Destiny determined on the day of Lester's funeral that she, like her rock, would be a survivor.

Stephanie Rodriguez was on the phone when the detectives knocked on the door again. It was the fourth time they had come to her apartment that day. This time she would answer, according to the instructions of the person on the other line.

"Fine. I'll call you when they're gone. Bye."

She waited for another series of knocks before answering.

"Yes?"

The bruise on her face had darkened, blemishing an otherwise flawless face. Inspectors Garner and Harris closed on the door as Harris began.

"Are you Stephanie Rodriguez?"

"Yes."

"Inspectors with the San Francisco Police. We spoke at Jordan's house yesterday. I know this is a rough time, but can we please come in and talk with you?"

She hesitated, examining the men's faces.

"Maybe I'll just let you stay out there. You tricked me yesterday morning. I'm not gonna let it happen again."

Garner's voice was insistent.

"Ms. Rodriguez, we just want to come in and *talk* with you. No tricks. We promise."

She stepped outside and closed the door behind.

"I just don't trust you guys. It's out here or nothing."

Harris was frustrated.

"Ms. Rodriguez, we have Jordan Alexander in our jail right now. All we're trying to do is get all the facts surrounding the death of his wife. As I understand, the DA wants to charge him for murder. Maybe you know something that can *clear* him. Now you can either help him by cooperating, or you can let him stay down there forever. Either way's fine by me. It's been a long day and I'm ready to go home."

As Harris turned away, Stephanie seemed to be on the verge of relenting.

"No wait! I said I'd talk to you. Why can't we talk out here?"

Harris seemed even more annoyed.

"Fuck it! I said I was tired. I just don't feel like standing out *here* talking to you. If you don't want us to come in, that's fine. We'll just come back in a few days. Jordan'll keep until then."

Stephanie was nervous because of her earlier dealing with Osaka. The situation Harris described seemed like another set-up, but she wasn't sure what to do. She wanted to go in and make a phone call, but if she did that, the inspectors might leave, and if they left, she wouldn't be able to tell them that Jordan *couldn't* have murdered Lynette. It would have been impossible!

"Wait!"

She closed her eyes in resolution.

"Okay, you can come in. But no looking around. And no *tricks*."

Garner stifled a jaded smile.

"No tricks. We promise."

Stephanie sat on the white Italian leather loveseat while the inspectors settled across her on the matching sofa. It was a nice apartment, a flat near California Street and 23rd, and it was obvious someone had spent a good sum of money furnishing the interior.

On the table were an assortment of fashion magazines, two of which featured Stephanie on the cover. All along the walls in the room were matted and framed photos of Stephanie in an assortment of provocative poses.

Muted salsa music played in the background as Garner, notepad open and pen ready, began the inquiry.

"Ms. Rodriguez, how long have you known Jordan Alexander?"

She took a deep breath, mindful of the process that had begun, and answered.

"Probably about three years, but we've been together for a year and a couple months."

"You're his girlfriend?"

His writing made her nervous.

"Uh, yeah, I mean yes. I said we've been together for a year."

"When'd you see him Sunday night?"

She closed her eyes, trying to be as accurate as possible.

"I think a little before eleven. No, no. He called me at about 10:45, but I didn't actually see him till I picked him up at around eleven."

"Where'd you pick him up?"

Her eyes snapped open, and she looked from Garner's face to Harris' face. She was like a nervous fourth-grader answering a test question.

"I, I picked him up near the wharf, by a parking lot not far from Pier 39, you know, by the Vagabond."

"What kind of condition was he in? What'd he look like?"

She was becoming unraveled. She felt an enormous sense of guilt for not telling the truth about where she picked him up, the same sense of shame she felt as a child when she lied to the priest at confession. The priest could always tell when she was lying.

"I don't know. He was beat up, I guess. His eye was swollen and his face was bleeding. They threw him in a garbage bin."

"What did he say to you?"

"He told me that two black guys beat him up and took his wallet and car. He said he thought they we're gonna kill him, but they beat him up and dumped him in the garbage bin instead."

Harris' face scowled at the suggestion that *two black guys* had committed the crime. It was the same disrelish he felt when, in newspaper stories and television coverage, editors mentioned the race of criminals only when perpetrators happened to be black. It was just easy to believe the guilt of these generic black guys regardless of any actual evidence.

Annoyed, Harris cut in.

"Did he describe these guys to you? Did he tell you what they *looked* like?"

"I don't know what you mean."

"Did he say they were tall or short? Did they have any scars? Were they wearing gang colors? Did he say anything about them?"

She closed her eyes again, remembering.

"No, he didn't say anything about that. They were just two black guys, two really big black guys."

Frustrated, Harris moved to the next area of questioning.

"How many times has he beat *you* up?"

She looked at him in shock.

"He never beat me up."

"So what happened in the room at the house yesterday afternoon never happened? And that bruise on the side of your face isn't there?"

She sighed.

"He was mad at me yesterday afternoon, and he had every right to be. So he just pushed me around a little. He didn't beat me. Jordie knows I would never put up with that."

Harris persisted.

"But you know he beat his wife. We all know that. So I just want to be clear. Are you saying he never hit you in all the time you've been together?"

"Now you're changing it. He may've slapped me a few times when I deserved it, but he never beat me."

She spied the mini tape recorder sitting on the glass table.

"Have you been taping this whole thing?"

Harris answered.

"Yes, but if you have a problem with the tape, we'll turn it off. It's not a trick. Its purpose is just to help corroborate what we write in our report. On or off?"

She studied his steady expression.

"You can leave it on."

Harris sat forward on the sofa.

"Ms. Rodriguez, as you probably know, the DA believes Jordan killed his wife. He's going to put Jordan on trial for murder."

He paused to punctuate the next question.

"*Did* Jordan kill his wife?"

"No. No way!"

"How do you know that?"

"Because, because he would never do anything like that. Believe me, I know. He still loved Lynette. He would've never killed her. I know he—"

Harris cut her off.

"No, I wasn't asking you that. Would it have been possible for Jordan to have gone over and killed his wife, to have driven to Golden Gate to ditch the car, to have caught a cab to the wharf and to have called you with a story about being mugged and thrown in the trash bin? Do you think it's possible something like that could've happened?"

She was insistent.

"No, he would've never murdered his wife. He's not a killer."

"After he told you his story, did he tell you what to say in case anyone started asking questions?"

Again she seemed nervous.

"No, he never said anything like that."

Harris stood.

"Ms. Rodriguez, now I don't want you to take this the wrong way, but I just want you to realize that if Jordan *did* kill his wife and you know something that you're purposely withholding from us, you could be viewed as an accessory to the murder. You could go to jail. So I'm asking again, is there anything about Sunday night that you think you need to tell us?"

She was in a near state of panic. However, taking a breath, she answered.

"No, it's just like I told them yesterday when they asked. I picked him up at about 11:15 and drove him to his house. He called the police to report the mugging right after he got there. Then he got cleaned up and went to bed."

Garner, who had been scribbling notes during Harris' questioning, looked up.

"Did either you or Jordan, or both you and Jordan leave the house for any reason after that?"

She choked on the word.

"No."

The high-pitched chirping of her telephone interrupted the silence that followed.

"Excuse me."

Springing up from the loveseat, Stephanie rushed into the kitchen to answer the call.

"Hello?"

The rest of her conversation was too muted to understand, though she sounded agitated. Garner leaned forward, trying to get the sense of what she was whispering. Wrinkling his sunburned and freckled brow, he muttered to Harris.

"She lied about not going anywhere. It's in Osaka's report. She knows something."

"She knows Jordan did it, and she's covering for him."

Stephanie, standing in the doorway, cleared her throat.

"Excuse me, but I'm gonna have to ask you two to leave now, and you can't come back unless you have a subpoena or court order."

The inspectors exchanged expressions of confusion. Garner managed the first sentence.

"Ms. Rodriguez, now I don't know who was on the phone, but we're not here trying to trick you into saying anything. We're just trying to get the facts down as you understand them."

Her voice grew louder.

"You two are not my friends, and you're not friends of Jordan! *You're* the ones tryin to build a murder case against him. I want you out of my house now!"

The inspectors stood and headed toward the door. Harris stopped in the doorway.

"You are a liar, and the fact that you lied to us is going to hurt Jordan in court. You would have been better off telling us the truth."

"Get out!"

She was sure she had injured the inspector's shoulder when she slammed the door. After locking the deadbolt, she leaned back against the door, sliding down so that her rump rested on the floor. Summoning a tortured expression to her face, she lipped inaudible mournful words, buried her bruised face in her clammy palms and began to cry.

CHAPTER 9

Rikki entered the inner sanctum of the District Attorney's office unannounced. The receptionist tried to stop her, but she was never one to listen to subordinates. Pushing the door open, she found Peter Granucci in conference with Destiny and Brett. She made her purpose clear in her typical abrasive manner.

"Whatever you two are doing in here, deal with it later. I need to speak with Peter, alone."

Destiny and Brett looked to Peter for direction, who after shooting an angry look toward Rikki, nodded to indicate they should leave.

Satisfied she had been given the respect she deserved, Rikki shut the door and turned on Peter.

"What's this I hear about you announcing murder charges at your press conference at five?"

Peter didn't stand. He sighed.

"Great. Why am I not surprised that you have access to the most private discussions in my office? Who told you? Ted Waters?"

She ignored the question and settled into the seat.

"You know it's political suicide, don't you? And I thought you wanted to run for mayor?"

His voice took a cold, angry tone.

"Look Rikki, I'm playing this the only way I can."

Rotating the chair, he turned away from her, irritated that she had been so brazen in her entrance.

"Don't get me wrong. I would like to be mayor of this city someday, but I didn't seek this office just to someday run for mayor. I came here to prosecute crimes committed in this jurisdiction, and that's what I'm going to do. And if that means I can't be mayor, then so be it."

She reached over and grabbed his wrist.

"Sounds like a campaign speech. I Should have known! You're already running."

Successful at getting him to turn back toward her, she smiled.

"Let me guess. You want to prosecute Jordan Alexander to make a name for yourself, while at the same time you want to link Jordan's murder charges to his relationship with the mayor? You're trying to make Martini look dirty, aren't you? You'd do anything to become mayor, wouldn't you Peter?"

He struggled to keep his composure.

"No that's more your style, Rikki. Screw or screw over anyone to get ahead."

He stood, turning away.

"Look, I've got a busy day. Do you have a specific purpose for being here?"

She stood.

"You might resent me, Peter, but I'm here to help you, to stop you from making a mistake. Off the record. I've talked to the mayor, the police chief and various media people. We all think murder charges today would be a little premature. The investigation's only just begun. Give it a few days, and if you still feel you've got enough, bring the charges then."

She was right. He did resent her. And his rancor increased as he learned the mayor and others had discussed his private decision among themselves, a hard wrought decision that had somehow been leaked to the outside by one of his attorneys. Beyond that, the mayor and whoever else knew had the gall to send Rikki over to dissuade him for announcing charges against Jordan.

"You know, the mayor and the rest of you are going to show how morally bankrupt you are once this story comes out. Instead of insisting on an impartial investigation, which treats Alexander like any other citizen in this state, you're doing your best to hinder the process."

Rikki was in his face.

"Aw, save your fucking speeches, Peter! They don't mean shit! You obviously don't have a clue about public relations. You can't just go out and say what you want to say and do what you want to do with no regard for the way it's going to affect people in this city, the way it'll affect the gears of this city! These matters have to be handled with some kind of finesse, which obviously you have none of!"

Her voice took on a threatening tone.

"Now get on the phone and cancel that fucking press conference!"

Offended by the tone of her voice and the language, Peter walked to the door and pulled it open.

"Get out of my office!"

She hesitated a moment before moving toward the door, stopping to issue a final warning.

"Now we can do this your way or mine. If you don't cancel that press conference, believe me, I will!"

Though he wore jailhouse-issued jeans and a well-worn once-blue canvas shirt, Jordan looked good as he sat awaiting word or a visit from his lawyer.

No books, no pens, no clocks, no music, no television, no telephone, no one to talk to. It was torture. His stomach felt unsettled the entire day, and the unpalatable jail food didn't help. There was no way he was going to use the stainless steel toilet sitting out in the open at the other end of the cell! Barry just had to come through.

The guards went out of their way to be rude, went out of their way to make him feel like a worthless criminal. For moments at a time, he felt he was losing his mind.

He thought of Lynette's face often, of the day he met her, of conversations he had enjoyed with her over the years, of their first Christmas, of the birth of each of the girls, of a magical winter they had spent in Vienna.

He thought of the way she used to duck under his arm on long walks, when she'd snuggle close to his body and purr like a kitten. He thought of the feeble attempt she made at singing for her cousin's wedding, of the riotous way she laughed when she watched Sam and Diane on *Cheers*, of the way her lip trembled when she cried on the night that she first discovered he'd been unfaithful.

Then he thought of her in death, her body cold, stiff and bloody as it rested on some cold marble slab in the morgue. It was more than he could bear. Sitting on the bed, he pulled his knees up to his chest and sobbed.

Barry Divine arrived at 3:30, and while he tried to remain upbeat, Jordan knew his cousin concerned about the situation, that the predicament weighed heavy on the lawyer's mind. Barry sat on the bench against the wall, put a monocle onto his face before a squinting right eye, opened the briefcase and withdrew notes and documents, which he began reading and sorting. After a couple minutes of silence, he pulled the *Mont Blanc* writing instrument from his shirt pocket and made occasional notes.

While Barry wasn't a man most people considered handsome, his confidence and personal charm compensated, giving him extraordinary presence. Unlike Jordan, who was tall with medium brown hair, Barry inherited the form and physical qualities of his father's family, the Divines.

Standing barely 5'6" in shiny dress shoes, Barry's features were heavy and his complexion was darker. His lips were fuller. His curly hair was jet-black and wavy with flecks of gray. There was a small mole on the left side of his forehead that disappeared every time he wrinkled his brow.

Barry was stocky, and at 33 years old, he was still in good physical shape. His shirts, handkerchiefs, pens and briefcase always displayed his ubiquitous monogram: B.A.D.

Yet the most distinguishing feature about him was the black leather patch he wore over his left eye, a roguish peculiarity that had become his trademark. He ridiculed unrequested advice about a prosthetic replacement eye, which would have amounted to a "silly marble rollin around in my head." Instead, he had a sense of humor when colleagues and friends referred to him as *Long John Silver, the Oakland Raiders' official mascot, One-eye Jack* and *Cyclops*.

Jordan modeled for Macy's men's ads during college breaks from Stanford, but that was when he was much thinner and he seemed slightly effeminate.

While his face was well-proportioned, a square jaw, strong forehead and full lips, his eyes were his most striking feature. They were set in such a way that Jordan struck anyone who looked into them as a deep, sensitive and tragic figure. Those eyes watered as he watched Barry flip through another set of papers retrieved from the briefcase.

It was hard to imagine that only one incident from one day, only one little slap across Stephanie's face could result in so much paperwork and trouble. Jordan determined right then he would never hit a woman again.

Apprehensive in the silence, he interrupted his document-engrossed cousin.

"Come on, Barry. Tell me, what's it looking like?"

"Just a second."

Barry wrote, alternating between a yellow legal notepad and one of the bundles of papers resting in his lap. After about three minutes of the sustained frenzy, he looked up.

"Now, what was that?"

Finally! For a moment, Jordan forgot what he wanted to ask. Eager to express what he felt, he stumbled in speaking.

"Well, when can I get out of here? I can't take it in here! I'm losing it!"

"Jordie, just sit down! Get a grip!"

"That's easy for you to say! You're not locked up in here."

Barry's briefcase crashed to the floor as he stood.

"Sit down, Jordan! I have something to tell you, and I'm going to be straight with you."

Jordan felt like a man who'd just been diagnosed with a terminal illness. Yielding, he sank onto the cot.

"What is it?"

Barry removed the monocle.

"Papers I got from the court about 45 minutes ago. It's an Information to the court filed by District Attorney Peter Granucci's office. They want to charge you with Lynette's murder at a press conference at five today."

"Peter Granucci? Didn't we give money to his campaign?"

"Nothing to do with it. This is a legal matter here, and it looks pretty bad, Jordie. Besides, we actually gave a larger share to his opponent."

Barry knelt beside the briefcase, collecting papers and re-organizing its contents. Standing, he read from a thick document.

"They've got blood that matches your blood type at Lynette's, a match on her blood type in the Rolls, your blood type in the Rolls, her blood type at your house, footprints that could be yours leading away from the Rolls, a blue or black swatch of material found snagged in the bushes near the car with blood on it, a bruise and scratches on your face, something that could be skin under her fingernails. They obviously think they have enough for a judge to grant a trial. Believe me, Granucci wants to prosecute you on this."

Jordan hung his head and looked toward Barry.

"Granucci's just the district attorney. What's Tony Martini doing for me?"

"All that he can. The mayor's office has no direct influence on criminal investigations, especially those conducted by the DA. Thing about it, I think Granucci wants to use this murder and your relationship with Tony to steal Tony's job in the next election. The mayor's doing what he can."

Jordan crossed his arms as tears swelled in his eyes.

"I've got to get out of here, Barry. I *swear* I've got to get out!"

He blinked back the tears in his eyes as he approached Barry, who was collecting his belongings, preparing to leave. He grabbed his cousin's arm.

"Lynette's funeral's tomorrow. I've got to go to the funeral! They can't keep me away from the funeral!"

"Calm down, Jordie. Technically, they *can* keep you in here, but I'm working on getting you out for the funeral. Just trust me. I don't know if I'll be able to pull it off, but I'll give it my best shot."

When Barry knocked on the door for a sheriff officer passed, Jordan grabbed his shoulder.

"Wait! Don't leave! Don't leave me alone in here, please. I'm going crazy!"

Barry smiled at his cousin as the guard opened the door.

"Look Jordie, if I'm in here, *who's* going to be fighting all your battles out there?"

He winked.

"See you at the funeral."

CHAPTER 10

"I know it sounds a little futuristic, but it's going to be the biggest single advancement in forensic science in 100 years. It's on the level of fingerprinting. In fact, that's exactly what it is, a genetic fingerprint."

Destiny passed a copy of the newspaper excerpt to Peter and a second copy to Brett.

"Scientists in England used it to solve a double murder case just this year. They're able to extract the DNA from a blood or semen sample from a crime scene and analyze it to match it against known samples from accused criminals to either prove or disprove guilt. It's pretty incredible stuff."

Peter scanned the article.

"Yeah, but that's England. Who's doing it here?"

"I'm not sure, but I understand the FBI crime lab in Washington D.C. has spent millions of dollars on the equipment and they've hired expert DNA scientists to put together a standard testing procedure."

She flipped through a report, stopping at a page in the middle.

"According to this summary, Maryland courts are considering allowing it in. Looks like Virginia courts might consider it within the year."

Brett, engrossed with the article and subject, motioned for the booklet in her hands.

"It is incredible stuff. Has anyone tried to introduce any DNA evidence in California?"

"Paternity cases only, but nothing in criminal courts."

Peter, checking his watch, brought the discussion back to the case at hand.

"That's all well and good, Destiny, but even if the courts here were to allow results from DNA testing, how would you expect to use it to prove anything?"

Sporting a powder blue Halston blazer and skirt suit, she sank into the gentle embrace of the leather armchair, answering.

"I brought this up as a sort of behind the scenes corroboratory. We already have enough in this case in terms of the status quo. Jordan's blood type is AB negative. Pretty rare, about five percent of the U.S. population. And as you know, a few of the samples at the scene were also AB negative. That fact and various other rare coincidences put us in good shape, but everything we've got is circumstantial."

She closed the thin booklet, tossing it onto the table.

"We know how good Barry Divine has been at raising reasonable doubt in similar cases, and we know, given Jordan Alexander's celebrity and status in this city, most jurors will be inclined to give him the benefit of any such doubt. I was just thinking that if we could send some blood samples from the crime scene to the FBI lab along with blood from Jordan—naturally, we'd have to *pay* to have them tested—if those blood samples matched conclusively, maybe we'd have a little more than just circumstantial evidence to put up."

Peter contemplated while Brett flipped through the booklet. Brett cleared his throat and spoke.

"I don't see what it could hurt. The only problem is, how are we going to get a blood sample from Alexander? Cyclops would never allow it."

Destiny smiled.

"I've got a plan for all that, but only if Peter is willing to allow for the time and expense required to pursue the DNA angle."

Peter opened a notebook and organized papers as he answered.

"I'm not saying anything one way or another on any DNA angle for now. Right now, my primary focus is on the press conference in 90 minutes. Now, I'll make the initial statement announcing my intent to formally charge Jordan with Lynette's murder. I'll tell the public how I agonized over the matter, how like everyone else, I resisted initially, how being a elected official entrusted by the people, I felt an added burden, an added responsibility to stand outside myself and the personal respect I felt for Jordan in order to treat him no differently than I would any other person in San Francisco."

He shrugged.

"I'll add that being charged doesn't automatically make a person guilty and conclude with something about the process. You know, given the set of circumstances, the process dictates any person at this point in an investigation should be formally charged and a preliminary hearing should be scheduled."

He looked up from the notes.

"You Destiny, have to attack on his credibility. You've got to hammer at the fact that there's been a brutal murder. You've got to put the tragic figure of Lynette and her murder before the city. You said earlier you were going to tie in the domestic violence issue, and that's good. Tell the city what you believe happened and what you believe you can prove. Make them feel the passion you feel to see justice is done in this matter."

He turned toward the other lawyer.

"Now Brett, this is going to sound worse than it is, but I had three reasons why I chose you to work on this case with Destiny."

He snapped up from the report and listened as Peter continued.

"First, you're the only man in this city who could give Jordan a run for his money in a beauty contest. I think you're better-looking, actually. None of this should matter, but unfortunately it does. Second reason: you're a bisexual."

Brett started to protest, but Peter went on.

"You've been circumspect about it, but everyone in this city believes it. They believe it about you, but they're suspicious about Jordan. As a result, he'll play well with gays on the jury, and while I'm not trying to suggest anything by putting you up front, I just think that having a perceived bisexual on the prosecution team in a city like San Francisco couldn't hurt."

Brett settled himself in the seat as Peter finished.

"The third and most important reason I chose you, Brett, is that you're one of the best young lawyers I've ever had the pleasure of working with. In fact, whether you believe it or not, I think the two of you right here are hands-down the most highly skilled prosecutors in this office.

"Ted, Chester and Janice have experience on you, but even they know it. You're smarter, more resourceful and more in tune with the diversity of this city. They know that with a little more experience, you'll be *better* than they are. That's why I chose the two of you."

The room was silent until Brett mustered a sarcastic smile.

"So in other words Peter, you don't want me to say anything at this press conference. You just want me to smile, nod, sit back and look pretty, right?"

"Exactly."

Peter and Brett engaged in a brief staring contest before both broke out in laughter. Peter spoke, struggling to regain composure.

"Say anything you feel like saying, Brett. Find your angle. Just keep in mind that—"

The door swung open, as Lydia, Peter's personal assistant, backed her way in, pulling the gurney with the television behind her.

"I'm sorry to bother you, Mr. Granucci, but I was monitoring the news and I thought you just had to see this."

Lydia plugged the television into an outlet and shot the necessary signal from the remote. The television crackled as the picture began to stabilize. The face that appeared froze Peter's expression. The cameras pulled from a close-up to a medium 2-shot of Rikki Thomas and Dennis Webber. Rikki was speaking.

"Once again, the San Francisco Police Department is confirming that an arrest has been made this afternoon in the Sunday night murder of Lynette Alexander. Two African American males have been arrested in connection with the murder of Mrs. Alexander. They are being held without bail in the county jail. The suspects, whose names are being withheld at this time, were arrested at about three o'clock after almost 18 hours of police surveillance. A concerned neighbor who overheard the two men discussing details of the murder in their backyard alerted the police department.

"Officers on the scene have recovered a large double-edged knife that has been sent to the medical examiner's office for analysis. Police have reasons to believe that the same men assaulted Jordan Alexander early Sunday evening and stole his car before murdering Mrs. Alexander in her Pacific Heights home. We'll have more on this story as it develops."

The three lawyers sat there, dumbfounded by the announcement. The news commentator's voice continued as the station ran footage of Jordan's arrest from his Haight Ashbury home.

"This afternoon's arrest goes a long way toward lifting an air of unspoken suspicion by police and city officials that Jordan Alexander was the primary suspect in the investigation into the murder of his wife. At the jail just moments ago, Jordan's lawyer and cousin, Barry Alexander Divine, predicted Jordan's immediate release."

The familiar eye-patch identified Barry standing in the crowd.

"This has been a trying time for Jordan. The man has lost his wife and the mother of his three daughters. It was unconscionable for anyone to have thrown him in jail for being understandably emotional during such a loss. The police department owes him an apology."

He looked toward the cameras, smiling to warm his audience.

"And in light of the arrests, those of you in the media and various public officials who have besmirched his good name by suggesting he was somehow involved in Lynette's murder— you should be ashamed of yourselves. We're demanding that Jordan be released immediately so that he can grieve with his daughters as the family prepares for the funeral tomorrow. It's the least we expect."

"Turn it off!"

Lydia, still holding the remote pointed at the television, resisted, still listening.

"But it's not over, I wanted you to see the part about—"

"Turn it off! Now!"

Peter called the orders to Lydia even as she pushed the television aside.

"Lydia, I need you to get on the phone with the television stations and newspapers. We have to cancel our press conference."

"Yes, sir."

"No, on second thought, tell them that we're postponing it until further notice. Tell them we'll be rescheduling in the next few days."

He picked up the telephone and dialed.

"Yes, this is Peter Granucci. I want a copy of the complaint against the men arrested for Lynette Alexander's murder delivered to my office immediately if not sooner."

Peter slammed the table.

"That bitch Rikki Thomas! She came in here this afternoon and told me she was canceling my press conference, and that's exactly what she did! There aren't many things I'd bet my life on, but I'd bet anything that when we investigate the two black kids arrested this afternoon, we'll find they might be guilty of something, but not of Lynette Alexander's murder. That'll bring us right back to where we were an hour ago."

Peter retrieved his briefcase from the floor. Standing, he fumed.

"Rikki knew what she was doing. The arrests bought Jordan freedom for a few days. For the funeral, that's all. We'll reschedule the press conference for Monday."

Destiny stood, incredulous.

"So you're saying the police are capable of arresting these two black guys, knowing that they didn't murder Lynette, just to cancel our press conference and get Jordan out of jail for a few days?"

"That's what I'm saying."

She sighed.

"Makes you think about who it is we're going up against by prosecuting Jordan Alexander. It'd be good to know."

Peter nodded his head, fidgeting with his pen.

"It's a good thing you *don't* know, Destiny, because if you did, it would scare the hell out of you."

CHAPTER 11

Neither Tyrell Briggs nor Deondray Carter graduated from high school, but both were street-smart enough to know it was better to talk to a lawyer before answering the tricky and loaded questions posed by the police.

Separated after the arrest, they sat in adjoining cubicles at the jail, each with a cellmate. A pale thin, bespectacled, bearded beadle of a man arrived almost four hours after the two were booked and informed of charges filed. Presenting a card to Deondray, he identified himself as Bob Levine, an attorney working for the public defenders' office. After a brief interview and a subsequent visit with Tyrell, it was agreed that each would submit to a separate police interrogation with Bob acting as the attorney for both.

Bald, Deondray was the larger and more muscular of the two, standing at least 6'4". His disposition was nasty and mean, while his eyes were wild and full of hatred. He seemed so much a killer that deputies in the jail feared him and gave him space. He had been arrested before: twice for armed robbery, nine times for assault, once for threatening a judge, twice for nearly beating men to death and four times for forced sodomy.

While at 34, Deondray had spent most of his adult life in prison, Tyrell, 29, had only served six years for slitting his stepmother's throat and stabbing her face beyond recognition. Tyrell, at about 5'5", was smaller, though he tried to play the situation just as hardcore. It was Tyrell who resisted the arresting officer, flooring her with a right cross, landed on her left temple.

Yet despite his desire to be considered a gangsta's gangsta, Tyrell was intelligent. In the six years that he'd been out of prison, he had developed a complex and lucrative little cocaine and crack business, which extended all along Fulton Street between Divisadero and Fell. He also supplied select areas of San Jose and Oakland.

The money from street sales flowed back to Tyrell, who usually made a 1,000% profit on each *kilo* he bought to the tune of about $900 every day. He profited after he paid off Deondray, who ran the pager business, collected moneys and forced a strict adherence to payment schedules.

In order to enjoy and bank the money, Tyrell ran it through a restaurant called *Mama's* in Oakland that sold fried fish, gumbo and barbecued ribs. According to an agreement with the owner, he was an employee and silent partner. *Mama's* owner Lucille DuBois and her husband, however, were engaged in a protracted battle with the government, as they fought against being shut down by the IRS for evasion and/or gross errors in the payment of taxes.

Tyrell was the first to be interrogated. Shackled at the wrists and ankles, guards led him down the hallway and took him and his lawyer Bob Levine up by elevator to a small room, in which two men were waiting.

"Tyrell, is it? Tyrell, my name is Bryan Osaka with the police and this is Hector Aguirre with the District Attorney's office. I think we all know why we're here."

Of the four men in the room, three sat. Tyrell remained standing. Bob Levine urged him to sit by grasping his shoulder, but Tyrell shouldered his hand away.

"You better keep yo mother-fuckin hands off me, man! You work for me. Rememba?"

His long Jheri-curl was becoming dry and unruly for lack of curl activator. Throwing back his head to clear the puffy curls from his face, he stared at Bryan.

"Go ahead an axe yo punk-ass questions, cuz I ain't done nothin!"

Rolling his eyes and sighing, Bryan began.

"Mr. Briggs, can you account for your time last Sunday night between 6 p.m. and midnight?"

Tyrell fell silent. This was one of the questions he wanted to avoid until he talked to Deondray. The arrest was so sudden and unexpected that there hadn't been any time to agree on an alibi. He wasn't sure if they had already interrogated his partner, and if they had, of what Deondray had said.

"I plead the Fifth."

"You can't plead the Fifth."

Tyrell shouted.

"I ain't no chump, you Chinese mother-fucker! I *said* I plead the Fifth! To everythang!"

Bryan looked toward Bob Levine who, intimidated, just shrugged his shoulders. Sighing, the detective continued.

"Were you involved in the Sunday night murder of Lynette Alexander?"

"Hell no! I don't get it. Seem like ever'body in San Francisco but the police know who kilt that white bitch! It was her mother-fuckin husband an y'all tryn ta pin it all on a couple of niggas ta save his sorry wife-beatin ass! You know he done it!"

He gestured with his shoulders because his wrists were restricted.

"Shit ain't goin down like that. I got an alibi, but like I said, I plead the Fifth. So if y'all wanna waste y'alls time tryin ta put it on me when I could prove where I was, do it!"

He turned back toward Bob.

"I'm ready to go back to ma cell."

Hector cleared his throat, ready to speak.

"Mr. Briggs, if you can prove where you were, do it. Pleading the Fifth is no protection against a conviction in court. And let me just tell you, if you don't come clean and you're guilty, the District Attorney is going to do everything he can to impose the death penalty on you."

Tyrell stood there, glaring at Hector, who continued.

"The District Attorney's office doesn't necessarily believe you were involved, but you're going to have to work with us here. You have to account for where you were that night. It's as simple as that."

No response.

"Is there any reason why you don't want to tell us where you were and what you were doing that night?"

Tyrell turned toward the door.

"Hey look! I said I was ready ta go. You my lawyer or what?"

Bob Levine scrambled up from the chair.

"Uh yeah! Of course!"

Rushing toward the door, he knocked. Within seconds, a guard opened the door and Tyrell shuffled out, followed by his nervous, frustrated and embarrassed attorney.

The somber bells rang on Saturday morning. Their steady and dull ringing could be heard for miles all along the tree-lined sidewalks of California and Taylor streets. At 11:00, traffic was at a near standstill all along Sacramento and Jones streets as expensive automobiles idled, waiting to get into one parking lot or another. The cold sky was clear and azure, a picture-perfect backdrop for the understated magnificence of Grace Cathedral on Nob Hill.

The stately edifice, an actual replica of Notre Dame in Paris, was deceivingly modern compared to the original. While construction began in 1925, the cathedral was not completed until 1964. Its walls and the towers, though from a distance they seemed as stony as those Quasimodo scaled in the City of Lights, were actually made of steel-reinforced concrete in accordance with California earthquake standards.

After leaving the hearse, the casket containing Lynette's body was carried through the crowded cathedral, past the *Gates of Paradise* and to a spot before a 15th century French altar in the *Chapel of Grace*.

Allegra Benson, Lynette's mother, veiled in a gossamer black headpiece, wept aloud in a private seating area nearby as a host of other older women bustled about her.

None of them could understand what she felt. No one else at the funeral had been there when Allegra gave birth. Not one of them remembered how she cried with joy on first seeing Lynette's beautiful little face. Not one of them could understand how complete Lynette had made her feel. It was impossible for anyone to know the instant bond formed between this mother and this daughter. None of the other ladies had awoken from sleep to feed Lynette at 4 a.m., not one of them had felt the stress and worry when baby Lynette sneezed or when she was feverish.

There were so many little things, like how embarrassed Nettie was the day her mother announced the onset of her first menstruation to grandparents in a crowded restaurant. There were boyfriends, betrayals by best friends, insecurities in the teenage years and long heart-to-heart talks complete with disagreements and tears. There was high school graduation and college.

There was Nettie's wedding day, *the happiest day of her life so far*, and mother, daughter, and granddaughter at each childbirth. Then there was the painful realization of the loss Lynette suffered for never having a father around. Her father had been a Marine colonel, killed in Viet Nam at age twenty-nine. Allegra raised Lynette all by herself in Los Angeles. They were all each other had.

Then along came Jordan Alexander from San Francisco, rich, good-looking, full of promise for wealth and happiness. He was the exact picture of magnanimity throughout the courtship and through the first year and a half of marriage right up until the time Caitlyn was born. That's when the cheating began and soon after that, the violence.

Every time the couple had one of their big blowouts, Lynette would come back home to Los Angeles. Jordan would arrive soon thereafter and, until he got her to agree to return with him, he was the perfect husband and father. Lynette never outright told her mother that Jordan hit her, but Allegra was neither blind, deaf, nor stupid. She knew her daughter was in an unhealthy and abusive relationship, and she had perhaps been *too* non-interfering.

She could have done more, she should have done so much more! Instead of telling her daughter to get the hell out of that dysfunctional situation, she remembered an occasion when after one such fight fifteen months earlier, she counseled Lynette to "stick in there and try to work things out for the sake of the girls." Allegra wanted the girls to have the father Lynette never had, but she never imagined her advice might have left them without a mother.

Looking up, her eyes rested on Jordan, who held stoic little Lyndsey in his lap as he sat between Caitlyn and Denver. Both sobbed bitterly. Lyndsey seemed an exact copy of Lynette at her age, except Lyndsey's hair was beginning to turn brown.

Standing, Allegra walked over to Jordan, who was also crying, and lifted Lyndsey from his lap. As she pulled little Lyndsey close, her eyes and Jordan's locked in an intense exchange.

Tears spilling onto his cheeks from the outside corners of his face, he mouthed silent words.

"I'm sorry."

Without thinking to respond, she blurted,

"I'm sorry, too."

Allegra was sorry she hadn't saved her daughter from all the pain and grief Jordan caused her. Regardless of whether or not he killed her, Jordan had made Lynette's life miserable in many ways. Was his apology an admission of guilt? It didn't matter, because Allegra was never going to be able to hold her baby again. She was never going to be able to talk with her, to laugh with her, to cry with her. Lynette had been taken from her, and nothing, no apology, no confession, and no conceivable punishment for her killer or killers, was going to change that.

Clinging to Lyndsey, Allegra turned and, vision blurred by tears, she stumbled, swooning, back to her place across from her murdered daughter's closed casket.

It had been twenty-four hours since the so-called interrogation by the "game-playin" police, seven since he called his lawyer and ordered him back for a meeting. What was going on out there? Tyrell was no stranger to being locked-up. He had paid his dues, he served his time.

He could never stand being locked up alone or being alone, period. The cellmate from earlier, he figured, was a plant by the police. Why else would he have asked so many questions about Sunday night and that murder up in Pacific Heights?

An hour after being questioned, Tyrell was forced to go downstairs and stand in a line-up for possible identification. When he came back, the cellmate was gone. His thoughts returned the line-up. He didn't know whether the person on the other side of the wall identified him as the killer or one of the other black men in the line, but he was becoming nervous.

Over the previous few hours, he began to believe the police were trying to frame him for killing "that rich white bitch up there," and he knew the public would demand the worst punishment for a black man guilty of doing anything to a white woman, let alone murdering a rich, proper one. It would be easy. Let the "gangsta nigga" convict take the fall so the rich white boy could go free. It happened all the time.

He knew it would be easy for people to believe he killed that Alexander woman after the media started talking about what he had done to his own stepmother, stabbing her all those times in the face after he slit her throat.

Even during his own murder trial nine years earlier, no one even considered how much she had hurt him. From the time she married his father when he was nine until he was sixteen, she never let a day pass where she hadn't beat him, slapped him or hit him with something. He remembered.

Though Mamie resented all six of the kids, she transferred the majority of her hate onto Tyrell, the oldest. While she beat him daily with belts, wire coat hangers, fan belts from cars, extension cords, fiberglass fishing rods, sticks, hot wheel toy racing car tracks and occasionally her fists, the physical torture didn't begin to approach the level of mental anguish she caused. Most of the physical scars healed, but the deep emotional wounds she caused still flowed blood, would never stop bleeding.

Mamie was a cruel and evil woman who knew what she was doing to her oldest stepson. Early on, she asked him questions about what he feared, about what made him insecure, about what he valued most. Using this information, she was brutal in her verbal attacks on his vulnerabilities. She did her best to destroy his soul. His father worked all the time and ran the streets on his time off, so explaining the problem to him was useless.

But Tyrell was intelligent and tenacious. At twelve years old, he set out to discover Mamie's fears and insecurities, and he used these to counter her cruel comments. She was fat, piss-colored, ignorant and she had her only son at thirteen, out of wedlock by a preacher at the church. In moments when he felt wounded, he'd let slip a comment on one of her insecurities. A sound beating followed, especially if his observation had been acute and revealing, but hitting at one of her vulnerabilities always made him feel better.

Yet he never thought to physically harm her until he was sixteen, when she discovered his greatest vulnerability. He had hid it so well over the years, pretending not to care, but one day shortly after his sixteenth birthday, he decided he wasn't going to put up with it anymore. Mamie had beat and abused him, but he wasn't going to let her do the same thing to his three brothers and two sisters, one by one.

At sixteen, Tyrell had become too big for Mamie to abuse without fear of retaliation, so she turned her violent attentions to fourteen year-old Zack, the next boy in line. Snatching the bulky nylon rope from her hand, Tyrell warned Mamie never to beat on Zack again. The warning only served to increase Mamie's joy in meting out punishment to all the children. The situation grew more agitated until the day Tyrell threatened to kill Mamie if she continued beating the children.

Duly concerned, Mamie told Tyrell's father of the threat, and his father threw him out of the house. He lived in the streets. The gangbangers, the very "niggas" his father told him to avoid, became his new family. Three months later, his sister paged him Christmas day, telling him that Mamie beat Zack and had just broken his arm. When Tyrell appeared in the kitchen doorway that evening, Mamie knew why he was there. She had been sitting at the table shelling black-eye peas for New Year's Day dinner. On seeing him, she began apologizing for everything she had done to him.

"Shut the fuck up, bitch!"

"Dear Lord, Lord Jesus! Please protect me! Please save me! Save me, Jesus!"

She was either reaching for the phone or the drawer with the knives when he caught her. Grabbing a handful of her oily hair, he yanked her head back and slit her throat.

He was surprised at how much she bled. Looking at the wound, he watched her desperate heart pumping, watched the blood spurting, rising a little lower each time than before.

Mamie's corpulent, farting body jerked. Her fists were clenched, tonic, thumbs inside, the way she held them as a baby. Her face held a look of panic as she gasped, spitting up a mouthful of blood. Her eyes were wild and distant, looking to something beyond the precious life that was so suddenly abandoning her.

In her final ironic moment, her eyes fell on Tyrell, the last person she would ever see, her last link to life and humanity, the last connection to everything she had known and experienced.

Her final ambivalent grimace had the appearance of a mocking smile. Wicked Mamie, even in death her demon taunted him. The specter of that hideous grinning face took possession of his soul.

Sanity slipping, he struck at the face with the knife, but it seemed she only smiled more. He stabbed again, but she appeared to be laughing at him, so he stuck the face again and again and again until it just seemed to disappear. When he looked up, his hands, shirt and face all covered with Mamie's still-warm blood, Zack and the others were cringing in the doorway, crying, horrified. Her face was gone.

"She ain't gonna hurt cha no more, guys. She ain't nevva gonna hurt y'all no more!"

CHAPTER 12

Rikki smiled as she considered Kiyomi's question.

"There was nothing illegal about the search. The department had information from a reliable source that Tyrell Briggs and Deondray Carter left Mr. Briggs' home on Hayes shortly before five on Sunday and didn't return until about 4 a.m. Monday morning. The source, a neighbor of Mr. Briggs, called us saying she overheard a conversation between Mr. Briggs and Mr. Carter in which they were discussing explicit details of the murder."

Kiyomi started to speak, but Rikki cut her off.

"Will you let me finish, please? The alleged conversation by itself wasn't enough, but officers who went over to investigate inadvertently discovered a light blood smear on the inside passenger window of Mr. Briggs car. When they knocked on the door to question him, Mr. Briggs was combative, forcing the officers to subdue and detain him. Within the hour, a search warrant was issued, and that's how we went in and found the knife."

The room used for the police press conferences was located in City Hall. Its limited size, dark redwood-paneled walls and classic design complete with great columns and intricate cornices made it ideal for briefing.

Rikki stood behind a podium at the far end of the platform while Dennis Webber stood to the left side of the wooden hand-carved dais. The mayor's spokesperson stood to Rikki's right. There were six rows of chairs for reporters and standing room, which stretched back to the door on either side of a set of elevated cameras.

At 1:00, there was no place to sit or stand. The local reporters and writers got the prime seats, and behind them sat or stood community leaders and special interest groups. Filling out the room were free-lancers, small and alternative press reporters and interested college journalism students.

Leaning toward the microphone, Rikki prepared to take another question. Ignoring Kiyomi's hand, she called on an older, large, dark black man whose poor tired suit was too small for his big belly.

"Excuse me, but why is it every time someone get murdered or raped, or any kinda crime go down in this city, the police and the media gotta blame it on black people?"

Rikki paused. This question was easy to answer.

"Now I can't speak for the media, but the police department is not at all concerned with the race, nationality or religion of anyone in this city. We simply respond to reports and complaints as they relate to criminal activity. I'm not saying this is true, but if blacks are getting more than their fair share of attention from the police, it may be because blacks, for whatever reason, have been involved in more than their fair share of crime in San Francisco."

The man sighed, disgusted, arguing.

"No, it's because it's easier for the police and white people on juries to believe blacks are guilty if we get accused of anything. And by the same token, you all wanna believe white folks are innocent even when it's obvious what happened."

She smiled.

"You are certainly entitled to your opinion, Sir."

Looking past two other blacks who waved their hands, she called on a conservative seeming middle-aged white man she hadn't seen before.

Standing, he stepped toward the podium.

"Thank you. While I realize the investigation is ongoing, I just have to ask. There's a story going around where witnesses are saying they saw and spoke with Tyrell Briggs and Deondray Carter in *Oakland* Sunday night at around the same time as the Alexander murder. Are you investigating those claims?"

Disappointment showed on Rikki's face. However, she was never long without a response.

"We've heard rumors of that sort and are in the process of investigating them. But let's not forget what we have here. We found a good quantity of human blood in Mr. Briggs car and in his house, we found a large knife smeared with human blood in his house and we found a bag of his clothing soaked with human blood.

"Despite several attempts at questioning them, neither Mr. Briggs nor Mr. Carter have been willing to talk to us about their whereabouts or actions on Sunday night. Both are felons, and the crime Mr. Briggs was convicted of was especially heinous, similar to Lynette Alexander's. He slit his own mother's throat, and then he stabbed her in the face over forty times. The evidence against them is mounting, and right now, we're just waiting for the District Attorney to file an Information with the court to begin the process of bringing them to justice. We—"

A commotion and loud shouting near the door interrupted Rikki's comments. Looking across the room, she and the rest in the front could see an object causing the crowd bounce back and forth, like a steamer cutting through the choppy sea.

As the person neared, his features became recognizable in small glimpses. It was was another black man. He was obviously an over-eater. His hair was straightened, in a style similar to activist Reverend Al Sharpton's. He was loud, and judging from his comportment, very agitated.

Early on, Webber signaled three uniformed officers who moved between the man and the stage, stopping him 15 feet short of the stage.

The man called to Rikki over the officers' shoulders.

"It's all garbage! What you're sayin is all garbage! Tyrell an Dray ain't had nothin ta do with killin Jordan Alexanda's wife. I been tryin ta tell you guys that all week long, but nobody wants ta lissen! They ain't kilt Jordan Alexanda's wife. They kilt *ma* wife! They kilt Lucille. I *know* it!"

Rikki glanced toward the cameras through the corner of her eye and then back to officers who were restraining the man. She raised her eyebrows and nodded, indicating that they should escort the man out of the room. The young officers tried, but the man resisted.

"Hell no, I won't go! Nobody wants ta lissen. I been ta the police. I been ta the television stations, ta the newspapers! Nobody wants ta lissen! They kilt ma wife! Them two boys y'all got kilt ma Lucille! They ain't kilt that white woman."

After considering the situation, Webber gave one of his stern nods, and the officers took the man to the ground. Rikki sighed as she watched the cameras following the commotion. Breaking the pencil in her hand, she looked over at Webber, wagging her head in disapproval. He responded with a blank face that yielded to a mild smile as Rikki turned back to address the reporters.

"This would obviously be an emotional time for anyone who's lost a wife or other family member. The murder of Lynette Alexander has forced the whole Bay Area to focus on the crime of murder and how it can disrupt, unsettle and tear apart an entire community, let alone an individual or family."

She smiled as she watched the door close behind the struggling man, concluding.

"As I said before, the San Francisco police department remains committed to solving the murder of Lynette Alexander, but beyond that, the department would like to assure the public that we are equally resolved to seek answers for all the other as-of-yet unsolved murders in this city."

Her eyes remained on the door as she watched reporter Kiyomi Yamakita rise and head outside, pursuing the disturbed man and the lurid details of his peculiar claim.

Unsettled, Rikki ignored the waving arms and annoying questions.

"I'm sorry, but that's it for now. I apologize for not getting to all of you, but you're welcome to phone me or my office anytime and we'll do our best to keep you informed of where we are in the investigation. Thanks for coming."

After walking over to Webber and whispering something into his ear, Rikki hurried from the platform, scurrying toward the door through which Kiyomi and "Lucille's" husband exited.

"I hope you don't mind, Peter, but I took the liberty of sending a few of the blood samples to the FBI crime lab in Washington. There was a lot of blood, so hopefully the six samples I asked them to analyze won't be missed."

Once again, Destiny, Peter and Brett were seated around the clipping-cluttered and brief-covered conference table. Impatient, Peter cut her off.

"Just document everything, okay? What I'm trying to figure out is not *whether* I'm going to schedule a press conference and announce formal charges, I've just got to decide when. I could do it today, but everyone's at the service, and arresting him at his murdered wife's funeral wouldn't exactly earn us any points with potential jurors. Besides, today's a terrible news day. People don't watch news on Saturdays. They're all out doing things. What do you two think about Monday?"

Brett looked up from the document he was writing.

"Monday's fine. Gives us a chance to come to some kind of deal on the DuBois matter."

Destiny chimed in her own comment.

"Monday works better all around. There are a lot of things that are still unresolved, like this police report here. One big question is, do you think Jordan might run?"

Peter groaned.

"No! But to tell you the truth, I wouldn't really mind if he did. It would make our job easier. Eventually he'd be caught and prosecution would be a cinch."

Brett continued in his line of thought.

"What about the DuBois matter? Where is Mr. DuBois he and what are we doing with him?"

Peter laughed.

"I heard Rikki Thomas and Yamakita at the *Chronicle* went fists-to-cuffs trying to get to him."

Smiling as he imagined the scene, he continued.

"We ended up getting him. As a matter of fact, he's with Hosea right now. It's a little ironic. It turns out Hosea is somehow related to Deondray Carter. I think he said Deondray was his second cousin's son or something like that. Hosea said he wanted to do what he could for him, so I told him to go over to the jail and see what he could do."

Destiny looked up from her notes.

"The police report I've been reading here says the blood found in Tyrell Briggs' car and house matches Lynette's blood type. I also understand the medical examiner is saying the double-edged knife found in Briggs' house is somewhat consistent with the wounds Lynette suffered."

She removed her glasses, placing them on the cluttered table.

"Now I know you want to go on with the press conference on Monday, Peter, but unless Briggs and Carter come clean, you might be forced by the abundance of circumstantial evidence to charge and try them instead of Jordan."

"Hate to say it, but I think she's right, Peter."

Peter sighed and nodded, his left hand covering his mouth and chin.

"That's why we've got to make those two boys an offer they can't refuse."

Jordan remained at the gravesite even four hours after the service, his head bowed low. He spoke to himself. Everyone else had gone—the girls, Allegra, his parents, his employees, relatives and friends, everyone. Although it was late August, early evenings in the Bay area were cool, if not cold. The fog had rolled in, obscuring the city save a few skyscrapers in a blanket that seemed to shimmer, gossamer white.

Flask of cognac in his hand, he sipped, staring at the fresh uneven rectangles of sod covering the place where the casket had been suspended.

"It should have been me."

Six feet under that neat little patchwork of new grass, Lynette's butchered body was beginning to decompose, her flesh beginning to turn to a sort of wormy mush. The lips he kissed on their wedding day were blue and cold, the body he made love to, stiff, unyielding and rotting. He sobbed aloud.

Sucking in another large mouthful of the XO, he closed his eyes, remembering her smile.

"I want to die. I can't go on."

"You don't have a choice, Jordie. You can't quit now."

He didn't have to guess whose firm left hand was squeezing his shoulder. Barry walked around the chair and extended his right hand, reaching for the flask. The lawyer sipped, pursing his lips as he finished.

"We've got a battle ahead."

"I don't want to go back to jail! I don't want to be locked up again! I'll die first."

Barry sipped again.

"No you won't. We're going to win this thing and we'll be able to put it behind us, but we've got to work within the system. In the next few days, there'll be things you'll have to do, and you won't have any choice. Your life won't be your own. You're going to hate it, but you'll get used to it. Trust me, Jordie. If you follow my advice, I promise you, you'll be out in six months, twelve months max."

"You don't understand, Barry. I can't go back to jail!"

"No, you don't understand, Jordan! You don't have a choice right now! Now if you want me to represent you, you're going to have to do what I *tell* you to do!"

He adjusted the patch over his damaged eye, scanning the area with the other to make sure no one was listening in. The cold air was creeping in from the bay.

"I'm going to level with you. You might as well face it. You're going back to jail, period! No question about it. And you'll be there six months to a year depending on when we go to trial and how long the trial lasts."

Jordan looked up at his cousin.

"What about the two black guys they arrested?"

"There's no way in hell they could have murdered Lynette. Vic says those two have an airtight alibi. DA never believed they were involved anyway. He's been after you from the beginning."

Jordan hung his head, wrapping his coat tight to stay warm.

"So what do we do now?"

Barry sighed, a diaphanous cloud of vapor billowing from his mouth.

"We wait, Jordie. That's what we do. It's all we can do for now. We wait and see what happens."

Bryan Osaka and Hosea Carter sat in the small room, awaiting the second of two meetings they had scheduled that afternoon.

The jingling chains outside the door indicated that their uncooperative opponent in the critical game had arrived. Bryan began the dialogue.

"Mr. Briggs, when we met before, you were in a position to remain silent and make us prove we had enough evidence against you to warrant charges. Unfortunately for you, you are no longer in that position."

Still standing, Tyrell answered.

"Fuck you! Nothin's changed. I wasn't guilty then, and I ain't guilty now."

Bryan's voice took on a ruder edge.

"Apparently, you need to consult with your lawyer. Guilt has nothing to do with this now. The question is, *does the DA have enough on you to bring you to trial?* The answer is yes."

Tyrell looked over at Bob who nodded in the affirmative. Hosea broke his silence.

"Tyrell, tell me something. Do you know anything about a woman by the name of Lucille DuBois?"

"Who are you, you *Stepen-Fetchit-lookin* mother-fucker?"

Hosea sat back in his seat.

"My name's Hosea Carter with the District Attorney's office, and I'm the last chance a dumb nigga like you is gonna ever get."

Tyrell turned on hearing the name.

"Waitaminute! Waitaminute. Carter? I knew you looked familiar! Aren't you Dray's uncle or somethin like that?"

"Let's just say Dray and I are related. For both your sakes, I hope you're a little smarter about the predicament you two are in than he was."

Tyrell studied the older man's face, searching for a flinch or a break that would belie the weight of his words. Remembering his own murder trial, he considered how the system was set against him. Closing his eyes to build resolve, he began.

"Okay Bob, you're my lawyer, but cha gotta go. An Chinaman, I don't remember your name, but ya gotta go too. I wanna talk ta Dray's uncle here, black man ta black man."

Bob protested.

"Not a good idea, Tyrell. As your attorney, I advise you—"

"Nothin personal, Bob, but y'all public defenders send more black men ta prison than the DA. I'll take my chances with my own good sense and this black man here."

Bryan stood, offended for being excluded. After receiving a reassuring glance from Hosea, he followed Bob to the door and into the hallway.

In the silence, Tyrell, chains rattling, backed to a chair and sat.

"Now I really don't know you, but I figure you're here for a reason. Cuz the DA thinks you can cut the deal he wants with us two niggas where his white boys cain't. I need to know now, are you the DA's nigga or are you here as a black man?"

"I've been a black man for as long as you've been alive, Tyrell."

"Then tell me, what is it y'all got on me?"

Hosea referred to a notebook.

"Blood's the worst. The blood type in your car? It matches Lynette Alexander's blood type."

Tyrell shrugged his shoulders.

"Yeah, but there gotta be over a million people in this city with that same blood type."

"That's not the problem here. The problem lies in your lack of an explanation. Why did you have so much human blood in your car, on your clothes and in your house? Why did police find a knife covered with human blood in your possession? Where were you on Sunday night and what were you doing? *Those* are the problems."

Tyrell sat forward.

"Okay, you're right. Those are problems, but they don't prove nothin."

"They don't *have* to prove nothing!"

Hosea sighed, disgusted.

"Let me just tell you what we're looking at here. We got a dead white woman. And not just any dead white woman, but a gaddamned socialite white woman. All right? Her rich white husband says a coupla niggas beat him up and stole his car on the night of the murder. Now the police find the niggas, two incorrigible criminals, the kind that give white folks nightmares. Anyway, one of these dumb niggas killed his own stepmother, cut her throat, stabbed her in the face forty times. All right?"

Hosea could see he had Tyrell's attention.

"The police find what could be this white woman's blood all over the nigga's house, all over his clothes and his car. Then they find a knife that the medical examiner says could be the murder weapon, all covered with human blood that matches her blood type. All right?"

Hosea leaned toward the prisoner.

"Now there are two possible explanations here. On one hand you got the husband, but he's rich and white, he's got everything he needs. The mayor's his homey, hangs out with Joe Montana. Why would he wanna kill his wife? Then on the other hand you got the two niggas. One of em butchered up his own Mama, and the other's got a rap sheet longer'n Methuselah's beard for crimes that have been violent and sexually perverse. Ta cap it off, neither one of these niggas wanna talk ta anyone about where they were and what they were doin on the night of the murder. All right?"

Hosea stood.

"Now I could be the sorriest-ass lawyer in the world, but tell me, what do I gotta prove for a jury of twelve mostly white folks to send your sorry black asses straight on over ta the gas chamber at San Quentin?"

Noting a flash of alarm in Tyrell's eyes, the prosecutor continued.

"Yeah, that's right. I said the gas chamber, or the needle, you can choose. If we've ever had a case where the death penalty was a slam-dunk, this is it. And we're gonna go for it, black man."

He paused for effect.

"Unless of course, you're willing to deal with us. We think we already know where you were and what you were doing that night, so all we need is for you to confirm it for us."

For the first time since being arrested, Tyrell seemed receptive to the possibility of cutting a deal.

"Confirm what?"

"Confirm or help us fill in the blanks in the story as we see it. In most cases a simple yes or no will suffice."

"And what's in it for me?"

"Your life. Tyrell, my boss gave me his word on it. If you help us out here, no matter what you did, we'll make sure you don't get the death penalty. We'll even work in your behalf to get you a lesser sentence."

Tyrell sat for a minute before speaking up.

"Alright, what do I gotta do?"

Bryan Osaka and Bob Levine back in the room, Hosea turned on the tape recorder and began the interrogation.

"Mr. Briggs, do you know or have you known a woman by the name of Lucille DuBois?"

"Yes."

"And would this be the same Lucille DuBois who was the owner of *Mama's Restaurant* on 13th Street in Oakland, California?"

"Yes."

"Were you and Mrs. DuBois involved in some sort of a business relationship?"

"Yeah."

"Are you aware of the fact that Mrs. DuBois was under federal indictment for tax fraud and money laundering?"

Tyrell hesitated before answering.

"Yes."

"Did you know she named you as an accessory in the money laundering operation?"

"Uh, uh no, I didn't know that."

Shifting his weight in the uncomfortable chair, Hosea flipped the page in the notebook and continued.

"Did you see Lucille DuBois on the night of Sunday, August 17th?"

Tyrell closed his eyes.

"Yeah."

"Did you two have a disagreement?"

"No."

"Okay, did you and Deondray Carter forcibly take Mrs. DuBois from her home at approximately ten thirty that night?"

"Yes."

"Mr. Briggs, I want you to consider the next question I ask, and I want you to answer it very carefully."

Tyrell glanced over at Bob who stared straight ahead.

"Okay."

"Mr. Briggs, did you and Deondray Carter kidnap and murder Lucille DuBois on Sunday, August 17th?"

Tyrell tightened his jaw, bowed his head and answered.

"Yeah, we did."

Hosea sighed with a sense of accomplishment.

"All right, so where's the body?"

"In the hills behind the Coliseum."

Tyrell stood.

"I did my part. Now you do *your* part."

Turning, he shuffled for the door with Bob following. Within a minute, he and his lawyer were gone. Reaching over, Hosea turned off the tape recorder.

"Don't that just beat all?"

Bryan snapped up from the daze.

"What?"

"I've been at this for over 25 years, and I thought I'd seen everything. This is the first case I've ever heard of in history where a person accused of a murder brought in something like this as his proof of his innocence. In essence, Tyrell Briggs' assertion to the state of California is, 'I couldn't have murdered Lynette Alexander, because I can prove that, at the time she was murdered, I was busy across the Bay murdering someone *else*.'"

CHAPTER 13

Frantic, he dialed the phone number, rushing the receiver to his ear. Once again, no answer. She had to be on her way. Hustling up the stairs, he went to his room where, on his bed, a half-packed suitcase lay open.

On the television in the corner, Bryant Gumbel was discussing the case of Tyrell Briggs and Deondray Carter. He was interviewing a lawyer who predicted a probable arrest in the Alexander matter that afternoon.

Cash! He needed the cash. The safe was in a wall of his bedroom. Fortunately, he had withdrawn $20,000 in cash from the bank, taken in four separate $5,000 increments on Friday, Saturday and Monday. He stacked the $20,000 plus an additional $10,000 from the safe in a fireproof security briefcase.

Hurrying into the closet, he took a couple of suits, two pairs of shoes, a few white shorts and a handful of ties. From atop the chest of drawers, he removed a case full of shorts and summer clothes, emptying its contents into the suitcase. He closed the suitcase, struggling to draw the zipper closed. Securing the lock, he dragged the oversized bag from the bed and down the stairs.

He just placed the suitcase and briefcase case on the white marble foyer at the right side of the entrance when the doorbell rang. It was odd, because she never used the doorbell. She had a key.

"Who is it?"

No answer. He called louder.

"I said, who *is* it?"

The doorbell rang again. Nervous, he attached the security chain and yanked the door open as far as the chain would allow. Peeking out, he saw a large, muscular black man, dressed in a suit. Next to him stood a white man with brown hair, just as large. Both wore dark sunglasses.

"Excuse me. Who are you?"

The white man answered.

"Why don't you just open the door, Jordan, and let us in."

Jordan thought he could see the shoulder harness for a gun inside the black man's jacket.

"Why don't you just tell me who you are?"

The white man smiled. He sounded like a New Jersey gangster.

"Relax Jordan, we're friends. We work for Barry Divine. He sent us over here. Come on, open the door, please."

"Just a minute."

Jordan closed the door and went for the phone. Barry answered after the first ring.

"Hey, Barry. What's this with the goons outside my door? What are they here for?"

"Private security. They're for your protection. Just let them in."

Why didn't you ask me? I don't need—"

"Just let them in, because I gave them very specific instructions. They're not going away, and they're bigger'n you. Let them in, Jordie."

Barry was gone before Jordan could respond. He sat on the sofa for a moment before going to the door. Unlatching the chain, he pulled it open and stood aside. The henchmen stepped in, casing the room. The black man spied the suitcase and briefcase.

"Looks like your cousin was right, Jordan. He warned us you might be thinking about taking a little vacation."

The New Jersey wiseguy plopped down on the sofa.

"Looks like your little trip's gonna hafta wait, brother, cuz you ain't goin nowhere."

❖❖❖❖❖❖❖❖❖❖

"Could you have chosen a place that was a little *more* public? It's not like I won't be getting more exposure than I'll ever need today."

Kiyomi smiled across the table.

"You call this public? It's a cafe at an art school."

The late morning summer sun filtered through the trees along the edge of the terrace restaurant, affording diners an extraordinary view of the city.

"You know of course, Kiyomi, once the trial starts, we won't be able to meet like this."

"Aw girl, we're sisters. They've got to know we're going to talk."

Destiny tore off a piece of bread and dipped it in the garlic and balsamic vinegar-tainted olive oil.

"Yes, but things are going to come up, details of the trial. Some you won't be able to write about and others I won't be able to tell you about."

Kiyomi dropped her fork in the half-finished garden salad.

"Destiny Marie Mitchell! Don't tell me you think you'll be keeping secrets from me once the trial starts, girl. You have to tell me everything."

Destiny pushed her salad aside, sighing in disbelief.

"Oh, now come on, Kiyomi. You've been doing this long enough. We both know I'm barred from sharing information that might compromise the State's case. The only thing I could even think about sharing is a narrow band of information, which on its face, is irrelevant."

Kiyomi smiled.

"Hours before the press conference and your head's already started to swell?"

She laughed.

"Just what makes you think that I'll be coming to you for the juicy little tidbits? I mean, I'm the reporter. I hear everything that goes on in this city. What makes you think you won't be coming to me?"

Destiny crossed her arms, tilting her head.

"Now who's got the swollen ego? I'll admit it. You're tapped in. But this is a legal case, and some of the information will be so guarded that even Kiyomi Yamakita won't be able to penetrate the court-ordered protections in place."

The female server reached in, taking the salad plates and placing a glass of El Dorado county Zinfandel in front of Kiyomi. Standing behind each woman, she pulled the salad plates with her left hand and plopped down the entrees with the right. Kiyomi sampled a bite of the fish. Returning her attention to Destiny, she cleared her throat.

"So I suppose you're trying to say that you won't be needing to use me as a resource during this trial?"

Self-assured, Destiny nodded, chewing a mouthful of spinach pasta.

"Not to be disrespectful, but what could you possibly know about this case that I don't already know or have access to?"

"I know that one of your key witnesses has bolted."

"What?"

Kiyomi watched her best friend gulp from the water glass to keep from choking.

"Now I'm not a big-shot lawyer like you, so of course I'm only *guessing* this person is a key witness."

Destiny feared Kiyomi's swagger. Studying her friend's steady eyes, she sighed.

"All right Kiyo, we've got a press conference scheduled for two o'clock. I need to know whatever you know."

She pushed the plates away so that nothing rested between Kiyomi and her and extended her palm, turned upward.

"I'm asking you best friend to best friend, as a sister. Which witness is gone?"

Kiyomi took the hand.

"I'm not trying to play reporter games with you, Destiny, but I just want you to understand that you're not in this alone. You need me and I need you. We won't break the law, but we need to talk to each other."

Destiny nodded.

"Okay, I agree. Which witness is gone?"

"Stephanie Rodriguez. She was unstable all along, nearly fell apart whenever anyone asked her a question. Bank teller called the paper and said she cleared out her checking and savings accounts on Friday afternoon. When I called the modeling agency this morning, they told me she phoned just before I did. She didn't them give a reason, but she quit."

Destiny glanced at her watch, which indicated noon.

"I don't believe this!"

"Went to her house right before I came here. It was sealed like a vault. Don't count on having her around for the trial."

Retrieving her plate, Kiyomi took another bite of fish as Destiny sat back, sinking in the chair.

"Like I said, we're in this together, just like old times. We'll find her, Destiny. I understand she has a sister who lives in Pacifica. I'll drive over there tomorrow."

Destiny was considering a worse possibility.

"I know we'll find her, unless there's something bigger going on here. The big question is, did she leave by herself, or is Jordan Alexander with her?"

In a long final sip, Kiyomi finished off the chalky Zinfandel.

"I got a bigger question. Did she leave by herself, or did someone with an interest in the case instruct, order her or pay her off to leave?"

Always the reporter, she concluded.

"And if someone that big has a stake in what happens to Jordan Alexander, just how far will they go to protect him?"

CHAPTER 14

"This is it. This is where you've got to make it count, Jordie. This may be the only chance you'll ever have to tell your side of the story. We've got all the right people here. The whole city'll be listening, and that includes the people who'll decide this thing. Give them a big dose of that Alexander charm you're so famous for."

Jordan bowed his head and managed a smile.

"I think I'm ready."

"You think you're ready? Half-assed ready ain't good enough, Jordie. Not right now when it counts. Look, I'll call this thing off right now if you're not—"

"No, I'm ready. Let's go."

The constant clicking of camera shutters and a paparazzi effect on the walls animated the room even before Jordan and Barry turned the corner. The imposing microphones jabbed in at chin level and questions shouted from reporters began. Moving front and center, Barry held his right hand up, palm out, calling for quiet.

"We're here and you're here because we expected this to be a civilized proceeding. Jordan regards all of you as guests in his home, but I'm afraid if you continue to behave like a disorderly flock of half-starved turkey buzzards, we're going to have to ask you all to leave!"

The crowd of reporters grew quiet, though there were a few murmurs.

"First a statement. Jordan?"

Running his fingers through his hair, Jordan neared the cluster-head of microphones, cringing at the flashes of two dozen cameras. The clipboard in his left hand held the text of the prepared statement. Glancing toward Barry and then to the clipboard, he began.

"Ladies and gentlemen, journalists and other media representatives, family and friends, fellow San Franciscans and fellow citizens of the world, when in the course of life in America, it becomes necessary for an ordinary man like me to submit to the brusque and inimical demands of the criminal justice system, to humbly submit in the wake of the greatest tragedy I've ever experienced in my short life, and that is the death of my wife, my dear daughters' mother, a decent respect for public opinion requires that I declare the circumstances which have made me a suspect. Beyond that, I am impelled to proclaim my innocence before all men."

He took a breath as he scanned the attention-rapt faces in the room. A smile indicated of his growing confidence.

"Sunday, August 17th was tragic day for me, but I would learn it was even more tragic for my wife Lynette. After dinner at Alioto's at seven o'clock with Bernard Katz, I was assaulted, I was mugged by two large black men in a parking lot across from the wharf. My best guess is that it happened around eight-thirty. After beating me for over ten minutes, they threw my naked body headfirst into a garbage bin.

"They took my car, a silver shadow Rolls Royce, they took my wallet, they took my keys and they took my clothes. I must have been unconscious for over two hours, because when I gained enough strength to crawl out of that slime-filled, maggot-infested dumpster and call a companion to pick me up, it was eleven o'clock. Dante himself couldn't have created a hell worse than that garbage bin. After arriving home at eleven thirty, I phoned the police to report the attack and the theft of my car."

He paused, his tired eyes filled with emotion.

"I just felt lucky to be alive. The car, my wallet—they meant nothing. I was just happy I would be able to see my daughters again. I was happy to be a part of their lives for another day."

A tear rolled down his cheek.

"I slept uneasy that night, knowing the guys who assaulted me had my keys, but I—"

His voice broke. He wiped his eyes.

"I just... it never crossed my mind that they would go over to Lynette's. Upon reflection, I realized they had her address from my driver's license and the keys to get in."

Batting his eyes, he wiped his runny nose.

"Detectives came over at about five-thirty the next morning and told me Lynette was dead, and I've been numb ever since. I just keep going over it again and again in my mind. I should have thought to warn her. In that sense I blame myself."

Looking down, he searched for his place in the text.

"Lynette and I had been separated for the last year. I think many of you know that. Our marriage, like many marriages in this city, was not perfect, but Nettie and I loved each other. It might sound strange, but we separated because we loved each other and didn't like the direction our marriage was headed.

"In the year before the separation, we fought a lot, and yes it got physical. There was violence, unfortunately on both sides. We didn't like what it was doing to us as individuals, and we especially didn't like what it was doing to our three daughters. So we decided to separate and seek counseling, but we promised we would remain a family and do things together as a family, for the girls."

He closed his eyes, pain in his expression.

"I don't know how many of you have ever gone through it, but it's a horrible thing to lose a wife, a mate, someone you thought you were going to have forever, someone you'd always dreamed of growing old with. I thought it was the most horrible thing that had ever happened in my life, and it was... until my cousin Barry Divine told me the district attorney named me a suspect. I thought it was the cruelest thing anyone could have ever done. I felt the despair of Job, to hear them suggesting I was in any way involved in Lynette's murder.

"But Barry assured me it was nothing personal. He said in most cases like mine, the husband is always a suspect. He said I had to have faith the criminal justice system, that I had to work within that system to clear my name. That's why I'm here today."

Besides reporters, the room was filled with Jordan's supporters and friends of the family. Their sympathetic sighs and expressions became part of the message.

"Within an hour, I will go to the police department and submit myself to arrest and certain confinement. I am willing to sacrifice my freedom to clear up any suspicion that district attorney, Peter Granucci, might have about me. While I have great faith in the criminal justice system, I have an even greater faith in the good people of San Francisco who have been so gracious and generous of heart to my daughters and me in our time of need. Confinement will be very difficult for me. I'll need your support."

In the front row of the audience, a woman reporter for the *San Jose Mercury News* daubed her moist eyes with a tissue.

"I'll conclude with this. For the record, I did not murder my wife, Lynette, nor was I in any way involved with her death. I loved her. I was myself the victim of a violent crime on the night of her murder, and I call on the police and district attorney Peter Granucci to spend more of their efforts trying to find the real murderers, who are probably the same two black men who attacked me. Thank you."

Barry approached the microphones as Jordan backed away.

"The text of Mr. Alexander's statement will be available to you as you exit the door."

A tall, burly *Time* magazine reporter standing next to the fireplace was the first to interrupt, his baritone voice booming.

"Mr. Alexander, so far the story as you told it is compelling, but do you have any explanation for the blood that matched your wife's blood type found in your home on the day after the murder?"

Jordan flinched and leaned toward the microphone.

"Sir, because I am apparently being charged by the district attorney, my counsel has advised me not to answer that question or other questions of similar subject matter."

Shouldering Jordan aside, Barry spoke into the microphone.

"Ladies and gentlemen, fortunately our courts have set a higher standard for corroboration and proof than some of our news media editors. Now you're the very persons who write and report the stuff. You of all people know that you can't always take what you read or hear as truth. All we ask is that you suspend judgment and look at all the facts presented in court with an open mind. And please remember that in America, a person accused of a crime is presumed innocent until proven guilty."

An older man standing mid-room called out.

"Maybe I wasn't listenin, but I didn't hear it. *Who* did ya say picked ya up when ya crawled outa the garbage? An did ja have anythang on or were you just standin there necked?"

"I'm sorry, but counsel has advised me not to answer those questions or questions on similar subject matter."

Another woman spoke up.

"Was Stephanie Rodriquez the person who picked you up?"

"I'm sorry, but I can't answer that."

The old man was still standing, shaking his head in disbelief.

"Well, Mr. Alexander? What question can ya answer?"

Jordan ignored the question, looking straight ahead, but the man continued.

"Is Ronald Reagan still the President of the United States? Or do ya hafta check with ya lawya ta answer *that*?"

The throng of reporters in the room reacted in laughter. Some called out similar questions.

"Well, *is* he still the President?"

After Barry whispered something into his ear, Jordan's face erupted in a smile.

"Well Sir, if you don't know who's President of the United States, then I think you're at the wrong event. I understand the district attorney's doing his press conference over at City Hall."

The loud feedback from the PA system resonated through the room, causing many of the reporters and city officials seated or standing to clap their hands to their ears. The conference room at City Hall was full, but the District Attorney was late. A sound technician hurried onto the stage, making adjustments to the microphones while an assistant altered the direction of the speakers.

In the small office adjoining the stage, on the other side of a closed door, loud, excited voices dominated the muted din of a television. Inside, Peter Granucci walked over and turned off the set, pivoting to address his four employees seated at the table. Destiny and Brett were on one side, while Ted Waters and Chester Douglas sat across from them.

"That's what's wrong the whole fuckin system! They give that arrogant asshole time on television to tell that story to the potential jury pool! And people blame us when we don't get convictions!"

"You're in over your head, Peter."

All eyes in the room darted toward Ted Waters who sat, elbows on the table, hands folded, fingers steepled.

"You still have time. Cancel the press conference and give me and Chester a chance to review the work your rookies have done on the case. Between the three of us, we've got the savvy, experience and the balls to *win* this thing."

Brett recognized the reference to his sexuality.

"Hey fuck you, Ted."

"Nothing personal, Brett. You're a good lawyer. Both you and Destiny are good lawyers, but you haven't been at it as long as I have. When you get my age, I hope you're a better lawyer than I am. But I'm just telling Peter that while it's magnanimous to give two inexperienced lawyers a crack at what'll be the biggest case this city's seen in forty years, if he wants to win it, he's going to have to go with experience. Chester and I would be willing to let you two assist us, and at some point I'm sure you'd be able to get up and argue on evidence."

"Fuck you, Ted."

This time it was Destiny who voiced the objection.

"Excuse me, young lady—"

She kept her eyes focused on the knuckles of her clenched fists.

"You heard me. I said fuck you, Ted. Brett and I have already worked too hard on this case!"

"And you two young idiots are going to lose this case! You're in over you heads! You'll make fools of yourself. If Peter doesn't have the common sense to see it, then *you* two should. Neither of you are competent enough to walk into the same courtroom going up against me or Chester, let alone Barry Divine!"

With a nod, Ted summoned Chester up from his seat. Chester's voice was slow and ominous.

"This is it, Peter! Now we all get to see what you're made of. Are you going to buck conventional wisdom and put your faith in a black woman and a gaddamned homosexual or are you going to come to your senses and turn this case over to the only two lawyers in this city who can win it?"

Brett defended himself.

"I've told you. I am not a homosexual!"

Peter stood, slamming his notebook on the table.

"That's enough! All of you!"

He turned toward Chester.

"You and Ted weren't invited to this press conference, so I want both of you to leave the building before we start."

Ted faced the door, his back toward Peter and the rest.

"Like I said earlier, you're all in over your heads. You just made the biggest mistake of your life."

Never looking back, Ted pulled open the door and exited. Angry, Chester stood beside the table. Glowering, he turned toward his boss.

"You're an asshole, Peter. Ted spent his life in this office doing the shit work for you and all those other political bastards here before you. He busted his ass to make you look good, and how do you reward him? You pass over him and give the plummest case any prosecutor's seen here in fifty years to a couple of amateurs!"

Destiny cringed at the sound of the door slamming. No one spoke for a minute. Finally, Peter sighed, sitting.

"You don't like being called a homosexual or faggot, do you Brett?

"It's not that. It just isn't—"

"Yes or no."

Brett relaxed.

"No."

"And Destiny, does being called an amateur and an incompetent, affirmative-action, nigger bitch lawyer irk you?"

She answered.

"Of course it does!"

"Well, get used to it. Get used to a whole lot worse. Ted and Chester were just a dress rehearsal. You have no idea about how bad it's going to get in the months to come."

He went to the door and pulled it open, looking out into the crowded room.

"What are you two still sitting there for? It's showtime."

Jordan flinched in response to the bright flash of the camera and batted his eyes in an attempt to focus them. He lowered the make-shift sign displaying his last name, first name and social security number. A guard snatched the sign and directed him to a table where another guard waited.

"What are you standing there for? Get your ass over there!"

He already wore the baggy, blue, jailhouse-issued pants and shirt. Barry Divine took measures to make the arrest as low-key and possible—no cameras and no reporters. Other arrangements were made to keep Jordan away from the general jail population and to provide for his comfort for the duration of his confinement. One of the trustees was displaced so that Jordan could have a cell with improvements, among those a television and a real mattress.

Jordan and Barry entered the jail from a rear access door used and known by only the Sheriff and a few other city officials. The arrest was made in a private office where Jordan was able to change from his suit to the rags he wore.

A guard led him along a yellow line painted on the floor, past glass-windowed holding cells, around the corner and over to an elevator near the end of the hall.

"This is the last time I'm gonna tell you to keep your hands where I can see em. I'll just start whackin em next time. Get in."

Jordan stood against the back wall motionless, his hands suspended in front of his face. The elevator jerked and began to rise, gaining momentum with each passing second. It stopped with a jolt, locking itself in place as the doors opened.

The face was familiar, though Jordan wasn't sure why.

"Well, if it isn't Jordan Alexander, the fuckin toast of San Francisco. I told you when you got in my face that day. One of these days you were going to make a big mistake, and when you did, I was going to do my best to fuck you. Well buddy, today's the day."

He walked into the elevator, stopping when his face rested four inches away from Jordan's.

"I just came here to welcome you to the kind of life you'll have to get used to for the next twenty, thirty years."

"Who are you?"

The man laughed.

"Don't tell me you don't remember me? Commander Webber? You swore you were going to have my job when I had you arrested three years ago. Instead it's *your* ass, and all your big shot bastard lawyers won't be able to get you out of this one, believe me. But they won't tell you that, cuz they're fuckin vultures, all of them. They see you in trouble and smell all the stinkin money they're going to be making if this thing goes to trial."

He stared Jordan in the eyes, certain he had shaken him, and then Webber turned, calling back.

"Save your money and plead guilty, cuz we got enough on you to keep you locked up till you're eighty-five."

It was the first time she ever saw Peter nervous. He spoke faster than normal and his voice sounded higher-pitched. He wiped his brow four times in the first two minutes.

"Jordan Alexander murdered his wife and then wove an elaborate alibi hoping to escape justice."

He paused.

"You know, most of the time I like to think I have one of the best jobs in San Francisco County, but that's not true today. Today I have the toughest job in the city, a duty you all charged me with when you elected me. And that is a legal duty to release or prosecute those persons who are accused of crimes.

"When there is insufficient evidence or the lack of a clear motive, I am forced to drop charges against persons, even if I believe they're guilty, but when I have dozens of irrefutable, damning facts staring me in the face, plenty of opportunity, and a motive that makes sense, I have no choice to do anything other than that duty you charged me with."

His left hand went to his forehead, this time stopping near his left temple.

"San Francisco is the greatest city in the world. Like the rest of you, I love this town. Today my love for San Francisco comes into direct conflict with my duty to her. Today it is my duty to bring down one of her icons, one of her greatest sons. But no one is above the law. Jordan Alexander, in careful premeditation and with full intent, took the life of his wife, Lynette, and for that, he must be held accountable."

He glanced toward Destiny and then scanned the crowd.

"By accountable, I mean he's got to stand up before a judge and a group of his peers and answer. He'll have to answer the difficult questions I'm sure Deputy District Attorney Destiny Mitchell here is going to ask him."

He paused.

"Like the rest of you, I appreciate all the wonderful things the Alexander family has done for this city. In fact, if San Francisco had a royal family, Dottie Alexander would be our queen. We are indebted the family, but I think even Dottie, being the principled person she is, would agree that no son of this city is above the law."

He wiped his forehead a final time.

"And that is why, San Francisco, I am charging Jordan Alexander for the murder of Lynette Alexander. This is a first degree murder charge that could put him in prison for life, without the possibility of parole."

He bowed his head.

"So today is a sad day for San Francisco. But if I were Jordan Alexander and I was dealing with the charge he's facing, I'd want to be prosecuted by the fairest, the most open-minded and professional attorney the county had to offer."

He smiled.

"And that's what he'll have in Destiny Mitchell."

She took a step forward as he continued.

"From the list of eminently capable prosecutors I had to choose from, she was my first choice. Ms. Mitchell possesses the unique combination of trial savvy, energy, passion and sensitivity I was looking for in a prosecutor for this case. You the people should be pleased to have her working in your behalf."

Motioning in her direction, he concluded.

"Ladies and Gentlemen, Ms. Destiny Mitchell."

She walked to the microphone in the suffocating silence. Clearing her throat, she began.

"Lynette Alexander was murdered on the evening of August 17th. She was brutally cut off from a life she had only begun to reclaim. Through successful counseling, she had managed to move beyond a painful, violent marriage and shattered dreams to a new exploration of herself and all that life had to offer a person with her youth, energy and compassion.

"When she talked to her mother on the last Sunday afternoon she lived, she said for the first time in all her adult life she felt happy and complete in herself. Lynette was a wonderful mother who read *Anne of Green Gables* to her three beautiful daughters before putting them to bed that night."

Destiny scanned several faces in the crowd. It seemed they were with her, so far.

"Less than two hours later, she was stabbed by a large knife so many times that her bones lay exposed in several places and her room resembled a slaughterhouse. Feebly, she fought back, scratching her attacker's face and neck, but she succumbed to the sheer punishment of the blood frenzy."

A woman reporter in the front seemed uncomfortable with the description. More than five television news cameras followed Destiny as she continued.

"Almost as unfortunate as the murder itself, she knew her attacker. He was a man who promised to love and protect her for the rest of her life. He was her husband, Jordan Alexander. Why? Because she found a way to move beyond their painful and violent marriage, because she had found a way to be happy without him."

More confident, she tapped the rostrum.

"Ladies and gentlemen of San Francisco, as we go forward, let us not forget that the trial before us is *not* about Jordan Alexander, though as Peter said, he must be held accountable. It is an inquiry into the brutal murder of gentle, caring woman who was just beginning to live again, a woman who had the life she loved savagely pounded and drained from her body. It is a trial about justice. While Lynette has been silenced for all time, I vow today to be her surrogate voice.

"I will tell you about her life and her pain, of how she feared her husband, Jordan Alexander. I'll share the events leading up the night of August 17th. Then I'll tell you how Jordan Alexander took a knife and butchered her. Finally through me, Lynette Alexander is going to demand justice for the loss of her precious life, and I believe the people of San Francisco are going to demand that justice will be served."

She bowed her head.

"Thank you."

When the bold reporter from the *L.A. Times* stood to pose a question, her response was short and to the point.

"You should have been informed. We won't be taking questions today. As for anything else on the matter, we'll say it in court, and we're asking Jordan Alexander and Barry Divine to do the same. If Barry Divine is half the lawyer they say he is, then he understands the rules. And I'm sure we won't be seeing any more media shows like the one he orchestrated earlier today."

She forced a labored smile.

"Thank you all very much for your time."

She turned and walked toward the conference room. Brett followed, but Peter remained with the crowd where he made himself available to reporters for private comments on his political future.

CHAPTER 15

"So who *is* Destiny Mitchell? That's what I need you to tell me. I want to know where she comes from, about her parents, about where she went to college and law school, her politics, the married-single stuff, all that. Oh, and I want briefs on any big case she's worked on."

"No problem, Divine. Good as done."

The private detective on his way out the door, Barry returned to his office, plopped into the leather armchair and lifted the phone receiver from the cradle, tapping the intercom button.

"Marybeth, get me Destiny Mitchell in the District Attorney's office. Just ring me when you've got her."

He returned the receiver to the base and bowed his head, thinking. Barry had been in many offices during his career as an attorney, most of the time because he was working with other lawyers. Because he never felt comfortable with partners and their intrusions, he had always dreamed of going out and opening his own firm.

His office in the distinctive, pyramidal Transamerica Building was his sanctuary, a reflection his inner self. No one, not one person had ever been invited in. A few secretaries had caught glimpses of arranged bookcases and the huge mahogany desk over the years, spawning hours of inter-office gossip and heightened curiosity. However, all personnel knew Barry Divine's private office was off-limits.

The office also had a bathroom and closet space, because sometimes Barry would go in wearing one suit and come out in another, freshly-showered.

On that August morning, Barry sat at his desk waiting to speak with the young black deputy district attorney who would be prosecuting Jordan. He was lost in his thoughts, reliving a poignant memory. Through his ruined eye behind the patch, he watched, he remembered.

It was a foggy, fate-filled Friday night, May 17th, many years ago. Barry, in his first year of classes at Stanford, was with a black college friend and they had gone over to Chinatown to buy an ounce of blow for a party.

They parked off Jackson and Grant and walked over to the alley behind the restaurant where the exchange was to take place. They never made it to the restaurant, because just as they turned the corner onto the alley, six or seven members of a Chinese street gang accosted them.

The leader of the group knew where they were going and knew how much money Reggie had in his coat pocket. Reggie was a pretty big guy who played defensive end on the Stanford football team.

He punched the teenager who whirled num-chucks toward him in the forehead, sending him banging into the building wall where he slid down and did not move again. Four of the other gang members went after him, obscuring his form in a blur of fists, sticks and kung-fu shoes.

Barry's attacker was a guy with a congenitally deformed face who had a small metal hook attached to the little finger of his right hand. Barry kicked his opponent in the knee, though he was aiming for the crotch area.

The teenager grimaced in pain and swung wildly toward Barry's face as he fell, tearing the cornea of his eye with the hook. The pain was searing, intense. Barry fell to his knees, his left hand bracing his upper body, his right hand gripping the left area of his face, fingernails digging into his cheek.

"My eye! My eye!"

His deep, throaty, agony-laden screams were guttural and resounded through the alley, attracting instant attention. He could feel the tear as he batted his left eye under his right hand. It was a tear! But the pain! The eyeball burned like hell! No, it was worse than hell! He wanted to snatch it out of his face and throw it on the ground where it could hurt no longer hurt.

"Someone please! Someone please call a doctor!"

He heard a siren not long after, and yet to his disappointment, the vehicle that pulled into the alley was not an ambulance. It was a police squad car, and the officer who approached had his nightstick drawn.

"You down there! Up against the wall! And spread em!"

Barry did not move.

"Call me an ambulance! I'm injured! Chinese bastard cut me in the eye! He tore it open with something!"

The officer gripped the back of Barry's jacket, pulling him to his feet, and slammed him into the building.

"Maybe you didn't hear me the first time! I said against the wall, lowlife!"

Gripping Barry's left wrist, he slapped on the metal cuff.

"And just what were you and that nigger doing over here in the first place? You were buying drugs or something else illegal! Whatever they did to you serves ya right."

Grabbing Barry's right arm, he twisted it back and applied the other cuff. Groaning in pain, Barry glanced over to see the other officer pushing Reggie into the back of the squad car.

"My name is Barry Alexander Divine! Dottie Alexander is my grandmother! So if you sorry fucks don't get me a doctor right this minute, I swear to you, you won't have jobs on Monday morning!"

Clutching Barry's shoulder, the officer led him toward the car, answering.

"Look kid, this ain't the movies. Now your grandmother might be rich, but she don't run the police department, and neither of ya can threaten my job."

He opened the car door, shoving Barry inside.

After over thirty minutes of questioning, the officers took Barry and Reggie to the county hospital emergency room where doctors went to work on the eye.

On Saturday morning, a specialist told Barry the eye was injured beyond saving. He removed it on Monday morning. Ironically, the two officers who denied him medical treatment were also removed on Monday morning after harsh rebukes from the mayor, the police chief and Dottie Alexander, who began a lawsuit.

Monday, May 20 was a morning of epiphany for Barry, who decided in the recovery room that he would be a lawyer. Sitting up in his hospital bed, his grandmother nearby, he voiced his intention.

"I hate cops! They're are assholes! I'm going to spend my life making them pay."

True to his promise, he built a reputation as a defense attorney by persecuting any police officer unlucky enough to be examined or cross-examined by him in open court. Law enforcement feared him and he loved it. It redemption of sorts, though it was hollow. He would have rather had a good left eye.

The ringing was distinct, indicating the call was coming from the reception desk. Snapping up from the daze, Barry lifted the receiver.

"Yes?"

"Deputy District Attorney Destiny Mitchell holding for you on line one."

Smiling, he readjusted the eye patch and depressed the button. His voice was sarcastic.

"Hello Ms. Mitchell! I have to tell you. I enjoyed your little press conference. Nice opening argument, but what are you going to do when we go to trial? You've already spent your wad."

He recoiled at what she said on her end, though he smiled, doodling with a pen and pad.

"And you seemed like such a lady! Now is that any way for a woman in such precarious position to talk?"

He paused, listening.

"No, don't hang up. Please, let's talk. What would you and your boss say to a plea of temporary insanity? Mandated psychiatric treatment and probation, but no jail time. Jordan cops to a crime of passion and saves the State a lot of trouble and money."

He listened for a moment.

"What's wrong, Ms. Mitchell? You're stuttering."

Still doodling, he smiled.

"Maybe it's just that you're in over your head this time. Maybe I should be talking to your boss instead, or do you want to deal with me on this? It really doesn't matter to me."

He paused, listening.

"Okay, so are you willing to deal on the temporary insanity plea?"

She responded on the other end.

"Fine. That's all I wanted to know. Thank you very much. Goodbye."

It was Thursday morning, and though the place was less than an hour's ride from downtown San Francisco, it seemed a foreign country. The neighborhood was old and run-down, abandoned by whites twenty years earlier, patched together here and there by boards and artifices reminiscent of towns south of the border.

A group of five shirtless young men sat and stood along the stairs and the porch. One dribbled a basketball. Four of the guys were thin and muscular, though one was fat. All wore blue bandannas and sported gang tattoos.

Drawing a breath, Kiyomi turned off the car and engaged the emergency brake. Nervous, she locked the door twice with the remote. All eyes were on her as she approached.

"How's it going, guys?"

The young men responded with smiles and slang greetings as they parted, allowing her to approach the door. She knocked. When the door opened moments later, an old woman's face appeared. Her teeth were black and her hair was white. She looked Indian.

"Hello Mrs. Ximenez, my name is Kiyomi Yamakita from the *Chronicle*. Would you mind if I asked you a few questions?"

The woman's expression remained blank.

"No speak Eenglish."

Kiyomi put her foot in the door's threshold to keep the old woman from closing it, enunciating slowly.

"*Yo trabajo por el Chronicle. Yo ando buskando Stephanie Rodriguez. Tu no saves donde estas?*"

The woman wagged her head and attempted to close the door again. Kiyomi found the name on her notepad.

"*Aida Rodriguez! Vive aqui Aida Rodriguez!*"

"*Vete de aqui!*"

Angry at the reporter's insistence, the woman forced the door shut. Kiyomi turned around however, to a sympathetic audience. The fat young man shook his head.

"Don't mind *Abuela*. She don't trust people comin round askin questions. She thinks you're *policia*."

Kiyomi sighed and smiled.

"Thank you."

She scanned the faces, realizing the young man knew why she had come.

"Is she Stephanie Rodriguez's grandmother too?"

He nodded.

"So you're her cousins?"

"Just me. The rest of these *cholos* are my homeys from round the hood."

Kiyomi acknowledged the other young men by smiling before returning to the largest.

"Do you know where Stephanie Rodriguez is? I'm a reporter. I just want to talk to her."

The black wife-beater he wore covered very little of his bulk as he crossed scarred and tattooed arms, skeptical.

"You said you work for the *Chronicle*, yo? What ya wanna write about her?"

Kiyomi crossed her arms.

"Oh nothing! Nothing really about her. I'm working on a story about Jordan Alexander, and as far as anyone can tell, she's the only person who can confirm what time he got home and where he was on the night his wife was murdered."

He nodded.

"So you're tryin ta *help* Jordan Alexander?"

"Not necessarily. I'm just trying to get to the truth. I just want to write about what happened that night."

"Excuse me, y'all."

The group leader turned and disappeared down the steps, returning to view in the distance as he walked toward Kiyomi's car, his shorts wedged in the crack of his wide posterior.

One of the other men standing there nodded toward Kiyomi.

"You're supposed ta follow him."

Clutching her purse, she slipped between the young men and hurried down the stairs. By the time she reached her car, Stephanie's cousin was sitting on the hood, smoking a cigarette.

He spoke, a street gang accent flavoring his pronunciation.

"Ya know, man this is the third time someone come by here lookin for Stephanie. First time it was a woman with some kinda badge, you know. Second time it was two big guys in black glasses who looked like the Mafia or somethin. They tried to scare us, but that didn't work. Nobody told em nothin. Didn't talk ta em."

He spat onto the sidewalk and drew a drag on the cigarette, holding it in before blowing through his nose.

"If you write this story, man are you gonna dig up all kinds of shit on Stephanie and make er seem like she's some kinda *whore* or somethin?"

Edgy, Kiyomi took one step in the direction away from the spit.

"No. I'm not interested in her story. I just want to find out what Jordan Alexander did that night. I give you my word. If you tell me where she is, I promise I won't tell anyone."

The red sports car rocked as he stood. He brushed his hand across his cropped hair, exposing a dime-sized mole on his scalp.

He turned away.

"All I can tell you is that she's somewhere in San Jose. You're a reporter, right? You should be able to find her there."

She called out as he started back toward the house.

"Where? Tell me where? San Jose's a big city."

He didn't turn.

"That's all I'm gonna say."

"Hey! Waitaminute. Hey! What's your name?"

He stopped, turning.

"Xavier. It's Xavier, but man if I see any bad shit about me or my cousin in your paper, me and my friends will come lookin for ya. There'll be no place where ya could hide. And ya can take that straight ta the bank."

"Destiny, don't worry about it. You've got too much work to do preparing for the preliminary. I can handle it."

The smirk on her face dissolved into a wry smile.

"It's nice of you, Brett, but we're a team. Besides, I don't want you or anyone thinking I'm dumping all the grunt work off on you. I can *be* there, really."

He stood, fastening his briefcase.

"Do you really think Chester Douglas or Ted Waters will change their mind about us based on whether or not you show up at this arraignment?"

Assuming the question to be rhetorical, she pursued a new point of consideration.

"What if something goes wrong?"

"Loosen up a little, will you! What could possibly go wrong? Wow, Barry Alexander's cagey, but it's just an arraignment! They'll plead not guilty and at the worst we'll be on our way to the preliminary."

She nodded.

"You're right. I'm sorry. I guess I just let Barry Alexander get to me yesterday afternoon."

He smiled as he pulled open the door.

"I'll be fine. I just hope your friend's had some luck with our key witness."

Destiny pulled the phone closer and checked her watch.

"Oh I'm sure she has.. She's got good instincts. If Stephanie Rodriguez is anywhere on this planet, Kiyomi'll find her."

Already dialing, she spoke without looking up.

"Oh hi, this is Destiny again. Did Kiyomi make it back yet?"

She smiled as she reached for a pen and notepad.

"Kiyo! You shouldn't have me holding for so long, girl! What happened? You find her?"

Her face showed disappointment. After listening for a moment, she responded.

"San Jose? It could take forever finding her there. I might as well forget about having her for the preliminary."

She paused, listening.

"Well, maybe you can and will, but I'm not going to count on it. Preliminary hearing will be next week. I've got to put something together by then or the Cyclops will end up with grounds for the dismissal he's been demanding."

She stood, walking around the desk.

"Well, thanks anyway Kiyo. And let me know if you hear anything."

Parting her lips, she sighed and hung the receiver, scanning the specious disorder of the table. Because she was familiar with each brief, note, report and document, only she could make sense of it. On the left was all the *time-line/theory* information, arranged chronologically from bottom to top.

The *motive-opportunity* notes and evidence were at center, though she hadn't decided their final order. On the right were extensive notes, reports and photographs on the most important *physical evidence* aspects of the case.

Three separate stacks of legal books sat in each area, pink, yellow and blue flags jetting out from pages in various places, indicating relevant cases worthy of review. Against the wall on the right was another table, straining under the weight of additional legal books marked in the same manner. A table next to it held piles of pamphlets and was marked DNA INFORMATION.

Sliding a chair over to the right side of the table, she sat. At length, she picked up a file folder labeled *Medical Examiner's Report*. It contained two documents, the first being a more attenuated autopsy report while the other, the investigator's report was only two pages long.

Because she had gone over hundreds of autopsy reports over the years, she knew where to begin the analysis. The abstruse, methodical, more comprehensive autopsy report made for torturous reading. Void of description of scene or circumstances, it was a slow, systematic physical examination of Lynette's butchered body in intimate detail.

In expository medical language, it included the angle at which each of the two of her fingers on her right hand had been severed. It also detailed the size and nature of the large bruise to the sub-cranial area on the left side, the number and angle of puncture wounds to the pelvic/ genital region and left thigh.

The report also noted the degree to which her vegetarian lasagna dinner had been digested, her body temperature at the crime scene contrasted to the reading made at the lab two hours later, and the degree of *postmortem lavortis* during the initial examination. Finally, there were toxicology findings, the visceral puncture, the subsequent damage and the overall condition of the innards, musculature, skeletal integrity and brain.

While she perused the report for possible leads and clues, her greatest interest was in the medical examiner's estimated time of death and the process he used in arriving at such a time.

While "*in between 9:50 and 10:10 p.m.*" seemed a little broad, it would have to do. At the foundation of the prosecution theory would be the presupposition that Jordan Alexander had to be at the crime scene during the medical examiner's *window of opportunity* in order to commit the murder. If she and Brett couldn't place him at Lynette's at or around that time, they would have little hope of convincing twelve jurors of his guilt.

With or without Stephanie, Destiny felt confident that she'd be able to bring a reasonable jury around to get a conviction. But this case was different because it involved a prominent person. Jury selection would be a problem. She didn't want to think about jury selection. Not yet.

Sliding over to the right side of the table, she scanned other reports and documents before picking up the preliminary report by the police. She thumbed through it, stopping at a report written by Inspector Bryan Osaka. This Lincoln that arrived and pulled into the garage at 4:59? What was *that* about? Was Jordan in the car? Was it Stephanie? Or both? Where had the car come from? It was suspicious.

Notwithstanding, Destiny had scheduled a meeting with Inspector Osaka within an hour. Hopefully, this actual observer would be able to provide more for clues than the sterile, policy-conforming, one-dimensional report she held in her hands.

Closing the folder and returning it to its place in the chaotic order of the table, she stood and walked over to a table against the wall with the DNA information. Flipping through a stack of photocopied newspaper and magazine articles, she extracted one that came from the *British Journal of Preventative Medicine.*

Unfortunately however, results from such a process, because the process was new, would be met with a degree of skepticism by California judges who would rely on *Frye v. United States*. Under the Frye standard, judges asked to consider scientific evidence are compelled to defer judgment and the ultimate acceptance of such evidence to the scientific community.

Because Mr. Jeffrey's process was so new and untested, getting any such DNA evidence in would be a long shot. However, if she could get it in, the impact of "DNA fingerprinting" on the California court system would be extraordinary. She was steeped in an explanation of Jeffrey's patented *Restriction Fragment Length Polymorphism* process, or *RFLP*, when her secretary, Faith, called in on the intercom.

"Uh, Destiny? You have a visitor."

She picked up the receiver.

"Who is it? Inspector Osaka?"

She listened in silence.

"Oh really? By all means! Give me about two minutes and send her in."

Ignoring the mess on the table, she went to her desk where she sat and began straightening files.

The woman knocked and pushed open the door. She was an older woman, but she seemed refined. Her hair was mostly gray, though there were traces of light brown throughout. Her well-ordered face seemed stressed and tired despite the smile she mustered. Even her eyes held a contradiction.

"Ms. Mitchell, I know you're busy. I'm sorry to bother you. I just wanted to tell you I'm happy that you were chosen to prosecute this case. I was hoping it would be someone like you."

Destiny smiled.

"Well, I meant everything I said. I want to be Lynette's voice to the world. I'll try to be fair, but I have to admit something to you. I'm biased. I don't like Jordan Alexander one bit. I think he's a sick asshole. I'm convinced he murdered her, and I'm going to do everything in my power to make him pay for it."

Allegra smiled, almost crying.

"And I hope you do. I don't like him either. I never liked that damned bastard! Even if he was my son-in-law."

CHAPTER 16

Brett McPherson felt more at home in the courtrooms of San Francisco than in any of the actual homes or apartments he ever occupied. Because both his parents were criminal defense attorneys, he grew up in conference rooms, courtrooms and visiting rooms at the county jail.

When he was younger, he wanted to be an actor, but his parents had a more ambitious future planned for him. He always fantasized about playing the part of *Hamlet* on the big stage. Closing his eyes, he could see the enraptured audience, mouths hanging open as he, scolding his mother, stabbed the meddlesome Polonius through the arras.

"How now! a rat? Dead, for a ducat, dead!"

Brett knew Hamlet's and Horatio's lines as well as many of the play's other great lines and speeches. From the first time he read the play, Hamlet and his feigned madness intrigued Brett. *The madness was the thing!* Brett understood the madness, he understood the prince's pain; he understood the inner torture. And yet while Hamlet hated his Uncle Claudius for murdering his father and violating his mother, Brett hated his own uncle for violations no less perverse and deplorable in his mind.

Brett's Uncle Terrence was at a time one of the most respected judges in the city, but he was a sick man. Judge Terrence McPherson had no children of his own by slight Aunt Marjorie, so the couple sometimes asked Brett's parents to let him stay the weekend for special outings and other events. Because his parents worked all the time, they accepted Terry's offers with genuine relief and appreciation. They had no idea about the horrible behavior that began when Brett was 12, a seventh-grader just about to be an eighth-grader.

He was a good-looking boy. That's when it started. At first it was just prolonged, frequent and unnatural touching, patting and stroking. It made Brett uncomfortable, but Uncle Terry was a powerful judge. Brett felt there was nothing he could do. He thought he was the cause or had done something wrong.

Then, when Brett was thirteen, his uncle, drunk during the St. Patrick's Day weekend, cornered him in the garage and raped him. While Brett felt abused and ashamed, he told no one, and his uncle, once the act was over, pretended nothing had happened. The raping and forced oral copulation continued until Brett was almost fifteen, when during sophomore English class, he began reading

William Shakespeare's *Hamlet*. He identified with the Danish prince and through him found a way to end the abuses of his uncle.

Thus at age fourteen, Brett feigned madness. Stabbing his uncle in the left shoulder with the sharp, 4-inch blade of a pocketknife, he began speaking in strange, mocking terms of his uncle, aunt, parents and teachers. The aberrant behavior got him three years with a therapist, but his uncle never bothered him again. Like Hamlet, only by feigning madness was he able to save his sanity, a bitter irony.

At seventeen, he got a scholarship to Notre Dame, his father's alma mater, so he moved to Indiana after graduation. He took a few acting classes in college, but he finished with a degree in political science and a secured admission to the law school at UCLA.

Acting was a dream deferred and sublimated. To him, the courtroom was *a stage, and all the men and women merely players; they have the exits and their entrances; and one man in his time plays many parts.* Court was theatre at its finest.

The stage was set on that warm early September afternoon. Brett and Hosea Carter sat at the prosecutor's table on the right, awaiting the entrance of the lead player and his supporting performer. The court recorder, and older woman, had taken her place *up/center* in front of the bench. She looked perfect for the bit part. Two overweight bailiffs, near the door at *right/center*, whispered to each other, ad-libbing occasional laughter. Behind Brett, the audience had already begun to arrive. First came the reporters and community representatives, followed by circumspect city officials and police personnel.

"Give em hell, Brett!"

The voice belonged to his father, Bob, who always sat behind him in court. Bob retired with a heart condition in the same year Brett passed the California Bar examination. Bob taught occasional law classes at Boalt Law School in Berkeley. Behind him sat Allegra Benson, her niece and several friends. A wave of silence ran over the room, directing all eyes and attention to the entrance of Dottie Alexander and her procession.

Dottie's face was stony, her salt-and-pepper coiffeur pulled back in a bun beneath a cream-colored pillbox hat. She wore a conservative, Paris-tailored, beige business suit, the skirt falling to a place a little below her knees. She was eighty years old, and though she looked every bit her age, her health seemed excellent. She chose a place behind the table on the opposite side of the room, and she sat. Her two daughters and daughter-in law followed.

Her daughters, Elizabeth Alexander Purdie and Victoria Alexander Divine, took their places on her left and right sides. Her daughter-in-law, Jayne Alexander, leading Jordan's three daughters past their great-grandmother, assumed a place further down and sat, a girl on one side and two on the other.

Philip Alexander, Jordan's younger brother, was the last of the family to sit. Philip wasn't as tall or good-looking as Jordan, though he was far more conservative, stern and serious. His wife was pretty in a plain sort of way while his ten year-old son, sighing and rolling his eyes, had already begun to take on his father's boorish ways.

Kiyomi and the other reporters watched the family from the rear of the room, scribbling observations without ever looking down.

Finally, a door further up stage swung open to reveal the entrance of Jordan and Barry. Jordan recoiled, smiling as he observed the bustling, standing room only crowd on hand. He wore a midnight-blue Brioni suit purchased by his mother from the Wilkes Bashford store days earlier. His silk tie appeared to be maroon, though it was red with an intricate black or dark-blue design.

Barry's suit was olive-colored, accented by a gold and black-colored tie with a matching handkerchief. The two men approached the table, stopping to pull out their chairs. Barry smiled and nodded toward his grandmother and then toward his mother before turning and sitting.

Catching his beaming daughters' eyes, Jordan tried to lend reassurance with a calm expression he knew they would understand. Earlier he had argued with his mother about bringing the girls to the arraignment

Notwithstanding, Jayne had brought them because Dottie had insisted that, despite the family's censuring of what the girls were able to see and read, they were precocious and mature enough to know what happened and needed to be present to hear their father's answer to the State's charges and insinuations.

Caitlyn and Denver smiled toward their father while youngest Lyndsey hung her head, staring at the shiny patent-leather shoes on her tiny feet. Glancing toward reporters who were at work writing descriptions of the visual exchange between father and daughters, Jordan sighed, rolling his eyes in disgust before turning to sit.

"All rise!"

Then came the judge. Judge Harold Rosenthal was an old man near the end of his legal career. Over the years, he sat on notable cases involving racially-charged issues, drug trials, the hippie movement and other trends, police homicides and murders like Lynette's.

Though he was in his late sixties, his mind was sharp and active through constant stimulation. He had retired from the bench in order to teach classes at Hastings Law School, but the County persuaded him to return to the court system to assist with its chronic backlog of cases. His pallid eyes scanned the room as he nodded and sat, clearing his throat.

"The court will come to order. Please be seated."

He waited for the murmur and din to dissipate.

"Will the defendant please rise?"

Jordan stood, his face beginning to shine with a thin sheen of perspiration. Barry stood beside him, confident, smiling.

"Jordan Alexander, you have been accused of violating California Penal Code 187, that being the willful, deliberate and premeditated killing of Lynette Benson Alexander on the evening of August 17th.

"Count One of the indictment alleges that in the commission of the crime therein described that you, using a deadly or dangerous weapon, with specific intent to inflict such injury, did personally inflict great bodily injury on Lynette Benson Alexander. I take it your lawyer, Mr. Divine, has advised you of your rights with respect to this proceeding?"

Jordan nodded, flexing and opening the sweaty fingers of his fists in an effort to stay calm.

"Yes he has, your Honor."

The judge looked down at the defendant over the rim of wire-rimmed bifocals.

"And how do you plead?"

"Not guilty, your Honor. I did not kill my wife."

The judge frowned at Jordan and then at Barry before looking down at his notes.

"A simple 'not guilty' will suffice."

"I'm sorry, your Honor. Not guilty."

The judge sat back in the seat, not looking up. Instead, he read from his own notes.

"Very well. We'll schedule a preliminary examination exactly one week from today. Mr. McPherson?"

Brett stood.

"Yes, your Honor?"

"I'm denying your motion to postpone the preliminary hearing. A week is ample time for you to prepare for the hearing. It isn't a trial after all."

Brett's face was beginning to turn red.

"Yes, I know your Honor, but we're having a problem with one of our key witnesses. We—"

The judge cut him off.

"If you're referring to Ms. Rodriguez, all I can suggest is that you find her or proceed as best you can without her. She's imminently recognizable. I'm certain she can be found."

"But—"

"That'll be all, Mr. McPherson."

Judge Rosenthal flipped to the next page in his notes.

"Mr. Divine?"

Barry stood, smiling as the judge began.

"I've considered your request to have your client released on bail. It was filed late and nothing in it convinces me of your claim that Mr. Alexander will be irreparably harmed by continued incarceration.

"Furthermore, in light of the fact that this is a high-profile case plus the frustrating propensity you have for staging media events that make the State's task of finding an impartial jury more difficult, I think it's in the State's best interest to keep Mr. Alexander safely stowed away until the hearing. It's only a week away."

Barry could see Jordan's nervous fidgeting from the corner of his eye. Walking around the table, he began in bombastic protest.

"If it pleases you, your Honor, I must reaffirm the main assertion in my—"

"I've already made my decision, Mr. Divine."

Barry continued, ignoring the judge.

"In my motion, your Honor, a licensed psychiatrist documented my client's tremendous suffering during—"

"Mr. Divine, I told you I already made my decision."

"Yes you did, and I'm asking, no I'm *begging* you to reconsider! Jordan Alexander has had to undergo psychiatric treatment as a result of the initial incarceration and—"

The judge slammed the gavel, his voice trembling in a sustained angry tone. His bald head, beginning to sweat, shone in the light.

"Mr. Divine, do you think by arguing you're going to change my mind? Sit back down! There will be order in this court."

Out of breath, the judge wiped his forehead with a handkerchief.

Brett stood.

"Mr. McPherson? What do you want?"

"For the record, the State opposes granting bail for reasons stated in our written opposition."

"Very well. Is there anything else?"

Brett looked toward Hosea Carter shook his head.

"Nothing from us, your Honor."

"Mr. Divine?"

"No. No, your Honor. Nothing else from us. Thank you very much. You've been very kind. Thank you."

Guards already in place behind Jordan, the judge concluded the arraignment, and guards escorted Jordan and Barry from the room.

Even as Brett and Hosea re-packed their briefcases, Brett's father patted him on the back, commending him on his incredible poise. The preliminary hearing already on Brett's mind, he and Hosea rushed from the courtroom to report on the arraignment to Peter and Destiny.

Little Lyndsey, rocking, stared at the empty chair where her father had been sitting, oblivious to the emotion and commotion around her. Allegra, worried and teary-eyed, walked toward the little girl, wanting to take her up in a comforting embrace, but she couldn't even get close. Her other grandmother Jayne Alexander saw to that.

Family members huddled around the girls as they were escorted past Allegra and out the room. Dottie had instructed the girls not to even look in Allegra's direction. In the empty courtroom, Allegra collapsed into a chair and wept, not for Lynette or the girls, but for herself. She was so alone.

CHAPTER 17

"Frankly, Ms. Mitchell, the police department believes your boss acted pre-maturely. Neither the department nor your office have enough on Jordan to even think about going to trial."

Rikki had barged into the inner office uninvited. She eyed the layout of the room, noting the quantity of supposed evidence on the tables. Destiny, offended by the rude intrusion, held her ground.

"Ms. Thomas, that's why people like you aren't lawyers. The purpose of the preliminary hearing is to establish whether or not the evidence brought forth, if believed, merits a trial. If we don't have enough, I'm certain the *judge* will let us know."

Irritation showing in her voice, Destiny continued.

"I still don't understand why you're here in Inspector Osaka's place. It is imperative we interview him before the hearing."

Ignoring the comment, Rikki walked toward the window, her back toward the fuming lawyer.

"Destiny? You don't mind if I call you Destiny, do you?"

No answer.

"Anyway, Destiny. You seem like a smart young woman with a promising future ahead of you. That being said, I'm certain you know the vast implications of this particular case."

"I know that, but the Alexander family won't be on trial. Only Jordan will."

As Rikki turned, her face held the practiced composure of a professional dealmaker.

"One in the same."

She closed, placing her left hand on the skeptical lawyer's right shoulder.

"Destiny, I'm equally certain that, as intelligent and pretty as you are, you don't want to be in the District Attorney's office for the rest of your career. You'd be wasting your talents."

Remembering a rumor she heard about Rikki's relationship with a local female news anchor, Destiny glanced at the hand on her shoulder and answered.

"I wasn't planning on spending my career here, but I'm comfortable with where I am at the moment."

Uneasy with the proximity, Destiny turned and went to her desk, pretending to examine her notes. Rikki followed and remained close, though not touching.

"What if I told you that I've talked to one of the largest law firms in Los Angeles about you? What if I told you they were impressed with you? That they are prepared today to offer you a job with a six-figure salary for starts plus perks? Would you be willing to consider it?"

Destiny wondered how Rikki knew about her desire to live in the Los Angeles area and about her recent interest in law firms down there. And for at least the next two years, Charles Covington was down there. It was everything she wanted, but it was a catch.

"It all sounds good, Ms. Thomas, but let me ask you one question."

"Ask away."

"If I indicate I'm interested and I tell this firm you've talked to I can't start until after the Jordan Alexander trial, would the offer still be good?"

Rikki was quick to answer.

"Afraid not. Trial could take a year or more. No, you'd have to start immediately."

Destiny turned toward Rikki, who stood close.

"Exactly as I thought. Great offer, but I'm not a sellout. My father taught me better than that."

She took a deliberate step backward.

"I've got to get back to work. Anything else?"

Rikki smiled, dragging her eyes down the length of the young woman's body. She whispered.

"Not for the moment, but I'll look forward to talking with you again."

Backing again, Destiny was certain the woman was trying to make her uncomfortable. Nervous, she remembered.

"What about Inspector Osaka? When will I be able to reschedule the interview?"

Rikki was all-business again, her posture and overall composure changed in an instant.

"Inspector Osaka is very busy on a special assignment, so if I were you I wouldn't make any plans for him before the hearing. Anything he could tell you is in the record anyway."

Rikki headed for the door, but she stopped, turning before exiting.

"Oh by the way, Destiny, going for and getting what you want isn't selling out. It's just good business."

Commander Dennis Webber insisted on a table in a remote corner of the quiet North Beach restaurant. He smoked a Marlboro red, sipping a clear liquid from a tiny flask.

At five thirty, the after-work regulars were just beginning to arrive. A single blond woman in a tight leather skirt sat at the bar, her eyes following the bartender's every move. She may have been a shopper employed by the restaurant, but the eye-play between the two made it more likely that she was a new girlfriend, visiting him at work.

The bartender, Paoli, had lots of them, a new young college coed every week. Two stools away, an older man and young woman whispered to each other, his hand on her inner thigh. He wore a wedding ring, but her fingers were bare.

At a table near the bar, three good-looking, dark-haired Italian youth in expensive suits sat watching the room, only mumbling to each other at times. Webber and others on the force knew of occasional mobster influence in North Beach, but he hadn't heard anything lately.

He didn't care either way. He wasn't even a regular in the place. He usually hung out up the street at the Washington Square Bar and Grill. Everyone knew him over there. But today he didn't *want* to be known. It wasn't a secret meeting, but he wanted it to be a private one.

Six o'clock straight up, and Bryan Osaka walked through the front door, adjusting his glasses as he scanned the room. Webber nodded as their eyes met, looking away to light another cigarette. Bryan cased the room as he crossed over to Webber, studying the clientele. He fanned the cigarette smoke as he sat.

"Couldn't you have found something in non-smoking? This place is like a gas chamber."

Dennis only blew more smoke in Bryan's direction.

"What're ya drinkin?"

Bryan looked toward the flask on the table.

"What's that?"

"Grappa."

"And grappa is?"

"Italian for *sake.* You'll love it."

With an expression, a hand motion and a nod, Dennis ordered the drink for Bryan from a server who stood in the distance.

"So what happened with Chief McGuire?"

Bryan removed his glasses, relaxing a little.

"Well, it's like you said. First scare tactics. He busted my ass. Said my career was over, that Internal Affairs was going to ream me a new asshole and all that."

Listening, Dennis didn't blink.

"Okay, when he finished all that, he gave you a way to save your career, right?"

"Yep."

The server delivered Bryan's drink and a second for Dennis. Webber sipped, finishing the first flask.

"What'd he offer?"

Bryan made a face after sampling.

"Said if I wanted a career, I shouldn't let you drag me down. That you're using me and everyone else around you to advance your own private agenda. He said you don't care about us."

"He's right."

Bryan grinned.

"He said I could be in big trouble for getting myself inside Jordan's house and searching around. He said I might face departmental discipline and a probable lawsuit."

"Bullshit."

Bryan sipped again, grimacing.

"*Sake* it ain't. Anyway, he kind of suggested that I could redeem myself during the preliminary hearing by being less certain about my observations when I testify than I was in my written report."

Webber used the spent cigarette to light another.

"He's such a predictable dumb-ass prick!"

He gulped half the drink.

"So how'd it all end up?"

Bryan sipped again, like a child forced to swallow bitter medicine.

"I told him I'd think long and hard about the situation and that in the end he could count on me to do the right thing."

The bar was filled, almost to capacity. A man with his wife and secretary at the next table was speaking louder than required. Two brunettes, probably lawyers, sat at the far end of the bar, laughing and joking with Paoli, much to the displeasure of the blonde at center.

"Did you ever call Destiny Mitchell?"

“Not yet, but I will.”

Bryan laughed.

“Would you believe McGuire told me not to talk to anyone at the DA’s office?”

“I believe it. They see it coming, but they won’t be able to get out of this one, an we’re gonna get them all, Alexander, McGuire, that bitch Rikki, Martini. All of them.”

He took a last drag from the cigarette, pinching it between his thumb and index finger as he dropped it into what was left of the grappa, where it hissed.

“And the beauty of it all—no matter how he fights it, that asshole Jordan did it. He murdered his wife. He’s going down, and he’s gonna drag all those other son’za bitches with im.”

CHAPTER 18

Barry had come into the conference room to meet with Vic Ehlers, the private detective. To Barry, Vic was more than a contractor. He was a friend who had been of great assistance over the years. Theirs was a friendship based on mutual benefit and respect. Vic was neither large nor tall. He was slight and bald on the top. He wasn't what anyone would expect one of San Francisco's top private eyes, but he knew the business.

A soldier during the Viet Nam conflict, he worked in MP internal affairs as an investigator. His phlegmatic personality and cynical outlook on human nature lent itself well to his profession. His abrasive nature sometimes made him unpleasant to be around, but those few friendships he had were genuine and enduring.

Unlit cigarette trembling between his thin lips as he spoke, he shoved the file toward Barry.

"There she is. Destiny Mitchell. Typical ambitious black broad on a mission to prove to the world that 'spades ain't so dumb after all.'"

Flaming matchstick between the fingers of his cupped left hand, he lit the cigarette, inhaling and blowing out the smoke, sighing with pleasure.

"Father was Air Force. He's dead. Mother's a retired teacher."

Barry was already scanning the file, though he looked up to indicate he was still listening.

"Older sister's a microbiologist-slash-geneticist working in a lab over in Emeryville. Her brother dropped outa college to become a preacher."

Barry read from the report.

"UCLA law school, *magnum cum laude*. Well, we knew she wasn't dumb. And the casework I asked about?"

"It's all there. She's good, thinks on her feet. Does lots of homework. Nine major cases in seven years. Five of em circumstantial. Never lost one. Hard ta say exactly why Granucci chose her, but out of all those bastards over at the DA, she's probably got the best chance of winning this thing."

Barry closed the file, returning it to the table.

"There's got to be a man."

Vic smirked, wryly.

"Isn't there always?"

He paused, opening a small black notebook taken from his shirt pocket. The book contained his personal notes, acquired information he didn't always share with clients, secrets no one had any business knowing.

"Colonel Charles Covington, United States Army at Fort Irwin down in the Mojave Desert training facility, West Point grad, near the top, clean record, several commendations, ambitious. Wants ta make General one day, upper middle-class family from a Boston suburb, father died in Nam. Fools around a little."

"Is he black?"

Vic shook his head in condemnation.

"Is he black? You fuckin libs are so funny! Yeah, he's black."

"What about the relationship? I mean, it can't be serious with them living so far apart."

Vic closed the notebook, returning it to his pocket.

"As I understand, she likes him a little more than he likes her. He isn't sure she'll fit the bill as a General's wife. Thinks she's a little too feisty and headstrong, but she's a good fuck. Moans a lot."

Barry's one eye held a look of incredulity.

"And how would *you* know about that?"

Vic grinned, self-satisfied.

"Trade secrets of an ex-soldier."

Vic shifted his weight in the chair, turning to get a direct look into the lawyer's eye. He lit another cigarette.

"Did Jordan tell ya?"

Barry was withdrawn and cool.

"I didn't ask. I don't want to know."

"Course you do. It's natural for you to wanna know—you more than anyone else. Now if you tell me it's *best* for you not to know, I can believe that, but don't tell me you don't wanna know."

Barry was standing.

"That's what I'm telling you. I do not want to know."

Sensing he had worn out his welcome, Vic stood.

"Well that says it all. You don't wanna know because you believe he's guilty. Want me ta tell ya what I think?"

"No, Vic. I don't want to hear another word about it."

The lawyer escorted the detective to the door, stopping on a thought.

"What about Stephanie Rodriguez?"

"I've had a guy down in San Jose for a week now. Says the town's cold. No leads, no trace of her, but I got another guy on her grandmother. I'll let ya know as soon as I hear somethin."

Barry patted Vic's shoulder.

"Fine. Now when are you going to let me look in that little black book you keep in your shirt pocket?"

Vic laughed.

"Like I've always said, it's privileged information. Biddin starts at about, uhm, two million, cash."

"*Arigato.*"

The middle-aged server backed away from the table, bowing as she disappeared. Of all the many tucked-away mom-and-pop owned little restaurants in Japantown, this one was Destiny's favorite. Kiyomi always told her to go where the "real folks" go to eat, and this place was full of nothing but the authentic folks.

The room was packed with little old Japanese couples and two or three young families in the booths along the wall. The table settings were Spartan, though practical. The tea on the table was still steeping in the ornamental urn, teacups looming large against the austerity of the stark tabletop.

"Why'd you invite him here? Isn't this like someone inviting you to a place like Big Bertha's Soul Food Kitchen just because you're black?"

Without looking up from the menu, Destiny answered.

"Doesn't matter. Food's great here. Besides, he's here against the wishes of the chief. We didn't want this to be a public meeting."

Brett scanned the room.

"Well, we accomplished that. Might as well be in Japan."

"Exactly."

The server, smiling at Destiny, poured the steaming tea.

"Maybe you ready to order now?"

Destiny looked from the door to her watch.

"*Mo suko shi matte ku da sai.*"

"*Hai.*"

As he watched the little woman tiptoe away, he was amazed.

"What? You speak Japanese?"

"Not really. I've studied it enough to say a few little things."

Brett hardly remembered asking the question. Even as she answered, his mind was on the preliminary hearing.

"So, in spite of the fact that you weren't there, you think Cyclops was up to something at the arraignment?"

"Come on, the way I heard it, he was nothing better than a half-assed lawyer. He filed the petition late? In Rosenthal's court? And you think that was an accident or a slip on his part?"

Brett was becoming defensive.

"It wasn't like that. You weren't there. You didn't see it."

She sighed, regretting she hadn't accompanied him to the arraignment.

"Look, a person wouldn't have to be there to know Divine was up to something. He filed the petition for bail late because he didn't *want* Jordan out of jail."

"And why's that?"

"I'm not sure. Because maybe he thinks Jordan would run, maybe he thinks Jordan would lead us to Stephanie Rodriguez."

Brett took a breath, saying nothing. Finally, he spoke.

"Maybe you're right. I hadn't really considered it, but I did hear a rumor this morning that they found packed suitcases in Jordan's downstairs closet, and they said there was a passport and over $30,000 cash in the safe."

She was quick to move for a conclusion.

"And you think Barry Divine isn't dialed in on that one?"

Signaling befuddlement, Brett shook his head.

"I don't know. Maybe he was acting, but if he was, he's good."

"Well, that's why they say he's one of the best."

She sipped from the steaming teacup.

"Anyway, if for some reason we don't find our witness, all we can do is hope Peter is able to help us by playing politics with the system. With no Stephanie Rodriguez, we can only hope he'll get us a sympathetic magistrate."

The detective walked toward the table, his eyes fixed on Destiny.

"Hi. I'm Bryan Osaka. I watched your opening statement on TV. I was really impressed."

Her face evinced irritation as she stood, responding to his attempt at humor.

"It wasn't an opening statement. I was just leveling the field. Destiny Mitchell."

Her co-counsel, standing beside her with a crumpled napkin in his left hand, extended his right.

"Brett McPherson. Thanks for coming."

All sat. The server returned, insisting for an order on what seemed like a busy night. Destiny ordered the *Udon*, while after some discussion Brett decided on the *Tonkatsu* and Bryan opted for an assorted plate of *Futomaki*, *Hamachi*, *Taki*, *Tobiko* and *California Roll*.

Readying her pen and notepad, Destiny began the interview.

"First of all, have you spoken with any investigator or lawyer for the other side?"

"This afternoon I spoke with Barry Divine at his office. Answered general questions, elaborated on unclear references in the report."

Destiny wrote.

"What time were you there?"

"About two."

"Tell him anything that differs substantially from what's in the report?"

He paused, thinking before answering.

"No. Nothing. I take great pride in turning in thorough, well-written reports that are accurate in every respect."

She put the pen and pad down.

"Well, did he tell you he's filed a motion to suppress everything you wrote and all the evidence obtained during the search of Jordan's home?"

Bryan sat back, surprised.

"What? He can't do that!"

She took a breath and continued.

"He can file the motion, and he did. In it he says you entered the home illegally and deceitfully, and that based on your warrant-less observations, the search warrant obtained was based on exaggeration and false innuendo. Wants it all suppressed during the preliminary examination. Without it, we've got nothing."

Bryan drew a breath and exhaled, shaking his head.

"I didn't know about any of that, but it's all bullshit! I entered that house legally. She practically begged me to come in and look around."

Brett broke in.

"Is that the way you'll tell it at the hearing?"

He turned to Brett.

"It's exactly what happened."

Destiny, writing again, looked up.

"Well, we've got one thing in our favor. Doesn't seem like Stephanie will be around to dispute anything you say."

Brett nodded.

"Besides that, officers at the house during the search reported that Jordan slapped her around when he got there for inviting you in and asking you to look around. It's all in the record."

Bryan relaxed a little.

"Yeah. That's right."

The server, slipping between Bryan and Destiny, placed the *Udon* in front of her. Within the space of a half-minute, all were served.

After a minute, Bryan, squinting from a wasabi rush, balanced his chopsticks on the edge of the plate.

"So, which one of you is going to question me during the preliminary?"

Destiny finished her mouthful, patting her lips with a napkin.

"I am."

"Anything I need to know?"

She turned toward him.

"Only that the defense is going to come after you. They'll question your motives, they'll ask if you were ordered by anyone to find a way in, about what information you relied on when telling Stephanie you thought the murderers could be still at large and possibly headed to the house. They'll ask if you carried any pre-existing animus, probably delve into your record on file and your personal life, that kind of stuff. Maybe they'll try and set up a way to impeach you by ambushing you during the trial. If you're anything but a choirboy, they'll know it."

Bryan sighed. He'd been on the stand over thirty times in his career, but no one had ever come after him before.

"You think it'll be Barry Divine?"

"Absolutely."

He wasn't hungry anymore. Instead, his stomach began to muddle in anticipation of the stress that was to come.

"So the preliminary's on Wednesday?"

Brett answered.

"No. The suppression hearing's on Wednesday, preliminary begins on Thursday."

Worried by Bryan's loss of composure, Destiny offered a more positive spin on the situation.

"We'll learn a lot from the preliminary. If we're lucky, the defense will give us a better idea about what strategies they'll be using during the trial."

Bryan shrugged, retrieving his chopsticks.

"So what exactly are you trying to accomplish at this preliminary?"

She answered, manner-of-fact.

"One thing. Putting on as little of our case as possible, we want to convince the magistrate there's sufficient probable cause to warrant a trial. That's all."

He sat back.

"Well, that shouldn't be too difficult. Should it?"

Brett answered.

"Not if we prevail at the suppression hearing. If we lose that, Jordan will walk."

A summation by Destiny lent a somber perspective.

"And if Jordan walks, it'll be time for all three of us to start looking for new jobs, maybe even new careers."

Brett differed.

"I think you're being overly-optimistic, Destiny. If Jordan walks, we'll have to pack our bags and leave this town."

Judge Harry Chow's day had been long and excruciating due to an overbooked schedule, but it was Wednesday, so he went over to *The Club*, a tiny room in the back of Sonny Long's little restaurant on Stockton Street in Chinatown to play *supsam jahn*, or thirteen cards.

The game was a Chinese version of poker, which was more complex than any American version of the game. Seated at his left was Councilman Norman Kwong while Financial District developer Johnny Wong sat across from him.

A liter bottle of Johnnie Walker Black Label sat in the center of the table next to a shallow dish containing pickled pig's feet. Johnnie brought the *sui jee* and *sui mei*, which were consumed. Only empty plates with traces of hot mustard and chili paste remained. Edward Hom, heir to the largest family laundry business in Chinatown, was late or missing again, so the three who waited were irritated.

A boombox on the chest-style freezer next to the door played nostalgic Chinese standards from the old country. Johnny hummed along, occasionally singing a lyric or two he remembered his mother chanting so many years ago. Norman and Harry were already gambling, engaging themselves in a game of casino-style blackjack for $20 a hand.

All three figured the commotion in the hallway outside was just Edward, drunk again, joking with the waiters about how much money he had taken from them in bets, but this time they were wrong.

The man who poked his face around the door wasn't Edward. It was a *lo fahn*, a round-eye, a white man, probably the only white man in town whose presence at such a game would be tolerated.

He smiled as he stepped into the open.

"Hello Harry, Norman, Johnny. I see you have an open seat. Mind too much if a white boy sits down with you? I've got money."

Harry looked from Johnny to Norman and then back to Peter Granucci who was already seating himself in Edward's empty chair.

Harry made the call.

"Five hundred dollars to get in *supsam jahn*, thousand dollar bank for *Shingaroo*."

Peter pulled a two-inch thick wad of folded fifty dollar bills from the inside pocket of his jacket and tossed it onto the table.

"I expected nothing less. As always, *fay doy*, I came ready to play."

Thirty minutes later, Peter's wad was smaller owing to the fact that few white men had mastered the game well enough to win money at it, especially from the likes of Harry Chow and Johnny Wong. Peter recouped a fraction of his losses during *Shingaroo*, but he finished down by about $900.

Harry laughed to himself as he and the district attorney were cloistered at a booth in the restaurant for private conversation, as he broached the subject.

"Don't get me wrong, Peter. I love taking your money, but that's not why you came. You're here about the suppression hearing tomorrow."

Ego still stinging for his losses, the district attorney answered.

"Well, I didn't just let you guys take me for a grand for the fun of it. What can you do?"

The judge sighed.

"I don't know. Just looking at the facts, it could go either way. It's all going to depend on what's brought in and what's argued. I've got my staff working overtime researching relevant cases. I'll finish reading all the lawyers' arguments and briefs in the morning."

His subtle belch smelled of pickled pig's feet mixed with scotch.

"What is it you want me to do, Peter?"

"Deny the motion to suppress. *Find* a way to do it. If you don't, you're going to have to find insufficient grounds for a trial when the preliminary's over. You'll be the one who let that bastard get away with murder."

Peter and Harry met while attending Stanford Law School almost three decades earlier. Peter was already in his third year when Harry arrived as a bewildered transfer student, halfway through his first year. They were never close friends and ran in different social circles, but they had engaged in legal discussions over the years through necessity. As a result, they respected each other, and both being liberal, they had similar legal ideas.

Peter knew about the poker game because, some eight years earlier when he was first elected, Harry invited him to sit in on a single session. He lost two thousand dollars that night and swore to those ruthless Chinese gamblers that it would be a cold day before they ever saw him or his money at their table again.

"I'll do what I can, Peter. You just make sure your lawyers are well prepared and that their arguments are logical and coherent. I don't want to end up having to coach them through it, especially when they're going up against Divine."

In his twelve years on the bench, Judge Harry Chow had never encountered a case with so many profound political undertones and such behind the scenes maneuvering. In example, the District Attorney had just crashed "the boys" weekly poker game to lobby his case.

And just that afternoon, Judge Chow received a surprise visit by Rikki Thomas, the police spokesperson, who took a pro-defense position. She suggested Osaka, her own detective who went in, was in violation of written department policy.

And Mayor Tony Martini called at five reminding the judge about the wonderful vacation they had shared two years earlier in Hong Kong and the Canton province. All this while he denounced

Granucci's political motives for bringing the complaint. Even Dottie Alexander called, telling Chow she respected "his people" for being fair and honest. She added that, however he decided the motion, she was sure he would consider the Alexander family.

Sitting across from Peter, Harry realized he was on the brink of making the biggest legal decision of his career. He tried to stand outside himself, his relationships and all the political bullshit involved in the case. By granting the motion and excluding the evidence discovered at Jordan's residence, he would essentially exculpate the man. Without the blood, the hair, the fingerprints and footprints, the State would never be able to bring Jordan up on charges. In the absence of another suspect or other suspects, any further investigation into the murder would be stalled or run aground altogether.

On the other hand, if Harry denied the motion and the prints and samples collected at Jordan's home came in, Jordan would have an opportunity in court to explain the damaging circumstantial evidence against him by mounting a vigorous defense, advanced by Barry Divine. The judge was already leaning toward denying the motion, but he wouldn't let Peter know it.

"Your lawyers will have to hold their own."

He sighed, testing the district attorney's resolve.

"You think they're up to it?"

Peter nodded.

"Destiny Mitchell is a little spitfire, and she feels personally involved in this thing. If she's able to hit her stride during the trial, I'd put my money on her against anybody. You watch and see. If Barry Divine comes in thinking he's up against some lightweight amateur, he'll end up flat on his ass and he'll never know what hit im."

CHAPTER 19

He and the general got on late, so they were only able to play 14 holes before shadows crept far enough onto the course to hide all but the highest hilltops. The desert day was warm for September, in the mid-90s, but the air had cooled to the 50s as they walked toward the clubhouse, bags on their backs and arms goose-pimply, their metal cleats clicking and crunching along the loose, gravely asphalt walkway.

The afternoon was productive for Charles Covington, though it was his first day off in almost a month. Leaving the base at five in the morning, he drove down Highway 15 toward San Bernardino before picking up the 10 over to Palm Springs. He attended an informal briefing at eleven before lunching with three Generals.

Two of the Generals were visiting from Washington D.C. Both were Pentagon personnel. The higher-ranking man, Major General Douglas Weaverly, Jr., had for many years maintained a powerful presence in the politics of the nation's capital, though he escaped any association with Colonel Oliver North and the Iran-Contra scandal. Weaverly's assistant, Gordon Bancroft, was himself a general, distinguished as a colonel for his role in U.S. withdrawal after the fall of Saigon. General Ted Deitler, Charles' boss, was responsible for all operations at Fort Irwin, which sat in the desert north of Barstow. Not surprising, the fort was one of the main domestic facilities for training troops in desert warfare.

General Deitler, a veteran of the Korean War and the Vietnam conflict, at a little more than five feet inches, was not a large man, though most soldiers at the fort considered him a hard-ass. When he met Charles four years earlier, he liked him right away, taking the tall, good-looking, young Negro major under a protective and directive aegis.

Ted was harder on Charles than any of the other colonels in his command, but the higher expectations and the greater responsibility helped develop character in the young general-to-be. Thirty-nine-year-old Charles was assigned to oversee desert training operations for the infantry and cavalry divisions.

By four o'clock, the driver for Generals Weaverly and Bancroft arrived to transport the two over to the Hunter Liggett Military Facility up in Monterey County, leaving Charles and Ted three to four hours of daylight for a hurried round of golf. When the game was called off due to poor visibility, Ted had Charles by two strokes.

After walking ten minutes along the meandering trail, they arrived at the clubhouse, shivering as the darkness extinguished the last traces of daylight, which glowed like red-orange embers on the horizon. It was already eight o'clock. Conscious of the time, they showered, changed and drove over to a restaurant on the strip to enjoy dinner and discussion.

Ted, as always, offered advice. He savored his last bite of blackened catfish.

"Weaverly was impressed by you. I know that because he told me so."

Charles kept his mouth shut. He listened, nodding, as Ted continued.

"Seems the only piece missing now is a *Mrs.* Covington."

Charles' anxious eyes widened as Ted sipped from the wineglass, studying the younger man's reaction.

"You knew it would come to this, and there's a practical reason for it, so you might as well plan it and execute."

Charles sipped from his glass, still saying nothing.

"What about Destiny Mitchell? She's pretty, she's black—thank God she's black. She's intelligent, carries herself like a lady."

Clearing his throat, Charles spoke in a deliberate tone.

"She's all those things you say she is and I really like her, Sir. But she's got a career, and I don't know if I'm ready to be second to anything where a wife's concerned."

Ted laughed.

"Oh, come on, Chuck. You're 39, not 93. Of *course* women have careers now, and it's a good thing. One of the downsides of being a general is that you're away from home for weeks at a time. These days you want a wife who can stay busy doing something."

Resolute, Charles maintained.

"I think a general's wife should be a good soldier, under the command of her husband, helping fight *his* battles, trusting in the direction he goes and following him without question."

He sighed, disgusted.

"Not in some courtroom where he amounts to nothing but a spectator on the sideline."

Charles continued, reacting to the scowl on the general's face.

"Your wife never had a separate career. Betty never worked outside your home."

Deitler pushed his plate away, wiping his mouth with the napkin.

"Different set of circumstances, different time."

He signed the credit card slip, glancing up.

"Listen, there's no escaping it. You have to get married, and right now Destiny Mitchell seems like your best prospect. Opportunity's an impatient bitch—she waits on no one."

After hesitating, Charles' face signaled slow acquiescence.

"Yes, Sir."

General Deitler smiled, patting Charles' shoulder as he stood.

"I like Destiny, Son, and so does Betty. She'll make you a good wife. It might be a little uncomfortable the first few years, but I think you'll learn to love it like I did."

Charles looked toward his mentor, forcing a smile.

"Yes, Sir."

"Hey? Have I ever steered you the wrong way?"

"Absolutely never, Sir."

The general glimpsed toward the front door and then back to his surrogate son.

"Good. Now Betty and I'll expect to hear some kind of announcement from you soon. See you back at the fort."

With the general gone, Charles slumped in the seat, staring ahead. He saw himself at a major crossroad in life. While he knew he loved Destiny, knew he loved her intelligence and her independence, he also knew she was too intelligent and independent to make a good wife for a general.

On many of the occasions he visited her in San Francisco, *he* was forced to wait for her to finish a hearing, a deposition or an argument in court. In restaurants up north and down south, *he* was forced to sit at the table, waiting for her as she worked the room. Even formal military functions were problematic events, especially when she was outspoken on political and legal issues.

However, he wanted to make general, and if that meant marrying Destiny Mitchell, he resolved do it, unless a replacement prospect came along soon.

The server steadied the drinks on the tray, as if the snifters contained nitro glycerin.

"Louis the Fourteenth!"

Even as he placed one in front of Charles and the other in front of an empty seat, the colonel objected.

"Waitaminute! I know how much this stuff costs! I never ordered cognac!"

"I know, Sir. Lady at the bar sent them over. Enjoy!"

Charles looked over at the bar as a dark-haired woman stood, smiling. As she walked over, Charles stood, pulling out the chair on his left.

The emerald colored velvet gown she wore flattered her bare shoulders, her ample bust line and well-shaped legs, subtly shadowed in gossamer black. She touched his forehand as she walked around the chair, smiled and sat, taking up a snifter and passing it beneath her nose. Upon that cue he sat, eager to find out who she was.

"Thank you very much. I admit I have a weakness for Louis the Fourteenth, but how'd you know? Do we know each other?"

Her deep burgundy-colored lips pouting, she crossed her legs toward him, sliding closer.

"I don't think you know me, but I know you, Charles."

He was apprehensive. Scanning the restaurant, he discreetly sought confirmation that the general had left. Turning back toward the intriguing woman, his eyes traced the outline of her soft, smooth, alabaster-white shoulders. They seemed moist in the soft light from overhead that washed over her tantalizing body.

The contour of the gown led his eyes to the cleavage between her large, luscious breasts, which were held together and pushed up toward him. She wasn't a pro. Pros didn't buy $150 shots of cognac.

"May I ask *how* you know me?"

"Mutual acquaintance. That's all I'll say for now."

She lifted his snifter, offering him aromatic persuasion.

"But being I'm down here all by myself, I really don't want to spend the night alone. And somehow I get the feeling you don't want to spend it alone either."

He could hardly believe what was happening. Her hand under the table was creeping along his inner thigh. He thought to stop her, but he had never felt so intimidated by a woman before. While it was uncomfortable, it was also exciting. If she was playing some kind of a strange Palm Springs sexual game, he wouldn't be the first to flinch.

"Really? And just what makes you think I don't want to spend the night alone."

She smiled, leaning forward.

"Oh, I know one really *big* reason."

In that instant, her fingers grasped the swollen bulge in the front of his pants.

"What do you think?"

Thirty minutes later, the muted sound of mattress springs squeaking and heavy breathing actuated the stillness of the darkened and otherwise empty hotel room. In a ray of faint moonlight that streaked through an opening near the top of the curtains, his black skin was barely visible, while portions of her legs, held high in the air, seemed florescent as they passed back and forth through the light. The air in the room was sultry, containing the distinctive scent of an excited woman. The moans, sighs and groans persisted for more than an hour and stopped.

He awoke at six a.m. with a jolt and sat up, disoriented. Thinking, he remembered where he was. He remembered the restaurant, the cognac, the woman and the seduction. He groped the sheets in the place where she fell asleep, but she was gone. In the light escaping the bathroom he could sense a person inside.

Rising from the bed, he approached the door and turned the corner to find her dressed in a conservative dark-blue business skirt suit, her white blouse buttoned to the neckline. Still nude, he recoiled.

Stepping toward him, she laughed, her eyes running the length of his body as she saluted.

"Good mornin, Soldier, rise and shine."

Squinting, his face beckoned an explanation.

"You don't remember me telling you last night? I've got an eight o'clock flight back up to San Francisco. Told you twice."

She flirted, her eyes lingering in the area below his waist.

"But you had something else on your mind."

Make-up all repacked in a clear zip-up bag, she turned back to the mirror, spraying her short black hair with liquid from a white aerosol bottle.

"Probably don't remember my *name* either, do you?"

"Did you tell me?"

She gripped his waist on each side, pulling herself against him and reaching up for a kiss. Patting his buttocks, she backed away and pivoted, heading for the door.

"My name's Rikki Thomas. I work for the San Francisco Police Department. Ask around next time you're up my way."

As she turned, her facial expression became cold and professional.

"On second thought, just ask your girlfriend, Destiny. She'll know where to find me."

Though it was only 8:15 a.m., the attorneys had spent 45 minutes waiting for the magistrate to appear. Judge Chow called the hearing for seven-thirty and warned counsel for both sides that he was intolerant of tardiness, regardless of excuse.

Destiny sat in the seat nearest the center of the room, at the table she shared with Brett. On the left side of the courtroom sat Barry Divine, closest to Destiny, while Teri Gonik, his red-haired co-counsel, sat next to him. Next to her was the distinguished and venerable Paul Previn, a bearded and gray-haired Santa Clara Law School professor who was a recognized expert on Fourth Amendment issues. While Previn framed the main arguments of the motion and was prepared to argue and answer on points of law, Barry Divine would handle the motion before the judge.

The room was quiet except for the sound of pages turning as lawyers read and wrote. Harry Chow closed the hearing, excluding all but court-required personnel. A court reporter arrived at eight-thirty, signaling the probable readiness of the magistrate.

The judge arrived ten minutes later, tired and irritable as he took his place on the dais. He examined both sets of lawyers who studied him, hoping to pre-determine his decision. There were some days where it was *just the tits* to be a judge. "This," he thought, "ain't one of them days."

"Counselors, I apologize for being late."

He checked the courtroom to make sure all were present.

"Certainly, you of all people know the complexity of the issues being argued and the Herculean task imposed on me as I've tried to consider all the arguments you've submitted in addition to my own research on the matter."

He paused, studying the expressions on their faces.

"And the fact that there are various political and celebrity undertones in this case hasn't made my job any easier, thank you."

He sipped from the water glass on his left.

"Just so you know, I've basically made a decision on how I'll rule. It's an initial, though not unchangeable determination based on what you've submitted and relevant cases I've considered. But the very purpose of you being here is to clarify and strengthen your arguments as you answer questions that come to my mind. That being done, I can render a final decision."

He looked toward Destiny.

"We'll begin with you."

She stood, waiting for the judge to begin.

"We've all read Osaka's report, Ms. Mitchell, and one of the central questions pertaining to this hearing is the determination of whether or not Stephanie Rodriguez actually asked him to go into the residence and search it in the manner that he went about searching it. Her statement is rambling and vague, but in it she says that she invited him in because, under false pretenses, he frightened her into believing she was in some sort of immediate peril. My question to you is, 'did Inspector Osaka have any information or any report from which he could have drawn a conclusion that she was somehow at risk for being there?'"

Destiny was flipping through a notebook as he spoke. After flagging a page, she answered.

"It's in Inspector Garner's report, your Honor. During the interview with the defendant that morning, Mr. Alexander told detectives that his vehicle registration listed the address at his *Haight Ashbury* residence. Based on that information, several of the detectives believed that, if the defendant's car had been stolen by the same persons who had murdered Lynette, then their next stop might have been Jordan's house. The Pacific Heights address was listed on Jordan's license, but the Haight Ashbury address was listed on the registration."

The judge nodded.

"And Inspector Garner somehow communicated such a suspicion to Inspector Osaka?"

She flipped back one page.

"We have records of a call made to Osaka at six-fifty that morning, and Garner will attest to the nature of a conversation at that time in which he submitted such a suspicion. Page eight, Elliot Garner."

Harry scribbled something on his pad, ignoring the fact that Barry Divine was standing.

"Very well."

Ignoring protocol, Barry interrupted the judge.

"If I may on that issue, your Honor? I just would like to remind your Honor that Garner's report is the one we referred to in our argument as *altered*. By his own admission, Inspector Garner initially listed the time of the interview with Jordan at seven-thirty and later changed it after reading Osaka's report, which indicated the interview happened an hour earlier."

The judge nodded, interjecting.

"So your argument is that, if the interview wasn't until seven-*thirty*, Osaka couldn't have known at *seven* that Jordan would suggest the killers were the same men who stole his car and that the registration listed the Haight Ashbury address?"

Barry finished the thought.

"Which only serves to prove our chief argument. Osaka was there because he is part of a rogue faction of the San Francisco Police Department bent on injuring an innocent man for personal and political reasons. When Jordan wouldn't let inspectors Harris and Garner in at five that morning, the detectives put their heads together and *invented* an exigency, which took the form of an illegal and unwarranted search. The Fourth Amendment was purposed to circumscribe such a reckless—"

Harry Chow interrupted.

"Mr. Divine, as you can see, there is no jury seated. You can step off the constitutional soapbox any time now."

Barry turned toward the judge.

"According to the language of the amendment, which is unequivocally instructive and unambiguous, every piece of evidence obtained in the search of Jordan's home should rightfully be excluded in the preliminary examination. That should include detective reports, all physical evidence and testimony relating to this contemptible abrogation of Jordan Alexander's personal and civil rights."

The judge listened, writing all the while. Barry tightened his jaw, smirking, and sat.

Looking up, Harry spoke, mindful of word choice.

"Ms. Mitchell, would you care to respond?"

She was speaking even before he finished asking the question.

"Absolutely, your Honor. First of all, there is no question that the interview with Jordan happened at six-thirty. That fact has been independently corroborated by Harris' report, which lists the correct time, *and* by a statement from the clerk who issued the key for the room, at six-fifteen on her log. We have documentation on every detail of that morning, and defense counsel is aware of it. The detectives didn't have to make up a lie to explain anything. Jordan Alexander had already done that."

Barry Divine interrupted again.

"Your Honor? The issuance of a key by a clerk is hardly proof of the time the interview occurred. The detectives could have held the key for forty-five minutes or even an hour before using it."

Offended by the interruption, Destiny broke in.

"Your Honor, I frankly resent the insinuation by counsel that the detectives are somehow corrupt to the point of lying to frame Mr. Alexander for his wife's murder. Counsel has lost all sense of objectivity in the matter. Any suggestion about corruption has no factual basis and reflects more of counsel's own *myopic* view of the police and the world than anything else. Can we stick to the facts of this case, please?"

Barry laughed as he responded.

"*Myopic*? Your Honor, if counsel wasn't so green and inexperienced, she would have known 'myopic' has been used on me already. It's hackneyed. Beyond that, one of these days if counsel tries a case from the *defense* side of things, perhaps then she'll realize that some of us can't afford to believe facts just because police tell them to us."

He paused to change direction.

"There's no question detectives wanted to get into Jordan's home at five o'clock on the morning of August 18th. There's no question he told them they were not welcome inside for any reason. There's no question they knew he was gone and that Stephanie Rodriguez was there alone at seven o'clock when Osaka knocked on the door. There's no question Osaka told her something that intimidated her into submitting to a general search of the property. And finally, there's no question Garner's report was altered."

He paused to take a breath, surprised he hadn't been interrupted.

"One must however, question the motives and actions of the detectives, which were far from generous and fair as far as Jordan Alexander was concerned. That fact would lead prudent individuals to ask if there was some pre-existing animus on the part of the police department or the detectives involved. If not, no one is harmed for the asking, but if there *is* some sinister motive in operation, we would all be party to it if we didn't ask the difficult questions and demand complete answers on details involving the essential facts of the case."

Concerned that the judge was losing interest, he concluded.

"The main reason for this hearing is determine if Jordan Alexander's Fourth Amendment rights were violated, and we happen to think we've proven our argument. At the bottom line, the police went in without a warrant and without probable cause. Under the exclusionary rule, we believe the court is constitutionally bound to disallow all evidence and reports arising from a search that was patently unwarranted and illegal."

He sat, patting Teri on the shoulder and whispering into her ear. Destiny still stood, seething anger betraying her affected smile. Her nostrils were flared, her breathing shallow and irregular.

"As we see it, your Honor, the only person who has been deprived of guaranteed constitutional rights is Lynette Alexander. She's dead. Her life was taken. Now Mr. Divine can stand up here and cite the Gettysburg address if you let him, but it, like his far-fetched police corruption scheme and his Fourth Amendment references are completely irrelevant in this hearing."

She placed her notebook on the table and walked into the aisle, approaching the judge.

"Lynette Alexander is dead, and we know the *police* didn't kill her in some kind of a conspiracy to frame the defendant. When Inspector Osaka went to the defendant's residence on August 18th to tell Stephanie of legitimate police concerns for her safety, he wasn't part of some elaborate political or personal scheme. He was just doing his job. When she asked him if he would come in and look around, he put himself in harm's way to put her at ease. When he inadvertently found sticky blood in the defendant's room, he immediately ceased all searching and called for a warrant, for which a magistrate like your Honor determined there was probable cause. Everything he did was by the book. For that reason, your Honor, the State is certain you have a solid legal basis for denying the defense's motion to suppress legitimate evidence that clearly identifies the killer in a murder case. Thus with great confidence we await your ruling on this matter."

Harry Chow's body heaved beneath the black robe as he drew a breath, exhaling through tightened lips.

"As I said before, when I came into the room, I was prepared to issue a decision based on your written arguments, but what I think it's best to do now is *postpone* my ruling until some of the facts-in-dispute can be settled."

He removed his glasses and massaged his eyeballs through closed eyelids before looking up.

"There's no doubt that Inspector Osaka will be called to testify during the preliminary examination, and because he's so central to the State's case, I'm hoping he'll be one of first persons called. I expect that many of the questions in my mind will be settled during his testimony. That being done, at some appropriate time during the preliminary, we'll reconvene and I'll render a decision on the suppression motion then."

He turned his body toward Destiny.

"Until that time counsel, I'm going to ask you to limit the scope of your case to the investigation at the crime scene, the detectives' interviews with Mr. Alexander and any other relevant interviews. Certainly you'll be able to bring Inspector Osaka on and discuss the circumstances that led to the search of Mr. Alexander's residence, but all discovery from the residence once he was inside will be off-limits until the suppression motion is settled."

Barry Divine stood.

"Thank you very much, your Honor."

Turning toward Destiny, he smiled, lips tight and closed, before winking his right eye and stepping toward her, right hand extended.

"Good job, Counsel. Somehow, I get this feeling that you will be a worthy adversary."

His voice was low and controlled.

"I look forward to the challenge."

Irresolute, she grasped his hand, still not certain whether or not she wanted to exchange pleasantries. She wanted to say something witty or sarcastic, but the judge's non-ruling was disappointing. What it meant, she didn't know. Either Peter Granucci had failed at persuading the judge to deny the motion or perhaps someone more powerful in the city wielded a greater influence on the proceeding.

As her eyes focused on the scarlet embroidery of his white shirt cuff that advertised *B.A.D.*, she wondered if Barry Alexander Divine had found a way to influence the judge. Her response, delivered in an undertone, was icy cold, without a trace of a smile.

"Challenge? And for some reason, I thought you were here because you believed your sorry-ass cousin wasn't guilty."

CHAPTER 20

The phone's ringtone was inaudible in the bustling newsroom. In fact, the call would have never been answered if a receptionist, searching the room for a reporter, hadn't seen the line blinking.

"Oh no! It's no problem. She's here. Let me find her for you."

As she placed the call on hold, she cursed to herself. Now she would have to track down *two* errant reporters!

She peered into the office to find the woman she sought, black stocking-covered legs crossed and up on the desk. Yamakita was on the phone pressing some poor convicted felon for details of the plea bargain.

"Excuse me, Kiyomi. You have a phone call. Line eight. He wouldn't say who it was, but he wanted to talk to you and he said it was very important."

Cupping the mouthpiece with her hand, she pulled her legs off the desk and sat up in the chair.

"Thank you, Theresa. I'll take it in here."

Kiyomi curtailed her questioning, warning the felon that she would call back. Flipping to a fresh page in the notebook and readying her pen, she pressed the button corresponding to the tiny blinking red light.

"Kiyomi Yamakita. How may I help you?"

Her face erupted in an excited smile.

"Oh hello, Charles! Wow! To what do I owe the pleasure? How are you?"

She tossed the pen aside.

"I'm fine. Busy as always, but fine. Destiny tells me you're coming up this weekend."

She swiveled in the chair, closing the door with an extended leg.

"A favor for a future general? Okay, but you know you might end up owing me, and I drive a hard bargain. I might ask you to start a war!"

She laughed.

"Oh really? Well, I'm not sure if I'm your person, but I do know most of the players in this town. Who do you want to know about?"

Her countenance changed, all joy extinguished from her aspect.

"Oh I *know* her all right, and she's bad news. She's a wicked, conniving little bitch whose known in this town for two things, fucking people and fucking people over. Why? What do you want to know about her?"

She glanced over at a gold-framed five-by-seven of Destiny and the colonel embracing at a formal military function photographed four months earlier.

"Well, in what context did this lieutenant of yours mention her? I mean, has she been down there?"

She stood, turning toward a mirror, checking her make-up.

"No, she'd never date a lieutenant—she likes women. But if she was down there, rest assured she was up to something."

She paused, biting her bottom lip, thinking.

"Waitaminute! I get it now, Charles. She didn't go down there to see one of your lieutenants, did she? She went down there to see *you*!"

Her eyes squinted as she listened to his long explanation.

"So you're saying you just sort of met her by happenstance? *I'm* saying it was no accident. What happened? You *talk* to her?"

She sat on the edge of the desk.

"All right, that's fine. We can talk about it in person. You're coming up Friday night, right?"

She opened her appointment book and began writing.

"Well, I just happen to know for a fact that Destiny will be busy most of the time you're here. Preliminary hearing for that big case she's got starts tomorrow morning. Maybe we can squeeze in a lunch on Saturday?"

She sighed, closing the book.

"What's that?"

Her face frowned.

"Well I, I don't know. Destiny's my best friend and I'm a little uncomfortable keeping secrets from her, especially—"

She listened for a moment and nodded.

"All right, all right! I won't say anything about it, but you *will* tell me everything on Saturday, won't you?"

Kiyomi hollowed her cheeks, pursing pink-lipstick-faded lips.

"Okay, we'll do that. See you on Saturday."

Worry transformed her face as she hung the receiver. She glanced down again at the photo of Destiny and Charles. Destiny was looking into his eyes, heart fluttering and eyes beaming the way they did when she had it bad. Kiyomi, of all people, knew how much Destiny loved that man. "It'll be all right," she whispered to herself, and yet her reporter's intuition contradicted her optimistic affirmation. Deep inside, she was certain, if Rikki Thomas was involved in any way, her best friend was headed for major pain and heartache.

"Mr. Mayor. Thank you very much for coming. It'll mean the world to Jordan."

Tony Martini shook the extended hand, looking about, noting the cameras that followed his every move. He smiled in his practiced fashioned, nodding as he entered the gauntlet of reporters crowded at the entrance to the jail building.

"Mr. Mayor!" one man shouted, "Does your presence here mean you believe Jordan Alexander is innocent?"

He stopped, and ignoring the reporter, he answered the cameras.

"That's an issue for the judicial system to decide. I'm here because Jordan Alexander is my *friend*. I have a great deal of respect for the Alexander family. Let it never be said that Tony Martini wasn't there for a friend in his time of need. That's all I'm going to say for right now."

Ignoring the cacophonous clamor from the chorus of reporters yelling garbled questions, the mayor and his entourage entered the building only to find another garrison of cameras and reporters stationed inside.

"This way, Mr. Mayor."

A guard directed the group along a private route that led to the visiting area. After winding through a series of hallways, stairwells and upwards in a private elevator, the mayor entered a room where haggard Jordan sat in the distance, his head drooping and eyes held low. It was not the Jordan Alexander he expected to see, not the friend he had known. Instead of upbeat, Jordan looked beat-up. He looked defeated, he looked... *guilty*. Tony extended his arms.

"Jordan! My friend! How *are* you, *pisano*?"

Jordan held the mayor for a long time.

"I'm going crazy in here, Tony. You've got to help me!"

Tony patted his shivering friend's back, sliding his hand over Jordan's shoulder before leading him over to a table where the two sat. His left hand on Jordan's shoulder, Tony looked toward Barry and the others.

"Why don't you give us a little privacy? We need to talk alone for a few minutes."

With Barry, Rikki and three others seated at the other end of the room, Jordan and Tony whispered together. In the early going, Jordan became agitated and cursed aloud on several occasions, but Tony always managed to settle him. They talked for a little more than twenty minutes before Tony stood, motioning for the others to come over.

"It's going to be all right. Jordan's going to be all right. He'll be fine."

Jordan looked up at the skeptical audience.

"Yeah, I'm going to be all right."

Tony placed his hand on Rikki's shoulder.

"Okay, why don't you and my staffers head on back to the office. I need to talk to Barry about a few things on the way out. I'll catch up with you in a few minutes."

Barry lingered with Jordan for a few minutes, giving last minute directions on courtroom decorum. All instructions being given, Barry and the Mayor watched the guards take Jordan away.

Tony crossed his arms, leaning back against the wall.

"So what do you think, Barry? Is this thing going to trial?"

"I'm doing everything I can to avoid it, but if the judge denies the suppression motion, I'm afraid a trial's unavoidable."

Tony grabbed the attorney's left shoulder.

"Look Barry, you and I both know that you get *off* on this going to trial stuff. It might be the ultimate orgasm for you, but it's serious business for me and Jordan. I got an election next year and Jordan's stuck in this shithole of a jail while *you're* doing television interviews."

Barry pried the Mayor's fingers from his shoulder.

"It's *your* shithole. Do something about it!"

He readjusted his coat and continued.

"Like I told both of you! I'm doing everything I can for Jordan. Granucci's all over his ass. If either of you think you can find someone better, do it and I'm outa here. If you can't, you both need to shut-up and let me do my fuckin job!"

Tony softened. He extended a hand to calm the lawyer.

"Look Barry, I didn't mean—"

Barry slapped the hand away.

"Keep your fuckin hands off me, Tony. You can talk to me, but keep your fuckin hands off me!"

Tony raised both hands to face level, flicking his pinkies outward in a resigned gesture.

"Sorry. It's just that it's been rough for all three of us. I just wanted to make sure you were doing all you could."

"Bullshit, Tony! You're just trying to cover your ass."

He studied the mayor's face.

"What he tell you? Did he tell you all about that night? Did he tell you whether or not he *did* it?"

Not knowing how to respond, the mayor remained silent.

"Never mind! I don't want to know. All you're concerned about is how a trial will affect your re-election."

Tony cocked his head, nodding.

"Of course I am, but that doesn't mean I don't care about Jordan. I'm just—"

Barry cut him off.

"What you ought to be worried about is the verdict, because ya gotta know is if Jordan goes down, it won't be long before Peter Granucci carves up your fat ass and serves it up to all your enemies in this town."

CHAPTER 21

"Please state your name and spell it for the record."

"Gloria Applebaum, G-l-o-r-i-a-A-p-p-l-e-b-a-u-m."

Magistrate Judge Harry Chow sighed before setting the proceeding in motion.

"Ms. Mitchell? You're on."

Destiny stood, stunning in a lime-green and cream-colored St. Johns knit suit, straight skirt flattering her shapely hips.

"Thank you for coming, Mrs. Applebaum."

The woman smiled, glancing sidelong at the judge before bowing her head.

"Mrs. Applebaum, first of all, while the State is grateful that you've come forward to help us in our struggle to sort out what happened on the night of August 17th, I have to ask you as I'm sure Mr. Divine will ask you. Why have you come forward so late?"

The apprehensive witness looked toward a stern-faced, balding man in the audience and then back at Destiny.

"Harold."

"Harold? Who's Harold?"

"My husband. Says I'm a busybody."

"So you're saying you called the police so late because your husband objected to you coming forward earlier?"

Barry did not look up from his notes as he spoke.

"Objection. Leading."

"Sustained."

Destiny sighed.

"Mrs. Applebaum, can you tell us why it took you so long to call the police?"

"It's like you said. Harry my husband there told me not to call. Said if Jordan had it in him ta kill his wife like that, what would stop him from comin after us next?"

Barry voiced the interruption as he was still writing, never looking at the witness.

"Move to strike the entire last response, your Honor. And can the court direct our witness to limit her responses to the questions being asked?"

The instruction given, Destiny smiled at Gloria, trying to appear reassuring.

"Mrs. Applebaum, what is it that made you ultimately disregard your husband's severe warnings and finally call the police?"

"The girls."

"The girls?"

Gloria nodded.

"Lynette and Jordan's daughters. Especially that little buttercup, Lyndsey. They use to sometimes play on the sidewalk in front of my house. Harold and me live next door. Anyway, every day that went by with the news reports an all, I just felt guiltier and guiltier until finally I just had to call and say what I saw."

Destiny glanced up from the legal pad.

"Are you referring to something you saw on the night of August 17th?"

"Of course I am. Otherwise I wouldn't be here, would I?"

Destiny leaned against the table.

"What did you see?"

"Like I told you, I saw Jordan Alexander's car—his, his Rolls Royce. It was parked in front of the house for forty minutes, maybe even an hour."

"What time did you see it there?"

"Nine-thirty, exactly."

"Exactly? How can you be so sure?"

Gloria answered, her growing confidence and personality beginning to show.

"Because Harold's a stick in the mud. Him and me do the same thing every Sunday night. At six o'clock we watch Mike Wallace on *60 Minutes*, then we eat dinner and get the kitchen clean in time for Angela on *Murder, She Wrote*, and then I listen to my self-improvement tapes for an hour until ten when we go to bed. The tapes are an hour, thirty minutes on each side. And I had just turned the *Assertive Seniors* tape over when I saw Jordan Alexander pull up in his Rolls."

"Do you know if the person who pulled up was in fact the defendant?"

"You mean Jordan? I couldn't see close up, but I think it was him."

"Objection. Speculative."

"Sustained."

Destiny stood, approaching the witness.

"Well, at any time did you see two large black men get out of the car and go into the house?"

"No. It was just one person. And besides, you can't really see a black person in the dark. No offense intended, but it's a known fact. The man I saw wasn't black."

Destiny glanced over her shoulder toward Brett before walking over and conferring with him. She looked back toward the witness.

"Thank you very much, Mrs. Applebaum. But one more question. Do you know what time the Rolls left the front of the house?"

"It was still out there when I went in to take my shower at 10:15 like I always do, but it was gone at 10:30 when I got out."

"Thank you."

Destiny sat, signaling she had no further questions as Barry stood, indicating he was prepared for cross-examination. Judge Chow introduced him before allowing him to begin.

The lawyer's voice was gentle, though professional.

"So you're a fan of Angela Lansbury's *Murder, She Wrote*, are you?"

Gloria became withdrawn.

"I watch it."

"Faithfully every Sunday, according to what you said earlier."

"Yes."

"Do you like murder mysteries?"

"I guess so."

"Would you say you are *fascinated* by them?"

"I wouldn't say that exactly, but I like em well enough."

Barry had gone back to the table and wrote as she answered.

"What about other shows? Ever watch *Ellery Queen*? *Mystery Theater*?"

"Yes."

"And books? You read Agatha Christie and Sir Arthur Conan Doyle?"

"Yes. Okay, I like murder mysteries."

"And you like spying on your neighbors. You told us your husband called you a busybody. Why would he call you a busybody?"

Destiny looked up from the pad.

"Objection, your Honor. Calls for speculation and the question's irrelevant."

The judge sighed, turning toward Barry.

"Before I sustain the objection, are you going somewhere

definite with this?"

"Your Honor, she volunteered her husband called her a busybody. I think it might be helpful to know why."

Barry smirked, certain his argument hadn't won over the magistrate.

"Anyway, it'll be my last question along that line."

Harry Chow contemplated before acquiescing.

"Ask the question."

"Why would your husband call you a busybody, Mrs. Applebaum?"

Angry, she looked toward her husband. Here he was in court, with his mouth shut, and he was still humiliating her.

"Oh I don't know. You'd have to ask him that."

"Mrs. Applebaum, how's your health?"

"Fine."

"And your memory?"

"Fine. I have a great memory."

"Are you under a physician's care?"

"No."

Destiny sighed aloud.

"Objection. The question is irrelevant."

"Objection's irrelevant. She's already answered the question."

Barry sat.

"I have nothing else."

Harry adjusted the glasses on his face.

"Okay. Ms. Mitchell?"

"Nothing else, your Honor."

"Very well. Next witness?"

The act being over, both sat up in the bed, the flat, white cotton sheets sticking to their sweaty bodies. They were long-time friends, and while some intimate acquaintances got together over lunch or drinks to discuss details of their personal lives, these two took the same room in the same hotel at least once a month, twice or three times in exceptional or unduly stressful months.

The sex was a prelude that inspired candid discussion, the nudity a symbol of honesty and openness.

The mayor was still breathing hard minutes later as she sipped the Asti Spumante from a tulip-shaped flask she took up from the nightstand at bedside.

He panted.

"It's been a busy week. I never made it to the gym."

Rikki smiled, patting his rounded, pudgy stomach that quivered like gelatin, though he did his best to suck it in.

"I can tell, but then, I didn't go to the gym either."

She teased, stretching one of her shapely legs high into the air for a moment. Then she gently arched her back, drawing his attention to her delicate, sculptured waistline, yielding to firm though graceful hips.

"Your wife feeds you too much on purpose. She likes you fat."

Minutes later, as he alternated between a cigarette and the sparkling wine, the strategy session began.

"Why is it you can get to just about any man who's a player in this town, but you can't do anything for me with that asshole Divine? And that's what he is, a divine asshole."

Though she didn't usually smoke, she took the cigarette from him and managed a long, blissful drag, her face resigning as she blew it out.

"Cuz he's a freak. He'll never let anyone anywhere close to him. No one, not even his own mother, has ever been allowed up in his office! Besides, we don't need him. I think we got enough with other people."

"What do we got?"

She took one last drag before handing the cigarette back to him.

"Listen Tony, I've told you this before. As far as the things I do for you go, the less you know, the better. You've just got to trust me."

He leaned over her, grasping her shoulders with his hands.

"You know I trust you, but this is different. This is my ass. I didn't want to go anywhere near that jail yesterday, but I had to. Dottie Alexander asked me to go as a personal favor to her. She's my biggest backer. How could I say no?"

She rolled toward him, leaning on her right elbow.

"And what did I tell you?"

"You called it political Russian roulette, but what would you have done?"

She closed her eyes, contemplating.

"Well, I guess I would have gone too, but that will have to

be the last contact or comment you ever have about Jordan and the charges against him. You have to distance yourself."

He shrugged, confused.

"How?"

"You just stay silent. Over the next few days, I'll leak a story to the press about what happened at the jail. It'll come from one of the guards who watched you and Jordan with the rest of us. The story will go that you two had an argument, that there's a major rift between you. I'll have sources say you two haven't gotten along over the past two years, that it's never been the great friendship people thought it was."

"And his grandmother?"

"Fuck Dottie Alexander. She'll be dead in a few years. Besides, you don't need her anymore. You're the incumbent mayor. If you cut your ties to Jordan, you'll be fine."

Tony nodded as he leaned back, sipping the wine.

"That's all well and good, but we're still going to have problems if this thing goes to trial. Granucci is going to jack this thing off so the trial will start in February or March, which coincidentally is the beginning of the mayoral campaign. He wants to make it a big fuckin orgasm right in the middle of the election."

Rikki covered his mouth with the fingers of her left hand.

"Leave that to me. If we can avoid a trial, we will. If it does go to trial, I'll screw up Destiny Mitchell's world so much that she'll be a basket-case out there. She'll make herself and Peter Granucci look like shit, and Granucci'll be sorry he ever thought to bring this case."

CHAPTER 22

Barry sighed, disgusted. Bryan Osaka was lying to the judge. And yet, to a judge wanting to be convinced, the detective's testimony probably seemed credible. It would be an uphill battle, but Barry preferred it that way, heated and hard-fought. He looked over at Jordan who had been gripping his shoulder, contradicting the detective in angry undertones.

Leaning toward his cousin, Barry whispered.

"Let me do what I do, okay Jordie?"

Jordan was handsome in the dark blue *Nino Cerruti* suit. Owing to Barry's advice, he appeared composed, confident, and innocent.

"Ask him when he got there!"

"Again, let me do my job, Jordie."

The magistrate judge interrupted the quiet discussion.

"Mr. Divine, as I said before. Your witness?"

Barry stood, bowing his head in deference to the magistrate. Smiling toward Harry Chow, he began.

"Inspector Osaka, your credentials and your many commendations from the police department are impressive, but will you tell the court what every last document and award you presented have in common?"

Confused, Bryan stuttered.

"I, I don't think I understand your question."

Barry's voice was insistent.

"It's a simple, straightforward question, Inspector. What is it that every last document and commendation presented to this court have in common? I mean, you're supposed to be this great detective, aren't you?"

Studying Bryan's comportment, Destiny interrupted.

"Objection, your Honor. The question's too broad. The witness couldn't possibly know what counsel's getting at. No one could."

"Sustained."

Harry removed his glasses, speaking to Barry.

"Start again, and try something a little more pointed."

Barry sighed and continued.

"Very well. Mr. Osaka. Is there a signature on each document and commendation presented to the court as proof of your record?"

Bryan was apprehensive.

"I, well I... Yes, I guess they're all signed."

"And do you know whose signature is on each of those?"

Taking a breath, Bryan answered, staring straight ahead.

"I would guess they're all signed, but I've never really checked to see if they were all signed by the same person."

"But you wouldn't be surprised if I told you they all were, would you?"

"No."

Barry retrieved a sheet of paper from the desk.

"I have here the last commendation you received back in May. Can you look at it and tell me who signed it?"

Destiny called out as Barry approached the detective.

"Objection. This whole line of questioning is irrelevant."

"Overruled."

Though Bryan did his best to appear calm, the paper shaking in his hands revealed his nervousness. Barry continued.

"Inspector Osaka, do you know who signed that commendation and all the others you brought before the court?"

"Yes."

"Will you tell the court the name of that person?"

Bryan glanced toward Destiny before he answered.

"Police Commander Dennis Webber."

"And how well do you know Commander Webber?"

"Fairly well. He was my teacher when I attended detective school."

Barry tugged the document from Bryan's fingers, turned while speaking, and passed it to the judge.

"Have you at any time discussed the testimony you would give in court today or any future testimony with Commander Webber?"

"No."

At his desk, Barry retrieved Osaka's report from a stack of documents piled on the table's edge.

"What time did you arrive at Jordan's Loma Vista Way residence in the early morning of August 18th?"

"It's in the report. I remember distinctly. It was few minutes before five."

"And why were you there?"

By this time, Bryan seemed a little more at ease.

"I had orders to watch the house."

"Really? And did you know *why* you were watching the

house? What were you watching for?"

"Nothing specific. The orders weren't that specific. I guess since we had information that Jordan had been mugged that night and his wife had been killed, someone thought it might be a good thing to watch the house."

"And who is that someone?"

Bryan shrugged.

"I don't know. Could have been any one of a few people at—"

Approaching the witness, Barry cut him off, his voice becoming hostile.

"There's no jury present, Osaka. Don't pretend you're stupid! You know what I'm asking. Who gave you the order to watch the house?"

"Move to strike, your Honor. That comment was uncalled for."

Harry Chow spoke to the excited recorder who typed with raised eyebrows.

"Please strike the comment. You can leave the question."

He turned back toward Barry, reproachful, shaking his head.

"You're not winning points employing these in-your-face tactics. Just ask the questions."

Barry nodded, though traces of a trembling smile tugged at the left corner of his mouth. He had already achieved more than he hoped for. He wanted to test Osaka's poise, but he had shaken the uneasy inspector.

"You're right, your Honor. I'm sorry."

Barry spoke toward the empty jury box.

"I'm sorry if I was in your face, Inspector Osaka, but can you please tell us who at the police department gave you the order to watch the house?"

"Objection! Asked and answered."

"Overruled."

The magistrate judge turned toward Bryan.

"Answer the question, Mr. Osaka. Who gave the order?"

Bryan's flinching was perceptible.

"Commander Dennis Webber. He gave the order."

Barry returned to the desk and was prepared to launch a new line of questioning, but the judge, noting it was already five o'clock on Friday night, ordered the proceeding *in recess* until

Tuesday. On Monday, Harry would conduct an *in limine* Frye hearing on Destiny Mitchell's petition to admit preliminary DNA analysis of blood samples found in the Sacramento Street and Loma Vista Way homes, as well as those found in the Rolls Royce.

"I don't know if I like this, Charles. Where are you taking me? Where are we going?"

"It's a special spot, my favorite place in the whole world."

It was six o'clock as he drove along Fell Street in the rented charcoal-gray Lincoln Towncar. Destiny sat in the passenger seat, her head against the red leather headrest and a blindfold covering her eyes.

Charles showed up at court in a tuxedo just as the session recessed. Conjunct with excited Neiman-Marcus store clerks, he picked out an exquisite sapphire *Givenchy* gown with matching shoes and hosiery, and as he gave it to her, he insisted she should put it on right away. He told her he had reservations at "the coolest restaurant on the face of the earth."

Before leaving the court building, he asked her to put on a blue satin evening mask he purchased. Flattered about all the effort and expense he put himself through, she argued half-heartedly and let him cover her eyes with the silky blindfold. Her briefcase in his left hand, he led her along, right arm around her waist, as he guided her down the steps and over to the car.

The interior of the car was still warm and new, though she caught the subtle scent of Charles' cologne and the sense of his unique body pheromones, which she knew well. The leather seats were soft, holding her body in a firm embrace.

He started the car and pulled out into traffic. She could hear the sound of cars passing even as he turned on the stereo cassette. The song was recognizable as soon as the lead-in began. It was Destiny's favorite song of all time, sung by her favorite singer, *Moon River* by Nancy Wilson. Under the mask, tears ran from her eyes, causing the fabric to stick to her face. Reaching over with her left, she squeezed his extended right hand.

"Charles, I love you."

"I love you too, Destiny."

He made a few turns, but after that he drove a direct course for almost twenty minutes before pulling over and parking. Turning up David Sanborn's *Love and Happiness*, he opened his door.

"Don't move a muscle and don't peek. I just need to check on our reservations."

She wasn't about to peek and ruin the wonderful air of mystery he worked so hard to create. She thought she felt the car rock once or twice, but she figured the sensation came from cars passing by too closely. After ten minutes, she heard a key trip the lock and felt her door come open.

"Our table awaits."

The day was warm for September, so the air hadn't cooled. As he led her along, she thought it strange that the ground under her feet was grassy. Restaurants usually had paved walkways leading inside. She took careful, cautious steps for about seventy-five feet with him before he stopped. The chair pushed against the outside of her left leg and positioned behind her was a cue to sit. He guided her into the seat and took her left hand in his, slipping what felt like a ring onto her third finger.

"Okay, Destiny. You can remove the blindfold."

As her pupils adjusted to the light, the first thing to come into focus was a crystal champagne glass, a sculptured frosted-white dove at its base. Tiny bubbles, appearing from nowhere, snaked their way through the golden nectar in the fluted vessel, creating a delicate mousse at the surface. The tablecloth was white with polished silver place settings that gleamed in the light.

Then she saw Charles' handsome face, illuminated by the glow from the setting sun, as he knelt beside her in the full regalia of a U.S. Army colonel.

The sky was clear and blue. At once, she began to recognize the surroundings. The table sat in an enormous grassy area perhaps 100 feet long and 40 feet wide. Traffic flowed all around the green island in a creeping single-file fashion. Many drivers were staring across the grass at the spectacle of a formally dressed couple sitting at a fancy table right in the middle of the park.

That's when she realized where she was. Just behind the tall hedge in the distance in front of her was the Japanese Tea Garden. On the right, beyond the trees and over in the distance was Steinhart Aquarium, and the Planetarium.

At left, the sun was setting in glorious fashion on the Pacific Ocean. As she looked around, feeling the sensation of a breeze that carried the essence of the sea, she realized that Charles was right. It was the coolest place on the earth! Charles had set up the table on a bright grassy traffic island right in the middle of Golden Gate Park.

A small group began to assemble from those who passed by, and many stood about at a distance, admiring the scene. Several drivers honked their horns to indicate approval. Down on one knee, Charles began.

"Destiny Marie Mitchell. Before the whole world I ask, will you marry me?"

She looked from the ring on her finger to his serious aspect before her face blossomed in a smile.

"This is the happiest day of my life so far! Yes, Charles. Of course I'll marry you!"

"Yes!"

He stood, his arms extended as he addressed the crowd and others who watched, shouting.

"She said 'Yes!'"

"Awww!—" was the response in unison before many of the observers began in applause.

CHAPTER 23

Peter Granucci smiled as the cameras swung in his direction. A young woman with a face powder compact patted his forehead and cheeks to dull the sheen in the bright lights. Unlike the mayor, who was short and stocky, Peter was tall and in good physical shape. Anthony Martini, the mayor, was of a swarthy, ethnic complexion while Granucci had the whiteness of Anglo-Saxon Americans.

Shying away from a full-blown press conference, he invited three key television reporters with cameramen and a news director into his office in order to make a statement. At six-thirty on Friday night, he hoped the statement would be aired on the eleven o'clock news and broadcasts throughout the weekend.

In the grander scheme, he wanted to attract the attention of news agencies beyond the region. He wanted the nation to know what was happening in San Francisco. Looking at the main camera, he listened to a director who held up a hand with fingers spread out wide.

"Okay, in five, four..."

The last three were counted in silence, simultaneous with emphatic hand gestures. Cameras rolling, Peter began.

"As I promised all of San Francisco at my press conference earlier this month, I will not rest until there is justice in the Lynette Alexander murder case. Even as I speak, we are in the process of a preliminary examination to determine whether or not the facts in evidence indicate her estranged husband Jordan should stand trial for that heinous crime."

Turning his head, he adjusted his focus to the camera at left.

"However, as ardent as we may be in our pursuit of justice, we can never allow our great zeal to blind us of our duty to protect the rights and reputations of persons who have *not* been accused."

His head and focus moved back to center.

"Recently, there have been rumors involving my office and the possible indictment of Mayor Martini on charges related to the Lynette Alexander murder. In fact, I read a story in one of the papers just this morning that said the mayor had been under investigation from day one. Now I don't know the source of any of these rumors or reports, but I assure you none of them have come from my office.

"Like all of San Francisco, I realize Mayor Martini and Jordan Alexander have been best friends for years, but for anyone to make an assumption about any possible involvement of the mayor based on nothing more than friendship would be wrong. It would be guilt by association. Investigators did in fact *question* the mayor early on and were satisfied by his explanations and responses.

"So once again, let me reaffirm that my office is *not* in the process of indicting the mayor or conducting any investigation on him. In the name of justice and in fairness to the mayor, I hope that all the rumor and innuendo we've all been hearing can now be put to rest. Thank you."

Lights out and cameras packing, Peter approached the news director.

"I'm not sure what the rest of them are going to do, but if you can splice in the footage of Martini going to the jail to visit Jordan, I'd really appreciate it."

The younger man grinned, patting Peter's shoulder.

"You'll get all that and more from all of us. This is the biggest story of the night!"

Looking through the large window, she could see the Berkeley pier stretching out into the bay. The afternoon sun was high above, causing the rippling water to create a paparazzi-like effect on her eyes. Brown pelicans stood on some of the poles, leaving occasionally to dive for fish while hundreds of gulls and turnstones performed an air show over and about the pier, landing to scavenge scraps of bait and small fish or crabs from people with poles and lines angling over the wooden railing.

"Would you care for another *sauvignon blanc*, Ma'am?"

Kiyomi snapped up of the daze.

"Oh! No, I'm waiting for someone, and he's late. I'll probably be leaving before long."

She gazed again on the pacific scene in the distance. It was a living portrait, beautiful in color and contrast, in brightness, balance and natural understated grace. She wondered why she never allowed herself more moments of solitude to appreciate nature. She was alone so much of the time, but she spent all her solitary time either writing stories or on the exhaustive research required for the articles she wrote. Writing was such a lonely life.

"On second thought, I think I will have another glass.

Thanks."

Cedric, her live-in boyfriend and a pilot with American Airlines, was away flying six of seven days. Cedric was her best friend's first cousin, hand-picked for Kiyomi by Destiny six years earlier. He was a kind and remarkable man, though he was only average-looking. He loved her and made the most of every moment they spent together. Their wedding was planned for next June. As she sat at the table staring out into the bay, she wished Cedric could have been there beside her, but being less tenured than many of the other pilots, he always had to fly on weekends.

"Kiyomi, I'm so sorry. I had a long night that wasn't over until an hour ago. I take it you've heard the news?"

Re-animated, she embraced him.

"Of course I did! Congratulations! Golden Gate Park! That was so sweet!"

Charles Covington lifted her from the ground as he hugged her, the twelve-inch height difference making both compensate to achieve the affectionate display. Minutes later, he sat across from her, his right index finger drawing designs through the condensation on the tall glass filled with club soda and lime. He struggled to answer the question.

"I, I spent a few hours with her. That's all I can tell you. I just want to know who she is and what she was up to."

Kiyomi was quick to respond.

"She's the most conniving and cold-hearted bitch I've come across in all my life. Her job is with the police department, but everyone in this town knows she's still working for the mayor. She's the one who got him his job in the first place."

"So what do you think she'd want from me? I don't live up here."

Kiyomi sighed and lowed her voice, leaning in.

"In case you haven't heard, the mayor's best friend was accused of murdering his wife, something that isn't flattering for the mayor, especially when he's up for re-election next year. So you can understand that neither the mayor nor Rikki Thomas want this thing to go to trial. And if it goes to trial, they're going to do everything they can to make sure there's no conviction."

Charles was doing his best to follow, struggling to make a connection.

"I still don't see what any of it has to do with me."

She sipped the wine and continued.

"There's been no announcement yet, but we're all just about sure that our district attorney Peter Granucci will run to become San Francisco's next mayor. If he gets a conviction in this murder case, he'll try to tie Jordan Alexander to the current mayor and he'll probably have the job sewn up."

Understanding flashed in Charles' eyes.

"Don't *tell* me this murder case is the big trial Destiny's supposed to be involved in for the year?"

"It is, Charles, and the stakes are high. If Rikki has anything on you, she'll probably want to use it to force Destiny off the case."

He nodded.

"Why is she so worried about Destiny? Doesn't the district attorney have other lawyers?"

She answered, glancing aside.

"The lawyer who would have normally gotten the case, Ted Waters? Word is Rikki had something on him. Granucci wouldn't have gotten as far as a preliminary hearing if Ted Waters was on it."

"Aren't there other lawyers?"

"Of course there are, but this is Destiny's kind of a case. It's circumstantial, her specialty. She's probably the only one at the district attorney's office who can realistically win it. Her boss knows that."

She paused, gazing into Charles' eyes.

"You have to tell me. Does Rikki Thomas have something on *you*?"

His eyes fell below the table line as he struggled to keep memories of that night with Rikki from his mind.

"She's got nothing on me. I don't know her and she doesn't know me."

Kiyomi grasped his fidgeting hand.

"You can tell me. You can trust me. Is there anything about you she could use to force Destiny off the case?"

He looked up, glaring into her eyes.

"No, there's nothing."

"Good. As a friend, I'd suggest that you have nothing to do with Rikki Thomas in the future. You'd be better off dealing with the devil."

Charles clenched her hand, nodding.

"You're probably right. I'll do my best to avoid her at all costs."

Discussion about Rikki Thomas completed, Kiyomi and Charles talked and joked about future weddings and life thereafter, about kids and other ambitions. They ate lunch at leisure, remarking about the beauty of the setting outside. After lunch, they walked along the pier, stopping on occasion to examine abandoned sand sharks and skates wriggling about or melting on the deck.

Kiyomi remained near the pier's edge, soothed by the constant washing of the surf. She sat on a huge granite stone, her ankles crossed and knees pulled close to her chest, staring out over the water. As she heard her lunch partner drive off in the smooth-sounding rented car, she sighed for Destiny, for Charles, for all the wonderful, hopeful people in the world who weren't sitting at that pier that evening as the brilliant orange sun began to set on the shimmering bay.

CHAPTER 24

"And at the moment you went in, Inspector Osaka, were you aware of the fact that Jordan Alexander expressly told Inspectors Harris and Garner he didn't want police to go into his house under any circumstances?"

"Not at the time I went in. I became aware of what he told Harris and Garner at a much later time?"

Barry was examining Garner's report, though he continued his questioning.

"Really? And do you recall when they told you?"

Bryan raised his eyes toward the ceiling as he thought.

"I think it had to be when I got back to the station."

"And what time was that?"

"It was at, it was sometime after noon. It was somewhere around three."

Frustrated, Barry sighed, slapping the report down on the table.

"Inspector Osaka, do you expect us to believe that at six fifty-six on the morning of August 18th, when you supposedly talked to Garner about the possibility of two big black murderers somehow sneaking unnoticed into the house, he just somehow failed to mention the fact that Jordan said he didn't want detectives inside?"

Bryan addressed Judge Chow.

"He said nothing about it. That would have been something I would have definitely remembered."

Barry sighed.

"And did you definitely remember believing there were two big black guys roaming around or hiding in that house?"

"I remember thinking it was possible."

Barry leaned against the rail in front of the jury box.

"How possible? Highly possible?"

"Well..."

"Slightly possible? A long shot?"

"Slightly possible."

Barry paused, nodding his head before continuing.

"And you thought 'slightly possible' gave you probable cause to force yourself in?"

Bryan turned to face the lawyer.

"It wasn't like that at all. It's like I told Ms. Mitchell earlier. I was invited in."

"Ms. Mitchell wasn't there, but the person who *was* there said you 'tricked' your way in."

"Objection. Not in the record. Argumentative."

"Sustained."

Barry crossed the room to refer to notes on the desk.

"Inspector, you had to know that Jordan was away. Why did you knock on the door in the first place?"

Bryan thought for a moment, answering.

"Well, Garner told me he thought there was a woman in the house. I was ready to head on back to the station, so I just wanted to warn her."

"But you'd been watching the house since five o'clock that morning, is that right?"

"Yes, that's right."

"And you didn't see any big black guys sneaking by you, did you? I mean you *are* a trained detective. You didn't see anything suspicious?"

"No."

"Did you see any Rolls Royce pull up?"

"No."

"Inspector, what did you think you would find when you went in to search the house? Were you looking for anything specific?"

Bryan glanced toward Destiny, hoping she might find a way to object, but he was on his own.

"Well, after checking the front rooms, I checked the back door and lower windows for evidence of forced entry, and then—"

"And did you find any evidence of forced entry?"

"No."

"No? So if no one came in through the back, which was locked, and no one came in through the front where you were watching, why did you then think it was necessary to search the upstairs, and specifically Jordan's bedroom?"

Again Bryan made his answer to the judge.

"I really, I'm not one hundred percent sure. I was just being thorough."

"Did you carry blood into that room, Inspector Osaka?"

"No."

"Objection. No foundation."

"I'll allow it."

"Did you smear blood on that wall, Inspector?"

"No."

"Are you aware of derogatory statements made by Police Commander Dennis Webber about Jordan Alexander and the Alexander family?"

"Objection. Beyond the scope.

"Overruled. I'll allow him to answer, but I'll advise counsel to move on."

Barry nodded.

"I will. Thank you, your Honor."

He spoke to Bryan.

"Are you aware of any derogatory statements?"

"Not specifically."

"Did Commander Webber give you orders saying he wanted you to gain access to Jordan's house at any cost?"

"No."

"After receiving your assignment to watch the house, did you go directly there?"

Bryan paused before answering.

"Yes."

"Did you visit the crime scene on Sacramento Street?"

"No."

"Who has your greatest loyalty, Inspector? Commander Webber or the San Francisco Police Department?"

"The police department."

"And did the police department give you a commendation for that piece of work you did at Jordan's Loma Vista Way residence on August 18th?"

"No."

"No? The truth is that you've received a departmental reprimand in that matter, haven't you?"

"Yes."

"Did the police department find you went in illegally?"

"No."

"But your actions that morning are under investigation by Internal Affairs, aren't they?"

Bryan bowed his head and answered.

"Yes, I believe they are."

"Thank you."

Barry went back to his table, stopping before sitting.

"I have nothing else, your Honor."

As Barry sat, Jordan patted him on the shoulder and whispered something into his ear. Judge Harry Chow looked toward

Destiny and Brett who were engaged in a conference of whispers.

"Care to re-direct, Ms. Mitchell?"

"Just a few questions, your Honor."

At first she started to read from a notepad, but she placed it on the table instead.

"Inspector Osaka, are you the only person at the department who has a commendation or document with Commander Webber's signature on it?"

"No."

"Why's that?"

"Because it's Commander Webber who signs all the commendations."

"And was there anything unusual about the Commander asking you to watch the house on Loma Vista Way?"

"Well, not really. In my years with the department, I've watched a lot of houses."

"Okay, and when you went to the door to warn Stephanie Rodriguez to be careful, were you secretly trying to find a way inside the house?"

"No."

"And when you agreed to go in and search for a possible break-in, were you hoping to discover some dirt on Jordan?"

"No."

"To whom do you feel the greatest sense of loyalty, Inspector? To the San Francisco Police Department or to the people of San Francisco?"

"To the people of San Francisco."

"So if you felt not searching the house would have put Stephanie Rodriguez at risk, were you willing to suffer any consequences the department might impose on you in order to provide for her safety?"

"Yes."

She smiled toward the judge.

"One last question."

She approached the witness.

"Can you tell us one last time the only reason you went into that house?"

Bryan trained his eyes on Barry as he answered.

"Because Stephanie Rodriguez *asked* me to."

The bulk of testimony heard on Wednesday morning involved establishing the actual time and manner in which Lynette had been murdered. Attorneys interviewed the county medical examiner and two criminologists. On Wednesday afternoon, Judge Harry Chow ruled in favor of the prosecution on the suppression motion involving the search of Jordan's Loma Vista Way residence.

Thus all the evidence from the crime scene at Jordan's residence, the hair and blood splotches, were allowed in. This paved the way for testimony from police officers and a serologist on the blood and physical evidence found at Loma Vista Way as well as Sacramento Street and in the Rolls Royce.

Destiny devoted the latter part of Thursday morning to presenting evidence that served to establish Jordan had both the opportunity to commit the murder and a motive based on jealousy and an established proclivity toward violence.

By Thursday afternoon, Judge Chow asked both lawyers to present final arguments before the court recessed for the day, and he promised to announce his ruling on the matter on Friday morning.

Unlike Thursday morning, where only a handful of reporters and observers turned out to hear more of the dry, boring testimony, Friday morning saw the courtroom filled to capacity. Even the hallway outside buzzed with excitement as reporter after reporter recorded story lead-ins for the news event that would take place inside. Judge Chow pounded the gavel to still the whispering that survived his announcement and entrance.

"Ladies and Gentlemen—"

Clearing his throat, the judge began in a somber, unwavering tone. After opening remarks, he first summarized the facts presented to the court during the preliminary examination.

Next, he began a definition of terms, which included The Fourth Amendment, the exclusionary rule, the poisonous tree and its fruit, exigent circumstances, the charge of first-degree murder leveled at Jordan and the penalties it carried, the object of the preliminary examination, the duty of a magistrate in a preliminary examination, burden of proof and probable cause.

Consequently, it was fifteen minutes into the decision before he gave any inkling of which way he would rule. Jordan sat in the uncomfortable seat, looking up at the judge, his fists clenched in nervousness, his breathing shallow. Next to him, Barry seemed to be taking notes, but as always, he was doodling. Doodling was

Barry's way of detaching himself to abridge the stress and pressure.

Across the aisle, Destiny had turned toward the judge and away from Brett while Brett sat, his hand on the back of her chair. Rikki Thomas sat in the first row for spectators beside Police Chief Bill McGuire, who was present as a sign to Jordan that the mayor was doing all he could to help. Kiyomi Yamakita sat behind Peter Granucci, listening as the judge spoke. A great swarm of reporters and community activists filled the seats in the back.

Though the ceiling was high, the courtroom was became warm and stuffy due to overcrowding. Dottie Alexander and the rest of the family sat behind Jordan and Barry, flanked by city and county officials, who came to show appreciation for the monetary support Dottie extended to them over the years.

While it seemed the entire city and its power structure was behind Jordan, it became apparent that Judge Harry Chow was going the other way.

"The issue of the blood found at the Loma Vista Way residence is clearly the most damaging of all the evidence. The fact that it does not match Mr. Alexander's rare blood type isn't as significant as the fact that it does match with Lynette Alexander's blood type, and that Inspector Osaka reported it appeared sticky, or not completely dry."

He flipped the page, concluding.

"Add that to the fact that Mr. Alexander's whereabouts, his physical condition and the time he arrived home can't be substantiated by anyone, and I'm afraid I have to find sufficient probable cause for a trial."

He looked down toward Jordan.

"Mr. Alexander, you will remain in custody until the trial is over. I'm certain your attorney will let you know what rights and options you can exercise prior to and after the time the district attorney issues his Information to the court. Counsels, Ladies and Gentlemen, this hearing stands adjourned."

CHAPTER 25

They came from the Mission District, from Western Addition, Potrero Hill, South of Market and Haight Ashbury on that second Monday in October. In mid-September, all six hundred persons crowded in that unventilated room at the criminal courts complex at 850 Bryant Street had received a summons to appear for jury duty.

While California skies would remain clear and blue until mid-November, the temperatures had begun to fall off by an average of one degree per day.

This was no ordinary attempt to impanel a jury for a crime committed by some common criminal. Rather, it was the jury selection process for what many were calling the trial of the century.

Some were excited about the prospect of being chosen while others warned of a lengthy trial and possible sequestration. The bailiff closed the door at 9:15, and shortly thereafter clerks gave each prospective juror a thick questionnaire.

A woman in the front explained the questionnaire, its importance, and the need to be as accurate. They were to answer the eighty questions under the penalty of perjury. Judge Helen Morgan, the upcoming trial judge, had written many of the questions. Right before the potential jurors were excused for the day, the clerk confirmed the rumor. Jordan Alexander's attorneys and the State would begin jury selection on Tuesday morning.

"I'm glad you reconsidered and agreed to meet, Charles. You can't afford to believe everything you've *heard* about me. I bark loud, but as you know from experience, I never bite."

Apprehensive about the tryst, Charles had flown into San Jose, taken the 17 to Highway 1 and driven down along the coast into Monterey. He pre-arranged for a 12:45 tee time at the Pebble Beach Course where he played poorly, owing to jittery nerves. The idea of meeting with her was crazy! What if it was a set-up? While it was against his better judgment, he took 17-Mile Drive over to Carmel, determined to find out what she wanted.

The posh little restaurant was public, but it was far enough from San Francisco to assure no accidental encounter with Destiny or any of her friends.

Rikki continued.

"Sit down. I understand congratulations are in order, though something tells me it'll never happen."

Charles sat, still wondering who the other woman was. She was beautiful!

"Why would you say that?"

"Because Destiny's not right for you, Charles, not right for a man who's going places. You'll be a General some day, and while Destiny's nice, she wouldn't make you a good wife."

He said nothing because in his heart he knew she was right. Rikki Thomas was insightful, if nothing else. The beautiful light-skinned woman cleared her throat, nudging Rikki, who laughed and began.

"Oh, I'm forgetting my manners. Charles, I'd like you to meet a *friend* of mine. This is Claudette Boveé. Claudette, Colonel Charles Covington."

Even as Charles reached over to shake the woman's hand, he noticed she held Rikki's white fingers clutched between her brown thighs. Pretending not to notice, he sat back.

"It's very nice to meet you, Ms. Boveé."

"*Monsieur*, the pleasure is all mine. Rikki tells me you are a truly wonderful man, Colonel."

Embarrassed about the intimate reference, Charles lowered his eyes and listened as Rikki went on.

"Claudette's quite a remarkable lady. She has a Ph.D. in literature from Dartmouth. She teaches over at Dominican College in Marin County."

Claudette's light brown complexion lent itself well to her keen facial features. Her eyes seemed Asian, owing to some Native American ancestry. Her cheekbones were high and angled, while her lips and nose were evidence of the enduring the racial integration of New Orleans. She was a pretty woman with long, wavy jet-black hair and a smile that was provocative, captivating. Her breasts seemed slight in the blouse she wore, though her waist was small and her hips and smooth legs were shapely enough.

Notwithstanding, Charles hadn't taken leave of the camp to admire Rikki's gorgeous little girlfriend. He came up because Rikki called him with an implied threat that if he *didn't* meet her, she was going to tell Destiny about *their passionate night together in Palm Springs.*

When General Deitler asked him about his sudden need to

jaunt up North, he explained the trip was necessary to secure a venue for his upcoming wedding.

Charles distrusted Rikki's motives.

"That's wonderful. So why did you threaten me to get me up here? What do you want?"

Rikki smiled.

"Oh come on! I never threatened you. Look, I know you don't trust me. But if you just give me a chance, you'll find out you and I are on the same team. We both want the same thing."

The waitress offered Charles a drink, but he refused, crossing his arms after she left.

"Okay, so what is this thing both of us want?"

"Isn't it obvious? I mean you did have lunch with that Yamakita woman on Saturday, didn't you? She must have told you what I'm after. You and I both want your new fiancée off the Alexander case."

Charles sighed, relieved, and continued.

"Why is it you think I would want her off the case?"

"Because if she's on the case, you two won't be getting married for at least a couple of years, something that probably doesn't jibe well with your promising military career. Timing is everything. You can't afford to wait for her."

He couldn't disagree, yet he was surprised at how well she had assessed his situation. Had she done the research, or was she that smart? Anyway, what she was asking seemed easy.

"And I suppose you have some sort of a plan to make sure Destiny doesn't try this case?"

Rikki turned toward Charles, her back toward a patient Claudette.

"All you have to do is apply a little pressure and I'll do the rest. Tell her you want to get married and you can't wait for her. Tell her you're a rising star and you can't put your life on hold for two years waiting for her to finish this trial. Ask her what's more important, this unwinnable case she's intent on pursuing, or you?"

She leaned toward Charles.

"I mean, do you know?"

He was staring away, contemplating.

"Do I know what?"

"Do you know which is more important to her, you or this murder case? Ask her to choose."

He maintained silence to guard his thoughts. Was this all she was asking? For something he planned on doing anyway?

Maybe she wasn't as cunning or devious as Kiyomi warned.

Nodding, he answered.

"Seems we *are* after the same thing. I had already planned on asking her to forego the case."

She extended her hand.

"Pleasure meeting with you, Colonel."

He shook her hand as he stood.

"Yes, and hopefully it'll be the first and only time I'm ever blackmailed into meeting with anyone for anything."

She turned back to Claudette and stroked the lovely woman's hair.

"Learn to keep it in your pants, and maybe it *will* be."

He started to walk away, but he stopped, turning.

"Just so I know. You said I'd be sorry if I didn't show up here. But what would you have done if I refused to meet with you?"

She turned, smiling.

"Oh, I was going to wait until the moment right before opening statements. I was going to slip into a seat right behind Destiny, and then, in great detail, I was going to tell her about all those wonderful things you did to me that night in Palm Springs, over and over again."

"She wouldn't have believed you."

She laughed to herself.

"Probably not. So that's why I took great pains to make sure I obtained proof of everything that happened. Of course Colonel, if you don't believe me, you're welcome to call me on it."

CHAPTER 26

Dottie wanted the meeting to be discreet, and so it was. No one saw her go into the county jail, no one saw her enter the elevator or slip into the private room where Jordan sat waiting. He stood, rushing to embrace his grandmother.

"I'm so glad you made it. I've missed you so much!"

Batting tears back in her eyes, she clutched him, sighing.

"Oh, I've missed you, too. I've missed my favorite grandson."

She backed away only after she drained the embrace of all its emotion. Removing the dark glasses, the wig and hat, she found a bench and sat.

"Oh, Jordan! Do you realize what a *time* I've had trying to keep up with the murder, the arrest and all this dreadful trial business? Don't be surprised if I drop dead any minute now. Oh!"

She removed her shoe, massaging her left foot with her right hand. Jordan sat beside her, taking her leg into his lap as he massaged the foot.

"I'm so sorry you've had to go through this."

"Don't be sorry. You're an Alexander. Alexanders built this town. We've got nothing to be sorry about."

She lowered the foot and leg, extending the other for equal treatment.

"On second thought, you do have *one* thing to be sorry about, but I hate to say I told you so."

"What's that?"

"For marrying that little tramp in the first place. I warned you many times. I told you she'd be trouble. She was a whore! You were sleeping with her anyway. You didn't have to *marry* her."

Jordan bowed his head, answering.

"I loved Lynette, Gran, and now she's dead. She's dead."

Dottie studied her grandson's demeanor before reaching over to stroke his face.

"Yes she is, and I know it must be difficult for you. This whole ordeal must be difficult for you."

If only she knew. If only she knew how he cried himself to sleep each night, how he was haunted by illusions and apparitions even during daylight hours, how his sanity and sense of reality was becoming unhinged.

August 17 seemed like a dream, the beginning of a dreadful, frightening nightmare where the lines separating fantasy and reality merged. The regularity of the preliminary hearing had been reassuring, so ironically, he looked forward to the trial.

"It's been hell, Gran. Why is this happening to me?"

The woman San Francisco referred to as "Earthquake Dottie" remained silent. She sat watching her grandson before moving to another subject.

"So how are you and Barry getting along through all this?"

"Well, he doesn't listen to me, but everyone keeps telling me he's the best in the criminal defense business."

"Fire him."

Jordan recoiled at the words, struggling for a response.

"I, I don't understand, Gran."

"Barry's my grandson, but I don't *trust* him. He's in it for himself, for whatever thrill he gets out of arguing in court the way he does. I blame him for this thing going to trial in the first place. We're Alexanders! Things should have never gone this far."

Dottie's favorite grandson, Jordan had never been afraid to disagree.

"Barry might be a little full of himself, but he's a great lawyer. I think I'll keep him."

"Well, you're going to have to get rid of him before this thing's over anyway. Might as well do it sooner than later."

The matter resolved in his own mind, Jordan chose to ignore the comment and move to another subject.

"How's the business?"

Feet on the floor, Dottie reached out, clutching both of her grandson's hands.

"The kingdom's fine, but we're missing our prince. We need you to get *through* this and come back to take the place that's rightfully yours."

Jordan knew she wasn't pleased his younger brother had taken over as CEO in his stead.

"How's Philip?"

Dottie sighed, disgusted.

"He's an absolute boor, and that wife of his is hideous. She's an embarrassment to the family."

"He married money, Gran. What did you expect? Marilyn Monroe?"

"I had a few good prospects for him, but he wouldn't listen."

She reached up, touching her handsome grandson's face.

"I'm going to do everything in my power to make sure you

win this trial, Jordan, and then you have to take back the company. I don't want Philip in charge. I'd just as soon sell it piecemeal and donate everything to charity."

He gripped her wrist.

"You won't have to, Gran. I promise I'll be back."

Dottie smiled, trembling.

"Good. And when you come back, you're going to have to clean up your act. You're going to have to listen to good ol Gran for a change."

"Nothing personal, Destiny, but somewhere along the line we're going to have to make a tactical decision here."

Janice Prescott and Gail Friedman sat at the table with Destiny and Brett, pouring over juror questionnaires. It was after midnight. Earlier in the evening, the four had gone over five hundred applications, setting aside potential jurors who would be challenged summarily.

Because the prosecution would rely on circumstantial evidence to prove its case, the lawyers decided to favor college graduates and those who had at least some college education. Persons who worked in the technical and medical fields were also considered with preference. Professional older white men and women were good prospects.

Slowly, the lawyers began putting together the profile of their ideal juror: white, female, educated, middle-aged to old, conservative, pro-law enforcement. While Destiny agreed with the profile, she had hesitations about eliminating candidates solely because of race, for simply being black.

"First of all, it's unethical. And second, what makes the three of you think all blacks feel the same way about everything? We've got pro-prosecution blacks in this town too. I happen to know a few."

Gail was sarcastic.

"And those few that you know, any of them in this jury pool?"

"Of course not."

"Then it's a pot shot, and we all know blacks tend to be pro-defense. Again nothing personal."

Destiny sighed, disgusted.

"You have to understand. This is one area where I have an

advantage over the three of you. I can read black jurors better than you can. And I can read them better than Barry Divine and anyone else on that defense team can."

Pushing away from the table, she continued.

"Same thing goes for winning them over. I've dealt with quite a few blacks on jury panels over the years, and I've done well with them. The record speaks for itself."

Destiny could tell her colleagues were listening.

"Now, we all know Barry's going to try to get a jury that looks like the East Oakland Baptist choir, and we also know *we* can't keep all the blacks off. That's why I think our key concern here should be to control not how many, but which blacks get on."

Janice was first to agree, removing her glasses as she spoke.

"Destiny's right. It's all a matter of reading them. Over the years, I've done pretty well with black jurors as well. It's a matter of rapport."

She paused for effect.

"I've never told any of you this, but I dated a black man once."

Destiny sat there, unsure about how to respond to Janice's revelation. As she looked from face to face, she was comforted to observe the other lawyers seemed just as confused.

What really mattered, however, was Janice's growing emotional involvement in the case. When Ted and Chester opposed Peter's decision to make Destiny lead counsel, Janice was silent, though according to Gail, Janice thought Peter had made a big mistake.

Over the weeks that followed and throughout the preliminary hearing, Janice warmed to Destiny, began giving advice and offered assistance in a genuine manner.

Gail, always caustic, was quick to respond.

"That's great Janice. That makes all four of us, and your point is?"

Upon reflection, Janice was embarrassed about the way her declaration must have sounded. Glancing sidelong toward her colleagues, she explained.

"What I really meant to say was that there are some identity issues when it comes to black people, and because Destiny's black, she has an advantage in terms of establishing rapport. And she's right. If Barry wants a mostly black jury, there's no way in hell we're going to keep them off altogether."

Gail raised her hands, abandoning the issue.

"Hey, I won't argue that. It's Destiny's call anyway. She's the lead attorney here."

Gail, busy writing, glimpsed up toward Destiny.

"Well, if that's the case, don't we want the *gays* too? I mean, if Brett played it right, he could have them squirming in that jury box. Don't you think?"

Brett started a protest, but he stopped. All three women in the room had already heard him deny being gay many times, so what was the use?

Destiny's response however, came as a bit of a surprise.

"I think you're right, Gail."

She turned toward Brett.

"Gay or not gay, the gays in the pool are going to like you, they're going to identify with you more than they will with Barry. You can call them pro-defense if you want, but if they like you, they're more apt to go your way."

Brett mumbled a response.

"I disagree, but Destiny, you're in charge."

Gail was first to comment.

"We could end up losing our asses, but it sounds workable."

Janice chimed in with her support, leaving Brett alone in his opposition.

Peter liked the Chinese. They watched everything and gossiped among and about themselves in their language, but whatever happened in Chinatown remained in Chinatown.

He had found a little, unremarkable place on Grant Avenue owned by an old couple who operated the restaurant in what should have been the small living room of their modest dwelling. In the corner opposite from where he sat, four old men were playing *mah jong*, crumpled stacks of money held in their left hands as they placed tiles with right hands.

The tiny brass bell on the door jingled, announcing the entry of Dennis Webber. Peter relished the astonishment that showed on Webber's face. The police commander had no idea there were places like *Shew Yee's* in operation. Grinning, Peter stood, extending his arm in Webber's direction and motioning with his hand. The men exchanged a handshake and sat.

"I took the liberty of ordering something light for us, turtle soup. Your wife'll appreciate it. Chinese say it gives you that extra..."

He gestured, showing his forearm with a tightened fist.

"...staying power if you know what I mean."

Webber's tone was sarcastic.

"Yeah, as if I really need that."

Peter laughed.

"What's that, the turtle soup or the staying power?"

Minutes later, as they consumed the soup, the men discussed the upcoming trial.

"All I can tell you is that Barry will be coming after you, and he knows police codes and regulations better than anyone on your force, so you and Osaka are going to have to come up with some pat answers that jibe."

Dennis chewed the tough meat, his throat bulging as he swallowed the poorly-masticated chunk of reptile.

"Barry Divine doesn't worry me. It's that black broad you've got handling this thing for you. I mean, I've heard she's good, but do you think she's *up* to it?"

"Apparently you didn't see any of her pre-trial work in this case. She'll give Divine all he can handle."

Frustrated with the soup, Dennis struck a match to light his cigarette.

"I wasn't worried about how she was going to deal with Divine. What I'm wondering about is whether or not she can deal with that Rikki Thomas bitch. If Rikki finds a way to get her hooks into your little lawyer, she'll rip her inta a hundred little pieces."

Peter nodded, signaling reluctant agreement as Dennis continued.

"Somewhere along the line, you and I are going to have to come up with a way to take Rikki out, and I guarantee she won't make it easy for us."

Peter thought before answering.

"Well, there *was* that scandal with Martini a few years back, with the campaign donations?"

Dennis disagreed.

"It's got to be something much bigger than that."

Peter pursed his thin lips, contemplating.

"Well, you and I both know Vic Ehlers and his little black book. If anyone can get us anything on Rikki, it'll be Vic."

Dennis nodded.

"Yeah, but it'll be expensive, which means that somewhere

along the way, one of us is going to have to find some money."

Peter set his spoon down and pushed his bowl away.

"Don't worry about the money. This is San Francisco. Every player in this town has a big money enemy somewhere. I'll find the money. It's just that when Rikki goes down, I can't afford to be anywhere near the scandal. I'll provide the information, you take her down."

He looked into Webber's eyes.

"Is that something you can agree to?"

Dennis had forked another piece of undercooked reptilian meat from the soup, chewing it vigorously before swallowing.

"Listen Peter, you give me enough to take Rikki down, and I'll gladly take *all* the credit for it. I hate that bitch, so if anyone else in this town wants to fuck her as bad as I do, they're gonna hafta settle for sloppy seconds."

"So are you willing to promise me, the judge and Mr. Alexander that your verdict will be 'not guilty' if the prosecution doesn't prove their case beyond a reasonable doubt?"

The twenty-something black man's eyes followed as Barry moved from the table to the rail.

"Yes."

"And what if you never get to see Jordan Alexander take the stand? Would that make you think he had something to hide?"

"Not necessarily. Person don't have to take the stand if he don't want to. Fifth Amendment rights or somethin like that?"

Barry looked toward Judge Morgan.

"Defense accepts this juror."

"Very well. Ms. Mitchell?"

At the table, Destiny and Brett were in a quiet though passionate disagreement. Hearing her name called, Destiny stood, approaching the jury box. She addressed the young man.

"Let's say I prove beyond a reasonable doubt that Jordan Alexander stabbed his wife to death on August 17th, but throughout the course of the trial, you never see the murder weapon. What would your verdict be?"

The young man answered, his eyes running over the attractive lawyer's shapely body.

"Well, if ya proved it beyond a reasonable doubt, I guess I'd hafta say guilty."

"What if no witnesses come forth to say they actually *saw* what happened, but I proved Mr. Alexander was guilty of murdering his wife by putting a lot of little pieces together like a jigsaw puzzle? What would you say then?"

"If it seemed like he definitely did it, I'd hafta say guilty."

Destiny turned toward the judge.

"The prosecution accepts this juror, your Honor."

Now there were eight accepted jurors in the box, five women and three men. Juror number 1 was a young white woman who just graduated from Cal Berkeley's school of Economics. Next to her in seat 2 sat a middle-aged Mexican housewife and mother of four. Juror number 3 was a black woman employed by the city for the last 26 years. An older black man sat in the fourth seat. He was a retired airplane mechanic.

This was the third day of *voir dire*, which in French has the equivalent meaning of *to see/to say* or *show and tell.* Both sides invested time, energy and resources for the purpose of gaining an advantage in the all-important jury selection process.

Barry hired a consultant and purchased a *jury book*, a resource used for examining potential jurors in light of the previous trial experiences. The prosecution, employing the wherewithal of the district attorney's office, had prepared abstracts for each juror, with a subjective rating printed in the top right corner of each page.

The juror who occupied the fifth seat was a 47 year-old white woman who had never been to college, though she worked as an escrow officer in the Financial District. In the sixth and last seat of the back row sat a 30 year-old Japanese man who worked as an accountant and small restaurant owner.

In the far left seat of the front row sat an outspoken, overweight black woman, a Macy's women's store department manager who had been mistaken for Oprah Winfrey on several occasions. Physically, she dwarfed juror number 8, the young black college student the lawyers just finished interviewing.

All in all, both sides were pleased with the way the jury was coming together, though Judge Morgan pressured attorneys to seat the jury seated before the day was over. Because Barry had used 18 of his allotted 20 preemptory challenges, he was loath to strike future candidates, except for a compelling reason. Destiny however, only used 11, providing her with opportunity to seat three of the last four jurors, unopposed.

Jurors 9, 10 and 11 were middle-aged white women, while

juror 12 was a black woman in her mid-twenties. The *voir dire* process, during the selection of alternates, moved along much faster so that when court adjourned for the day at 4:30, twelve jurors were seated along with twelve alternates.

While the behavior of the lawyers was exemplary, Jordan scored points with the jury. Per instructions from Barry, he sought to establish eye contact with each juror seated and to hold the gaze, evincing a trace of a smile.

The purpose of the behavior was to affect an individual bond of trust with jurors. It was Jordan's earliest opportunity to indicate he had confidence in each juror, that he had faith in every juror to return a proper verdict, a just verdict, a not guilty verdict.

It was Friday night, just a few minutes before midnight. Destiny and Brett were at the office working on her opening statement until 10:30 and picked up sushi on the way back to Destiny's apartment. It was a long, tortuous week, but it was rewarding. After dinner, Destiny invited Brett out to the living room where she had slipped a rented copy of *Back to the Future* into the VCR.

"You've seen this before?"

"No, but I've heard Michael J. Fox is pretty good in it."

Twenty minutes into the movie, Brett laughed to himself.

"Would you believe it? My parents are in London for the opening of Andrew Lloyd Webber's *Phantom of the Opera*, to which they bought me a ticket and paid the airfare. But no, I didn't go. Instead I'm sitting here watching Alex Keaton driving around in a *DeLorean*, getting picked-up on by his own mother! So much for the myth about lawyers living the glamorous life!"

He glanced over at Destiny, who seemed disappointed.

"What's wrong? I said the best thing about the night was the company."

She tossed a pillow at his head.

"You said nothing of the sort. Oh!"

She turned and headed for the kitchen, returning with a black and gold bottle, condensation on the glass gleaming in the light.

"I almost forgot. Peter sent this yesterday morning. *Dom Perignon*, the real shit! Wanna open it now or wait till after the trial?"

"Open it now! The charm of the bottle will be spoiled if we somehow don't get our conviction. No time like the present."

After peeling off the foil and placing a napkin over the cork, Destiny twisted the wire loop six half-turns, stretched it open, grasped the cork in the napkin and began turning the bottle. With each turn, the cork, under great pressure, worked itself further and further out until a muffled explosion startled her. When she removed the napkin and cork, the delicate mousse from the champagne bubbled from the opening, trailing a squiggly line of dry sparkling wine down the side of the black bottle.

She poured a half-inch of champagne into each of the frosted, fluted glasses and waited for the tiny tide of bubbles to ebb before filling each to almost three-quarters full.

She gave a glass to Brett and raised her own.

"Here's to the trial."

Brett followed her lead, raising his glass.

"To *winning* the trial!"

The crystal glasses resonated with a distinct hollow tone, and both lawyers were savoring the creamy crispness of that first sip when someone knocked on the door.

"It's after midnight. You expecting anyone?"

"No one I know of."

She didn't seem convinced of her answer. Worry lines showed on her brow as she placed the champagne on the table and crossed over to the door.

"Who is it?"

"It's me, Destiny. You going to make me stand out here forever?"

She recognized the garbled voice and began unlatching the door. Uncertain about what to expect on the other side, Brett backed away, complaining as he retreated.

"You're just going to open the door? Who is it?"

She stopped, just before twisting the last lock.

"Relax, Brett. It's just Charles."

When she opened the door, Charles stood there, glaring in Brett's direction and then at the champagne glass sitting on the table.

He stepped through the door.

"I'm sorry, Destiny. If I had known my fiancée was entertaining gentlemen callers past midnight tonight, I'd have phoned first."

Stepping to his side, she latched onto his stiff right arm, pushing the door shut with her left in the same motion.

"No! No, Charles. This is Brett McPherson. Brett's my co-counsel for the Jordan Alexander trial. We worked late tonight and came by here to eat and watch a movie."

His eyes were fixed on the fluted glass in Brett's shaking hand as she continued.

"Our boss Peter got us the champagne, and we were just celebrating the beginning of the trial. Would you like a glass?"

"No."

Brett took the tone of Charles' answer as his cue to make a discreet exit.

"You know it's getting late, Destiny. I'm just going to leave."

"Brett?"

Charles interrupted.

"Let him go."

Saying nothing, Brett placed his glass on the table, grabbed his coat and walked past the couple, his head and eyes bowed as he passed Charles. He opened the door.

"I'll call you tomorrow, Destiny."

"Okay. Do that."

As the door slammed shut, Destiny turned on Charles, her eyes narrowed in anger and her voice breaking.

"What the hell is *wrong* with you, Charles? What do you think you're doing? You show up unannounced at my house at midnight with this, with this bullshit attitude! You're rude to me, and you're even ruder to my colleague! What's gotten into you tonight?"

He didn't look at her. He only crossed his arms as he answered, his voice seething.

"*First* of all, a man shouldn't have to announce himself when he decides to travel 400 miles to visit his fiancée. And second, I don't know what kind of a world you lawyers live in, but for the rest of us, *any* man would have a problem if he went to visit his fiancée after midnight and found her sipping champagne with another man. Your pretty boy's lucky he made it out of here in one piece."

Destiny exhaled, disgusted.

"I don't buy it, Charles! You've not even the jealous type!"

"I've never been engaged before."

"Besides, Brett is *gay*! He'd have been more interested in you than me."

Charles turned away so that his face wouldn't betray the anger he wanted to project.

"That guy's not gay. He's interested in you. I could see it in his eyes when he looked at you on his way out. And if you two had gone through with this trial together, I'm sure he would have told you so."

She heard it. Somewhere in the back of her mind, she knew it was going to happen. She wanted to broach the issue earlier, right after she accepted the marriage proposal, but she was so happy. She didn't want to ruin the mood.

In her hopeful exuberance, she believed the strength of their love would have transcended the issue, but here it was. Emotionally unprepared though she was, the time had come for a showdown.

Softening the tone of her voice, she initiated the argument.

"Charles, I can't help being a little shocked hearing you say '*if* I went through with the trial.' I hope that doesn't mean you have some kind of a problem with me staying on the biggest case I'll probably ever get in my life. Especially after all the work I've already done."

He turned, and facing her, took both her hands in his and led her over to the couch. They sat.

He looked into her eyes.

"Destiny, I know you think it's a lawyer's chance of a lifetime, and I know you've worked hard on it, but it's just a case. Your boss gave it to you because you're good, which means you'll have many of the same opportunities throughout your career."

She opened her mouth to argue, but he didn't let her speak.

"Listen to me, Destiny. Don't sell yourself short. If you think this is a once in a lifetime shot for you, you're suggesting you got it as a fluke and never deserved it in the first place."

He stroked her face.

"But we all know better. You got the case because you *earned* it, and you'll earn others, maybe some that'll make this case seem petty and insignificant."

He smiled with perfect white teeth.

"Marriage to someone you love, on the other hand, really *is* a once in a lifetime opportunity. You'll be on this case for what? Two years max? And then you'll move on, but this marriage has to remain our first priority for the rest of our lives."

Destiny smiled, stroking the outside of the hand that

caressed her face. The smile dissolved however, replaced by a stern expression that emanated from deep within. Placing his hand into his lap, she stood, beginning the rebuttal.

"You're right, Charles. Marriage has to be the number one priority. But you can't have a marriage if you don't have two people getting married, and these people don't just leave their hopes, their ambitions and prior commitments at the threshold. The two become one flesh, but they can never stop being individuals."

She turned, staring into the darkness outside the window, out through time, through space and convention, to a poignant moment, a horrible event she believed forever changed her life.

"What you have to understand Charles, is that I made a commitment to a person before I accepted your marriage proposal. In doing so, I made a promise to myself. You know I love you more than anything, but I hope you're not telling me I have to betray that person and that vow in order to be your wife."

As he stood, approaching her, the tone of his voice was becoming more severe.

"So what are you telling me, Destiny? That I'm going to have to sit around on the sidelines for two years before you're uncommitted enough to marry me?"

She turned, facing him, raising her voice in gradual anger.

"Charles, you knew when you *proposed* to me I was working on this case. What? Did you expect me to just give up everything I've worked so hard for to run off and marry you?"

"Well, you knew when you *accepted* that I wasn't planning on putting my life on hold for two years waiting for you. I mean, why didn't you tell me right there in the park you weren't ready to get married yet? You could've saved both of us the grief!"

"Let me get this straight, Charles. Are you saying you don't want to marry me now?"

"I'm saying I'm not going to wait two years. I'll find someone else."

She glared into his eyes.

"And what's that supposed to be? A threat? I'm not saying the trial's going to take two years, but if you want to find someone else, go do it. Be my guest."

Uneasy because she called his bluff, he retreated.

"I didn't mean I was going out *looking* for someone else, but you have to understand something here. I'm going to be a general. There are a lot of women out there who would just *love* to be my wife, and here you are choosing a damn court case over me! It's insulting!"

By that time she was so furious she that wanted to take off his ring and shove it in his face. However, she had grown attached to the sparkle and glint of the large diamond, so she just turned the ring so that its jewel rested in the palm of her hand instead.

"I don't know what they teach you in the military, Charles, because your thinking is shallow and arrogant. This isn't about you, and it's not about the court case either. It's about a commitment I made to a murdered woman. Why can't you understand that?"

Frustrated with her, he headed for the door, stopping to answer.

"First of all, you can't make a commitment to a *dead* person! And second, even if you could, it's *your* commitment, not mine! If it means so much to you that you don't mind sacrificing me and marriage for it, then that's on you! It all boils down to a choice, Destiny. It's me..."

He yanked the door open.

"or this murder case. *You* decide what's more important!"

The door slammed with enough concussive force to rattle the plates and glasses in the china cabinet. Destiny at once thought to chase after him, but she convinced herself doing so would be at once stupid and demeaning.

Instead, her focus left the blank, inanimate door as she rushed to the window where, through a tiny opening in the blinds, she watched him get into his car and drive away, never looking back.

Her heart ached more every time she inhaled as she returned to her little living room, plopping down on the sofa. Tears began to stream down her face. She hadn't decided why she was crying, not knowing whether it was the anger or the hurt she felt. It didn't matter anyway. What did matter was the realization that, for the first time since this whole Jordan Alexander business began, she had regrets about having taken the case. Worse than that, she just wanted to quit.

CHAPTER 27

"Good morning, Ladies and Gentlemen. My name is Destiny Mitchell and I am representing the People of California for the prosecution in this very important murder case. For me, for my colleague, Brett McPherson at the table there and for the other attorneys who'll be assisting us, you will be the most important twelve people in the world over the next few months. We were all on our best behavior during jury selection, but now we're going to get a chance to really know each other. We attorneys however, had a little advantage. We read about you and got to know you in a sense from your questionnaires, but I for one realize there's more to all of you than what we gathered through those surveys and our pointed questions."

Pausing, she approached the jury box.

"As I look at you, I see twelve individual human beings, specially selected to fulfill a singular purpose. Certainly, one or two of you are apprehensive, perhaps a little nervous because you're unfamiliar with this process. Maybe a couple of you are excited to be a part of such a major case."

She smiled, taking the time to make eye contact with jurors in the back row.

"I'm hoping you're at least as nervous as I am because you are charged with the solemn and sober responsibility to be the triers of the facts of this case. My job is easy compared to yours. When it's all over, no one else is going to matter. You and you alone will have the duty to decide this case based on the facts we bring before you."

She walked toward an easel that displayed a 48"x 36" portrait of Lynette Alexander, waist up. Lynette was wearing a smart navy business suit, her curly blonde hair falling a little past her shoulders. She smiled, her eyes glistening with excitement. She seemed happy.

"After Mr. McPherson and I have presented our case-in-chief, and after Mr. Divine presents the defense case, duty calls on you to, in spite of your many differences, collectively decide whether Mr. Alexander did, as alleged in count one of the Information filed with the court, willfully, unlawfully and with malice aforethought murder his wife, Lynette Alexander, the woman whose picture we have before us now."

She centered herself before the jury.

"Lynette Alexander was a beautiful woman, and this is

indeed *seems* like a flattering picture. However, I have to admit to you, what you're viewing now isn't a picture at all. If you look very closely, you'll realize that what you're looking at is actually a puzzle. It's a jigsaw puzzle. I took Lynette's picture to one of those places on the wharf where they turn pictures into puzzles and this is what I got."

She approached the image.

"Now because jigsaw puzzles aren't exactly a hobby of mine, it took me much longer to put it together than it probably would have taken most of you. It took me three days. I finished it just yesterday. Only, when I had put all the little pieces together, I discovered something. At some time in the arduous process of organizing, categorizing, trying this or that, at some point in the trial and error process of putting it all together, I lost about a seven little pieces. Now, I could have gone back out to the wharf and re-ordered the puzzle, but I would have never finished it in time to show it to you today. It's a pretty picture, but if you come over and look very closely, you'll see where the pieces are missing."

She was standing next to the portrait, pointing as she spoke.

"There, right on the neck, a piece is missing. Two are missing in her hair. The fingers on her left hand—missing two pieces. As I said, there are about seven in all."

Through with the display, she approached the jury once more.

"Yet in spite of all the pieces that are missing, that *aren't* there, let us all ask ourselves, is there any question at all about what we have before us and who the subject is? No, not a question. It's the likeness of Lynette Alexander. We all know who it is because, while there are empty spaces, there's enough there for us to recognize what we're looking at."

Destiny's own appearance was pleasant and professional. She wore a conservative dark blue business suit with a lacy white blouse.

"Ironically enough, the case we're going to present before you is a lot like this jigsaw puzzle. It's a circumstantial case, which means it's not a clear, neat little photograph. We don't have the murder weapon. We don't have an eyewitness. All we have is a lot of little pieces, which individually tell us nothing, but if you put them all together and step back a little distance, a distinctive image emerges.

She nodded.

"Throughout the course of this trial, Mr. McPherson and I are going to put together another picture for you, the picture of a violent, married man who was a playboy on one hand and irrationally insecure and jealous on the other, the picture of a man who viciously beat his wife on many occasions, two for which he was arrested, the picture of a man who was afraid of losing a woman he had thrown away, a man who on August 17th took a knife and stabbed Lynette Alexander so many times that potions of her bones were exposed. The man who did that to her is sitting in this courtroom today."

She pointed toward Jordan.

"There. There, he is. He'll smile at you. His lawyers and others will say kind words about him. He'll try to charm you the same way he did Lynette, but if Lynette could speak, she'd tell you, 'Don't you dare trust that man! Don't let his good looks, his popularity and family connection fool you. Don't let Jordan Alexander get away with my murder!"

The old courtroom smelled musty because of the mold, which grew on the wooden support beams and under the tile of the floor. The dark, mahogany-stained panels on the walls lent an austere spirit to the room, reaffirming the severity of somber proceeding. All eyes followed Destiny until she directed them toward Jordan, who sat there discomfited, suffocating under the weight of the instant attention.

Closing his eyes, Jordan remembered Barry's admonition. A smile in that weighty moment would have cost ambivalence in skeptical jurors. A sulking, malevolent glare toward the woman prosecutor would have been even worse. A bowed head would have signaled contrition, or guilt. No, it was better to stare straight ahead. It was better to mimic Barry in his cool, analytical attention to the prosecutor's statement. Pen held between sweaty fingertips, he scribbled something unintelligible on the pad.

As Destiny continued, describing Lynette and her life in intimate detail, he noted two or three areas where her facts weren't correct. Even the smallest inconsistencies, according to Barry, could be useful at some later point in the trial.

"Finally three years ago, after years of similar visits, her doctor wrote her a prescription for Valium, one of many tranquilizers doctors prescribe for the type of high anxiety Lynette was experiencing. The Valium worked for the first year. Her mother, Allegra, remembers feeling her long lost daughter had come home. Nettie smiled again, she laughed, she talked about her life's ambition, a foundation purposed to assist San Francisco's women and children who were trapped in violent homes."

She glanced over at Allegra Benson.

"Lynette seemed herself for about nine months, but her mother as mothers do, Allegra Benson eventually sensed something wasn't quite right. Lynette had become addicted, or enslaved, to the very tranquilizers that liberated her, and once Lynette realized this, she determined to reclaim her life."

Dottie Alexander sat behind Jordan and Barry, with Jayne Alexander, Jordan's mother, at her left. At right sat Philip and his wife. Dottie scowled at the young woman prosecutor "who so disrespectfully painted her favorite grandson Jordan as a villain and the whore he married as an angel."

She sighed aloud as Destiny described the empowerment Lynette gained through therapy and grassroots community involvement, as Destiny detailed Lynette's volunteer work and monetary contributions she provided for the city's clinics, as Destiny called Lynette "the ultimate victim of the same violent and abusive domestic situations she worked so hard to eliminate."

Turning away from the jury, Destiny crossed to the center of the courtroom.

"She saved so many others, but in the end, she was powerless to save herself."

Her eyes fell on Dottie's irritated countenance.

"From all the foregoing, it is obvious Lynette Benson Alexander didn't live a perfect life, but tumultuous though it was, it was *her* life, and Jordan Alexander had no right to take it."

She turned back toward the jury.

"You see, from the very beginning of their relationship, from the fateful day they married in April of 1972, Jordan Alexander dominated Lynette. When he cursed her out in public, she politely apologized. When he stayed away with girlfriends for days and sometimes for weeks at a time, she asked him no questions. When he demanded she cut her mother out of her life for two whole years, she quietly complied. When he beat her face so badly that both her eyes swelled shut, rendering her blind for all practical purposes, she hid herself away in a wretched motel room, telling her daughters she was away on business or at her mother's. She endured all the pain and humiliation because she always hoped the situation would improve.

"And as I told you earlier, things did change in 1984. After 12 years of physical and emotional abuses, after the Valium addiction, after years of therapy, Lynette finally decided to take responsibility for the direction of her life. In November of that year, after Jordan slapped her, she ordered him out of their Pacific Heights home, concurrently filing papers for a formal separation and a restraining order. And the foundation she always wanted to set up—she did that in May 1985."

Approaching the rail in front of the jury box, she continued.

"But ladies and gentlemen, as my grandmother was always so fond of saying, 'You don't know the worth of water till the well runs dry.' Where Jordan Alexander had always taken Lynette for granted, suddenly he didn't have her anymore. He panicked at first, and then he began a series of alarming behaviors that grew progressively worse and culminated when he brutally murdered her on the night of August 17th. During the course of this trial, fellow prosecutor Brett McPherson will detail the defendant's desperation and his descent to depths of depravity in which warped minds actually begin to believe that the murder of another person is justifiable. Jealously of course, and the insecurity that accompanies it, is a powerful motive.

"The things you'll find out about Jordan Alexander and the heinous nature of the gruesome murder he committed will shock you. They will nauseate you, though what you'll see in photographs doesn't begin to come close to horror and gore of the actual crime scene. The fact that it was a vicious, brutal murder committed by an angry husband will become obvious as the medical examiner describes for you in detail the nature of the injuries Lynette's body suffered and the method and sheer force employed for inflicting them. It will be perhaps the most disturbing moment of the trial for many of us."

She returned to the prosecutor's table, bending over to unzip a large leather case from which she withdrew a chart. Upon her cue, Brett rose and, setting up another easel, he placed it before the jury. She followed, setting the chart into the metal slot. TIMELINE, in bold lettering, ran across the top of the chart. Moving down the display on the left side, in smaller lettering, was the heading TIME over a much larger area in which eight white strips of cardboard ran horizontally across the exhibit. Toward the center of the placard, across from TIME was the heading ACTIVITY.

"None of us would be in this room today if a murder hadn't been committed. That we know. The defendant wouldn't be facing you if there was no cause to believe he is the murderer. We know he had a violent history with her. We'll learn from acquaintances that he became increasingly desperate during the early weeks of August. So we have a murder and we have a motive. Thus we must also determine: Did Jordan Alexander have the *opportunity* to commit the murder? The answer is yes, and based on statements he and others gave, we've been able to piece together the chronology of the night. Here we're going to follow the defendant through the actual commission of murder."

She removed a six-inch piece of cardboard under the TIME heading, revealing *8:15* in bold print. Directly across, she removed an eighteen-inch strip under the ACTIVITY heading, which displayed, *Left Alioto's after dinner with Bernard Katz. He was wearing dark blue or black suit.*

"Witnesses confirm the defendant had dinner at Alioto's on the wharf at around seven and left at about eight-fifteen. They also confirm he was wearing a dark suit. We also know he consumed no more than two glasses of wine during that time."

The next line on the display read *8:30-9:20* and *Returned home. Drank large quantity of tequila. Got murder weapon.*

"One of the defendant's neighbors will testify he saw a light come on in the defendant's house at 9:00 and that it went out at about 9:15. Also, during a search of the residence, detectives found a half-full glass of tequila, which an analysis of its oxidation rate suggests was probably poured during that time."

Returning to the exhibit, she revealed the next time and activity: *9:30-10:00* and *Went to Lynette's home, gained entrance, argued with Lynette.*

"Witnesses will testify that Jordan's Rolls Royce arrived at Lynette's Sacramento Street address at 9:30 and that only *one* man quietly entered her home. You may also see or hear testimony from Caitlyn, Lynette's oldest daughter. She'll tell you that she remembers hearing her mother arguing with someone at 10:00 p.m. as she was drifting off to sleep. She assumed it was her father. During this time the argument became physical. The defendant slapped Lynette and Lynette fought back, scratching the back of his neck and employing a self-defense strategy to bloody his nose."

When Destiny removed the fourth cardboard strip from the display, the letters were printed in a blood-red color: *10:00-10-15* and *Jordan Alexander murdered Lynette.* The color of the line had been a source of contention from Barry, who argued the color of the line was unduly prejudicial. Judge Morgan however, who early on seemed to favor Destiny, disagreed, allowing it in.

"Based on degree of digestion, body temperature, and various other factors, the medical examiner will testify that the most probable time of death was about 10:00, though it could have been as late as 10:15. During this time, Jordan withdrew a knife."

Returning to the prosecution table, she reached toward Brett, who handed her a large knife.

"At this time, I'd like to introduce *State's exhibit A*."

With the knife clenched in her hand, she approached the jury.

"It's a large, single-edged hunting knife. The serrated blade is eight inches long, not unlike many of the knives the defendant used for deer hunting. We don't know exactly what the butt looked like, but it left a distinct impression on Lynette's forehead when the defendant slammed it into her face, finally knocking her unconscious. Of course, he didn't knock her unconscious right away. The first wound she received was in the right thigh. The second was a high-impact wound to the right shoulder. By this time, she was fleeing to escape him, thrusting out her hands to defend herself, but all in vain. Two fingers on her left hand were severed in the process. The defendant—"

A woman sobbing in the front row on the prosecution side of the room collapsed onto another woman's shoulder. It was Allegra Benson, who struggling in the earliest moments of Destiny's opening statement, yielded to the emotional undercurrent that eroded her composure. Her sister, seated next to her, tried to get her to stand in order to take her outside the courtroom, but Allegra stiffened, wiped her face and insisted on remaining seated.

Her eyes meeting Destiny's, she nodded to indicate she was prepared for whatever horror lay ahead. Destiny hesitated and smiled toward Allegra, clearing her throat before continuing.

"The defendant, in pursuit, finally caught her and knocked her unconscious with the butt of the knife."

She demonstrated the action as she described the scene.

"The evidence suggests she fell face-down onto the bedroom carpet. And then the defendant, standing over her, grabbed a handful of her hair, yanking her head back, exposing her bare throat."

The jurors were riveted in their chairs. Ten sat with horror-stricken faces while the other two glanced away, unnerved and reluctant to watch the description of the actual death stroke.

"He sliced with great force, ripping her neck open from ear to ear. Within seconds, Lynette's blood covered almost everything in the room and she was dead, but he wasn't through with her. No, not by a long shot. He continued to stab the body for at least a full minute or more. Yet the fact that he continued to stab her isn't nearly so disturbing as the odd fact that he began to direct his rage toward a specific region of her body. The medical examiner will testify Lynette was stabbed over twenty-five times in the vaginal area, so many times that her pelvic bone jetted out from the bloody, mangled, receding flesh of her lower abdomen. What he did to her body after he killed her was nothing short of mutilation."

Careful not to overkill the effect of the murder on jurors, Destiny went back to the board and removed the fifth strip of cardboard, which revealed, *10:15-10:45* and *Drove Rolls Royce into Golden Gate Park. Ditched the vehicle. Phoned Stephanie Rodriguez.*

"On a moderate traffic night, it would have taken approximately fourteen minutes to drive from Lynette's Sacramento Street home to the place in the park where the Rolls Royce was discovered the next day. We're trying to arrange a jury field trip so you'll be able to see the most probable route he took as well as the exact spot and position in which the car was parked. When the defendant left the vehicle, he was forced to fight his way through the dense bush that concealed the car's location. The bush was made of a plant species called *rosa pinetorem*, which is a favorite of zoologists and detectives alike for its natural tendency to snag fur or clothing. We'll discuss just what that dense brush snagged a little later."

Pointer in her hand, she re-directed the jury's attention to the board and specifically, to the information about the phone call.

"While we have proof the defendant called friend Stephanie Rodriguez at 10:45, we believe the evidence will show the call was placed from somewhere within Golden Gate Park."

She removed the sixth cardboard strip. *11:15-11:35* and *Arrived home. Phoned police to report car theft.*

"Police records indicate the defendant called in at 11:32 to report being mugged and having his car stolen. We know *that* call originated from the defendant's home on Loma Vista Way."

Seventh strip. *11:50 p.m. to 5:00 a.m.* and *Reported murder. Disposed of murder weapon and bloody clothing.*

"Records also indicate an anonymous caller phoned police at 11:58 to report the murder, complete with an address and a concern about possible children within. This call was placed from a pay phone near Clement and Park Presidio. Further, we believe Inspector Osaka of the San Francisco Police Department will testify that he observed a white Lincoln Towncar turn onto Loma Vista from the Masonic intersection and roll by his vehicle before pulling into the defendant's garage. This was at 4:59 a.m."

5:23 a.m. and *Inspectors Elliot Garner and Ed Harris arrive at defendant's home on Loma Vista Way.*

"Finally, at 5:23, unable to reach the defendant by telephone, Inspectors Garner and Harris arrive at his Loma Vista Way home to inform him of the murder."

Timeline detailed, she sighed aloud, her left arm raised as she motioned toward the exhibit.

"And there we have it. So now, after knowing the defendant had the means and the motive to commit this gristly murder, we now know he had the opportunity."

She glimpsed at the watch on her left wrist.

"As you look at the chart and all the times and activities listed, you might be saying to yourself: it tells a compelling story and all with great attention to detail, but she wasn't there. How could she possibly know what happened?

"Well, the truth is, I don't know everything, but everything I've told you is based on the little puzzle pieces investigators have been collecting since the night of last August 17th. The legal term for those puzzle pieces is *evidence*."

She walked toward Lynette's picture displayed on the easel.

"So far this morning, you've listened to the things I've had to say about what happened on the night of August 17th. I've talked about motive, method and opportunity. But when we come back after lunch, you're going to hear what the cold, hard *evidence* has to say about that night and the man who murdered Lynette, the man who is sitting..."

She pointed at Jordan.

"Right there."

Looking up toward Judge Morgan, Destiny nodded.

"This seems like an appropriate place to stop for now."

CHAPTER 28

It was already late June 1987, and while the rest of the nation was engrossed with the surreptitious activities of Colonel North, Admiral Poindexter and President Reagan with respect to illegal arms sales to Iraq, San Francisco was poised for the beginning of a lurid trial involving one of the most powerful and respected families in the city.

The population around the Bay was well-informed about many aspects of the incipient trial. They knew about the blood samples that had gone separately to the Washington D.C. crime lab and to the lab in nearby Emeryville for DNA PCR testing. They even knew suggested results of the testing. For two of the blood samples taken at Lynette's residence that appeared to be Jordan's, the incidence of a coincidental match was supposedly one in ten million.

Tests suggested a high probability that its owner was of African American ancestry. Yet it was clear the four samples had come from two separate human beings. The blood samples found at Jordan's Loma Vista Way residence however, were sent to Cellmark Diagnostics in Germantown, Maryland for RFLP testing. All the samples came back as probable matches for Lynette.

Nonetheless Judge Helen Morgan, after a Frye hearing held to determine the admissibility of such disputable scientific evidence, ruled that none of the results could be introduced during the State's case-in-chief or by the defense. Beyond that, she ordered sequestration of the jury for the duration of the trial. While opening arguments were set to begin in early spring, the DNA fingerprinting admission debate as well as other *in limine* arguments had pushed the start of the trial well into summer.

One of these arguments involved the *Tequila Test*. Destiny was hoping to prove that, based on a demonstrated oxidation rate for the Cuevro Gold Tequila found in Jordan's residence, the nearly full shot glass had been poured somewhere between 8:30 and 9:20. Investigators working for the district attorney had performed perhaps thirty to forty tests measuring oxidation rates in samples under varying conditions.

Beyond that, Destiny sent the sealed sample found in Jordan's home and the remains of the bottle to a respected professor at the California Institute of Technology in Pasadena for a more careful analysis. If the State could establish the tequila was poured by Jordan between 8:30 and 9:20, it would go a long way toward proving he was home planning the murder rather than lying unconscious in a garbage bin on the wharf.

Stephanie Rodriguez had been missing for ten months, and rumors persisted she was still in San Jose. Even Vic Ehlers, one of the best private investigators in the business, was unable to locate her. If she was maintaining any communication with Jordan, it would have involved Barry, since the origin of calls to and from the jail were monitored.

Media and legal analysts predicted Stephanie would miraculously appear at the onset of the defense's case, just in time to provide the framework of an alibi for Jordan, which could then be bolstered by other witnesses and evidence.

Under the rules of discovery, even if Barry conducted interviews with her, he was under no legal obligation to inform the prosecution or the court on the matter or share information he planned to use in Jordan's defense. The same rule applied for other interviews and evidence.

While Destiny had to supply Barry with all the material she planned to use in her case-in-chief, all Barry had to produce was a witness list. During pre-trial motions, Destiny, Brett and Janice railed about the unfairness of discovery rules, but they got little sympathy from rigid Judge Morgan and even less from Barry, who pointed out that the court system granted "unconscionable" advantages to prosecutors in criminal investigations and subsequent trials.

In early May of 1987, television and hard copy reporters found it newsworthy that Deondray Carter, one of the black youths accused of murdering Lynette, was stabbed to death in the Alameda County jail. His body was discovered on a Sunday morning clutching a copy of the *Koran*, with the butt of a steel shank extending from his back, the blade wedged between his ribs. Prison officials attributed the murder to gang activity.

Then in mid-June, Hosea Carter in the San Francisco district attorney's office received a call from a frantic and excited Tyrell Briggs who begged for another meeting. In his ranting, he insisted there had been a contract put out on Deondray and him and that "Dray's murder had pro written all over it." Hosea phoned the Alameda district attorney and the jail inquiring into the killing, but he could find no solid evidence involving foul play.

Shortly thereafter, Tyrell Briggs recanted his earlier confession involving the murder of Lucille DuBois, insisting he and

Deondray had remained in San Francisco on the night of August 17. He said they hired "young blood" to do the Oakland killing and that he never saw Lucille that night. He even went so far as suggesting that he had undisclosed information on the Lynette Alexander murder and that he was the only person who really knew the truth. When pressed for answers however, he balked, insisting on a deal that would make him a free man and give him a new identity.

The Alameda district attorney was working with Hosea on a counter-offer when guards found Tyrell murdered in his cell. He was castrated. His own penis was lodged down his throat and his mouth was full of his own testicles. His dark, bloody lips were sewn shut. The murder of Tyrell happened in the last week of June and was good for three news days of conspiracy theories advanced by the smaller, less established newspapers.

While the Alameda sheriff again blamed gang activity, the black community in Oakland grew agitated, angry and increasingly polarized with respect to the Jordan Alexander murder trial. Media analysts cited surveys revealing almost seventy percent of blacks interviewed in San Francisco and Oakland believed the defendant was guilty. Analysts advanced many theories for the polarity, the most prevalent being that blacks were merely identifying with San Francisco prosecutor Destiny Mitchell, who also happened to be black.

Destiny saw Charles on only one occasion since the argument at her apartment in October. She phoned him the next day and on six or seven times thereafter, but he never returned the calls. She knew she could never bring herself to say the words that would have elicited the response she wanted from him, words that would have made everything better.

She was unwilling to announce, "I'm off the case." She was also unwilling to humiliate herself by begging to a greater degree than she already had, so she gave up after two weeks, immersing herself in the daunting task of prosecuting Jordan Alexander.

Because her undergrad major at Berkeley was chemistry and because she always loved science, she was comfortable analyzing the scientific evidence for possible use in the trial. In fact, the tequila experiments were her idea. Since her sister worked at the lab in Emeryville where the DNA PCR tests were performed, she gained a thorough understanding of the process and for the interpretation of test results.

During mid-December of 1986, the world screeched to a halt as the labs and other support personnel slowed to indulge in the holiday season.

It was her first holiday alone in years. She really missed Charles. Agonizing, she called him, only to find he was unavailable, as always. One week before Christmas day, she got up the courage to take a flight down to Los Angeles and drive over to Camp Irwin. She had learned from General Deitler he wouldn't be going to Boston for the holidays because his mother was away at St. Croix.

She surprised him on a Friday, just as he was returning from the field. He *seemed* happy to see her. He said he sent numerous messages back to the base to let her know he got called into the field for desert maneuvers.

They had dinner in Destiny's favorite downtown Los Angeles restaurant and then drove up into the Hollywood hills to watch the stars in a clear, dark December sky, sprinkled with a million points of light.

Throughout the night, she tried to be more submissive and less headstrong than she had ever been. They laughed, drank cognac and discussed dreams of marriage and family. Happier than she could remember being in months, she fell asleep on his shoulder during the drive back to his house, apologizing profusely as the car pulled into his garage.

The sex was incredible that night, intense and frequent. They drove over to Las Vegas on Saturday morning to explore the new casino and to take in a few shows. Later in the night, even as Destiny toyed with the elaborate engagement ring on her finger, she and Charles flirted with the idea of a quick, forty-nine dollar, justice-of-the-peace ceremony right there in Vegas, but they never made it out of bed.

On Sunday night, Destiny had to fly back home to prepare for depositions scheduled on Monday morning. It was a wonderful weekend, and Charles promised to call to finalize plans for spending Christmas day together, but he never did.

When she called him on Christmas Eve day, a clerk told her he had left the fort. She spent Christmas with her sister, miserable as she babysat her nieces and nephew, such beautiful children.

Watching her sister and brother-in-law exchange gifts and tender affections made her feel even worse. Sick inside, she felt like someone had punched her in the stomach, so she quietly excused herself and drove home to her apartment where she cried through the night. Feeling used, she vowed to never call Charles again, and he never called her with an explanation. For all she knew or wanted to care, he had left the planet.

CHAPTER 29

"Ladies and Gentlemen, my name is Barry Divine, and I'll start by saying, Thank You. Thank you for the time and the liberty you've sacrificed in order to occupy the twelve seats you'll be using in the weeks to come. I thank your families for standing by you and supporting you as you perform the sacred civic service of jury duty."

He approached the twelve, smiling.

"Oh! And I better thank you in advance for putting up with me. You see, whether you know it or not, I've garnered a reputation with prosecutors for being a *divine* pain in the ass. Why? Because I ask questions, because I pick things apart, because I stand up and object when the rules are broken, because I completely insist on a presumption of innocence."

Dragging his fingers on the worn railing along the box, he stopped before the group.

"This presumption of innocence is a rule of law that states a person is not guilty of a crime he's accused of until and unless proven guilty beyond a reasonable doubt."

Three of the jurors, uncomfortable with the patch on Barry's face, avoided eye contact.

"Now, the *accused* doesn't have to prove anything. The accused doesn't even have to take the stand. The burden rests solely on the State to prove their case beyond a reasonable doubt. So really, it's not a matter of me being picky or difficult. It's actually a matter of law. If in the course of this trial you become frustrated with objections and minor arguments and delays for rulings, please remember that I just can't help myself. I'm only following the rules."

He lowered the volume of his voice, speaking in a courtroom whisper.

"Even the most minor argument you'll hear will be very important to Jordan Alexander sitting over there. After all, it's his life at stake."

He started to turn, but he paused.

"Oh, one more thing. The patch here. I lost my eye in Chinatown when I was in college."

He smiled.

"It looks harsh, but it doesn't hurt, really. It might make some of you a little uneasy at first, but we're going to be here for a while. You'll get used to it."

He turned and crossed toward the defense table, stopping short.

"We're all here because of a terrible tragedy that happened on August 17th of last year. On August 17th, Lynette Alexander was brutally murdered. She lost her life. She was the victim of a horrible crime, but as murders go, she wasn't the only victim. Jordan Alexander was also a victim. He lost a wife he loved very much. Three beautiful young girls, Caitlyn, Denver and Lyndsey, were also victims. They lost a mother. Allegra Benson was a victim. She lost her only daughter. Beyond that, the city of San Francisco lost a true champion, a person who had conquered many of her personal problems and had moved on to help others. She was an inspiration to us all. Ms. Mitchell came before you yesterday and described her life much more eloquently than I ever could, and I'm not here to dispute any of what she said about Lynette."

He glanced toward Destiny as he continued.

"I cannot help however, disputing her version of what happened on the night of August 17th as well as her portrayal of one of the victims. Jordan Alexander did not commit this crime. He simply wouldn't have. He literally couldn't have."

Passing behind the defense table, he patted Jordan's shoulder.

"I'll say it again: He simply wouldn't have. He literally couldn't have."

Barry smiled, his hand extended toward his cousin.

"It would be disingenuous for any of us to say we haven't *heard* of Jordan Alexander. It would be impossible to live in San Francisco and not know *of* him. We've all seen him in commercials and in ads, in the news, at major social events, at 49er games, at Giants games and in our communities. As a young man, he was instrumental in the revitalization of the Financial District. The Embarcadero Center we know today wouldn't have been a reality without him, and a few of the big developments along Dollar Block, California and Battery, may have been compromised had it not been for Jordan's insistence and influence with the city council."

Conscious of the jury, Jordan displayed a weak, distressed smile.

"Beyond that, Jordan was and *is* a wonderful father. His daughters have visited places, watched events and done things most of us can only dream of doing. Ask Caitlyn, and she'll tell you she's met Michael Jackson, Madonna and the Queen of England.

Ask any of the girls about their father, and they tell you he's the best dad a kid could ever have."

Barry approached the jury box.

"And ladies and gentlemen, despite what anyone comes up here and tells you, Jordan *was* a good husband to Lynette. Sure, they had their share of problems like the rest of us, but their marriage was basically a good one. It was a marriage that withstood the test of time, twelve years. It was a modern marriage that withstood the pressures of a CEO's busy schedule, one that withstood meddling from outside sources, one that withstood Lynette's drug abuse."

He stopped at the rail, before the jury.

"Let me tell you something about the drug abuse. Ms. Mitchell mentioned it to you yesterday, and maybe only because she didn't know everything, she didn't *tell* you everything. Lynette's Valium addiction brought on profound changes in her personality. During the two years she secretly abused the drug, she wasn't always the same wonderful Lynette we all remember. Witnesses will come before you and testify to that. They'll say that in odd moments she was irrationally angry, edgy, paranoid and sometimes delusional.

"And in some of those moments she was violent. Fortunately, the violence that resulted from the addiction was never directed toward the girls. Rather, it was always directed toward the one person who had committed himself to stay with her, to stand by her, to help her get over the addiction, regardless of the cost. The police came out to Jordan and Lynette's Sacramento Street home on many occasions to settle disputes. On some of those occasions, officers reported that Lynette suffered various injuries inflicted by Jordan.

"But ladies and gentlemen, these were injuries suffered as a result of Jordan only trying to defend himself, suffered as a result of Jordan trying to restrain her until help arrived. What most of the reports *don't* tell you, however, is that Jordan was usually more beat up and bruised Lynette ever was. Why don't we know about it? Because Jordan asked officers not to report his injuries, because Jordan didn't want her Valium addiction to become public. During the course of the trial, not just one, but a few officers will come before you and attest to that."

Barry turned toward the judge, his back to the jury as he paused for effect.

"Jordan helped get her the counseling she needed, and

Lynette came back stronger than ever. Unfortunately though, the same influential counselor who convinced Lynette that she didn't need the Valium also convinced her that she didn't need her husband. In fact, this counselor told Lynette that she could never be a complete person unless she got rid of Jordan. Lynette filed her restraining order not long after."

He turned toward the jury.

"Jordan didn't fight it. He told friends he was hoping the trial separation would make her realize how much she missed him and cared about him. His friends will tell you he wanted badly to be a complete family again. He even helped her find the money to establish *Aegis*, the foundation she opened to provide protection and shelter for victimized women and children. Witnesses will testify they were on the best terms ever during the few months before the murder."

His voice was steady, gentle, reassuring.

"Finally, before we let anyone label Jordan as a violent spousal abuser, perhaps we should ask ourselves a few important questions. Are there any reports of violence between Jordan and Lynette that pre-date the substance abuse? Were there any incidents after she got out of therapy? Has Jordan acted in a violent manner toward any *other* woman or women other than Lynette? Those are the objective questions we need to ask ourselves before automatically accepting anyone's portrayal of Jordan as a violent man. Simply put, Jordan is not and has never been a violent person. He simply wouldn't have. He simply wouldn't have murdered Lynette."

He sighed, scanning the faces in the room.

"But you have to ask yourselves as you listen to the inaccurate portrayal of Jordan that you'll hear from prosecution witnesses: If he's *not* a violent person, why would the prosecution go through so much trouble to try to make you believe he is? Then ask yourselves if any of the prosecution's theories can be believed *unless* Jordan is somehow transformed into a violent, sadistic, women-hating killer. Keep an open mind as you listen to prosecution witnesses come before you in attempts to re-invent Jordan, as they attempt to re-cast his role and redefine his character. Keep an open mind and just remember, there are two sides to every story."

The jurors listened as Barry detailed the list of witnesses he promised would paint "a better picture of Jordan and of his marriage to Lynette."

It was mid-morning Friday in a stuffy courtroom filled beyond capacity. While the morning newspapers touted Destiny's opening statement from day one as well-developed and brilliantly-delivered, writers predicted if anyone could poke holes in the prosecutor's detailed case, it would be Barry Divine.

Barry wore a European-tailored chocolate brown suit with a crisp white shirt, accented by a red, green and yellow Salvador Dali-esque tie. His style and delivery was notably more relaxed and conversational than Destiny's, his face more malleable. He smiled more often than she did. He showed distress in his face when speaking about the murder. He played more to the jury. The jury responded with corresponding smiles, with winces on several occasions and with head nods. Seven jurors were taking notes as he spoke, while the other five just sat there, listening.

Defense team member Terri Gonik sat next to Jordan, whispering to him on occasion. Dottie and the other family members took the same seats they occupied while listening to Destiny a day earlier. Allegra was in her same seat as well, her face showing contempt and resentment as Barry described her daughter's relationship with Jordan as wonderful and loving.

A television sketch artist captured the expression on her face in a frame that featured Barry standing during his opening statement and Allegra seated in the background. Rikki Thomas occupied a seat right behind Destiny. Smiling throughout Barry's statement, she seemed enormously self-satisfied about something.

Outside the court building, the news vans and correspondents were in formation, reporting the story for local, national and international news agencies. In the parking lot, various women's rights groups had assembled with tables, volunteers, leaflets, speakers and a banner that read, *Jordan Alexander Must Pay For Crimes Against Womanhood!*

On the other side of the building, a group of about forty blacks also assembled, led by Roscoe DuBois, the husband of the late Lucille DuBois. Lucille was murdered on the same night as Lynette. Roscoe had become a visible spokesperson for the black community in the months before the trial.

The story of his wife's death and his crusade for publicity put him in the newspapers and on television news on a regular basis. He called his story "A Tale of Two Americas," a story in which the murders of two women on the same night had been handled and perceived so differently. It wasn't about money or status, he maintained, because "me and Lucille had both." The jailhouse murders of Tyrell Briggs and Deondray Carter, he asserted, were indicative of how far "the system would go to absolve this white man and denigrate black males all the more."

"Tyrell Briggs and Deondray Carter paid for their sins," he told reporters, "Now we gotta see to it that Jordan Alexander pays for his!"

"Once again, he literally *couldn't* have. We also believe that this same Stephanie Rodriguez will come before you to tell you she picked Jordan up at 11:30, battered badly, shivering and naked. She'll testify he was groggy and disoriented, not inconsistent with a person who had recently been unconscious. She'll testify he was emotional and she'll testify he was *not* covered in blood, that he was barely bleeding from a scratch on the back of his neck. She'll tell you that, after talking with Jordan, she went into the Vagabond Inn to ask if any of the employees or guests had seen a man being mugged in the lot nearby, if they had seen two African American males driving away in a Rolls Royce. The manager from the Vagabond Inn can confirm that. So you see, contrary to the prosecution's theory and timeline, if Jordan never left the wharf in his Rolls on August 17th, it would have been impossible for him to have committed a murder over in Pacific Heights. He literally *couldn't* have."

Barry paused, walking over to the table to retrieve a legal pad.

"The prosecution yesterday spent the entire afternoon detailing this vast 'ocean of evidence' linking Jordan to the crime scene and blood from the crime scene to Jordan's Loma Vista residence. The Rolls Royce may or may not have been there at Lynette's. That we have yet to determine, but *Jordan* was never there, and not one item of evidence the prosecution proffered can prove that with any degree of certainty, certainly not beyond a reasonable doubt."

He was standing before the jury, notepad in his left hand.

"The prosecution offered evidence from which inferences must be drawn, and they've hired, and I repeat, they've *hired* so-called experts to help you move from 'what's there' to what they'd like you to believe."

He smiled.

"Well, we found a few experts of our own who'll tell you differently. They'll tell you that sometimes more than one inference can be drawn from a single piece of evidence. So, as you listen to the prosecution's invitation to just sort of wade into this vast ocean of evidence, be careful, reserve your judgment. Because as we all know, the neat surface of the water doesn't always reveal the perils and currents which lie beneath."

He crossed his arms.

"No, the gentle surface sometimes gives us a false picture, it gives us no clue about the turmoil and treachery that goes on underneath or behind the scenes, and that leads me to the last thing I'm going to talk to you about. Now, you may be asking yourselves, 'Well, if Jordan had absolutely nothing to do with his wife's murder, if he wouldn't have and couldn't have murdered his wife, why was he arrested and why is he here standing on trial for it?'"

He paused for effect.

"On the surface, prosecutors may lead you to believe that this trial is only about Lynette and about justice, but there's much more to it than that. During the course of this trial, we intend to demonstrate that, from that very first night, a rogue faction of detectives on the San Francisco Police Department went about making sure Jordan was blamed for the crime. We'll demonstrate that he was a suspect from the beginning and that one inspector in particular, one Bryan Osaka, resorted to outright deception in order to gain access to his private residence.

"What did he do once he got in there? What you'll hear from our experts will shock you. Beyond that, we'll tell you how other detectives harassed Stephanie Rodriguez a few days after the murder, frightening her to the point that she quit her job as a highly paid model and went into hiding. You'll learn that the actions of these detectives are currently under investigation by police Internal Affairs.

"You'll also hear testimony from Rikki Thomas, the police spokesperson, about written police procedures and the improprieties carried out by the detectives in question. She'll tell you who in the department authorized their actions. Commander Dennis Webber, and make sure you remember that name. If you're taking notes, his is the first name you should write down. *He's* the man with all the answers, he's the man who can tell you why, if Jordan couldn't and wouldn't have, he's the man who can tell you why Jordan's here on trial today."

Ten minutes later, after Barry had summed up the most salient points of his statement, he and Terri set up an easel with a large board covered with a tan colored veil that obscured the image. At the very center, observers could barely make out the features of a man's face. It seemed to be Jordan.

"Ms. Mitchell showed you a picture of Lynette yesterday and promised she'd paint you one of Jordan. I ask you, is this that picture? You tell me. Look at Jordan and look at the picture."

He paused as the jurors stared at the display

"With Lynette's picture yesterday, a few pieces were missing, and yet you still recognized her, right? Does this look enough like Jordan to conclude it is him without any reasonable doubt? Better yet, would it serve the interest of justice if you or anyone convicted Jordan for the murder of his wife based on such a murky and indistinct portrayal of him like this one here? No, it wouldn't."

He approached the display.

"You see, sometimes, even if you have *all* the pieces, even if you're up till three in the morning putting it together like I was, even if you put them all together right and don't lose any pieces, the picture you get isn't always what it seems."

He lifted the veil from the large board, revealing the picture underneath. The startled audience viewing it reacted at once with gasps and surprise. The picture wasn't of Jordan at all. Rather, it was the portrait of a young African American man who, in his facial features and profile, bore an uncanny resemblance to the defendant.

"This isn't your murderer either. His name is Jim. He works for me as a legal clerk. One of the reasons I hired him is because he *looked* so much like Jordan. In fact, the running gag in our office is that Jim and I are distant cousins."

He smiled at Jim who stood and nodded toward jurors.

"All I'm asking, throughout this trial, is that you'll always ask yourselves the important questions, that you'll keep an open mind and that you'll remember things aren't always what they seem. Thank you very much."

CHAPTER 30

Judge Helen Morgan removed her glasses, her solemn expression indicative of the journey all interested parties were about to undertake.

"Are the People ready to proceed?"

It was Monday morning, June 29, nearly a year after the murder. Destiny answered, though she and Brett were both standing.

"We are, your Honor."

"Very well. You may call your first witness."

"Thank you, your Honor. The People call Heather Croftland."

The pretty young woman who took the stand seemed nervous as the clerk swore her in. She spelled her name wrong the first time.

Destiny smiled to reassure her.

"Thank you for coming, Ms. Croftland. I realize you're nervous, being the first witness and all. You'll do fine."

Once again the lawyer, she began.

"Ms. Croftland, where do you work?"

"Um, I um work at Alioto's restaurant on the wharf?"

"And what do you do at Alioto's?"

"I'm, I'm a waitress. No! I mean, I'm a server."

"Were you working on the evening of Sunday, August 17th, 1986?"

Heather took a deep breath, calming herself.

"Yes, Ma'am."

"Okay. By the way, do you know Jordan Alexander?"

"Um. Well, I don't actually *know* him, but I know who he is."

"Why's that?"

"Because I've waited on him a few times at the restaurant?"

"Is that an answer or is it a question?"

"An answer."

Destiny took her place along the jury railing, a position in which she could see both the witness and the defendant.

"Would you recognize Mr. Alexander if you saw him today?"

"Yes, yes I would."

"Do you see him anywhere in this courtroom?"

"Yes, he's right there at that table."

"Can you indicate which man he is by telling us the color of his tie?"

"Blue."

Heather pointed at Jordan. The judge, leaning over her desk so that she could speak to the court recorder, nodded her head.

"The witness has indicated the defendant, Mr. Alexander."

Destiny continued as the court recorder nodded.

"Ms. Croftland, did you serve the defendant on the night in question?"

"Yes."

"Do you remember what time he came in?"

Hands in her lap, Heather fidgeted.

"Not, not exactly when you guys asked me the first time, but after that when they showed me the check from the table I remembered. I opened the check at 6:58 after he sat waiting about five minutes, so he had to be there at about 6:50."

"Okay, so he arrived at about 6:50. Do you remember what he had?"

"The *Cioppino*."

"Was he by himself or was he with someone?"

"With someone."

"All right. Do you know the person he was with? Had you ever seen him before?"

Heather smiled, becoming more comfortable with the questions.

"No."

"Do you remember whether or not the defendant consumed any alcoholic beverage during dinner?"

"He had the Sangiovesse. Two glasses."

"Two glasses and nothing more? No tequila? How can you be sure of that?"

Heather turned toward the jury.

"Because he stopped me after I poured the second glass of wine. Said he didn't need anything else."

"Okay, do you remember what he was wearing?"

Heather closed her eyes, thinking.

"A suit. A dark suit with no tie. Open shirt."

"Any jewelry?"

"I, I don't remember."

"Do you remember what time he left the restaurant?"

She opened her eyes.

"He left at a little before 8:15."

"How can you be sure about that?"

Heather seemed embarrassed. She ran her fingers through her collar-length brown hair.

"Well, because one of my friends has a crush on him and she was coming down to see if she could get his attention, you know, being that he was single and all? And when she got there at 8:15, she missed him by only a minute or two."

Destiny sighed.

"Thank you, Ms. Croftland. One more question. After dinner, who left first? The defendant or the man he had dinner with? Or did they leave together?"

"The other man left first. I remember because I was hoping Jordan would stay longer. He sat by himself for about five minutes before leaving."

"Do you remember what sort of mood he was in?"

Barry interrupted.

"Objection. Calls for speculation."

"Overruled."

Destiny continued.

"Was he friendly?"

Heather glanced toward Jordan.

"No he wasn't. He seemed a little edgy, maybe agitated about something? He had this real intense look on his face."

"Thank you, Ms. Croftland. No further questions."

Barry stood, already asking questions as Destiny settled into her seat. There, on the table, right on in front of Destiny! It was a six-inch square, cream-colored envelope with her name printed on the front. Curious, she tore it open, hands shaking as she realized she was holding an invitation. Somehow she knew, but she read anyway:

Dr. and Mrs. Claude Boveé
and
Mrs. Arianne Covington

invite you to share in the joy
of the marriage uniting their
children, Dr. Claudette Boveé
and Colonel Charles Covington.
This celebration of love will be
held at 2:00 p.m. on Saturday,

August 8, 1987 at
The Saint Louis Cathedral
New Orleans, LA

Reading and re-reading in shock, Destiny could hardly breathe. It was only last December, seven months earlier, when she was with Charles in Las Vegas. She was *with* him! She had sex with him! They had almost gotten married right there!

He proposed to her in Golden Gate Park just last September, and now, less than a year later, he was marrying someone else! Her stomach became muddy again.

"So, how many *bottles* of the Sangiovesse were ordered at the table?"

"Two."

"Two, and knowing that, how can you say he only drank two glasses? Are you saying his dinner guest polished off two bottles of wine less two glasses?"

"No. The other man drank four and a half glasses, about a full bottle. Jordan had two glasses."

"So if a full bottle is about four and a half glasses, and Jordan only had two glasses, what happened to the other two and a half glasses?"

Embarrassed again, Heather looked toward the judge.

"I drank the rest of the bottle after the shift, me and my manager."

Destiny hadn't heard any of the cross-examination. Her thoughts were incoherent and capricious in the wake of the wedding announcement. She felt crushed, spurned and embarrassed. She felt love and hate for Charles, pity and loathing for herself and a new disgust for her job as a lawyer. Was it all for nothing? No matter how the trial ended, nothing made a difference anymore. She'd be by herself, and the man she loved would be married to someone else. Someone else would be the General's wife, someone else would be Mrs. Covington.

Judge Morgan's voice was irritated and insistent.

"Once again, will the State call its next witness?"

Uncomfortable in the lull, Brett nudged Destiny with his left elbow, arousing her from the tear-filled daze.

"I'm sorry, your Honor. The State calls, the State calls Patrick Kirby."

The middle-aged, overweight man who took the stand had

a long, red-haired ponytail, tinged with gray. His freckled and tanned face was round, though its outline was obscured by a heavy beard and sideburns.

Although he had a musty odor, the expensive wire-rimmed glasses and the Rolex on his wrist let on that his appearance didn't tell the entire story. He identified himself as Jordan's neighbor, in the house right across the street. A *Dead* fan "since before there was a *Grateful Dead*," it was the second time he had lived in the Haight. After college, he became one of the Silicon Valley's first computer software engineers, starting his own firm that he sold for a small fortune.

He told Destiny he was involved in software system consulting from a small office in his Haight Ashbury home. He testified he was working in that office from 8:00 to 9:30 on the evening of August 17. He was certain of the time because he was working for a client and he had logged the time in the client's file. He said his office faced the street and that he distinctly remembered a light coming on in the house between 9:00 and 9:25. When he saw the light, he recalled, he wanted to go over and tell Jordan that Lynette and the girls had stopped by a little after 8:00, but by the time he logged off at 9:30, the light had gone out.

Barry, in his cross-examination, asked Patrick if he made any reference to the light in his log, to which Patrick answered, "No." He also asked Patrick if he saw the Rolls parked in front of the house or in the driveway, and Patrick answered that, while he wasn't looking for the Rolls in particular, he couldn't recall seeing it. A Rolls Royce, Barry insisted, isn't just an everyday car.

"Certainly if it was there, you would have remembered seeing it?"

But Patrick maintained it *could* have been there. Destiny, in her re-direct, got Patrick to say that he was 100% sure he saw a light come on in the house that night. In a brief re-cross, Patrick admitted however, that, as a *Dead* fan, his memory was far from perfect.

It was a forty minutes after she got the shocking wedding invitation before Destiny began to suspect how it got on her table in the first place. Brett didn't know, though he said one of the court clerks stopped by the table during the direct examination of the first witness.

Destiny scanned the area around her table, her eyes finally focusing on Rikki Thomas, who had moved to a place behind her. As Rikki eyes met the lawyer's eyes, she smiled, her right hand patting, almost caressing the inner thigh of a very pretty black woman seated at her right.

That's when Destiny knew. That's when she knew the invitation wasn't just a ploy to throw her off-stride on the first day of the trial. She knew Rikki had brought in the *bitch* Charles was going to marry to prove the invitation's authenticity, and as much as it wrenched and racked her inside, she realized she had sacrificed Charles for the case.

Accepting the loss, Destiny felt a new resolve to pursue the trial to its end. She rationalized that she had lost a man she loved too well, though perhaps not too wisely. And though painful, it was something she hoped she'd eventually get over. But Lynette had lost so much more.

The next witness called was Gloria Applebaum, and her direct testimony did not vary much from her preliminary hearing testimony. She said she saw the Rolls parked in front of Lynette's house "for forty minutes, maybe even an hour," from 9:30 until at least 10:15. Destiny put up a board display of Sacramento Street so that Gloria could point out her own house, Lynette's house and the position and orientation of the Rolls.

Gloria testified that she had often heard arguments between Lynette and Jordan, though she hadn't heard one on that night. "Lynette," she maintained, "was a gentle soul. That Jordan— he was the mean one." She also said only "one person exited the car" and that he was tall and seemed white. Three police cars, she said, arrived at the house at about twelve-fifteen.

Barry, in cross-examining this "hostile witness," challenged Gloria's recall for times and dates. He asked about the color of the Rolls, about how many doors it had, about the wheels. He asked about her vision and her ability to see details in the dark.

While Destiny objected to a few of the questions, her witness held up, but then Barry began his final line of questioning.

"Mrs. Applebaum, and I should remind you you're under oath. Are you now under a doctor's care?"

"Objection. Question's irrelevant."

The judge peered over her glasses.

"Overruled, but you're getting close, counselor."

Barry nodded.

"Couple questions and I'll be done. Once again, Mrs. Applebaum, are you under a doctor's care?"

"No."

"Well then, let me put it this way, are you being treated by a physician for any specific condition?"

"Objection. Asked and answered."

"Overruled."

Gloria glared at Harold as Barry closed on her.

"Mrs. Applebaum, haven't you been diagnosed as being in the early stages of Alzheimer's disease?"

"Objection. Foundation, your Honor."

"Overruled."

Gloria just sat there until the judge insisted on an answer.

"Yes. And how would *you* know that?"

"Are you aware of the fact that Alzheimer patients like yourself have had problems remembering things?"

"First of all, Mr. Divine, I am not an Alzheimer's patient! I've been diagnosed, but I am not a patient. And second, I saw what I saw that night. I saw Jordan's Rolls Royce down there! And I know what he did to his wife! You, you are *not* a nice man."

"Non-responsive. Move to strike the last response."

While Destiny did her best to rehabilitate Gloria's credibility by pointing out that the disease wasn't diagnosed until February 1987 and that there had been no physical or mental effects to date, the implication of Alzheimer's disease on the trustworthiness of a witness' recall was unmistakable.

Vic Ehlers sat at a small table along the wall as he listened to the trumpet player running through a series of chromatic scales to warm his instrument. The sax player, practicing riffs, was a regular at the club's Monday night jam sessions. Vic drank Old Crow bourbon and smoked Winston regulars every night, a habit that identified him as a former military man to other retired personnel.

He was raised in Ripley, Tennessee, in a small town not far from Memphis. At sixteen he went up to Chicago to live with his father, who played trumpet. His father introduced him to many of the musicians who played *The Chitlin Circuit*, most notable among those, Mr. Louis Armstrong. Since that time, Vic went out of his way to take in a session or two of real jazz on a regular basis, and this little club in Oakland had been his favorite for the past few years.

As Vic tapped the cigarette on the ashtray, re-exposing the cherry, he blew the dust-like shards of gray off the goldenrod-colored legal-sized envelope on the table. Mid-way through the third song of the second set, Peter arrived, his eyes scanning the room. He carried a small black canvass briefcase, placing it on the table as he sat.

"It's all there. Want to count it?"

"I never count it."

Vic's eyes on the envelope, he nodded.

"What you wanted, it's right here. But like I said, it's sensitive stuff, so I got two rules."

Peter tightened his jaw, preparing himself for the conditions.

"And those are?"

"One, you can read it, you can take notes about it, but you can't physically take it away from here."

Peter thought for a while before nodding.

"Okay, I can live with that. What's the second rule?"

"You can tell her you know about it, you can threaten her with it, but if she calls your bluff, you can't use it."

"What do you mean, I can't use it?"

"Exactly that. You can threaten her with it if you know what you're doin, but I can't let you burn the other people involved. Be bad for business."

Peter sat back in the chair.

"So I wouldn't be able to actually use it? Now *that* one I'll have to think about."

Vic smiled, sipping the bourbon.

"It's your decision. Take your time. Of course, if you don't think you'll know how to make it *work* for you, you can always pick up your money and go back home. Like I told you earlier, for the money you're payin, all you *get* is a look."

He patted Peter's shoulder.

"Have a drink. I'm buyin."

Fifteen minutes later, Peter pushed the highball glass aside in order to grasp the envelope. Straightening the metal clasp, he opened it and slid out the document, dropping the envelope into his lap. He read for a few seconds before his eyes widened. His jaw slacked and his mouth fell halfway open moments later as he flipped to the second page. Midway through the second page he stopped, looking up at Vic.

Vic smiled, wryly.

"Think *that's* somethin you can work with?"

Peter nodded, his eyes falling again to the page. Flipping to the last page of the document, Peter read a minute more and put it down on the table.

"It's scary how anyone could have access to this kind of information? I mean, we all *know* there are people like you out there, Vic, but we don't really want to believe it. Where do you get this stuff?"

Peter steadied his shaking hands by resting them on the table.

"Don't get me wrong. I mean, you've given me more than I bargained for but Vic, you scare the hell out of me. Where on earth do you *get* this stuff?"

"It's my job. I'm in the information business."

Peter gulped a large mouthful of the bourbon and soda, wagging his head. Then his expression was transformed to one of concern.

"Uh Vic? You know I have to ask, but do you have anything like that on me?"

Vic was watching the trumpet player soloing during *Bitch's Brew*, a tribute to Miles Davis. Hearing Peter's question, he answered as he lit a new cigarette.

"Tell ya the truth, depends on who's asking and how much money they're payin."

CHAPTER 31

"What exactly do you do, Mr. Taylor?"

"Uh, they got me on security for the parkin lot right there next ta, I mean uh next ta the motel."

"And were you working security there on the night of August 17th?"

"Uh, yeah. Yeah, I was workin there that night, sure was."

"During the course of your patrol, do you remember seeing a silver Rolls Royce parked in the lot that night?"

"Yeah, I saw the Rolls. Yep, it was a silver Rolls Royce."

Destiny spoke to the court as she displayed a glossy three-by-five.

"State's exhibit D. Photograph of the defendant's vehicle."

She handed the picture to Marcellus.

"Do you recognize the car in this picture?"

"Yeah, that's Mista Alexanda's. Use ta park it for him all the time, right there."

"Did you park it that night?"

"Um, yeah, sure did."

"Were you assigned to watch the lot that night?"

"Uh yeah, I hadta watch the lot that night. Yeah."

"And were you watching the lot at 8:15."

"Un-huh, I was watchin it then. I take ma break at nine."

As Destiny glanced over at the jury, all but one juror seemed to be following the line of questioning. One juror, juror number 10, one of the middle-aged white women, seemed dazed, daydreaming.

"Did you see the Rolls leave that night?"

"Uh yeah. Un-huh. I saw it leave."

"Do you remember speaking with police detectives the next day about what you saw?"

"Yeah, yeah I do."

"Do you remember telling them you saw Jordan Alexander get in his car and leave the wharf at around 8:30?"

The uniformed security guard seemed reluctant and nervous.

"Uh, Wow. Uh..."

"When you told them you saw the defendant get into his car and drive away at 8:30, were you telling them the truth?"

The witness' seat became uncomfortable. Marcellus shifted

his weight from the back of his thighs to his rump.

"Yeah, I told em what I saw. I saw his Rolls Royce leavin at aroun 8:30, but then when they axed me later, I said I didn't exactly *see* him. I said I *thought* it was him."

"So you're saying you saw a man who *looked* like the defendant get in the car and drive away?"

"Objection. Counsel's leading the witness. He said nothing of the sort."

"Sustained."

Destiny sighed to herself and continued.

"Okay, Mr. Taylor. When you saw a man get into the defendant's Rolls Royce and drive away at 8:30, why did you think it was the defendant?"

"Uh, I dunno. Because it looked like him? Because he got in his car? I dunno for sure."

"Did you see two men?"

"Naw, it was one."

"Was he white?"

"I cain't say that for sure, but I think so."

While Destiny reworded and reordered her questions in the attempt to get a more definitive answer, Marcellus Taylor was unwilling to answer with any more certainty than he already had. Moving on, she questioned him if and then about what time he remembered seeing a white Lincoln Towncar in the motel parking lot nearby.

He confirmed it was 11:15 or 11:30 and said he remembered the car pulling into the lot from eastbound Embarcadero traffic. He said a good-looking woman got out and went into the motel, but she came out after a few minutes and left westbound on the Embarcadero. He said he didn't know if she was alone because he couldn't see into the car. Answering a barrage of questions, he said he hadn't seen or heard anything suspicious in the area the entire night. He said he never saw two black guys in the area.

Under a friendly cross-examination from Barry, Marcellus Taylor acknowledged that he hadn't actually observed who got in the Rolls Royce before it drove away at 8:30 and that he just sort of assumed it was Jordan. If a mugging or robbery had happened in the lot, he admitted there was at least a possibility it could have happened outside his view. When questioned about his certainty of the Lincoln turning into the lot from eastbound Embarcadero traffic, Marcellus reaffirmed his earlier statement. Destiny redirected, emphasizing of course, that the lot was on the *west* side of the turnoff. After Barry opted not to re-cross, the judge adjourned court for the day.

The four lawyers spent the next morning in Judge Morgan's chambers arguing before the magistrate. While one issue was the admissibility of the results from the tequila test, the biggest issue involved the spousal abuse evidence, and specifically, the disputed fact on whether Jordan slapped Stephanie Rodriguez on the morning after the murder.

Lieutenant Allenby's report included a brief narrative that described Stephanie coming out of a room after Jordan screamed at her and abused her. The report said her mouth was bleeding and her swollen eye was just beginning to show the typical discoloration. Brett argued the incident of violence was relevant because it happened twelve hours after the murder. In a brief he filed weeks earlier, he asserted the violence directed toward Stephanie that morning was indicative of the anger Jordan was feeling for women, and further that it was revealing in terms of his state of mind."

Terri countered that Allenby's report was subjective, especially in the description of what happened when Jordan arrived at his residence to find the police "turning the place upside down." She contended that, according to the report, Jordan and Stephanie argued out of Allenby's sight and that it was impossible to prove that Jordan was violent toward her at all. "Letting something so unfounded and prejudicial like that in," she warned, "would be grounds for requesting a mistrial."

The judge had grown perturbed with Terri and her manner, but after forty-five minutes of arguments and numerous case-law referrals by both attorneys, she ruled Jordan's alleged violence toward Stephanie was inadmissible in lieu of better proof.

The results of the tequila test, however, would be allowed in despite Barry's insistence for an additional Frye hearing to determine and dispute methods used and conclusions drawn from the experiments.

Judge Morgan was careful and contemplative, owing to her religious Lutheran background. She was born to the Petersen family in the northern California town of Yreka fifty-one years earlier, but the family moved down to Redding when she was ten. Her father was a supervisor in a huge lumber processing plant along the Sacramento River while her mother was an elementary school teacher.

Helen was a quiet, studious, average-looking freckled-faced girl who grew into a spunky and adventurous young woman. She married the young coach of the high school's football team right after graduation. The marriage was ill fated from the beginning, and it all but ended when Helen gained admission at Sacramento State College. Unable to annul the marriage, Helen handled the divorce paperwork herself.

It was during the filing process that she decided she wanted to become a lawyer. Ironically, after transferring to the University of California at Davis where she finished her undergrad and after McGeorge Law School, the only area of law she never attempted was family law, or law involving divorce.

The move to San Francisco involved a man, Bob Morgan, a political fund-raiser who handled Democratic events in Sacramento and occasional high-profile affairs in Washington. They married in 1959 and had three children, two boys and a girl.

When informed she was being considered to sit on the Jordan Alexander murder trial, Helen was excited, but a few days later, doctors told her Bob had prostate cancer. Once chosen, she thought to recuse herself, but Bob insisted that she stay on, that she should continue to work while he went through the chemotherapy treatment in Los Angeles with their eldest son.

Stephanie Rodriguez's absence had a profound effect on the order of prosecution witnesses, and by extension, on the trial. Destiny originally thought to bring on the *crime scene* witnesses first, and then begin with the *Jordan Alexander time-line* witnesses, but Stephanie's absence and the lack of information from her left gaps in many places.

She and Brett decided to begin with the *Jordan Alexander time-line* witnesses because there were rumors going around that a guard had spoken to three jurors about a newspaper story on a Tyrell Briggs and Deondray Carter theory. The writer suggested the "two street thugs" had the time and opportunity to commit the murder for an underworld profit motive, despite the fact that there was no indication of any property missing from Lynette's Pacific Heights residence.

The *Jordan Alexander time-line witnesses* were purposed to establish up front that Jordan, first and foremost, had the time and opportunity to murder his wife, that there were no black gang members hanging around the parking lot on the night of August 17, that Stephanie Rodriguez picked Jordan up from somewhere *other* than the parking lot or its vicinity and that the story about the mugging and the theft of the Rolls Royce was unfounded.

During the afternoon court session, the criminologist who examined the Rolls Royce in Golden Gate Park came on and testified that Jordan's fingerprints alone were all over the vehicle's interior surfaces, indicating there were no fingerprints belonging to anyone else. He found blood that matched Lynette's blood type, Jordan's blood type and a degraded sample that matched neither. The faint footprints outside the car were analyzed after pictures were taken and casts were made. The dress shoe's size, "most likely 10½," just happened to match most of the shoes found in Jordan's closet.

After Destiny introduced a one-inch narrow swatch of black material, the criminologist identified it as a piece of evidence he found in the dense brush next to the car. He said the analysis yielded that it was dyed black wool, "probably from an expensive men's suit," and that it had been soaked in blood that matched Lynette's blood type.

Further, he said that under microscopic examination, he and assistants were able to determine a faint pattern in the fabric and had identified its manufacturer. The manufacturer, in an affidavit produced as a state exhibit and read by the criminologist, said only three designers had bought the exact fabric: Giorgio Armani, Arnold Scaasi and Hugo Boss.

During the course of the direct examination, Barry objected on more than fourteen occasions and asked for two sidebar conferences with the judge. Most of the objections were overruled and the sidebar distractions seemed to do nothing more than irritate Helen Morgan, but Barry's strategy was purposed to throw the confident prosecutor off-stride, which it did.

During the cross-examination, he posed a hypothetical to the criminologist, asking if fingerprints would be left by *car stealing thugs wearing gloves*. After suggesting that gloves could actually leave non-distinctive prints in some circumstances, the reluctant criminologist admitted that in most circumstances none would be left. When asked about how many people in San Francisco, how many people in California and how many people in the world shared Lynette's blood type, the witness said he couldn't cite exact numbers, but he admitted the number was large.

When Barry asked, "how large for the world," Destiny objected, asserting that any guess by the witness would be speculative. While the criminologist echoed Destiny's objection, Judge Morgan finally insisted on a general estimate. He answered, "In the hundreds of millions?"

Barry pursued the same line of questioning with regard to Jordan's blood type and his shoe size, and then he asked a few careful questions about the fabric found in the brush. When asked how he determined the fabric was left during the night of August 17, the criminologist explained that, when the material was discovered, it was still slightly damp from fresh blood, distinct from "dried blood that had become wet from sprinklers or dew."

Officer Kent Walker, the first of the *Sacramento Street crime scene* witnesses, came on the next morning, describing for the jury what he saw when he and Officer Trevor Price entered Lynette's house on Loma Vista Way a little after midnight. He testified that he saw partial bloody footprints as shined his flashlight on the steps leading up to the door. The doorknob itself was smeared with blood.

Apprehensive about going in alone, Walker said he waited approximately five minutes for Price to arrive before opening the unlocked door. He said his first concern was to find the children the caller said were inside. When he and Price went in, there were obvious footprints, bloodier than the ones outside. All the downstairs lights were off. Whispering, the officers agreed that until they could find the children, they would use the flashlights to search the house.

He said the amount of blood increased as he and Price moved from room to room, eventually coming back to the staircase. The girls, they thought, would be in one of the bedrooms upstairs. He and Price both had their guns drawn as they ascended the carpeted steps. Both officers were on edge as they reached the hallway of the second floor. Moving toward the back of the house, they finally arrived at a bedroom door. Walker twisted the knob and pushed the door open, peeking in, shining the flashlight.

Against the wall was a large wooden bunk-bed set, and in the lower bed he saw two little girls curled up, wearing oversized T-shirts. There seemed to be a body in the top bunk as well. Shining the flashlight along the walls, he made sure no one else was in the room, and then he and Price went in.

When they woke the girls, Lindsey, the youngest, started crying and asking questions. Price took up a blanket and raised it to limit what the girls could see as he and Walker led them out the house. Not long after, a patrol car pulled up and the girls were placed inside. A fourth car arrived just as the car with the girls sped away, and the two patrolmen who exited began blocking off the house and area outside it as an official police crime scene.

Walker and Price went back into the house and resumed their search, following the trail of blood up the stairs and along the corridor. Seeing light escaping the room under the door, they holstered their flashlights. Gun drawn, Price shoved the door open and leaned inside against the wall. He gasped aloud. Startled, Walker rushed in, pistol ready, but his knees became wobbly as he and Price stood there, staring.

Walker said he had never seen so much blood in all his life. His eyes moved around the room, stopping on the walls, then the ceiling, then on the severed fingers, then on the bloody bed sheet and finally on the body that rested on the other side of the bed in the dark-colored pool. Lynette's trademark blonde hair was stained red, much of it lying matted against her face. Her eyes were frozen open.

Though she was naked, her fair skin was stained in varying shades of red, bronze and brown. Her neck had been ripped open, exposing portions of her severed windpipe and esophagus. The puncture wounds were all over the body. Her body's vaginal area had been ravaged, stabbed repeatedly, as portions of its inner structure were exposed. A large puncture wound in the lower abdomen exposed a portion of her large intestine, which oozed a brownish-green substance that stained the area below it.

The smell was fetid, sickening. Walker heaved, cupping his hand to his mouth, and rushed out the room and down the hallway. Price, in an equal hurry to escape the scene, almost tripped over him as they descended the stairs. Walker turned on the light in the sitting room and dropped to his knees, closing his eyes tightly, rubbing them in a symbolic attempt to erase the horrible images etched onto them. Price knelt beside him for a moment before going out to the car to confirm that the homicide investigation unit was on its way.

Destiny asked probing questions and chose careful words as

she guided Officer Walker through his compelling testimony. Once he finished his story, she warned the jury that the two photographs she was about to show them were "disturbing and graphic" in nature. She said while individual jurors might feel inclined to turn away, it was important for everyone to examine these items of evidence in an effort to better understand just what happened on August 17.

Once again, Brett and Janice placed the easels before the jury. Careful not to reveal the 36"x24" photographs to the non-jury audience, they readjusted the pictures on the stands and returned to their seats. The jury's reaction was one of shock as the panorama of faces showed expressions ranging from horror and anguish to nausea. The jurors in the front row recoiled, pressing their bodies against their seat backs. Several looked away, while one of the middle-aged women looked up, simultaneously forming *the sign of the cross* with her right hand. A woman in the front row gasped aloud and began sobbing.

Destiny waited for the initial impact of the lurid images to dissipate before urging Officer Walker to describe the photos in compelling detail. Spending perhaps five minutes on each photograph, Destiny managed to achieve what she desired. It seemed the jurors understood Lynette's disgusting murder was the product of hate and anger, the product of an unstable and twisted mind. Now the task would be to make them realize the monster who butchered her so brutally was smiling at them from across the room.

The phone's ringer startled her awake. It was still dark outside. Looking over her shoulder across the bed, she could see the clock. 4:21 in the morning! It was either an emergency or someone was out of their mind.

"Hello?"

"Hey Destiny! Were you sleeping?"

This person *was* out of her mind!

"It's four in the fucking morning. I was up till one. What *is* it, Kiyo?"

"Oh, silly me. I forgot about the time difference. It's almost 6:30 here."

"Where *are* you?"

"You didn't get my message? I'm in San José."

Destiny sat up in the bed, turning on the light.

"San Jose? What are you talking about? There's no time difference between here and there."

"That's the mistake we all made. I'm not in California. I'm in Costa Rica."

Awake, Destiny sat up with a pen at the ready as Kiyomi continued.

"She's here."

"Who? Stephanie Rodriguez?"

"Yes. Found her yesterday. Haven't talked to her yet, but I've got the goods. I know where she's staying, what she's been doing, who she's been calling."

"Where are you?"

"I'm staying just outside San José at a *pension* owned by Orelda, a friend of mine from UPI. (506) 203-7524."

Destiny scribbled the number as she planned.

"Okay. I'll be down there tomorrow night. Can you pick me up at the airport?"

"Sure, but what about the trial?"

"Brett's on tomorrow morning. I can slip away for a few days. Besides, if we can get Stephanie to come back and testify, we'll be able to nail that bastard to the wall. And even if she won't come back, between you and me, I think we can get her to talk to us. What I need, maybe more that her testimony, is a few key answers."

Kiyomi's voice took on a lighter tone.

"All I want is the same thing, Girlfriend, but we're going to need something we can use as a bargaining tool."

"Look, we've got Jordan. He's all the bargaining power we need. Besides, she wouldn't be down there in the first place if Barry thought she was savvy enough to pull one over on the jury, let alone on you or me. She'll talk to us."

Kiyomi, as always, was tenacious.

"That's might be good for you, but I'd like to have a little extra insurance. I've got a little something on a few of her family members. What she'll need to understand that if she doesn't talk to us, I'm fully prepared to use it."

CHAPTER 32

"And Mrs. Drew, can you recall how many times your niece came down to southern California after having been beaten similarly?"

The sun-tanned, emaciated blonde's dark roots told the world her hair was badly in need of a touch-up.

"Must have come down seven, eight times at least, but it could've been more."

Brett, wearing a midnight blue Cerutti suit that morning, was more than merely handsome. He was pretty, though not in an effeminate way.

"And do you recall the nature of her injuries on any of those occasions?"

The woman seemed confused.

"I don't know what you mean."

Brett smiled toward the jury.

"What I mean is, do you remember what she *looked* like the last time you saw her all beat up?"

"Course I do."

Nora Drew demonstrated, raising a hand to her face.

"Left eye was swollen shut, all black and blue. And there was, I mean you could actually see the fingermarks Jordan left on her throat when he was chokin her."

Teri was quick to interrupt.

"Objection. Witness response assumes facts not in evidence. Move to strike."

"Sustained."

The judge spoke to the recorder.

"Strike the last response."

Brett moved to a place between Nora and the jury.

"Without mentioning any names, can you tell me if you saw marks on any place of her body?"

The woman glared at Jordan and answered.

"Course I did. On her face, on her neck, on her arms, on her body—black and blue all over. He beat her like that more than a few times."

Teri objected, yet unprompted, Nora responded.

"What? I didn't say any names. I didn't need to say a name. We all *know*."

Though hindered by frequent objections, Nora went on to tell the jury that the first time she noticed the bruising on Lynette was not more than a year after the wedding, that they saw injuries on her about once a year for the next four years. She said she was disgusted and she encouraged Allegra to talk to Lynette about either seeking counseling or divorcing Jordan, which Allegra did.

"That only made things worse," Nora admitted. Lynette wouldn't speak to or visit her mother after that for two years. Then, not long after Lyndsey was born, Lynette showed up at her mother's door with the baby.

Her left arm was fractured or broken, her jaw was swollen and both her eyes had black circles under them. She was having trouble breathing, so after making her mother and aunt swear they wouldn't tell the doctor the truth, she allowed them to take her to the doctor under the pretense the injuries had resulted from a car accident. Two of her ribs were cracked and a kidney had been bruised. She was hospitalized for three days before returning to her mother's where she rested for about six weeks.

Jordan came down with apologies for everyone and a promise he would seek counseling. In a surprise turn, he bought Allegra a new home in Pasadena and suggested she lease the other out for extra income. The whole family helped her move. Caitlyn and Denver stayed with Allegra and Lynette for five weeks that summer, while Jordan was there every weekend.

Finally, Jordan, Lynette and the girls returned home to San Francisco in time for the start of school. However, not more than six months later, Lynette showed up again. She was badly beaten, though "not as bad as the time before." Lynette told her aunt that Jordan was getting better, that the marriage was stronger than before. Then, on the other four or five times she was down there in the next three years with multiple bruises, she always made excuses for her husband's behavior.

On the last of those occasions, Nora and Allegra took Lynette to a psychiatrist who said she needed therapy as much as her abusive husband did and recommended a colleague in San Francisco. Dr. Judith Wendt of San Francisco, according to Nora, was the person who "gave Nettie her life back." Within two and a half years, Lynette had "gotten over Jordan for good" and had started up an organization purposed to "assist others like herself."

And then, "just when Nettie seemed her happiest," they heard the news that she'd been murdered. Nora sobbed as she told the details of the phone call from the San Francisco Police Department and of its devastating effect on Allegra. The black woman juror in the back row daubed her eyes with a handkerchief as she listened and several others seemed touched by Nora's grief. The court recessed after her direct testimony.

In the distance, the tall thick forest of trees swayed in the tropical breeze, bathed in blankets of moonlight that flooded through isochronal openings in the rolling clouds. The soft drops of water felt warm as they splashed on Destiny's engrossed, upturned, contemplative face.

A chaotic chorus of male frogs sang praises to the rain, each in his high-pitched, characteristic call, each individual in a passionate solo from near and far, from lofty and from subterranean enclave. The crickets sounded like hundreds of tiny un-oiled wheels, turning incessantly in the peaceful summer night.

"Destiny? You okay?"

Still staring into the heavens, she nodded, answering.

"I'm okay."

After a few minutes, she elaborated.

"It's just that, it's so beautiful here. Makes you want to forget everything you've ever known before."

Kiyomi, on the swing next to her, sighed, signaling agreement.

"Yep."

"I could be a lotus-eater. I could stay down here and never go back."

Kiyomi sighed.

"You'd be too bored down here. It's beautiful, it's peaceful, but there's not enough action and excitement down here for you."

Destiny turned her head toward her best friend.

"Says who?"

Kiyomi smiled.

"Says me. I know you. You came down here, and you're thinking about Charles, you're thinking about the trial, you're thinking about all the pressure you're under and you're wanting to just run away, but you won't."

"Oh yeah? Why's that?"

"Because you're Destiny Marie Mitchell, the most stubborn, the most hard-headed and the most competitive person I've ever known. Besides that, you've got *tits*!"

Destiny frowned, glancing down at the front of her blouse.

"What's that supposed to mean?"

Kiyomi smiled.

"Doesn't matter what they look like. I could have said balls, but it's so macho-centric. When they say a man's got balls, does anyone ever check his pants to see how big they are?"

Glancing sidelong at Destiny, she deadpanned.

"Tits. You got em."

She gestured, pretending to be holding objects.

"Huge tits! Giant tits!"

Destiny turned her body toward her friend.

"Well, if that's the case, Miss Yamakita, you've got the biggest tits in the whole Western Hemisphere."

Kiyomi laughed.

"I guess I'll take that as a compliment, coming from a woman with tits the siza yours."

Thirty minutes later, Destiny and Kiyomi plotted a surprise meeting with Stephanie. Kiyomi, through a housekeeper, learned Stephanie had a beauty appointment at an exclusive salon in the city the next day.

According to the plan, she and Destiny would also make appointments, and by bribing a few key people, could arrange to spend the entire day with her. But even as they perfected the scheme to the smallest detail, the wind began to animate the landscape and the rainfall grew heavier, sending both women scurrying back to the comfort and protection of Orelda's cozy *pension* on the hill, overlooking the Costa Rican capitol city of San José.

"Mrs. Drew, did you ever personally *see* Jordan strike his wife or otherwise abuse her in any way? Yes or no?"

Nora began an explanation, but Teri cut in.

"Answer the question. You ever see him *hit* her, yes or no?"

She responded after great hesitation.

"Well, no."

"You ever see him kick her, yes or no?"

"No."

You ever see him scream at her or threaten her physically?"

"No."

Teri went over to the defense table and whispered

something to Barry, who answered in her ear. Turning back, she approached the witness.

"Mrs. Drew, would you characterize Jordan as a generous individual? Yes or no?"

Nora's recoiling was noticeable. Destiny and the other attorneys had warned her about this sensitive area of questioning. Brett objected, but he was overruled by the judge, who pressed Nora to respond to the questions.

"Well, I can't really answer that question out right. I mean, I don't really know him for what he's done up here in San Francisco."

"Has he been generous with you, Lynette's favorite aunt?"

Her body stiffened as she answered.

"Yes."

"Didn't he buy you a duplex in Capistrano in 1980 after your husband died?"

"Well, yes."

"Did you feel indebted to him?"

"No."

"Did you believe he was abusing your niece in 1980 when you *accepted* the condo?"

"Yes."

"Did you report any incident of this alleged abuse to the police, the district attorney or any of the newspapers at any time?"

"No."

"Did the duplex in Capistrano buy your silence and implicit cooperation in the so-called abuses you said your niece suffered during that time?"

"No."

Teri sighed, smiling.

"No. All the money in the world couldn't buy your silence if you really thought your niece was being abused, could it?"

"No."

"Then why, Mrs. Drew, if you truly believed your niece was being physically beaten and abused, why didn't you report it to anyone?"

Nora was weeping, her head held down.

"I, I don't know. I should have. I don't know why I didn't."

"Isn't it because there was never any abuse in the first place?"

"No."

"Didn't you invent this entire history of abuse because you felt terrible about the murder and were searching for something or someone to blame?"

"No, it happened. He beat her."

Standing near the jury box, Teri paused, looking over at Nora.

"Mrs. Drew, that last time you saw Lynette injured, the time when you said she had two black eyes, a broken arm and a bruised kidney? Weren't those injuries in fact the result of a car accident?"

"Absolutely not. That was from Jordan."

"Well, isn't that what you told the doctor?"

"I told him what Nettie begged me to tell him, not what I thought."

"So you *lied* to the doctor?"

"No! I mean, yes."

"I see. So do you believe lying is okay under certain circumstances?"

The objection by Brett overruled, Teri pressed for a response.

"Mrs. Drew, do you believe lying is okay under certain circumstances? I mean, the story you told the doctor—if you're telling us the truth now, isn't that what you did? You told the doctor a lie?"

"Yes."

"So have you lied at any time during your testimony this afternoon?"

"No."

"Wouldn't you lie if by lying you thought you might be helping Lynette?"

"No."

"But in all the years you saw them together, you never saw him hit her, right?"

"No."

Teri smiled.

"So, for all you know, the last time you saw her all bruised up, the injuries she suffered really could have been the result of a car accident, correct?"

Nora rolled her eyes at the arrogant young woman, her natural sense of sarcasm beginning to show.

"Well, I guess you're right, Ma'am. I'd just like to know what model of car leaves impressions a *fingers* on a woman's neck!"

Stephanie, back arched, stretched her naked body sensuously along the smooth table, her large, firm breasts presented to an invisible audience. The masseuse, a pretty mulatto woman in her twenties, was squeezing and kneading Stephanie's buttocks and lower back. Stephanie took slow breaths, and on several occasions, she moaned.

On a table eight feet away, Kiyomi's held her eyes closed as another young woman massaged her thighs. As she leaned up, a little self-conscious, she glanced down at her own breasts, which were well formed, though not nearly as ample or round as Stephanie's were. Now *that* woman had tits!

An hour later, Kiyomi rested her head on a pillow, facing the young woman.

"So, what did you say you do again?"

Stephanie was reluctant to answer.

"Modeling."

"Down here on a shoot?"

"No. I came down here to get away."

"Get away? Get away from what?"

Stephanie started not to answer, but she did before turning.

"I came down here to get away from nosy people, people who ask questions. Know what I mean?"

Destiny's guileful attempts to get Stephanie to talk were equally unrewarding. Yet, it was Stephanie who broached the subject as Kiyomi and Destiny followed her into the whirlpool bath, sitting next to her at each side.

"Oh come on! You two aren't even sly! Besides, they already warned me about you. Newspaper reporter and DA, right?"

Destiny and Kiyomi exchanged sheepish expressions before admitting to the chicanery. Sliding away from Stephanie so she could better observe her reactions, Destiny began, trying her best to sound gentle and caring.

"You're apparently a smart woman, no doubt smart enough to realize that you're being used."

She continued, assured she had Stephanie's attention.

"Whatever they're telling you and promising you, I know you're not naïve enough to think you can just march back up there, testify the way they want you to and pick up your life and career where you left off. It's not going to happen that way. They know it, we know it and you of *all* people ought to know it."

Stephanie glanced toward the door before responding.

"Look, all I know is you all want something from me, so I don't think I'm ready to trust what you lawyers say. Barry already told me he wasn't promising anything, but he said I was the key to the whole trial. He said Jordie's future would depend on what I do from here."

The lawyer studied Stephanie's nervous habit of smoothing her hair back. At least she was talking! Zeroing in on Jordan, Destiny pried further.

"You do know he *did* it, don't you?"

"No, he didn't do it."

"What? Are you trying to convince yourself?"

She didn't wait for an answer.

"You were with him that night. You picked him up. If there's one person in this universe who could either clear him or help make him pay for what he's done, it'd be you."

Stephanie started a response, but following Barry's admonition, she stopped herself. Destiny continued.

"Please listen to me, Stephanie. Aside from all the bullshit you and I have been through since last August, aside from all the games and the politics, a woman was murdered. Jordan, *your* Jordan, took a knife and ripped her neck open with it. Then he took the same knife and stabbed her over and over again in the vagina. Now you may not have been exactly crazy about Lynette, but if you have any sense of justice and humanity about you, you'll come back up to San Francisco and do the right thing."

She could sense Stephanie was considering her words.

"Look, I'm not asking you to lie on Jordan. If you say you don't believe he did it, I'm willing to respect that. I won't question your faith in him. All I'm asking is that you come up and tell us the truth about what *you* did that night, the truth about what you saw."

Stephanie stared straight ahead, nodding as Destiny continued.

"Tell me something, Stephanie. I realize what you believe, but hypothetically, let's just say he *did* it. If he did, would you help him get away with it?"

Stephanie wiped the tears from her cheek and sniffed twice, though she didn't answer.

"Do you think he should get away with murdering Lynette, an innocent woman who could have been you or me?"

Stephanie began to mutter something that stopped mid-way in her throat. She groaned as she continued to listen to the prosecutor.

"You don't have to say anything, but I know he's hit you on several occasions, and I know you've had a lot of time to think about things since you've been down here. This whole issue isn't about how much you love him or how loyal you can be in spite of what he's done. It's about justice, because if it doesn't mean anything to us that a man just got pissed off and stabbed his wife to death one night, *who's* going to care when he or someone else decides he wants to murder you or me?"

Stephanie turned away, crying in silence. She pleaded.

"Don't you understand? I can't talk to you! I'm sorry!"

She stood, ready to leave, but Kiyomi grasped her right wrist under the water.

"Then talk to me! I didn't come all the way down here for this high school shit! Get real, Stephanie. You're sitting down here in at a tropical resort, living like a fucking movie star, and you've got the nerve to stand there crying like you're some kind of victim! You can save your tears, cuz neither of us feels sorry for you."

Stephanie stared straight ahead, shivering.

"Sit your ass down, bitch, because I'm going to write my story one way or another, and believe me, I've got enough on you and your family to make it pretty interesting. I know about Xavier's little methamphetamine laboratory and about your sister's working under the table. Now if you talk to us, I might let you have a say about what goes in and what stays out, but if you don't, authorities will find out about the immigration status of some of your relatives in the *other* San Jose. Your feisty little grandmother will be on her way back down to Villahermosa."

Stephanie turned toward Kiyomi, staring, as if trying to measure her resolve.

"You wouldn't *do* that."

"Believe me, I'll do worse. I'm a journalist—I *lie*. I'll write that I came down here and you told me you knew Jordan was guilty from the first night. I'll add details, make it sound believable. You know, stuff like how he was dripping wet when you picked him up in Golden Gate Park, about how you saw the scratches on his face and the blood in his hair, about the story he made up on the drive over to the wharf, about how you went out and disposed of the murder weapon. Of course, you know that makes you an accessory to the murder, don't you?"

"No, *I* didn't do anything!"

Kiyomi turned toward Destiny.

"Can't she be charged for that?"

Destiny hesitated until Stephanie turned to hear an answer.

"Well, it's not something I'd *want* to do, because basically I think you're a good person, and I know how you must feel. But yes, depending on what you've done, you could be charged as an accessory."

Stephanie sank into the watery seat as Destiny continued.

"Look Stephanie, we're not trying to force you to come up and testify. We just want to know what *you* know. And I promise—anything you tell me, if I use it, I'll make sure no one knows where it came from. If you tell the truth, no one can ever charge you with anything, but if you participate in a cover-up, then you're just as guilty as the person you're trying to protect."

She caressed Stephanie's shoulder and squeezed. Then, stroking Stephanie's cheek and turning her face, she forced Stephanie's eyes to meet hers.

"Do you know if Jordan murdered Lynette?"

Stephanie closed her eyes, crying.

"No. I don't know. I swear I don't. Sometimes I think yes, sometimes I think no. I swear to you I really don't *know*!"

Destiny held Stephanie's hand.

"Will you tell us what you *do* know?"

Gripping Destiny's hand, Stephanie sighed, at last relaxing. She wasn't sure why, but she believed she could trust this woman. It had been almost a year since she left San Francisco, and while the resort was lavish and beautiful, it felt like a prison. There was no one to talk to, no one to share with, no one to hold her hand.

And about the night of the murder—she had never spoken with anyone about it, though she wanted to. There were problems she had with various elements of the night and its chronology. She felt guilt about that night, but she had never been able to share it with anyone. She had never trusted anyone enough before. Barry didn't ask and didn't want to know.

Yet there, sitting in that whirlpool spa, Stephanie felt an overwhelming urge to share all she knew about that night with the reassuring woman who held her hand. For the first time in almost a year, it felt right. Sobbing, she closed her eyes and took a deep breath.

"All right. Where do you want me to start?"

CHAPTER 33

The next nine witnesses testified about the spousal abuse aspect of the marriage between Jordan and Lynette. The third was Lynette's good friend, Kristi Sherburne, who had seen Lynette's injuries in the year before she ordered Jordan out the house. Kristi became angry on one of these occasions and went over to confront Jordan, but he threatened even her. Next, a motel clerk came on and said that on all three occasions he checked Lynette in during 1981 and 1982, her face was swollen, beaten beyond recognition.

Then came psychiatrist Dr. Judith Wendt, who said she treated Lynette for a mental condition consistent with women in physically abusive relationships. She said, in her expert opinion, that Lynette was alone the victim, that Lynette was not the type of abuse victim who would fight back, let alone initiate violence for any reason. She described the Valium addiction as mild, emphasizing the problems and the physical and emotional abuses as its underlying cause.

After heated arguments in Judge Morgan's chambers and threats about an appeal to the ruling, Dr. Wendt was allowed to say Lynette feared someday that Jordan would go over the edge and murder her. In cross-examination, Teri challenged her credentials, questioning the merits and practices of the controversial institution where she received her doctorate degree.

She also asked the doctor if she was an activist lesbian and if she told Lynette to leave her husband, and Dr. Wendt answered in the affirmative. Beyond that, she said she would have given any woman in such a violent and precarious situation the same advice.

"Without professional help or an act of God," she told Brett in his re-direct, "abusers never change, and it *wasn't* like Ms. Gonik suggested. I wasn't trying to break up a God-ordained marriage. I fought to make Lynette realize that if Jordan didn't think she was worth humbling himself and submitting to therapy, then he didn't deserve her."

She also asserted that the insensitivity of the police and their unwillingness to take action in the face of obvious abuse made Jordan feel justified in everything he did, and further served to perpetuate the violence Lynette endured. She said the behavior of the police regarding the matter was "unconscionable and immoral," adding, "fortunately, because in most of these cases the abuser isn't so rich and so well-connected, an arrest would have been made."

She maintained that Jordan showed symptoms of insecurity

when Lynette began to have a life without him and he ultimately became obsessed with her. He threatened both Lynette and the doctor. "It was the classic, *if I can't have her, nobody will* syndrome." In the end, the doctor concluded, a person like the defendant could commit an act of extreme violence or murder and believe he was acting out of love.

Dr. Wendt was followed by a psychologist, Dr. Lori Cipar, who addressed the nature of the wounds to Lynette's body, especially the wounds to the vaginal area. She testified that the peculiarity of the vaginal attack suggested Lynette was attacked by no stranger. Rather, she asserted, Lynette's murderer was someone who knew her, someone who was very angry with her, someone who wanted to destroy her womanhood.

In rebuttal, Barry questioned Dr. Cipar about the sources she relied on in order to arrive at such an evaluation, and he questioned her methods for moving from the data to various conclusions, but the doctor held her own until Barry admitted to having no more questions.

After the psychologist came two reluctant patrol officers who responded to Lynette's 911 calls on separate occasions. The uncooperative first said she had bruises on her face and her back, though "she wasn't injured seriously enough to warrant medical attention." He said he didn't arrest Jordan because, "while she was definitely a little beat up, it seemed like the situation was under control and she wasn't in any further danger."

Under cross-examination, he said the condition Lynette was in when he arrived was common in San Francisco and all over, adding "I've seen a lot worse. Believe me, if I thought he was capable of killing her, I would have done something."

The second officer admitted that, from 1980 to 1985 when Jordan left, police responded to calls from the residence on more than twelve separate occasions. In the four times he had gone over, he remembered seeing bruises on Lynette's face. When Brett asked if Lynette insisted that Jordan be arrested for assault, the officer confirmed that she demanded an arrest.

"I think she asked us to once or twice. She was kind of hysterical about it."

Asked why he hadn't arrested Jordan on those occasions, he said he didn't because Jordan said she was drunk and on medication and didn't know what she was saying.

On the one occasion Jordan was arrested, the officer said he had no choice. He said Commander Dennis Webber called him on the patrol car radio and gave him orders to arrest Jordan if Lynette had the slightest bump or bruise on her face or body.

Under cross-examination, he said, while she wasn't beat up really bad, he complied with Commander Webber's order because the Commander wasn't "the sort of supervisor you wanted pissed off at you."

Teri's attempts to extract a comment on Webber's character or on a possible animus toward Jordan met with numerous objections from Brett—all of which were sustained by Judge Morgan.

When Brett asked about Jordan's behavior after his arrest, the officer admitted that Jordan became verbally abusive and threatening, that Jordan "got in my face, daring me to be stupid enough to throw away my career."

"Are you still employed by the San Francisco Police Department today?"

"No I'm not. Things started getting crazy for me around there after that, so I quit. I'm doing private security now."

The final witness Brett called was Jamie Khan, an attractive political consultant working for the *Aegis Foundation*. She recalled talking with Jordan over the telephone on a dozen occasions in the early summer of 1986. She said the conversations were innocent enough at first, but then they became "a little unnerving."

Early on, Jordan would ask about the foundation and about its various projects and goals, suggesting he could provide assistance if needed. Then, she testified, he started asking personal questions about Lynette. He asked if there were any men at the foundation, he asked if she ever said anything about being attracted to anyone, if she was dating anyone.

Jamie said she declined to answer such questions and told him they were inappropriate. She said he apologized and confessed he was asking the questions because he was convinced Lynette was seeing someone. He said he would have done *anything* to get her back. Feeling sorry for him, Jamie said she assured him Lynette was so busy with foundation duties and with raising her daughters that she didn't have the time or energy to see anyone.

During direct testimony, Jamie said he didn't call back for a while after that, but then in mid-July, he called her again, using coarse language to ask a series of questions about Lynette's personal life, which she refused to answer. She said he became angry, accusing her of covering for Lynette. Jamie said she asked him never to call her again and hung up the phone, but she said he called back and said he'd kill her if she ever disrespected him like that again. She said she feared for both herself and Lynette from that point on.

Direct testimony over, Teri asked Jamie questions about the length of the phone conversations and about their appropriateness. She asked why Jamie had been so friendly with Jordan early on. She asked Jamie if she remembered telling a friend "I'd be all over Jordan if he was available." While Jamie admitted that she was at one time thought Jordan was *attractive*, she said she never seriously considered anything beyond the friendly telephone conversations with him because he was married, and married to Lynette.

"Did you ever invite him out to an art exhibit that summer?"

"No."

"Did you ever tell him you were 'definitely available'?"

"Never."

"Are you testifying today because he rejected your advances?"

"Objection, your Honor. Beyond the scope."

"Overruled. The witness can answer the question."

Disgusted, Jamie looked from Jordan to Teri, sighing.

"That's ridiculous. No, I'm here today because Lynette Alexander was my *friend*, and because Destiny Mitchell asked me to come up here and tell the jury what I remembered."

Kiyomi's incessant coughing was disturbing and unusual in the particularly hot night. Destiny struggled to wake up, but her body felt weighted down. She fought to regain consciousness, which as it came, yielded way to panic. Something was not right. More than that, something was very, very wrong! As she opened her eyes, she saw Kiyomi next to her in the bed, her body heaving as she coughed.

As she struggled to sit up, Destiny's mind told her to reach over and wake her friend, but her arms wouldn't respond. The heavy air in the room was hot and hazy as she drew difficult breaths, struggling, fighting for oxygen. As she coughed, however, she could feel the control of her limbs and body slowly returning.

Arms still numb, she pushed Kiyomi's shoulder, slurring.

"Kiyo! Kiyo!"

Glancing at the door, she could see the smoke coming into the room from the hallway. Everything seemed in slow-motion. She could smell the hardwood oak furniture toasting in the intense heat of the next room. She could hear the fire crackling, shattering glass and treading steadily back and forth across the room, sucking fresh air out along the floor and returning it as smoke along the top of the doorway.

"Kiyo! Wake up, please!"

Kiyomi still only coughed. Tumbling barefoot onto the hot wooden floor, Destiny yanked her friend's upper torso into a position so that she could get her arms up to the joint under Kiyomi's armpits. Heaving, she dragged Kiyomi off the bed, slumping beside her, panting. Though the air near the floor was heated, it was cleaner, fresher, with more oxygen. Taking a deep breath, Destiny pulled Kiyomi's inert body toward the doorway. The heat had caused the wooden door to expand in the jamb, making Destiny panic as she struggled to yank it open. She stuck her head out into the hazy hallway to survey the corridor and living room.

Smoke filled the upper airspace of the little home. The fire burned in front of the window, on the couch, on the coffee table and in the kitchen doorway. Though the little rug in the entranceway was aflame, the front door seemed the best way out. Scooting her body forward and anchoring herself, she pulled Kiyomi along before inching forward and anchoring again. In this way, she brought Kiyomi almost to the door before she was struck with an unsettling memory: the Robinson murder case.

As the hot room grew smokier, she hesitated by the door, remembering. In the hallway, a beam came crashing down, spraying sparks and embers from the place it fell in a shower of fireworks. The sparks ignited an elaborate hand-woven Persian rug, which burst into flame. Destiny shuddered. The back door was a long shot with no guarantee of greater safety, but it was better than the alternative, so she began the slow, tortuous process of dragging Kiyomi along again.

Though the kitchen floor was covered with shards and fragments of broken glass, she continued on, her own body clearing a path toward the back door. Ignoring the pain from the cuts and scratches as she went, she reached the exit at last, dragging her body up along the door. When she yanked the heat-sealed door open, the doorknob slammed into her eye socket, causing intense pain and temporary blindness. Grimacing, she lunged one last time, dragging both herself and Kiyomi out into the much cooler and cleaner night air.

She drew a breath of the beautiful cool, clean air before pushing Kiyomi's body off the deck into the darkness of its shadow below. She followed, crashing onto the sticks, pebbles, scurrying creatures and mud along the edge of the little house. Not more than a minute later, there was an explosion in the kitchen that caused the entire *pension* to glow and burn more vigorously than before. Scrambling to Kiyomi's side, Destiny rolled her onto her back, straightening her neck. She slapped Kiyomi's face.

"Kiyo! Kiyo, talk to me!"

Left hand on Kiyomi's forehead, she pushed down, simultaneously lifting Kiyomi's chin with the index and middle fingers of her right hand and tilting her head back. Taking a deep breath, she placed her mouth on Kiyomi's mouth and blew, her eyes monitoring her friend's diaphragm as it rose. Backing, she watched the diaphragm fall as Kiyomi exhaled the air.

Mouth on Kiyomi's, she repeated the process, only on the second time, Kiyomi's body jerked and she began to cough again. After a third attempt, Kiyomi, though still coughing, began to breathe by herself. The breathing however, was troubled, irregular and punctuated with coughing spells during the twenty minutes that followed. Recovering, Kiyomi opened her eyes, stupefied by the scene of Orelda's *pension* burning behind the shivering silhouette of Destiny.

Then, as if the scene had been queued, rain began to fall, gently at first, then with great intensity as the women watching the house shuddered on the muddy earth in the insect and rodent infested shadows.

"What do you think, Destiny? Someone who knows us came down here and wanted us dead?"

Destiny's face trailed a line of blood from a cut on her cheek. She answered, never looking over, her eyes watching the road as curious neighbors approached from the path coming up to the *pension*.

"No. They don't want us dead, because if they did, we wouldn't have stood a chance. You ever hear of *pickin off fireflies*?"

Kiyomi pushed the wet mass of her hair from her face as she responded.

"No, what is it?"

"Murder case I tried in '84. James Robinson—shot five people in four different incidents. What, what he would do is go out to someone's house and throw a Maltov cocktail in a back window. Then, when the fire started burning and the people in the house started rushing out the front door, he'd be across the street with a rifle and scope where he could shoot whoever he wanted at his leisure. In all the confusion of the fire, he'd be gone before anyone realized what happened."

Kiyomi became apprehensive, her eyes scanning the perimeter shadows as she pulled her knees into her chest.

"Thanks for telling me that. What do you think they want?"

"I think they wanted to send us the message that they mean business, that we've crossed the line by going after Stephanie, that it's time to go home!"

Kiyomi sighed as she watched the area toward the left side of Orelda's *pension* crumble under the assault of fire and flood. Turning back toward Destiny, she studied the landscape.

"Well, if that's the message they're trying to send, how do we let them know that we received it? I know *I* have. Let's get the hell out of here!"

CHAPTER 34

Gail Friedman, looking professional in the black skirt suit, red scarf at her neck, held her glasses in one hand as she posed the series of questions.

"And your doctorate degree is in what area?"

"My doctorate is in the area of organic chemistry from MIT."

"And what type work do you do now?"

"I am the chairman of the chemistry department at the California Institute of Technology, down in Pasadena."

Dr. Flessner was poised as he sat in the chair beside Judge Morgan's bench, owing to the sheer number of times he had been called as an expert witness. His credentials were impeccable, as he had written chemistry textbooks for technical schools across the country. Moreover, he was a respected member of the global scientific community.

"And how have you come to be involved in this particular case involving Mr. Alexander?"

"Well, last summer, on September 14th, I received a telephone call from Ms. Mitchell, who asked me if I could determine the approximate time that a fixed amount of an alcoholic beverage was poured based on the amount of oxidation it had undergone in a given period of time."

"And what did you tell her?"

"I told her it was an interesting question. And I said that if collection methods were reliable and if she could assure that the collected sample was immediately placed in an airtight container and protected from extremes of temperature, there was a reasonable possibility."

"A possibility for what?"

"For determining, to within a half hour, the time the beverage was actually poured."

Dr. Flessner, who seemed to be in his mid to late sixties, was affable and relaxed despite the calculating, analytical aspects of his personality. His hair was long and mostly gray, though it had obviously been black years earlier. He didn't seem like a professor. Unassuming, he possessed the air and informality of an old family friend.

"And is that possible? Is it possible to determine what time an alcoholic beverage was poured based on its oxidation rate?"

"Oh yes, absolutely possible."

Gail walked toward the professor.

"Dr. Flessner, are you aware, or have you become acquainted with methods criminologist Desmond Collins utilized for collecting the sample in question?"

The doctor smiled, unable to resist the opportunity to deliver a waggish line.

"Why yes I am! I have complete faith in his work. After all, he's a graduate of CIT."

A few in the audience laughed for his gratuitous plug for the school.

"Are you familiar with the methods that Desmond Collins described in his written notes and explained in detail to the court yesterday?"

"Once again, yes."

"All right, and based on those methods, do you consider the sample you received last October to be the product of careful collection work and handling?"

"Yes, I do."

Destiny sat at the prosecutor's table, listening to Gail's direct examination. Though she had applied a liberal amount of make-up to the bruising around her eye, its shape was still distorted due to prolonged swelling. The two cuts and various scratches on her face were invisible, but she kept a bandaged left hand in her lap. Kiyomi, also scraped and bruised, sat twenty feet away in the third row behind the table.

Gail pulled a document from a stack of papers and continued.

"Dr. Flessner, in October, November and December of last year, did you oversee a series of experiments conducted at the California Institute of Technology, on behalf of the State?"

"Yes."

"Can you explain the object of those experiments?"

The doctor turned his body toward the jury.

"Yes. We performed a series of experiments that we called *the tequila tests*. The State had sent a sample of tequila collected from Mr. Alexander's residence as well as the remainder of the bottle it apparently had been poured from. So the first test involved an analysis of the sample collected from the shot glass, which measured exactly 42 milliliters. What we were testing for was the amount of oxygen the tequila in the shot glass absorbed from the air during the time it sat in the glass. Let me explain that in everyday terms."

Gail looked over at the jury, and then back to Flessner.

"That would be good. Thank you."

"Let's say for example you cut off a piece of apple, pear or banana and let it sit out on the counter for a while. If you watch closely, you'll see it becoming a little brown after five minutes or so. We've all seen it happen, and what we're witnessing is oxidation, or the result of the fruit surface reacting with the oxygen in the air. If you went on to test it chemically, you'd find that the fruit had actually *absorbed* oxygen from the environment."

He smiled as several of the jurors nodded, acknowledging that they understood.

"It's the same principle with the tequila that sat in a glass on the counter at Mr. Alexander's residence. From the moment it was poured, it began reacting with the oxygen in the environment, or absorbing oxygen. In the first experiment, we tested and recorded how much oxygen was absorbed in that 42-milliliter sample from the shot glass found on the counter at Loma Vista Way.

"In the next series of experiments, we poured fourteen additional 42-milliliter samples from the sealed bottle sent over from the residence. This was presumably the same bottle from which the first sample we tested was poured. The first eight samples were tested at one-hour intervals. Samples nine, ten and eleven were tested at six-hour intervals. Finally, samples twelve, thirteen and fourteen, the control samples, were tested in a separate lab at eight, eleven and seventeen hour-intervals respectively, though we we're unaware of the times on the last three."

Hoping to break up what she thought was beginning to sound like a discourse, Gail cut in as she placed a stack of charts on the easel.

"Is it all as complicated as it sounds?"

"Not really. It was actually easier than the work most people perform while putting together a meal in the kitchen. Until that point, it was just measuring, really."

Gail positioned herself so that she wasn't obstructing any juror's view of the chart.

"And then you tested them?'

"Yes, we tested them at those pre-set intervals I described and then we recorded the data."

"And what did the data reveal?"

The doctor removed his glasses, setting them on the table before him.

"The data revealed that all the tequila, at least the tequila from the particular bottle tested, oxidized or absorbed oxygen at a standard rate. In other words, from the results that came in after testing the first eleven samples, we were able to predict, with uncanny accuracy, the time of exposure in each of the three control samples based on the rate of oxidation alone."

Gail pulled the poster board off the easel, turning it around and replacing it. It revealed a detailed graph that summarized the experimental data.

"So you're saying that in the control samples, you were able to accurately determine what time each shot was poured based on the oxidation rate alone?"

"That's exactly what we were able to do."

"And the graph shows the oxygen absorption rate based on data that was consistent in every sample your researchers poured?"

"It shows that rate, which rises sharply in the first eight hours, slows over the next eight and levels off at about sixteen."

From behind the first chart, Gail pulled another, placing it before the jury. This chart showed a graph and a shot glass of tequila. The x-axis listed numbers that represented oxidation rates while the y-axis listed times, hourly. A red arrow pointed to a place on the graph that represented the shot glass sample of tequila recovered from the counter and the estimated time it was poured. Laser pointer in her hand, Gail led the doctor through a detailed explanation of the chart.

Finally, she came to the crux of the matter.

"Dr. Flessner, based on the rate of oxidation, or oxygen absorption in the sample recovered from the counter, is there any question in your mind about what time the tequila in the shot glass recovered on Loma Vista Way was poured?"

Confident, he answered.

"Based on collection practices detailed in the criminologist's notes and on solid scientific research, I can say conclusively that there is no question about when that shot of tequila on the counter was poured."

"And what time was that?"

"It was poured on the evening of August 17th, 1986 at a time between 8:30 and 9:00 p.m."

Gail and Destiny sighed simultaneously in appreciation for

the ground the State had gained with that statement. Now it was a matter of preparing the doctor for cross-examination.

"Dr. Flessner, if no one was in the home between 8:30 and 9:00 on August 17th, 1986, is there any way your research team could have arrived at an identical conclusion?"

Flessner replaced the spectacles on his nose, turning away from the jury.

"Not at all. Science aside, we all know glasses of tequila don't pour themselves. The tequila was in that shot glass in the state of oxidation I described because some *person* poured it into that glass during the specified time. Someone had to be in that house."

Gail, hoping to pre-empt rebuttal avenues available to Barry, asked the doctor about possible errors in the process of experimentation. She asked if the experiments would have been affected by differences between lab temperatures and the temperature of Jordan's home of August 17. The doctor replied that, right before testing in October, Desmond Collins went back to the house and recorded the temperature and thermostat settings, which hadn't been altered. Desmond Collins, a day earlier, testified the temperature of the home when he initially went in on August 17 was "comfortable, meaning not too warm and too cool."

Gail asked how the results would have been altered if the bottle had sat out opened on a counter weeks before the shot was poured, but the doctor referred to detective notes, which reported the discovery of an Albertson's grocery store receipt from August 17. It included the purchase of a one-liter bottle of Jose Cuervo Gold Tequila.

"Since there we're any other bottles of tequila in the house, we felt it was safe to conclude that the bottle of tequila we tested had been purchased at 3:17 that afternoon at the grocery store."

The doctor went on to testify that almost 300 milliliters of tequila were missing from the one liter bottle when he received it from the from the San Francisco Police Department in October. Collins recorded the fluid level in the bottle before he sealed it and turned it over to the police property division. In an attempt to be thorough, Gail asked about the space at the top of the bottle where the 300 milliliters had been displaced.

"Wouldn't the oxygen in that enclosed area above the liquid influence test results?"

"To a slight degree, but we accounted for it. It's in the

summary, though I think we estimated the oxygen in that space at just under 21% of the total displaced volume. It probably was an unnecessary precaution, but we adjusted for it anyway."

Finally satisfied with her deliberate thoroughness, Gail asked a final question.

"Dr. Flessner, just to put it all in some kind of perspective, would you mind telling us how many shots of tequila you would get out of a 300 milliliter sample?"

The doctor thought to himself for a moment before answering, smiling.

"The way I pour em? About five monster shots."

"Ted! Whatever it is, it better be good. I've been waiting for you here an hour and a half."

Ted Waters sat down at the table, grinning.

"Well, I'm here now. You didn't order me a drink?"

The middle-aged columnist, mildly perturbed, didn't even smile.

"It *evaporated* while I was waiting."

He checked his watch.

"What is it, Ted?"

Calling the waitress over, Ted ordered an Absolut double shot on the rocks.

"Got some juicy tidbits for you. You'll want to buy me lunch."

Teased to anticipation, Andrew Michaels, a *Guardian* columnist, became more amenable. When the waitress brought the drink, he insisted on paying for it.

"What's the story?"

"Got to keep my name out of it."

"No problem. Tell me."

Ted sucked half the drink down on his first sip.

"Okay. Well, you know Destiny Mitchell, don't you?"

"Yeah, black gal doing the Jordan Alexander trial, right?"

"Right. Well anyway, she's on the verge of being taken off the case. The word is she's going to be fired."

Michaels studied Ted with suspicion.

"You got that from Granucci?"

The waitress interrupted, causing Ted to order another drink before he answered.

"Let's just say I know."

Michaels tossed a pad onto the table, removing a pen from his pocket.

"Okay. Why?"

"He doesn't think she's the right man for the job. Thinks she's been ineffective so far. Then she's got a chip the size of a redwood tree on her shoulder."

Michaels scribbled, trying to keep up.

"Really? go on."

"Granucci confessed it was a mistake to put her on the case in the first place, that the case should have gone to someone who had more experience."

"Uh-huh."

"And he's unhappy with a trip she made down to Costa Rica last week trying to find Stephanie Rodriguez. Stayed with a UPI correspondent and ended up burning down the woman's house. The bandage on her hand, it's from the fire."

Michaels looked up.

"This is good stuff. You told anyone else?"

"No. Anyway, I personally think she's doing an okay job, but word is Granucci thinks she's on a crusade, that she's taking the whole thing a little too personal. Everyone at the DA's office is in agreement that she's a little obsessed with this thing."

Ted looked away, his speech casual.

"She was supposed to get married to some Army colonel this year, but I heard even he got a little freaked-out about her obsession with this case. Colonel's getting married to someone else next month."

Michaels set the pen down, captivated.

"And how's that affecting her?"

"Don't know. I really don't know, but she and Brett McPherson began spending a lot of time together after the colonel dumped her."

Unable to resist, the reporter grabbed the pen and began writing again.

"Now Brett McPherson? I've heard rumors that he's gay."

Ted interrupted.

"He is, or at least bi. Wants to hide it because he thinks it'll hurt him in his bid to be a federal judge one day. Personally, I think he and Destiny are fucking. She's trying the get over the colonel and he's trying to figure out what he is."

"And what about the case? Can you tell me anything about the case?"

"Only that there wouldn't be a case if Granucci wasn't ready to announce next week that he'll be running for mayor this summer. He's done all the preliminary stuff already. He's got the money all lined up, and he's got some key endorsements. All he's got to do now is make the announcement."

Ted gulped a mouthful of the second drink.

"Biggest thing prosecution will have to deal with is Inspector Osaka's report. In his report, he says he searched the whole house and found blood on a remote wall in the closet, but after he got the search warrant and the cops went, suddenly there was blood in all these other places. It seems if there was blood in all those other places, Osaka should have seen it, but he didn't, and the reason why he didn't is because it wasn't there. It was planted. Divine's going to carve his ass up into sushi when he gets him on that stand."

He sipped again, spitting small pieces of ice back into the glass.

"There's something funny going on at the police department, and I wouldn't be surprised if someone over there thought that because he's guilty anyway, planting evidence was okay. Probably saw it as nothing more than an insurance policy."

Michaels sat back.

"That's incredible."

"Isn't it? You think you can write it?"

"When did you say Granucci was making his announcement?"

"Saturday morning, next week."

Andrew Michaels nodded as he returned the pad to his pocket.

"Well, if I can get the editor to go along with it, you ought to see the story in the Friday morning paper."

Though Barry had been uncharacteristically quiet during the direct examination, he stood, smiling at the jury, confident. He looked at Destiny and winked. He liked the fire in her, her passion, the unmistakable shrewdness and mentality in the woman. He was enjoying every minute of the trial.

"Dr. Flessner, I must admit I was blown away by your

ingenuity and that of your researchers. Were the experiments your idea?"

The doctor smiled, shrugging.

"Actually no. They were Ms. Mitchell's idea. I was a little blown away myself. That is, until I found out she was a chemistry major in college. She's a smart young woman, in *spite* of being a lawyer."

Amused, Barry laughed along with others in the courtroom.

"I'm sure she is. Doctor, and I mean this in no disrespectful way, did Ms. Mitchell *pay* you or your school to conduct these experiments?"

Flessner sat back in the chair, answering.

"Counselor, *you* of all people know that no one does anything for free, and there were legitimate costs incurred for conducting the experiments."

"You didn't answer my question. Did she pay you?"

"Yes."

"And are you often paid by various prosecutors to perform experiments and then to come in and testify?"

"Yes."

"How often? How many times in a year?"

The doctor paused as he contemplated.

"Well, at my best estimate, a dozen and a half times, maybe more."

"And that's at least eighteen times a year, is that correct?"

"Yes."

"And if I told you it was twenty-one times last year, would you dispute that?"

"No. It probably was that many."

Barry walked over to the jury, again almost leaning against the rail.

"Of the twenty-one times you were an expert witness last year, how many times did you testify in favor of the defense?"

Gail interrupted with an objection, but she was overruled. Taking a deep breath, the doctor answered.

"None, that I can think of."

"And when you perform experiments and present results in court, would you consider your testimony to be objective?"

"Yes."

"Then can you tell me why last year, in the twenty-one times you testified, the results from your experiments always favored the prosecution side?"

Gail objected.

"Sustained."

Judge Morgan looked toward Barry in disapproval.

"Time to move on, counselor."

"Very well."

He smiled, raising his hands.

"Dr. Flessner, tell me. Did you take into consideration that the tequila could have had something *else* in it? Like lime for example? Or salt? Or *water* from a melted ice cube?"

"Yes we did. There was nothing in it."

"Okay, and if someone had covered the top of the glass with a napkin to keep dust or bugs out, would that have affected the oxidation rate?"

"It would have. It would have slowed the process, but there's no indication in the record that anything like that happened."

"What if Jordan say, had a drink at four o'clock that afternoon, left a half glass that oxidized until eleven-thirty, then he poured fresh tequila on top of the tequila that had already begun absorbing oxygen? Would something like *that* affect your analysis and ultimately your conclusions?"

"It might, but the scenario you described isn't very likely. In such a case, Mr. Alexander would have to have poured the fresh tequila on top of the old and then never drank any of it. If he had no intention of drinking it, one would have to wonder why he poured it in the first place."

"But you can't say that it *didn't* happen like that, can you?"

The doctor sighed and smiled toward the jury and then at Barry.

"Anything's possible, Mr. Divine. Every time I buy a lottery ticket, I'm a possible winner, but I'd be a fool to quit my job to start making plans for spending all that money. Your scenario would be an extremely long shot at best. Better off buying a lottery ticket."

Barry approached the doctor, standing close.

"So you're saying that people don't just pour drinks and then never drink them?"

"No, I'm saying people pour drinks in *order* to drink them. I don't profess to be an expert witness at boozing, but I've drank enough to know you don't open a bottle, fill a glass and then never touch it."

"Aren't you being a little inconsistent there though, doctor?

I mean, on one hand you say people don't pour drinks and leave them sitting, while on the other you wouldn't have had a tequila test in the first place if that very thing hadn't happened?"

"Objection, argumentative."

"Overruled."

Smiling toward the jury, the doctor responded.

"Oh it happens. It even happens to me on occasion, after I've poured my *fifth* drink."

"Isn't 42 milliliters of tequila," continued Barry, "the near-equivalent of a full shot?"

"It's close."

Flessner shrugged.

"I'm not an expert bartender, but I think you could call it a shot."

Barry had backed away. Now he stood across from the jury, hand on a rail behind him.

"So what your criminologist found was almost a full shot of tequila sitting on a counter in Jordan's home? Someone had poured it and never bothered to drink it, right?"

"That's correct."

"So once again, Dr. Flessner. You can't say that Jordan didn't have a shot of tequila at four, leave some in the glass, and then pour more in the glass at eleven-thirty when he got home, can you?"

Flessner hesitated and answered.

"No, I can't."

"Thank you, Dr. Flessner. That'll be all."

Gail, who stood before Barry was seated, was eager to repair the potential damage the skillful defense lawyer had caused.

"Dr. Flessner, all fantasy and hare-brained explanations aside. If that glass of tequila was poured and left on the counter untouched, can your experiments conclusively determine when it was poured?"

"Yes?"

"So if a person who was *with* Mr. Alexander that night were to testify under oath that one, she herself doesn't drink, and two, that Jordan never poured any tequila that night after he arrived home at eleven thirty—if that person testified he in fact refused a drink when she offered, if a person were to testify in that manner, would you be more inclined to trust conclusions that were arrived at after careful analysis of..."

"Objection, your Honor. Assumes facts not in evidence. Move to strike the question."

Gail looked pleadingly toward the judge.

"It's a legitimate hypothetical, your Honor."

Barry interrupted.

"Then it's misleading."

Judge Morgan contemplated a moment and started a response, but she stopped abruptly and summoned the lawyers over into the far corner of the courtroom for a sidebar conference.

Dennis Webber walked past the startled secretary and shoved the office door open without knocking. Inside, Rikki was sitting on a sofa with the same attractive black woman he saw seated next to her in the courtroom.

Rikki stood, her anger flaring.

"What the fuck do you want, Webber?"

Dennis walked toward the black woman, grabbing her shoulder.

"Excuse you!"

He led her to the door.

"This won't take long. I promise."

As he closed the door, Dennis undid his belt and the fastener at the top of his pants. Angry, Rikki walked toward him.

"What the fuck are you doing?"

Full of bravado, he smiled as he engaged the lock near the door handle and undid his zipper.

"Oh come on, Rikki. Don't tell me you haven't seen this before. I mean, isn't this what you *do*? Isn't this how you worked your way up? On your knees and on your fuckin back?"

She turned, went to the desk and picked up the telephone receiver.

"This is your ass, Dennis! I *promise* you that!"

She dialed an extension.

"Yes, this is Rikki Thomas. Get me security."

Pants open, Dennis had made his way to the desk. He took the receiver from her hand and placed it back on its base, holding it down.

"I wouldn't do that if I were you, Rikki. It would be a very bad career move, a bad life move."

He grinned with satisfaction, looking into her eyes.

"I've waited a long time for this, you dirty cunt! I've *got* something on you. So for the moment, I'm calling the shots. You're sucking *my* dick now, bitch. Got that?"

Rikki was ballsy enough to bait him, almost enough to call his bluff.

"You've got nothing on me. No one's got anything on me."

She studied his demeanor, searching for a giveaway or vulnerability.

"You're such a fucking retard, Dennis. What? Do you think you're the first sorry ass to come through that door, whipping his tiny little white dick in my face saying he's got something on me?"

Monitoring his face, she could see his confidence waning.

"And let me tell you something else, Dennis. You've got the smallest dick of all the assholes who've ever come in here, so you might as well stuff that tiny thing back in your pants."

She sat on the desk, accustomed to taking control of such situations.

"Fuck all this John Wayne shit! Whatever you *think* you've got on me, say it or get the fuck out. You came to play, so let's play."

His confidence was beginning to erode. He had nothing tangible he could show her, only what Peter had told him. But Peter assured him it was enough to take Rikki out. So putting on his best face, he began, following Peter's script verbatim.

"All right, I have a question for you. What do Martini's campaign in '83, a Hong Kong businessman called Wing Ma and a corrupt campaign manager by the name of Rikki Thomas have in common?"

Rikki looked toward Dennis in disbelief, though she remained silent. Up until that moment, she was certain the deal and transaction had been carried out in complete stealth. Only five people in the world knew, or so she thought.

Wing Ma and two other Hong Kong businessmen had contacted her with a proposal in the late spring of 1983. Between the three, they had invested and held over a billion dollars in assets in Hong Kong alone. They proposed a working relationship with Martini during his term as mayor, stressing the importance of San Francisco in the transfer of Hong Kong's wealth to other key cities, all in anticipation of its reversion to China in 1996.

When they flew Rikki in for the meeting, she was treated in royal fashion, pampered from the moment she arrived by private jet. She left laden with gold chains, charms, precious stones, stock certificates and a proposed campaign donation.

Of course, United States law prohibited Chinese nationals from contributing to candidates, but the proposal outlined a scheme that would have over time put more than two hundred thousand dollars in Martini's coffers while granting U.S. citizenship to Wing Ma. An individual with the State department was involved, though the woman had no idea about the vital role she played in the deal.

The plan worked and newly naturalized Wing Ma became one of Martini biggest supporters, but the deal, as carried out, was illegal. Webber suggested that an FBI investigation into the matter would result in deportation of Wing Ma and his friends and certain imprisonment for Rikki, not to mention a scandal of immense proportions involving the mayor's office, and a probable criminal investigation. Thus as Rikki stared across the room at Dennis, she did her best to disguise her profound concern. She would test to discover how much he knew.

"I have no idea what you're *talking* about."

Sensing her vulnerability, he closed for the kill.

"Of course you do, Rikki. I know all about the trip to Hong Kong, about the diverted funds, about the citizenship deal, the works. I have evidence. I've got at least enough to get some FBI boys I know all heated up and hot for you. Like I said, I've got your ass."

Her eyes fell to his crotch area and then back to his face as she crossed her arms.

"So what do you want, Dennis? If you really wanted to expose this so-called secret deal, you would have already done it by now. And somehow, I don't think you and whoever else is in on this went through all that trouble to get you a fucking blowjob. What's the deal?"

Sighing to himself, he was relieved she hadn't called his bluff. He smiled in triumph, and he spoke as though he had rehearsed the line a hundred times.

"I want your ass out of town by sundown tomorrow. Do whatever you've got to do, but as of sundown tomorrow, I want to make sure it's the last we all see of Rikki Thomas in San Francisco."

Chapter 35

"Do you have any more witnesses, Counselor?"

Destiny stood, relieved. She had anticipated the moment for such a long time.

"No, your Honor. With your permission, the People rest."

It was mid-August, six weeks since the start of the trial and all told, the State had put on forty-seven witnesses. The last witness to come on was the assistant criminalist who said he had tested the still-moist blood from a balled-up sheet in Lynette's room. He testified that it matched Jordan's blood type and had a notably high blood-alcohol level. The six weeks seemed like sixty.

It had been six weeks of stress and treachery, six weeks of objections and challenges and arguments behind the scenes, of second-guessing and commentary. The mayor had criticized Destiny on television, followed by judges, other lawyers and community leaders who portrayed her as *a bitch on a mission.*

Earlier in the month, Peter Granucci resigned as district attorney to run for mayor, leaving Janice Prescott at the helm. Janice however, having no special gift for leadership and administration, allowed Ted Waters to walk all over her. The numerous leaks from the district attorney's office were irresponsible.

There was a hit piece on Destiny, written by *Guardian* columnist Andrew Michaels. In it, Destiny's entire life story and her private relationship with Colonel Charles Covington was described, analyzed and editorialized in the public forum of newsprint and later on television. Rumors about a liaison between Destiny and Brett also cropped up, complete with pictures of Brett leaving her apartment at four in the morning. Bay area residents also saw images of Orelda's *pension*, burned to the ground, right next to close-up pictures of Destiny's cut face and hands.

Destiny got so frustrated by innuendo and misinformation that she stopped watching the news and reading the papers altogether. With the State's case-in-chief finally over, she hoped the media focus would shift to Barry Divine and the defense.

She felt confident about the case she had put on. While it would have been a major coup to have gotten the DNA fingerprint evidence in front the jury, she was satisfied the jury had seen and heard enough to find Jordan guilty beyond a reasonable doubt.

"Is the defense ready to proceed?"

An attractive younger black woman sat next to Barry as he stood.

"We are, your Honor."

"Very well. Call your first witness."

Like Destiny, Barry hadn't escaped the surprises and turmoil that accompanied all major trials. The testimony of several of his prospective witnesses had fallen apart during the course of the prosecution's case. One of the psychologists begged off due to pressure from one of the boards she chaired. There were damaging leaks to the media and irresponsible stories in the newspapers.

A reporter in the *Examiner* claimed to have interviewed Stephanie Rodriguez. According to the story, Stephanie would testify Jordan was drunk when she picked him up and that neither she nor Jordan had touched the shot glass of tequila on the counter after arriving at his home. What was worse, in the final days of the prosecution's case, Stephanie began refusing Barry's coded calls and didn't bother to return them.

Another major rag printed a picture of Lynette, face swollen and bruised, above a caption that read, "Car Wreck or Reckless Husband: You Be the Judge." Though the prosecution had put on a thorough, solid case, Barry was certain he could win over enough of the jury to get a hung situation at worst, or secure an acquittal.

Toward the end of the State's case, Dottie came into Barry's office and complained about the shoddy job she thought the defense had done at cross-examination. Barry, as usual, refused to argue with his critical grandmother and told her to watch and wait.

Insulted by her "least-favorite grandson's" insolence, Dottie disparaged his parentage, especially his father, whom she hated. She assailed his ability as a lawyer and threatened consequences if Jordan wasn't exonerated of the State's charges.

In the end, she wanted blood. She insisted that Barry fire Teri Gonik, "a sloppy girl who had shown herself incompetent going up against amateurs." Losing patience with his grandmother, Barry excused himself and told her that until she was trying the case herself, she wasn't in any position to make such demands.

However, a little over an hour after Dottie left, Barry got a call from Jordan who insisted that he replace Teri with another lawyer. With reluctance, Barry acquiesced and removed Teri from the defense team, replacing her with Lisa De Witt, a smart young lawyer he had worked with two years earlier on a Los Angeles murder trial.

Even that morning, as Barry prepared to launch the first of the defense witnesses, he suffered a final setback that affected his earlier exuberance. As he and Lisa discussed the day over coffee that morning, Rikki Thomas came into the room requesting a private conference with him.

In the privacy of a meeting room down the hallway, she began.

"Look, I don't believe in beating around the bush, so I'll just say it. I'm leaving San Francisco, and I'm probably not coming back. So suffice it to say, I won't be testifying at this trial."

In shock, Barry stood, staring straight ahead for a moment, before turning toward her.

"Are you sure about this? Do you know what this is going to do to me?"

"Absolutely."

He pursed his lips and hollowed his cheeks, blowing, nodding.

"Whatever Granucci's got on you must be pretty damaging."

Though she remained silent, her eyes signaled affirmation.

"Anything I can help you with?"

"Nope."

"Well then, I hope you know you're *killing* me on credibility."

"Sorry, but I can't help it."

He sighed, accepting her decision.

"So, what are you going to do? Where are you going?"

She closed her eyes to build resolve and spoke.

"Arkansas."

"Arkansas?"

"Yes, Governor there's launching a bid for the presidency, and I've got an inside scoop that he's got a pretty good chance in the '88 election. I figure maybe I'll work for him, and if he wins, maybe I'll move to Washington. It's where I've always wanted to be anyway."

His voice seemed concerned.

"Yeah, but god-forsaken Arkansas? What? You've got a job with his campaign?"

"No, but I don't think I'll have any problem getting on. I hear his weakness is my specialty. I think we'll get along just fine."

"The defense calls Bernard Katz."

Bernard's testimony was crisp and succinct. He testified that Jordan seemed relaxed and in good spirits as they ate dinner on August 17. He recalled a general conversation about Jordan's daughter Caitlyn, who was the same age as his daughter Julie.

As to character, he asserted that in the twenty years he had known Jordan, he had never seen or heard anything to make him believe Jordan was violent. He described Jordan as a concerned parent, a good and generous husband to Lynette and a fine, upstanding citizen of San Francisco.

In cross-examination, Destiny asked how often Bernard had been in the company of Jordan when he was with Lynette, which wasn't often. When she asked if he knew of problems the couple were having, he answered he was aware of the trial separation, though he didn't know the details because he hadn't asked and Jordan hadn't volunteered the information.

While Barry tried to portray Bernard as a good friend, Destiny sought to depict him as a casual acquaintance who hardly knew Jordan and was unqualified to answer questions on his character and on his relationship with Lynette.

The last few questions she asked related to Jordan's state of inebriation during the dinner. While Barry challenged the questions on the basis that the witness was unqualified to answer, the judge allowed Bernard to answer in general terms. He said Jordan didn't seem intoxicated at all, that he had probably *less* than two glasses of the wine. When she asked him if Jordan's speech was slurred or otherwise altered, Bernard insisted that Jordan didn't seem drunk.

The next two witnesses were an elderly black man and a city official, who Barry used to illuminate Jordan's generosity to the underprivileged and to the welfare of the city. Then came the middle-aged woman police officer who watched the girls until Jordan got to the station. She testified Jordan seemed genuine in his sadness about his wife's death, especially when he had to sit the girls down and break the news.

"They all just sorta huddled up on that little bench, crying together."

And next came the deputy medical examiner, who said he had performed various tests to determine whether or not Lynette had been raped in the final moments preceding her death. While he said he found no seminal fluid, he admitted the vaginal area was so horribly mutilated that he hadn't expected to find it even if it had been present. He also admitted that the vaginal mutilation might have been an attempt to hide evidence of a rape.

The last witness for the day was Gina Fasone, another of Lynette's Sacramento Street neighbors. In fact, she lived next door. According to her testimony, she was out watering her sunflowers and mums between 9:30 and 10:00 when she saw the Rolls in front of Lynette's house. She added that as she stood there, she saw "a strange, scary black man" coming toward her. She said he seemed to have come out of Lynette's house and was walking in a suspicious manner.

Frightened, she hurried back into the house and locked all the doors. She admitted she was even more alarmed the next day when she found out that Lynette had been murdered. As she gasped, she added,

"Very easily, it could have been me. He was looking right at me."

While she couldn't remember what the man was wearing, she recalled he had on glasses. When the detectives stopped by on August 18 to ask if she saw anything suspicious, she said she let her husband do the talking. She said was afraid to talk, afraid that if she did, the black man might come back to punish her and her family.

Notwithstanding, she did tell all on the evening Tyrell Briggs and Deondray Carter were arrested. She was unable to identify either as *the suspicious black man who walked by* when asked to view them in a police line-up. The man she saw was of a medium-to-slight build and of medium height, an older man. Finally, she testified that she recalled seeing dried blood drops on the sidewalk along the path where the black man had walked.

In her cross, Destiny asked the witness if she was afraid of all black men, and she asked what constituted suspicious behavior in Gina's mind. She also asked Gina if she remembered whether or not the man she saw was covered in blood. The witness responded that while she didn't remember seeing any blood on his clothes, he could have been bleeding. Gina said that while she did not recognize him among the blacks in the police line-up, she was certain she had seen him before, "either in the neighborhood or somewhere else. His face seemed really familiar."

Retrieving a newspaper from the prosecutors' table, Destiny held up the tabloid-style rag, which featured a story on Gina, titled, *I Stood Face to Face With Lynette's Killer.*

"Ms. Fasone, are you familiar with the story in the publication I just showed to the jury?"

"Yes."

"And did you allow a reporter to interview you in order to write it?"

"Yes."

"Have you read it?"

"Yes."

"Okay, and is the story, as written, consistent with what you told the reporter?"

"Yes it is, for the most part."

Destiny handed the newspaper to Gina, taking a place in front of the jury.

"Near the middle of the story there, the reporter quotes you as saying you saw the man *come out of Lynette's house and down the steps*. Accurate or not?"

Gina began to squirm in the well-used seat.

"Well, I don't know."

"Did you say it or didn't you?"

"Well yes, I, I guess I did... in a roundabout way."

She looked toward the judge, explaining, shrugging.

"I wasn't like I was under oath."

Destiny interrupted.

"No you weren't then, but now you are. Did you see the man in question come out Lynette's house?"

Gina hesitated before answering.

"Well, no."

"Did you see him come down the steps?"

"No."

"Ms. Fasone, do you have any idea where the man came from?"

Gina sighed, angry.

"No, I have to say I don't, but he came from that direction."

Referring to the newspaper in Gina's hands, Destiny continued.

"Further in the article, you're quoted as saying *the man's face was sweaty and that he stopped, his intense eyes running salaciously up and down my body*. Accurate quote?"

"Not, not entirely."

"Did you say it?"

"I, I remember saying some of it, not exactly in that way."

She shrugged.

"Reporters!"

"But you weren't under oath, right?"

While Destiny's argumentative comment drew a quick objection from Barry, the shrewd prosecutor had already shifted the focus of her questions.

"Did the publisher pay you for the story?"

"Yes."

"How much?"

"A thousand dollars."

"And have you been invited onto television news shows to describe what you saw that night?"

"Yes."

"You have actually become popular about town as a result of your story, haven't you?"

"No, not really."

"Didn't you embellish your story for the money and popularity you knew it would bring, Ms. Fasone?"

Gina's anger had become more obvious.

"I did not."

"Isn't it true that you saw a man walking down the street that night who scared you merely because he was black? And then, after you heard about the murder, you made up a sensational story about him to somehow involve yourself in this high-profile case for the money and publicity?"

"That's not true at all!"

Barry's re-direct focused on the dried blood drops in front of Gina's house. During the State's case, Barry got the criminalist to admit that while they matched neither Jordan's nor Lynette's blood type, they did match the third blood type found in the room and in the house. In the defendant's favor, one of the detectives on the scene testified that, with a little imagination, a person could discern a trail of blood, which began in Lynette's room, went down the stairs, out the front door and right past Gina's house.

Much more comfortable as Barry asked questions, Gina testified she knew the blood drops were left that night because she had a long-standing habit of washing down the sidewalk in front of her house every morning. The blood drops, for whatever reason, were deposited on that walkway on the night of August 17.

CHAPTER 36

On Monday, August 17, 1987, the first anniversary of the murder, Destiny had a quiet dinner with Allegra at a Lombard Street restaurant by the water that had been Lynette's favorite. Despite the sadness of the event that had brought them together, both were upbeat about the progress of the trial.

Taking Destiny's hands in hers, Allegra thanked her for the evident sacrifices she had made to stay on the case and predicted that in the end she would silence all the critics who so cruelly disparaged and discredited her.

Allegra wanted to move from the home Jordan bought her in Pasadena. The thought of spending one more night in a place he used in an attempt to win her over disgusted her. The house was a constant reminder of the shame and regret she felt. She wanted to move up to San Francisco where she could continue the work Lynette began with the *Aegis Foundation*. When asked what her plans were after the trial, Destiny responded,

"There's a tough question. In a lot of ways for me, this trial will never be over."

After dinner, Destiny drove west along the water on over to Lincoln Boulevard, which she followed down to her favorite little strip of shoreline near Point Lobo. Parking her car in one of the spaces on the hill overlooking the ruins of Sutro's baths, she descended to the beach, her arms crossed as she shivered in the chilled briny breath of the North Pacific.

Though it was becoming dark, she knew it would be there. Though she stumbled over sand hills, seaweed and irregularities in the inconstant alluvium along the shore, she knew it would be there waiting for her as it always had, as it always would, as long as she could remember, as it would long after she was gone.

Tracing its damp, stony outline with her hands, she turned and sat, sighing, looking out into a vast darkness that was the sea. She could hear the waves crashing in, unceasing, as they had from the beginning of time. She could smell the mineral salts in the air, could sense the essence of the ocean.

She could feel a second vaporous sea washing over her exposed skin, diaphanous surf that flowed beyond the water's edge. Its ephemeral breakers, composed of trillions of tiny droplets, cascaded a mile inland. As she took a deep breath, a sense of calm came over her. Staring out into the breathing blackness before her, she remembered.

Though summers in New Orleans were sweltering, August 8th had been cooler, actually pleasant. Destiny hoped for rain and gloom, but leave it to the girl who already had everything to get the best day of the entire summer for her wedding. At two o'clock in the church at Jackson Square, Claudette Boveé was going to marry the love of Destiny's life.

Destiny hesitated about going to New Orleans on that day, and she had no intention of attending the actual wedding. However, something drew her there, something in her searching for closure to the relationship she shared with Charles Covington.

He hadn't called her since before Christmas last year—not since that weekend in Las Vegas. He never told her it was over. He was such a bastard! And while she remained hurt, she was in New Orleans because she wanted to let go, because she wanted to see him one last time, if even from a distance, as he vowed his love and life to another woman. She needed the finality.

She envied Claudette, a woman from a privileged family. Her father was a respected cardiac surgeon and her mother owned a restaurant in the French Quarter. Her parents were good-looking, and only-child Claudette, disgustingly beautiful, had a Ph.D. from an Ivy League school.

The family was one among many rich and educated black families in New Orleans who looked down on the common blacks in the world. These families, though they resented white people, wore their lighter skin like badges of honor.

While that New Orleans society would have never approved of Claudette marrying a darker-skinned man, the family was impressed by Charles Covington's rank and his auspicious destiny. Destiny knew the wedding would be grand, but she had no idea how elegant southern weddings could be.

She arrived at one o'clock, taking a seat on a bench under a tall cedar along the path to the church. The procession began at one-thirty. First, she saw an elaborate, decorated horse and carriage roll by, and behind it, a pageant of fifty or more just like it. All the men were wearing tuxedos, and the women were dressed so fancy that Destiny felt dreary in the simple black Halston dress she wore. Her hair was up and snug in the pillbox hat while her face was hidden behind a lacy black fan.

She watched the excited wedding-goers pass by. There were older men and gray-haired women who moved in slow motion, the giggling children, the teen-aged girls who coyly checked out the older twenty-something men, the young men, back from college, the spinsters who had never been lucky enough to marry, the young hopefuls and finally, there was Colonel Charles Covington.

Ducking even further behind the fan, she watched him, groomsmen in attendance, proud as he stepped from the carriage and strode into the church. Then came Claudette, accompanied by her father. Her gleaming, iridescent gown was resplendent in the sun and shadows. Its train, almost twenty feet long, was carried by four handsome young girls. Lucky bitch!

With Claudette inside and the doors closed, Destiny rose and made her way over to the cathedral. Heart pounding and stomach tied in knots, she ventured past arrogant, disapproving carriage drivers to the door. Pulling it open, she looked in.

Slipping through the giant doors, she walked into an airy antechamber that sat before another set of doors. She could hear the somber priest speaking in Latin on the other side.

Hands sweating and fingers shaking, she pulled the door open just enough to look into the church. As fate would have it, Charles looked back at the exact moment she looked in. He sensed her presence and she knew it. In an exchange that lasted not more than a few seconds across infinite time and distance, she communicated the pain she felt while he communicated his regret. Eyes flowing with tears, she turned away and ran.

She ran and ran—past the carriages, past the trees, past the cars, out of Jackson Square. She ended up in a small bar, barefoot, hair mussed and mascara running, where she cried for two hours more. Summoning her strength with the aid of a straight bourbon shot, she managed to find the rented car and make it to the airport just in time for the 8:38 flight.

It was becoming cold on the dark beach as Destiny sat crying on that rock. Wiping her nose with the back of her hand, she turned, knelt and began digging in the sand under the rock. Though the grittiness of the sand destroyed her manicure, she continued until she had dug more than a foot down.

Fumbling in the hole, she found it. It was the ring Charles had given her, the large, two-caret, sparkling diamond ring he placed on her finger last September in Golden Gate Park when he got on one knee and begged her to marry him.

Gravel-covered ring in the palm of her right hand, she stood and walked toward the water. She had considered doing it before, but she was never able to let go, never able to throw away the man who would always have her heart. But things had changed. All hope lost, she proceeded into the water, ruining her shoes and silk slacks up to her mid-thighs.

The ocean rushed against her body as she stood there, weeping, regretting, until finally she flung her arm back, propelled it forward and released the ring. She didn't know how far it had gone and never heard it splash. It was simply gone. It was gone along with, in her mind, any hope of ever loving again.

CHAPTER 37

On Monday and Tuesday of the next week, a string of defense witness moved on and off the stand. Court was canceled on Wednesday due to a funeral for the sister of one of the women jurors. Barry finished with the first category of witnesses on Thursday morning, leaving the afternoon to set up an inevitable confrontation with Bryan Osaka on Friday.

First, he called San Francisco Police Department Internal Affairs Director Dexter Conaty to the stand, seeking testimony that would lay a foundation for discrediting and inculpating the detective. Conaty was a defense witness who went out of his way to suggest misconduct and hidden motives on the part of the three detectives involved in the initial investigation.

He testified that Internal Affairs had conducted an inquiry into the appropriateness of Inspector Osaka's actions in the early morning of August 18, adding that some on the board favored issuing a reprimand for what Conaty called a flagrant disregard for written departmental policy.

Specifically, he said Osaka deceived Stephanie Rodriguez into believing she was in some sort of imminent danger. Osaka, in Conaty's words, had created a false exigency purposed to gain improper access to Mr. Alexander's residence.

"And why, Mr. Conaty, does the San Francisco Police Department have such careful rules in place involving intrusions on private property?"

"Because the courts typically throw out evidence obtained in the manner Osaka went about getting it."

Brett's first question in cross-examination focused on Conaty's reference to the courts.

"Mr. Conaty, you said that courts generally throw out illegal evidence, right?"

"I said they do for evidence obtained illegally."

"And are you aware of any specific court hearing on the matter of Osaka's search of the defendant's home?"

An objection by Lisa caused an extended sidebar conference that extended to the lunch break. In Judge Morgan's chambers, the spirited young defense attorney argued that any mention of the suppression hearing and Judge Chow's ruling would be unduly prejudicial to jurors.

Brett countered that, in questioning Conaty on the appropriateness of Osaka's search, the defense had "opened the door" to prosecution questions on exclusions. The judge ruled in favor of the prosecution, acknowledging Brett's argument, though she limited the scope to questions on the object of the hearing and on the court's ruling. None of the specific facts from the hearing were to be considered.

"Once again, Mr. Conaty. Are you aware an evidentiary hearing conducted shortly before this trial relating to Inspector Osaka's search of the defendant's home?"

After looking toward Lisa for a possible clue about how to respond, he answered curtly.

"Yes."

"And are you aware of the object, or purpose of that hearing?"

"Yes."

"Perhaps you wouldn't mind enlightening the jury?"

Resentful, Dexter turned toward the jury box.

"It was a suppression hearing."

"And would you agree the purpose of that hearing was to determine if evidence seized by Inspector Osaka and other detectives was or was not in violation of the Fourth Amendment, relating to unreasonable and illegal searches?"

As Dexter Conaty hesitated, not sure about how to respond, Brett rephrased the question.

"In other words, was it a hearing to determine if Inspector Osaka searched the defendant's home illegally?"

"Yes."

"And are you aware of the judge's ruling?"

Conaty nodded.

"Yes."

"Didn't the judge determine that there was nothing illegal about the search?"

"He, he allowed the evidence in, yes."

Brett took his place before the jury box, almost posing, almost theatrical.

"One more question, Mr. Conaty. Who do you think would be better able to determine questions on violations of Fourth Amendment rights, a Superior Court judge?"

He smiled toward the jury.

"Or you?"

Lisa shouted, her voice full of contempt.

"Objection, your Honor. Move to strike. It's argumentative, it's improper impeachment and it's *way* beyond the scope."

Brett turned toward Lisa, emoting astonishment and disapproval for the loud outburst.

"No problem."

He turned toward the judge.

"I withdraw the question."

During the prosecution's case, Destiny limited the scope of Bryan Osaka's testimony to the bedroom and his discovery of the stain on the screen wall. Though Barry did his best to draw the witness out during cross-examination, through objections, Destiny was successful at limiting early liability. She even declined to re-direct when the judge offered the opportunity.

One of the key prospects of the defense's case-in-chief however, involved the greatly anticipated confrontation between the inspector and Barry Divine. During the break, after Dexter Conaty's testimony, the lawyers and judge discussed news of an alleged leak from one of the labs performing DNA testing.

Someone from the lab suggested the sample of blood from the room that matched neither Jordan nor Lynette's blood type had most likely come from "an African American male." This leak was printed in the newspapers and debated on talk radio, in articles and on television shows, which were off-limits to jurors. Thus after a guard overheard the middle-aged female juror discussing the leak with someone on the telephone, Judge Morgan called the juror in and dismissed her.

The alternate who took her place was a male in his late forties or early fifties. There was something about him that made Destiny uneasy, though she didn't exactly know why. During *voir dire*, he seemed a little too eager to get on the panel. His salt-and-pepper hair was cut short and conservative, while a pair of intense blue eyes sat fixed behind circular, wire-rimmed glasses. From his looks, she figured he was either gay or a Nazi. She was hoping for gay.

"The defense calls San Francisco Police Inspector Bryan Osaka."

It was the second time Bryan took his place on the witness stand to discuss his search of Jordan Alexander's home. During the State's case, he was apprehensive and careful during cross-examination, nervous that Barry would ask questions to set him up for impeachment during the defense's presentation.

Consistent with advice Destiny gave, he tried to keep his answers short, direct and unambiguous. In the previous two weeks, he met with Destiny on two occasions to discuss the questions Barry would most likely pose, the tricks Barry might employ and pitfalls to avoid.

Early on in direct testimony, his sanguine answers to Barry's innocuous questions lured him into a sense of false confidence, yet within minutes, he hesitated there, eyes darting back and forth, like a soldier upon the sudden realization he was standing in the middle of a minefield.

"During the course of that night, did you at any time visit the crime scene on Sacramento Street?"

"No, I did not visit the actual crime scene."

"What time were you called to duty, Inspector?"

Bryan thought back, hoping to craft an answer that would be consistent with his final report.

"I got the call at about 1:30 a.m., but I didn't get to my assignment until 2:45."

"And what exactly *was* your assignment, Inspector Osaka?"

Bryan looked at Barry, but he turned and directed his answer to the jury.

"I was assigned to watch Mr. Alexander's home on Loma Vista Way."

Barry had taken a position at the corner of the jury box so that he seemed to be among the jurors as he asked the questions.

"Just *watch* Mr. Alexander's home? On the night his wife was murdered? As a valuable detective, shouldn't you have been out pursuing possible leads?"

"Two other detectives were assigned to do that. I was directed to watch the defendant's home because Mr. Alexander reported being mugged and robbed sometime the night before."

"So you're saying that, as a trained detective, when a person reports being mugged and robbed in a public place, the most efficient way to solve the crime is to park your car and watch the victim's house?"

Destiny's voice interrupted Bryan's tentative answer.

"Objection. Argumentative. The witness already said he was there because he was directed there."

"Sustained."

Barry sighed, smiling.

"Very well. And who, Inspector, assigned you to watch Jordan's home?"

"It was, uh Commander Dennis Webber."

"Commander Webber? And did he tell you why you were watching Jordan's house?"

"He said there was a possibility the mugging and murder were related, so he sent me over there to monitor any suspicious activity."

"So you knew about the murder when you went over there?"

"Yes."

"And in your mind then, was Jordan a suspect?"

"Uh no. Well maybe, in the back of my mind. Husbands and boyfriends are typically suspects."

"All right, and is it standard procedure for detectives to make personal visits to notify next-of-kin in murder cases?"

"It happens sometimes."

"But more often than not, detectives stick to what they're good at, detective work. And they leave notifying next-of-kin to patrol officers, right?"

"Well, yes."

"Inspector Osaka, do you know why the two detectives assigned to investigate the crime scene left that scene to personally notify Jordan that Lynette had been murdered?"

"No, I don't"

"Is it standard practice? Is it 'by the book'?"

"Well, I don't know enough about the circumstances at the crime scene that night or at what point in the investigation they left. I really couldn't say."

"Did you see Inspectors Elliot Garner and Eddie Harris arrive at Jordan's home at 5:27 that morning, according to the report you filed with the department?"

"Yes."

"Did Jordan, at any time, allow them to enter his home?"

"No."

"And after Jordan left his home to find his daughters and tell them the news, did you speak with either of the detectives?"

"Yes."

"Did either of them tell you that, though they asked to enter the home on three separate occasions in their conversation with Jordan, he told them he did not want them in his house?"

"No."

"So you're telling us that neither of the detectives expressed any frustration or suspicion to you about being refused permission to enter Jordan's home?"

Bryan paused a moment before nodding.

"That's what I'm telling you."

"Did you see Jordan leave, Inspector?"

"Yes."

"Then, knowing he was gone, why did you proceed to go up and knock on his door?"

Careful, Bryan answered.

"Because in a telephone call with Inspector Garner, I learned there was someone *else* in the house. Then when I was called back to the station, I didn't want to leave without informing the person inside of the risk she might be facing by remaining in that house."

Barry laughed, shaking his head.

"Excuse me, Inspector. Would you mind telling us what *risk* you thought she might be facing?"

Bryan's eyes darted from the jury to the judge.

"Well, I knew Mr. Alexander had reported being mugged the night before and that he claimed his keys and car had been stolen. I knew Lynette had been murdered. I knew Mr. Alexander told detectives he suspected the men who mugged him had also murdered his wife, and I knew his vehicle registration listed the address on Loma Vista Way. If I had left without warning her and something had happened, I would have felt responsible for failing to warn her."

"Inspector Osaka, did you tell the young woman who answered the door that you had been watching the house since 2:45 and that there was no suspicious activity on the street throughout the night?"

"No, I did not."

"Didn't you in fact tell her that, despite the fact that you had been watching the house all night, someone may have slipped past your well-trained detective eyes and entered the house through a back door?"

"No."

"No? Well, isn't that why she let you in? To search the house for a possible intrusion from a back door or window?"

Bryan held his breath in an attempt to remain calm. After a moment, he sighed, answering.

"She said she'd feel better if I came in and searched the house."

Barry spoke to the judge.

"Your Honor, witness answer's non-responsive. I asked if she let him in to search for a possible intrusion from a back door or window, and he's failed to respond."

Judge Helen Morgan leaned toward Bryan, removing her glasses.

"Please answer the question, Inspector. Was that the reason?"

Bryan wiped the beaded sweat from his forehead with the palm of his hand.

"Yes."

Barry smiled.

"So I ask again, did you deceive the woman who answered the door about the level of risk she was facing just so you could to gain access to Jordan's home?"

"No, I did not."

"Did you lie to scare her into submitting to a search of Jordan's private residence?"

"No. No, I did not."

Barry walked back over to the defense table, exchanging the documents he was holding for another set.

"During the prosecution's case, we all got to find out about what a great detective you are, Mr. Osaka. We passed around the commendations and letters of appreciation and awards. In your own estimation, would you call yourself a capable, well-trained detective?"

"Well, I think I'm capable, and I think I was trained by the best."

"All right, and in line with all the great sleuthhounds of fact and fiction, whether it be Dennis Webber or Sherlock Holmes—what would you say is the most important quality for any detective to possess?"

Bryan sighed, certain about where the lawyer was going, though he couldn't help giving Barry the answers he expected.

"The trained eye, the power of observation."

"And do you possess that quality, Inspector Osaka? Are your eyes trained to notice irregularities and possible clues?"

"I believe they are, though I'm far from perfect."

"When you gained access to Jordan's private residence and began searching for this possible intrusion from a back door or window, did you initially search the first floor or the second floor first?"

"The first floor."

As Barry spoke, Lisa was preparing exhibits on two easels that stood before the jury box. On them were pictures displaying blood drops and smears.

"And when you searched the living room, did you somehow fail to observe the blood smear Inspectors Garner and Harris later discovered on the leaves of an artificial ficus tree next to the couch as we can see in defense exhibit P?"

Bryan's voice had taken on explanatory tone.

"I, I was searching for signs of a forced entry and possible persons. I wasn't looking for anything else."

"What about the blood drops on the foyer floor as shown in exhibit Q? From the picture, don't they seem to be in full view?"

"They were behind the front door where I wouldn't have seen them, since I left the door open."

Barry changed the exhibit.

"And the blood smear on the stair railing in defense exhibit S, you didn't see that either because it wasn't a person?"

"I wasn't looking for blood. I didn't notice it."

"And the same applies to the drops of blood found on the kitchen counter?"

Bryan nodded.

"Yes."

"Inspector Osaka, did you ever stop to consider that you didn't report seeing blood in any of those places because there *was* no blood there when you initially searched Jordan's home?"

"No."

"Have you since that time considered the possibility that someone later planted those drops and smears in an effort to frame Jordan Alexander for a murder he couldn't and wouldn't have committed?"

"Now *that*, that would have been impossible."

"Inspector Osaka? Are you yourself part of a coordinated effort by detectives and officers bent on destroying Jordan Alexander?"

"No."

"Are you part of a rogue faction of the San Francisco Police Department detectives who might sometimes bend the rules to insure a greater conviction rate?"

"No."

"Have your actions that morning, and the actions of the other detectives who searched the house, been under investigation by a police Internal Affairs board specifically in connection with the propriety of the search?"

"Yes."

Once again, Barry asked questions from the jury's physical perspective. He had taken control of the courtroom.

"Inspector Osaka, when you searched the first floor of Jordan's residence, did you discover any evidence of a forced entry?"

"No."

"No? Well Inspector, if no one came in through a door or window behind the house, and no one came in through the front, which you happened to be watching, why did you think there might be someone lurking in the closet upstairs? Why did you even search the upstairs for that matter?"

Fortunately for Bryan, it was one of the questions Destiny told him Barry might ask. Unless Stephanie actually testified, no one could refute his answer.

"Because the young woman in the house, Stephanie Rodriguez, she asked me to."

Barry looked toward Destiny and smirked, acknowledging her probable contribution to the response. Turning back toward the witness, he pressed on.

"Inspector Osaka, you said Commander Webber called you at 1:30, but you didn't get to Jordan's Loma Vista Way residence until 2:45. Is that because you went to the crime scene on Sacramento Street first?"

"Objection, your Honor. Foundation."

"Sustained."

"Okay Inspector, I have no intention of dragging this trial out no longer than I have to, but if my next witness is a patrolman who's willing to swear he saw you on Sacramento Street at 2:15 that morning, would he be telling us the truth?"

Bryan's face flushed. Panic shone in his eyes. Destiny, across the room, seemed concerned. He never told her or anyone else he had visited the crime scene on Sacramento Street. Thus, his hesitation provoked a greater interest in the answer. He stared straight ahead and spoke.

"Yes."

His response set off a rash of gasps and whispering in the courtroom. Barry, sensing his highest point in the trail, waited for the astonishment in the room to wane.

"Inspector, didn't you carry blood from the crime scene on Sacramento Street back over to Jordan's residence on Loma Vista Way?"

Instead of breaking, Bryan seemed emboldened by Barry's challenge.

"I did not."

"Didn't you carry blood and hair from the Sacramento Street crime scene into Jordan's home?"

"No."

"Didn't you carry that blood and hair into his bedroom?"

"I did not."

"Inspector Osaka, wasn't it *you* who smeared blood and hair from the crime scene onto the wall of the screen in Jordan's bedroom?"

"No, I would never do something like that!"

Barry stopped, glancing toward Destiny.

"One more question, Inspector. Have you been honest and truthful in your answers to this court and to the all attorneys involved?"

Bryan glanced toward Destiny, whose face seethed in anger, though she did her best to smile. He answered.

"Yes."

Satisfied with the theatrical tension of the moment, Barry turned to the judge.

"I have no more questions."

Helen Morgan turned toward Destiny.

"Your witness, Ms. Mitchell."

As the prosecutor rose, she uttered something unintelligible in the general direction of the witness.

"Bachiatari! Do she te uso o tsu ku no!"

The judge called her on it.

"Excuse me, Ms. Mitchell! *What* did you just say?"

Recoiling, Destiny looked toward the judge and then glanced over at the jury, especially at the Japanese juror who seemed astonished.

"Oh, oh nothing. I'm sorry, your Honor. I was just talking to myself, reacting."

Stern, the judge peered over her glasses, addressing the court recorder.

"Did you get any of that?"

The confounded young woman shrugged.

"Too garbled. Just *baka*-something."

Judge Morgan removed the glasses, issuing a severe warning.

"In the future, Counselor, I will not tolerate you saying anything unless we can all understand what you're saying. I will cite you for contempt. Do I make myself clear?"

Destiny bowed her head.

"Absolutely. I'm sorry. It won't happen again."

Bryan was more astonished than the juror. Unlike the rest of the courtroom, he understood what the lawyer had said. *Bachiatari!* It was something his father called him the time he got drunk in high school and totaled his little red corvette, the same thing his father called him when he lost his first job at Mikuni restaurant for getting in a fistfight with two Korean cooks. With that word came feelings from all the low moments of his life, moments of utter stupidity and disgrace.

At that moment in the courtroom, he felt a similar shame, a similar sense of humiliation. Yet most of all, he had betrayed a budding friendship and trust that had begun to develop between the attractive lawyer and himself.

However, he still had a job to do. As she approached, he was prepared to help repair some of the damage Barry had exacted.

"Inspector Osaka, did you for a fact go over to Lynette Alexander's Sacramento Street address and visit the crime scene?"

"I drove over there, yes."

"Did you go in the house?"

"No."

"Did you leave your car?"

"No, I didn't."

"So you never actually *visited* the area designated as a crime scene by the police department?"

"Objection. Leading."

"Overruled."

Destiny smiled toward Bryan.

"You can answer the question."

"No, I never visited the crime scene."

"Where'd you park, Inspector?"

He narrowed his eyes as he thought, trying to pinpoint the exact position.

"I parked about thirty yards away, on the opposite side of the street, facing east, I think."

"Did you speak with anyone from the crime scene?"

"No, I just sort of watched for a few minutes through a set of binoculars."

Destiny's voice was firm.

"Once again, did you have any contact whatsoever with anyone at the crime scene during the time you were there?"

"No, I was too remote. I had no idea anyone even saw me there."

She sighed, relieved, relaxing a bit as she moved away from Bryan.

"Why'd you go over there?"

"Curiosity, I guess. In a way, I didn't believe it. I couldn't believe Lynette Alexander had been murdered. I thought there had to be a mistake. I guess I drove over there to confirm it for myself."

"And did you pick up any blood and hair to carry over to the defendant's home?"

"No. That would have been impossible. I was never close enough."

"Inspector, do you hate Jordan Alexander?"

"No. I can't say that I even know him."

"Do you know of any plot or any conspiracy among detectives or the police to somehow frame him?"

Bryan shook his head.

"No. No, the San Francisco Police Department is made up of good men who proudly risk their lives for the people of this city. There's nothing like that going on."

Relaxed, Destiny leaned against the prosecution table.

"What about the young woman who was in the defendant's house. Did you ever come to know her name?"

"Yes. Her name is Stephanie Rodriguez."

"And before you complied with Stephanie Rodriguez's request to search the house, had you ascertained what relationship she had with the defendant and why she was there?"

"She was his girlfriend who often stayed overnight."

"And how'd you know that?"

"She told me and it's in her initial interview from Harris' report."

"And was Stephanie Rodriguez present the whole time when you discovered the blood and hair on the screen in the bedroom?"

"Yes."

"Was Stephanie Rodriguez present the whole time Detectives Garner and Harris searched the house after a warrant had been issued?"

"Yes, I believe so. It's in the report."

"So if the detectives were walking around the first floor of the defendant's residence, smearing and dropping blood in various places, Stephanie would have witnessed it?"

A sustained objection broke the rhythm of Destiny's questions. The judge, indicating how far the trial had run overtime that Friday, encouraged the prosecutor to wrap things up.

"I'll ask you one last question, Inspector. When and if Stephanie Rodriguez takes the stand to testify about what happened on the morning of August 18th, will her testimony, if truthful, contradict anything you've told us here today?"

"Objection. Calls for speculation."

"Sustained.

"Let me put it this way, Inspector, have all your answers been truthful today?"

"Yes."

"Have you held anything back?"

"No I haven't."

"Thank you very much, Inspector. That'll be all."

CHAPTER 38

It was 3 a.m. All the lights in Brett's Piedmont home were off, except those in the library where he and Destiny poured over pages of trial transcripts that numbered in the thousands. Three days earlier, after three and a half weeks of trial by ambush, Barry Divine-style, both were happy to hear him utter the phrase, "The Defense rests."

Behind the scenes, Janice and Gail had argued most of the points-of-law and prevailed in many, including a couple of key issues. Venerable Santa Clara law professor Paul Previn argued the other side. One hard fought debate focused on facts surrounding the murders of Tyrell Briggs and Deondray Carter at the Alameda County Jail.

Previn argued that in the end, Briggs recanted his earlier confession and was prepared to divulge the degree to which he was involved in Lynette's murder. The murder of Briggs in the jail, Previn maintained, was designed to end the federal investigation involving Lucille DuBois.

He said Briggs and Carter, after murdering Lynette, decided to cop to the DuBois murder for two reasons: 1) it was the lesser of two evils; and 2) to protect a shadowy, powerful underworld figure, who was the ultimate object of the federal investigation. He said when Briggs went back on the deal and started talking to the district attorney, it spelled certain death for both.

In a hearing outside the presence of the jury, Previn brought on a prison psychologist who testified on the "signature" of the Briggs murder. "The penis and testicles in the mouth with the lips sewn shut," he claimed, was the gang-related punishment for those who decided to roll-over. "It was a message to the prison-wide gang population about what happened to those who talked."

Janice however, pointed out that there was no evidence that linked either Briggs or Carter to the Sacramento Street crime scene, while the link to the DuBois crime scene in Oakland had already been established. She also argued the introduction of such a lurid and insubstantial theory wasn't probative at all in the case and would only serve to confuse the jury.

Judge Morgan let the lawyers argue back and forth until the

debate became repetitive. Then she brought the hearing to an abrupt close, ruling in favor of the prosecution. The other key ruling for the prosecution involved the exclusion of testimony by a renowned serologist/ DNA expert who was prepared to tell the jury that several of the drops of blood found in Lynette's room were black blood, or blood that had come from an African American male.

After Osaka's testimony, Barry proceeded to grill and accuse Garner and Harris, but owing to experience, the detectives pretty much held their own. While both denied planting evidence and the idea of a conspiracy, Garner went as far as saying he liked Jordan.

As he questioned Harris about planting blood evidence, Barry asked the detective if he had the same blood type as the blood sample that matched neither Jordan nor Lynette. An objection prevented the question from being answered, but the jury seemed to understand the implication.

After the inspectors, the defense called Commander Dennis Webber, a witness who had an unmistakable animus for the defense attorney. His answers were short, his tone disdainful. He said the idea of sending Osaka to Jordan's home was his, that it was discretionary and appropriate.

Barry introduced affidavits from six patrolmen who had at various times overheard Webber's inappropriate statements and criticisms of the Alexander family. Webber answered that he, in speaking, was criticizing the family as an institution in the same way he might criticize the *Chronicle* or the court system, but he had never felt animosity for individual family members.

During cross-examination, Webber admitted that while he realized the defendant had the right to a vigorous defense, he resented the way three of his finest detectives had been accused of evidence tampering.

Then came a series of expert witnesses purposed to refute the evidentiary conclusions of the prosecution's experts. The most memorable of these was a chemistry professor from MIT who poked fun at the idea of "tipsy, pimply-faced, geeky, bed-wetting" college students having the discipline to perform the tequila tests. His subtle sense of humor, his impeccable timing and his whimsical facial expressions contributed to perhaps the lightest and most entertaining fifteen minutes of the trial. Jurors laughed, spectators laughed and even Judge Helen Morgan laughed.

Finally came a decisive moment for the defense. For Barry,

it was a foregone conclusion, though he flirted with the issue in public. The idea of having Jordan take the stand was impractical. However, it was what Dottie Alexander wanted. Jordan, though he wanted to please his grandmother, was lukewarm on the idea.

As the three sat in a conference room on that Thursday afternoon, the argument raged between Barry and Dottie. Barry appealed to his law experience while Dottie appealed to family pride and the family name. In the end, Jordan sided with Barry, causing Dottie to unleash another one of her acerbic invectives against her "least favorite relative alive."

Minutes later, Barry stood before Helen Morgan and sighed, declaring, "The Defense rests."

By 3:30, both Destiny and Brett were struggling against mental burnout. It was just too much information to consider and too late at night. The brandy that Brett began pouring at 2 a.m. hadn't helped either. So leaving the well-ordered mess of papers and documents on the table untouched, they retired to a sofa, snifters couched in the palms of their hands between fingers. Brett turned the radio up on the smooth jazz of KMEL. Both relaxed, sipping.

After sitting for a little over ten minutes, Brett began at what had become a nightly ritual. He turned Destiny away from him and started massaging her back, shoulders and neck. She moaned aloud as always. His strong, sensitive hands worked, rubbing, pressing and caressing, only this time they ventured further. He dragged his fingers along her sides and over her hips and then back up along her shapely body.

She didn't seem to mind as his dexterous hands wandered along her ribs and up to the front of her body where he massaged her shoulders, the upper portion of her chest and the front of her neck. And she didn't seem to mind the sensual way he dragged his fingers along her taut skin, lingering in sensitive places. She didn't even mind the way, as he exhaled, his wispy and heated breath made the back of her neck tingle. She took deep breaths, sighing and relaxing her body. She did tense up however, when Brett began kissing her neck, though she didn't stop him.

He had embraced her from behind, and his hands ran over her body all while he kissed, nibbled and dragged his tongue along her neck. Eyes closed, she grasped his wrist, pressing his hand to the middle of her chest. He squeezed her breasts and slid his hand up to her neck, fingers clutching, turning her toward him.

Pulling her close, he kissed her mouth, teasing her open lips with his tongue. After kissing more than five minutes, he pushed her back onto the sofa, pressing his body on top of hers, undoing three buttons between her breasts. He had begun wedging his hips between her thighs to open her legs when she stopped him.

"What's wrong?"

"I'm sorry, Brett, but it's not going to happen. Not tonight."

"Why?"

Pushing him away, she swung her feet to the floor and sat up, re-adjusting her blouse.

"Because it wouldn't be right. Because it wouldn't be *real*."

He sighed, staring straight ahead.

"Wouldn't be real? And what's that supposed to mean?"

"It just means that you don't have to prove anything to me, Brett. You don't have to prove the *machismo* thing or anything else. I already think you're a handsome and awesome person."

His tone was sarcastic.

"Yeah, a really nice guy who does nothing for you sexually."

"That's not the case. It isn't that I don't want you."

"Then what is it?"

She clutched his hand.

"Want an honest answer?"

He turned toward her.

"Yeah, I think so."

"Well, you know about Charles. I'm not sure when or if I'll ever get over that relationship, but he really hurt me, and I'm not about to be hurt again, if I can help it."

She gazed into his eyes.

"You're a wonderful man and I could very easily fall for you, but somehow I think you have some unresolved issues involving your sexuality."

He began a response, but she cut him off.

"Now, I know you're going to tell me you're not gay or bi, and I know you don't want to be, but I've gotten to know you very well in this last year. Without going into details, which might be embarrassing, we both know there are some unresolved issues, issues you'll have to work out within yourself."

She smiled.

"I'm not trying to be selfish or insensitive, but right now I'm just too beat up and too hurt to start anything new, especially if there are unresolved issues. After Charles, I don't know if I'll ever be able trust another man. He really hurt me. He was never honest with me. I just need you as my friend right now."

Brett sat back on the sofa and swigged from the half-full brandy snifter. He seemed sad as he stared across the room at some invisible phantom crouching in the corner, at some demon that had taken a place there, squatting, mocking him, at the tragic reenactment of his most painful memories. His eyes glazed over, his voice was theatrical with a slurred British accent.

"I myself am indifferent honest; but yet I could accuse me of such things it were better my mother had not borne me: I am very proud, revengeful and ambitious, with more offenses at my beck than I have thoughts to put them in, imagination to give them shape or time to act them in. What should fellows such as I do crawling between earth and heaven? We are arrant knaves, all; believe none of us."

Across town, Barry sat alone in his sanctuary, table covered with documents before him. Hidden behind his many locks and doors, he removed the patch, exposing the hideous ruined eye socket. Over the years, he had grown accustomed to the appearance of his naked face, had even come to feel his deformity was part of his character, part of what made him a good lawyer.

In a college philosophy class, he read Homer's *Oddesey* and the play *Cyclops* by Euripides. In solitude, he often considered the symbolism involving Polyphemus, the crude and vulgar giant with one eye in the middle of his head. With limited vision, *abrupt of emotion, crude and clannish*, Polyphemus the Cyclops, lacked the balance, discernment, wit, wisdom and humanity of the two-eyed men he encountered.

For many years, Barry believed that when he lost his eye, he lost kinship with the human race. He believed this lack of affinity made him the superb defense attorney he turned out to be, unbalanced though he was. He was never comfortable with people. Rather, he felt at peace only when cloistered in his forty-fifth-story cave in the Transamerica Building, symbolic monolith rolled against the door.

Doodling on a tablet at the desk, he was startled when the

phone rang.

"Barry Divine."

He smiled upon hearing the voice and sat up in the chair.

"Oh yeah, it went as well as anyone might expect, especially since I never got a chance to put on my key witness."

Self-conscious, he put the patch back on his eye.

"No, she split San José and no one has a clue about where she is. She speaks Spanish. She could hide out anywhere down there."

He paused, listening.

"Well, I put her sister Aida on and got her to say Garner and Harris' were assholes and that their harsh tactics scared Stephanie into hiding outside the country. It saves a little of my credibility, but it doesn't help with the alibi."

He smiled, nodding his head.

"Thank you, Rikki, but because you're Rikki Thomas, I know you didn't call me at 4 o'clock in the morning to wish me the best. What do you want?"

Across the country in Washington D.C., Rikki sat nude on the down-filled comforter, rubbing cocoa butter onto her freshly-shaven legs. She had gone to Washington with Claudette, who had accompanied Charles there on business. Claudette lay asleep next to Rikki under the blankets.

In soft tones, Rikki answered the lawyer.

"Well, as you know, those assholes forced me out of San Francisco, and though I was going to leave anyway, I resent being blackmailed into it."

Barry's face showed puzzlement.

"Okay, so what are you telling me asking me to do?"

She sighed.

"Well, it was that asshole Webber who went out of his way to get something on me, so I went out of my way to get something on him."

"What did you get?"

She smiled.

"A story. A story complete with pictures."

"Well?"

"Well three years ago, a young woman by the name of Tasha Taylor was arrested for soliciting. She was a very pretty girl, went for four-fifty an hour and stayed busy. Anyway Webber, the married man that he is, saw her at the station the day she got arrested and decided to rescue her from her squalid lifestyle. He called in some favors and got her charges dropped."

Barry smiled, grabbing a notepad.

"Nice guy. Go on."

"Then he started hanging out with her, and somewhere along the way, he couldn't resist. Pretty soon, they were banging, in his office, in his car, in hotels, all over. And like all those other small-dicked assholes, he lost his head and got jealous, especially when she got the late night calls from regular clients. He wanted to get her a legitimate job, so he pulled some more strings and got her hired at the department."

She rose from the bed and opened the curtains to reveal a gray September morning sky. Charles was at the Pentagon, at a briefing on an attack by US destroyers and commandos on Iranian oil installations in the Gulf.

"Suffice it to say she didn't do well, couldn't type, couldn't do filing, wasn't even good at answering phones. She hated the job, especially since she was making less than five hundred a week. You still with me, Barry?"

"Yes. It's a good story so far. Go on."

"So what she did was trade a glamorous life of four hundred fifty an hour for a full-time piece of crap job paying five hundred a week, all so she could be Webber's little slut on the side. She was dumb, but she wasn't completely stupid, so it wasn't long before she was doing a little moonlighting in her off-hours. That lasted until it started affecting work, and then when she missed a few days, Webber figured it all out. Pissed off that she was cheating on him, he had detectives set her up and arrest her for prostitution."

Barry sighed, pen in his hand as he doodled.

"Well, that's Dennis Webber. Am I supposed to be surprised?"

"That's not the worst of it, Barry."

"Really?"

"I told you I *had* something."

She returned to the bed.

"Tasha swears the detectives planted an ounce and a half of cocaine in her apartment to make sure she did some time. She's still in. Got eight years."

"Oh really? Any idea who the detectives were?"

"Thought you'd like to know. The detective who found the cocaine was someone of interest to you, Inspector Elliot Garner."

Barry stood, contemplating, somewhat perplexed.

"That's interesting, Rikki, but as far as the trial goes, I've already rested, and even if I hadn't, Morgan wouldn't let it in. I wish there was something I could do with that information, but there's just no way."

After a pause, Rikki began.

"Well, probably not, but I called to ask you for a favor."

"And what's that?"

"I need you to somehow get to that reporter, that Yamakita woman. I need for her to go over to the prison in Vacaville. Tasha's sitting there waiting to go public with her story."

"Now Rikki, I'm a lawyer on this case. That could be construed as tampering. I'm barred from doing that. Why don't you just call Yamakita yourself?"

Rikki sighed.

"Because she doesn't trust me. She'd expect hidden motives. So if I asked her, she'd be skeptical of Tasha and lose any objectivity. In the end, she wouldn't trust the story enough to spend the time to investigate it, let alone go forward with it."

Barry nodded.

"You're probably wrong about her, but if all you want me to do is get someone to tell her to go over to the prison, consider it done first thing tomorrow."

"You're the best, Barry. And who knows? If the story breaks soon enough, maybe it'll somehow help you along."

He tossed the pen onto the table.

"I wouldn't exactly complain. At this point, I need all the help I can get."

CHAPTER 39

"Ladies and Gentlemen, I commend you all for the careful attention you've given to this trial, for your understanding, for your patience, for sacrificing your basic liberty to be here. Hopefully, you'll be able to go home in a few days."

Destiny stood before the jury in the navy blue business suit, her hair pulled back.

"Hopefully you'll be able to take a few days off to relax, have a dinner in your favorite restaurant, entertain or be entertained by friends and family."

"Living in San Francisco, there's one thing we all probably have in common. Because San Francisco's such a beautiful city, friends and relatives from remote places always want to visit us. As it's been my experience, many want to go to Alcatraz. So we go over to Pier 43, take a ferry, take a look at the island, examine the prison, hear about its history, and then we get back on the ferry and head home."

She turned, facing the jurors.

"You know, in many ways this trial is like that journey out to Alcatraz. It's like a trip to tour a huge island body of evidence. Remembering back to the first day of the trial, Judge Morgan called the court to order and there you were, sitting in those seats, waiting for the journey to begin. In our opening statements, Mr. Divine and I, your primary tour guides, did our best to carry you across to a place where you could best examine the evidence of this case.

"We did our best to prepare you for what you would see and hear when you got there. We promised you witnesses, who like additional guides, would provide key information. And we promised evidence that you would be able to examine with your own senses. You knew from the beginning that you would go on two separate tours of the same island: one that the State would provide; and one provided by the defense. So after our opening statements, you were there."

She neared the jury.

"You were charged with the responsibility of carefully examining that body of evidence for the purpose of rendering a decision when you got back home. So you heard the State's case, you saw the gory crime scene, you saw how Lynette Alexander had been violently murdered, you heard our witnesses, you listened to our experts. Then the defense presented their case, or their tour of the evidence. You saw their witnesses and you heard various explanations and theories from their experts."

She paused, nodded and continued from a more comfortable distance.

"So here we are, ready to board the ferry for the journey home. Now's the time to reflect on everything you saw and heard back there. Now's the time to put it all in some perspective. As I stand here before you, perhaps you should be reflecting on the job I've done as your guide. Perhaps you should be reflecting back to that first day and to the things the State promised to show you. Was the State's tour everything it promised to be? Did you see the evidence I told you about? Did you hear the witnesses I promised? But by the same token, how did the defense's case stack up to what you were promised? Did their tour live up to its expectations?"

She sighed, smiling with tight lips, mentally changing direction.

"And now, as we board the ferry for the journey home, Mr. Divine and I will provide a final service. We'll help you answer those questions in addition to the central question pertaining to this trial: Did Jordan Alexander willfully, unlawfully and with malice aforethought murder his wife, Lynette? According to the evidence you saw and heard over the past eleven weeks, the answer to that question is unequivocally, 'Yes.'"

She nodded toward Brett and Gail, who rose and set up two easels. Using charts and displays, Destiny began a point-by-point examination of the evidence brought forth in the trial. First, she reviewed key witness testimony involving the time and nature of Lynette's murder, including the medical examiner's theory for the actual sequence of the wounds inflicted.

She called attention to the testimony of various officers and detectives who investigated the scene, to a defense stipulation offering that Jordan had a key to Lynette's house, to the testimony of witnesses who remembered the many bruises and injuries she suffered, to statements by Inez Lopez, Lynette's housekeeper, about Jordan's behavior in the week before the murder. Then Destiny began a discussion of the physical evidence that included,

1) *Blood*: though the results from the RFLP and PCR testing weren't allowed in, Lynette's rare blood type indicated that the sticky blood found by Osaka at Jordan's Haight Ashbury home had most likely come from her. The chance of any coincidence was a long shot. Blood that matched Jordan's type was also found at both residences, on a balled-up pillowcase in Lynette's bedroom and in

his own bathroom at home.

2) *Hair and Fiber*: after testing, the hair found with the blood on the screen in Jordan's bedroom was judged to have "most likely" been Lynette's. Beyond that, there were hairs found in Lynette's room that were consistent with the samples Jordan had given in compliance with a court order. Because the murderer had yanked her by the hair, Lynette's hair was found in various places, including on the seats and floor of the Rolls, supposedly in Stephanie Rodriguez's car, and on the carpet of Jordan's bedroom.

The fiber evidence, in her words, was "equally damning." First, there were microscopic fibers from a dark blue or black garment found on the white sheets of Lynette's bed. These fibers were a so-called match with the shred of blood-saturated material found snagged in a bush next to the Rolls where it was found in Golden Gate Park.

Destiny made it a point to remind the jury that both the waitress from Alioto's and Bernard Katz indicated Jordan was wearing a dark blue or black suit at dinner on the evening of August 17, a suit that had disappeared. A single textile manufacturer, who testified the fabric had been sent to only three designers, had produced the subtle pattern in the material. One of the designers just happened to be Hugo Boss, a perennial favorite of Jordan as indicated by the volume of Boss apparel contained in his closet.

3) *Scientific Test Results*: The absence of unknown fingerprints in Jordan's car was noteworthy, according to Destiny. There were no prints in the car other than Jordan's, and the idea of someone stealing a Rolls Royce for transportation in order to commit a murder was absurd. Then there was the tequila test. Patrick Kirby, the witness who saw the downstairs lights come on in Jordan's house at 9:00 corroborated its finding. The traces of flesh found under Lynette's fingernails were determined to be human and could have likely come from Jordan, who just happened to have a scratch on his face the next morning.

Destiny's next area of discussion focused on "The Missing Witness."

"Remember back to that first day. Remember what the defense promised you? They were going to put Stephanie Rodriguez on. She was going to be their star witness. But what happened? Why didn't you see her? *That* is one of the questions you'll have to ask yourself as you decide this case."

She went on to suggest that Mr. Divine hadn't put her on

because her testimony "contradicted the story the defense wanted you to believe. If anyone in this world could have provided a credible alibi for the defendant, it would have been Stephanie Rodriguez, but we never saw her. Why? Because Jordan Alexander is guilty and she knows it."

Across the room, a tight-lipped Barry passed a note to Jordan who read and nodded.

"The lack of an alibi establishes the fact that the defendant had the time and opportunity to commit the murder, but what about the other essential consideration, motive? Why would Jordan Alexander murder his wife? Ironically, that's the easiest question I've had to answer throughout the course of this trial. Dr. Wendt, the psychiatrist you heard during the trial, probably put it best. She said it was the classic *if I can't have her, then nobody will* syndrome. Jordan Alexander had controlled and dominated Lynette from the beginning, and weak, she let him. That is why she put up with all the physical and emotional abuses.

"But Lynette, owing to the support of friends, family and licensed professionals, finally wised up. She realized how dysfunctional her marriage was, and she got out. When she rejected Jordan, he became obsessed with her. Not because he loved her, but as Dr. Cipar pointed out, 'in his mind, the rejection became a public judgment and a component of his self-definition.' In short, he wanted to undo the rejection.

"His behavior and comments to her co-workers are evidence of that fact, and from that point, his irrational jealously drove him to anger, to threats and ultimately to murder. It's a common theme throughout human history. Like Shakespeare's Othello, Jordan Alexander murdered Lynette because he only *thought* he loved her, when in truth he was just irrationally jealous and insecure. *He threw away a pearl richer than all the tribe.* So while we've already established time and opportunity, now we have a motive."

On Destiny's cue, Brett, who was seated at the prosecutors' table, withdrew a stack of posters or pictures from a leather portfolio, rose and placed them face-down on the table next to her.

"Unfortunately, for every person in this room except the defendant, there were no eyewitnesses to the murder of Lynette Alexander. However, if you indulge me a little, I offer you the opportunity to be eyewitnesses from a unique perspective. Albeit unwilling, you will be the witnesses to this gruesome and gristly murder. You'll witness the murder through the eyes of Lynette.

Taking all the facts gained through actual evidence and witness testimony, we were able to reconstruct the events of her life and of that fateful night in amazing detail. The story, as you already know, is a tragic one."

Taking a cardboard poster from the top of the stack, she placed it on the first easel at left. Glued to the poster was a portrait of Lynette, a much younger Lynette than the jury had seen in other photos. She seemed perky, girlish and thinner in stylish slacks and a sweater. Her smile was infectious.

"The year was 1969 and I'm a nineteen year-old college student who came to this romantic and glamorous city to pursue a career in painting at the San Francisco Art Institute. My name was Lynette Benson. I am blonde and about five feet six inches tall. My face is pretty, and I am often told I have a beautiful body. Compared to my new friends and classmates, I'm conservative, almost straight-laced. I love the Spaniards Picasso, Goya, Miro and Dali. I like to dance, especially to R & B. My father died in the Vietnam War and my mother lives in Glendale down south."

The photo Destiny placed on the other easel was one of Lynette and Jordan in a crowd, at a fancy social event. Because the crowd behind them was blurred and out of focus, the couple seemed to be the life of the party. They were embracing, posing. Jordan wore bell-bottomed slacks and a psychedelic shirt and sunglasses. His hair was long, nearly an inch below his collar. Lynette wore a floral mini skirt. Her long blonde tresses flowed over her bare shoulders and back.

"In 1971, during my final year of college, I met a guy I believed was the man of my dreams. His name was Jordan Alexander. He was tall, handsome and intelligent. He came from a powerful, wealthy family and he treated me like the princess my father always told me I was. It just seemed we had so much in common. We both loved art, we both wanted to see an end to the war in Viet Nam and we both loved children. It wasn't long before we fell in love with each other. We married a year later."

Brett placed the next photo over the first photo displayed. It was a recent one of Lynette posing with her three daughters, all four beaming with joy.

"Caitlyn was born in 1974, and she was precious, my oldest, the apple of my eye. She quickly became one of grandmother Dottie's favorites, being her firstborn great grandchild. Denver came in 1978, named after my only cousin. And then, in 1980, came

Lyndsey, my baby. Now Jordan had always been physical, meaning he sometimes slapped my face or slammed me into a wall when he was angry, but 1980 marked the beginning of a painful cycle of physical and emotional abuses.

"Where before he had slapped me, after 1980 he closed his fist and punched me in the face. He blackened my eyes it seemed at least once every month for one reason or another. He sprained my elbow and broke three of my ribs. He kicked me, he bruised me, he shoved me, he tried to strangle me on three separate occasions. And then, there was the so-called 'car accident.'"

Barry objected several times to Destiny's reference to the physical abuse, asserting she was *assuming facts not in evidence*, but Judge Morgan told him the court was inclined to indulge counsels on both sides during closing remarks.

The next picture was a waist-up photo taken by Allegra after the supposed car accident in 1984. In it, Lynette's eyes were swollen and dark. Her top lip was discolored and swollen on the right side, and her right arm was in a sling. There were bruises on the left side of her neck.

Barry and Previn had fought to keep Destiny from using the picture, but Judge Morgan had allowed it in with the stipulation that Destiny could not say the injuries depicted in the photograph were caused by Jordan. Despite the fact that Morgan had already ruled on the matter and other matters, Barry made numerous objections in open court to preserve rights to appeal in the event of a conviction.

"Why? you might ask, did I stay with him? Because I loved him. I loved him so much that I cared very little for myself. So, instead of telling friends and family about the abuses, I lied to protect him. And for those well-meaning friends who insisted he was wrong for the apparent injuries he caused, I became angry and accused them of trying to sabotage my marriage. He promised he'd get help, and I believed him, but with each passing month, the beatings grew more vicious and angry.

"In the summer of 1984, my mother was finally able to convince me to seek help, which I did. Through therapy, I learned to love myself and I learned it was never okay for anyone to injure me physically or emotionally for any reason. In November of that year, after Jordon slapped me, I forced him to leave. It wasn't easy. I was afraid, I felt guilty. I didn't know if I would be able to go on without him, but I discovered an inner strength I never knew I had, and I moved on."

Next, Destiny put up a portrait of a proud Lynette standing before the door of the *Aegis Foundation*, flanked by three women on each side. The other women seemed battered or impoverished in possessions and spirit, obvious victims. Yet as they stood next to Lynette, there seemed to be hope.

"More than that, I found the strength and the need to seek out and help other women who were in situations like mine. We had many wonderful success stories, and unfortunately, there were some tragedies."

Destiny's tone changed, becoming more somber, more melancholy.

"Jordan never got over the fact that I had found a new life without him. At first, he begged me to reconcile, swearing, promising to seek help, but I had heard his empty promises before. When that didn't work, he began threatening me and my friends, and he began accusing me of dating other men."

Destiny paused for effect.

"On August 1st last year, I served my husband divorce papers, which he ripped up and threw back at the person serving them. I believe he began planning an occasion to murder me at that time. During this trial, my housekeeper Inez told you he tried several times to get the girls out of the house by offering to keep them and by suggesting they visit his mother for a week. Frightened to be alone in the house, I refused. Inez also told you he left several messages on the answering machine inviting me out to discuss keeping the family together, and again I refused."

Destiny put on another photo of Lynette, shoulders up. Unlike the other headshots previously viewed by the jury, in it Lynette's ever-present smile was gone. Her expression was thoughtful, serious.

"I woke up on the morning of August 17th with an eerie feeling. On Sunday mornings, I always took the girls with me down to the foundation for a Christian service and then out to brunch, but on that Sunday, something didn't feel right. I moped. I called my mother to tell her something felt strange. Out of sorts, I missed the service at the foundation. In the hope of lifting my spirits, I took the girls over to the beach, and we stayed there all day.

"On the way back, we stopped by Jordan's because the girls wanted to personally remind him about a date they had with him to shop for school clothes. He wasn't there. He wasn't there because he was already well into the process of planning my murder."

Several of the jurors who listened were alternating back and forth from Destiny's face to Lynette's as they listened. All focused on her words.

"I can't say I know exactly what he did that day, but I'll tell you what I believe based on the evidence you've heard. At 3:17 that afternoon, he went to a grocery store specifically to buy a liter bottle of Jose Cuervo tequila. It was the only purchase on the receipt found in a crumpled brown paper bag from his garbage can in the kitchen. He bought it, but he didn't drink it then. When the bottle was found the next morning, there were over five good shots missing.

"If he drank that much tequila between say 3:45 when he got home and 6:30 when he left to go to Alioto's to meet Bernard Katz, and remember that's almost six shots in two hours forty-five minutes. If he drank that much, he would have been *drunk* when he got there. But both Heather Croftland, the waitress at the restaurant, and Bernard Katz said my husband didn't appear to be intoxicated in the least bit. No, he didn't drink any of the tequila before dinner. He had two glasses of wine at dinner.

"And then, after Bernard Katz left, he sat at the table brooding and agitated, working himself up to carry out the cruelest crime a person can ever commit against any person or society, the vile act of murder."

She stopped alongside the portrait, speaking from a place next to it.

"Heather testified he left the restaurant a little before 8:15, and Marcellus Taylor, the man who watched the lot, remembered seeing only one man drive away in the Rolls at 8:30. So where did he go? Well, according to the testimony of Patrick Kirby, his neighbor from across the street, he went home.

"Patrick testified he saw me and the girls drive up to Jordan's house shortly after 8:00, but he wasn't home. We stayed a few minutes and left. Then he said he saw a light come in the downstairs portion of the house at 9:00 p.m. He said that light didn't go off until 9:25. Inspectors testified that the lights weren't on a timer of any kind, so we know a *person* had to be inside the house to turn them on. That person was my husband. And what was he doing?

"It was during this time that he drank the five-plus monster shots of tequila. It was during this time he conceived the act, planned the act, that he developed malice aforethought. It was during this time it became a foregone conclusion he would murder me."

She paused again, letting the silence accentuate the last phrase she spoke.

"It was 9:20 and he was ready. He had poured a sixth shot, but he was already drunk. He didn't need it. What he needed was a knife, so he went over to a cabinet in the pantry and grabbed one of his large hunting knives, slipping it into the inside pocket of the dark blue or black suit he was wearing. He turned off the light. He left the house. He got in his car and he drove over to my house. It didn't take long, five minutes max. He was there at 9:30. Anyway, unknown to me, he had somehow managed to get a key, maybe from Caitlyn or Denver. I'm not sure how, but he went to the door and quietly let himself in.

"Hardly making a sound, he made his way through the house in the dark, finally reaching the stairs. I was up in my room reading, and the girls were in their room, completely knocked out after running all day at the beach. Moving deliberately, he came up the stairs and first closed the door to the girls' room, and then he tipped down the hallway to mine. He was already in the doorway when I looked up from the book."

Once again, Barry objected, complaining counsel was *assuming facts not in evidence.* He argued, "There is no way in hell she knows how Lynette felt and what happened in that room." Judge Morgan overruled his objections and suggested he'd be better off addressing and disputing elements of the prosecution's theory in his closing remarks.

Returning to the prosecutor's table, Destiny retrieved the State exhibit knife described as similar to the murder weapon and slipped it into the inside pocket of her jacket.

"Few people live long enough to describe the look in the eyes of a man whose mind is poisoned with the desire to commit murder. It is a look that will turn the blood cold in your veins. But it was exactly what happened when I looked up from that book. I wanted to run, but he deliberately stood in the doorway, blocking any means for escape. Then he reached over and turned on the radio by the door. When I saw the gloves on his hands, all hope vanished. No one wears gloves in the middle of August, not in California. I was afraid, but I didn't show it. Instead, I reacted angrily, telling him he had no right to let himself into my house.

"I insisted that he leave, but he stood there. I wanted to scream to awaken someone to help me, but his presence and his drunken condition made me worry for the girls' safety. I didn't want to make them a part of that terrible night unless I absolutely had to. He may have been bluffing, but I didn't want to take the chance. When he saw me glance over at the phone, he walked over and yanked it from the wall, careful to make sure I didn't dart past him. I spent the next fifteen minutes arguing with him, trying to reason with him, pleading for my life, though all in vain. His eyes glassy, he spoke in a slurred voice, condemning me for wrongs I never committed, accusing me of unthinkable acts and convincing himself that I had to die."

She withdrew the knife from her jacket pocket.

"He took the knife from his pocket and came at me, cornering me by the bed. Then he lunged. In an instinctive reaction, I threw my hands in front of my body to protect myself. The knife was sharp. It sliced off two of my fingers. At that point, I knew that if I didn't get out the door, I would die in that room. Jordan and I were both shocked to see my fingers lying on the floor, still twitching, and I took advantage of that moment in my attack. Remembering all I had learned from self-defense classes taught at the foundation, I surged toward the door, and finding him in the way, I clawed, I punched and I scratched to disable him long enough to make an escape.

"He was stunned initially, but he recovered. He stabbed me once in the thigh and another time in the shoulder. Despite pain that was horrific, all I could think to do was stay out of his way. As he chased me, I could smell the heavy tequila on his breath, I could feel my wounds flowing blood and I could tell I was becoming dizzy. I was all over the room. He stabbed me in flight four more times before he caught me, and then, taking the butt of the knife in his fist, he slammed me in the forehead, knocking me facedown onto the bed. I lay there helpless as he pinned me down and grabbed my hair, pulling my head back."

Knife in her hand, Destiny mimicked the actions she was describing.

"I watched the bloody knife surrealistically cross my field of vision from right to left before penetrating the left side of my neck under my ear. In one smooth motion, he dragged the knife across my neck, spilling distinguishable geysers of bright red blood onto the crisp white sheets. In the same motion, he lifted my body, pivoted and threw me to the floor. In my last moments of life, I watched him descend on me, knife stabbing furiously."

The tension in the room was powerful as Destiny put up the last two photos. One was of Lynette's nude, bloody and butchered body at the crime scene, and the other was of her in a casket with her daughters standing by, crying.

"The Lord was merciful to me. I didn't feel the majority of the 40 or more times Jordan stabbed me. I died on the floor in the exact position you're seeing in the photograph. Jordan, of course, left the scene in the Rolls, ditched it in Golden Gate Park and called his girlfriend, Stephanie Rodriguez, for a ride back over to the wharf and then home. That's when he called the police to report that he'd been mugged. But make no mistake about it."

She pointed toward Jordan who stared blankly ahead.

"That man murdered me. Jordan Alexander took my life! On August 17th, 1986, his purpose was to murder me. It was his intention to get away with it, and he will, but only if you let him. He robbed me of ever seeing my daughters grow up, of ever helping them get ready for their proms, of seeing them married, of being a grandmother, of all the joy and communion that mothers share with daughters. He took the life I counted as especially precious, but it wasn't only me. He robbed Caitlyn, Denver and Lyndsey. I was the only mother they had. He robbed my mother, Allegra Benson, of her only child. He robbed all the women I had dedicated my life to helping. He robbed the city of San Francisco of one of her citizens. And finally, ladies and gentlemen, he robbed you. He robbed you of my potential friendship and goodwill toward you.

"Now I don't know you, and though over the past 11 weeks you've only gotten to know me a little, I count you among my friends. The literal truth is, you're the last friends I'll ever have, the last twelve people in the whole world who can do anything for me. So I implore you: do not let my death go unpunished. Do not let the man who murdered me, that man right there, Jordan Alexander—do not let him walk away without answering for the terrible thing he did to me.

"You owe that to me as a woman, as a human being. You owe it to yourselves as individuals anointed as conscientious judges in this matter and you owe it to a spirit greater than yourselves, the spirit of justice. So as I fall silent for all time, my last words to you and the world are these, please hold Jordan Alexander accountable for what he did to me. Please hold him accountable for murder, which as you have seen and heard, though it have no tongue, will speak with most miraculous organ. Thank you."

CHAPTER 40

The Dennis Webber story broke in a big way, and the timing couldn't have been any more inconvenient for Destiny, and more benignant for Barry. Ironically, it was *San Francisco Chronicle* reporter Kiyomi Yamakita who wrote it.

Days earlier, Kiyomi received a visit from a well-known Madame in town who told her the sad story of Tasha Taylor and her inappropriate relationship with Police Commander Dennis Webber. She told Kiyomi about the strings Webber pulled and about the affair, with details more graphic than the reporter wanted to hear.

When asked about the timing of the revelation and a possible personal motivation, the woman said her conscience would not let her remain silent any longer. She insisted that Tasha was a tragic victim and that some responsible person really ought to look into the matter.

However, she did not tell Kiyomi that regular patron Barry Divine had asked her to call because he didn't want to be involved in breaking the story. Moreover, Kiyomi had no idea the story surfaced only after Rikki Thomas had paid a substantial sum to the Vic Ehlers Agency.

When Kiyomi visited Tasha at the prison facility in Vacaville, the story that emotional Tasha told was compelling. It was a story that begged retelling, that struggled for life, that longed to breathe before the jury rendered a verdict.

Kiyomi naturally, was torn between her journalistic duty to report the story and her friendship with Destiny. She realized early on that Tasha's revelation could influence the trial's outcome, but she felt compelled to go to her boss with it.

When the paper's chief editor caught wind of the story, she ordered Kiyomi to write it. Thus on the eve of its breaking, she had asked Destiny to meet her at the Fog City Diner for coffee, conversation and a surprise preview.

"Goddammit Kiyo! How could you *do* this to me? I don't believe this! You're, you're no better than the rest of them! Goddamn you!"

Frustrated with what she was reading, Destiny slammed the notebook on the table.

"I thought you were my best friend! I've confided in you all this time. I've told you my concerns about this case. You know what I sacrificed! How could you do this to me!"

Kiyomi sighed, stiffened her jaw and answered.

"Destee, I know you're angry, and I understand why, but this has nothing to do with you and me. I was ordered to write the story, and I just did my job."

"Bullshit! How long have I known you, Kiyo? You went after that story! You went after Webber! It's obvious from the way you wrote it!"

After a pause, Kiyomi acknowledged Destiny's assertion.

"Okay, and if I did?"

"Then that makes you a sleaze like all the other reporters. You assholes are the scourge of the modern world!"

Offended, Kiyomi answered in kind.

"And when we all go to hell, you lawyers will be one rung beneath us."

"Fuck you!"

Kiyomi's response was loud enough to make the nervous server move away from the table.

"No, fuck *you*! I don't understand what the problem is here, Destiny. It's just a *story*! The trial's almost over. You've already done your closing argument! Your jury's in a fucking hotel with no access to anything about anything! What difference is it going to make?"

"Oh please, Kiyomi! We both know sequestration in this case hasn't meant shit! They're not supposed to have access, but somehow they do. They're going to hear this story minutes before Barry's closing, and he's going to play up that Webber shit!"

Destiny batted her teary eyes, wiping the corners.

"I thought I *had* him. As a matter of fact, I'd never been more confident before about getting a conviction, but now you're giving Barry a chance to pick off a juror or two by playing up this piece of crap you wrote! I can't believe it! On what'll be the last day of this trial, someone I've called my best friend does this to me!"

She sighed, almost resigning, tears flowing from her eyes.

"After all I've sacrificed working on this case! Kiyomi, you of all people, knew what this meant to me!"

Kiyomi was beginning to cry. She reached for her best friend's hand on the table, but Destiny pulled away.

"Don't!"

Destiny stood, looking toward the exit rather than at Kiyomi.

"Don't! You've done your job. You've earned your thirty pieces of silver! You've written your story. You've been true to your sick, amoral profession."

She grabbed her purse from the table.

"But at what cost? As far as I'm concerned, we're no longer friends."

Kiyomi rose and started to follow, but she stopped, knowing it was probably best to let Destiny walk out the door and disappear into the cooling fog of San Francisco Bay.

He stood before the twelve for almost a minute before grinning.

"I don't know about you, but I'd rather be fishin. I'd rather be out on the bay. Sunny warm day, barefoot, out on one of the piers, line in the water, cold beer at my side, radio tuned in to the Giant's game. It just doesn't get any better than that."

He paused, his smile sarcastic.

"I guess I'm reminded of fishing because, like Ms. Mitchell suggested, we all got on a boat and went out to that huge island of evidence. I went to take you on a tour, but somehow I think Ms. Mitchell and the rest of the prosecution team brought along their fishin poles. You see, contrary to what she's suggested to you, not one person in this room, not you, not her, not me, not even Jordan Alexander knows the *details* about what happened in Lynette's room on August 17th last year.

"We know she's dead for sure, but nothing else is certain. This is a circumstantial case. All anyone can do is look at the evidence we've been fortunate enough to collect and guess about what the evidence might or might not say. Ms. Mitchell did yesterday what any good prosecutor would do. She put together a real good story or theory about what the State wants you to believe happened. She made it powerful, she made it realistic, she made it *tempting* to believe, and then she floated it in front of you, hoping you'd bite and get hooked.

"Now maybe some of you already have, but before you allow yourselves to get completely reeled in, you owe it to yourselves *and* to Jordan Alexander to resist for a moment. Don't get taken without a fight, stop yourselves dead in the water. Let's think this thing through, okay? You're all very intelligent. That's why you're here. So why don't we, together, go over the evidence of this case. And in the end, let's see if we'll be able to recognize the State's case for what it is: a flawed theory, a false lure."

He posed for effect, affected a tight-lipped smile and continued.

"Before we begin, I just have to admit to you, I don't have all the answers either. I can't tell or prove to you what happened on August 17th. No one can. We can however, get the sense of what *didn't* happen. For instance, no one can accuse any of you twelve of the murder because somewhere along the line in the investigation, whether you knew it or not, each of you were *eliminated* from the list of potential suspects. That's the way an investigation goes.

"When Lynette was murdered, the detectives were immediately faced with the question, *who could've done this horrible thing?* At first thought, *any*one in San Francisco could have done it, but then they began to see clues that helped them eliminate the vast majority of this city.

"When the detectives on the scene initially suggested that the murderer was most likely *a tall and powerful male*, they were able to eliminate most of the women, elderly persons and disabled persons who live here. The fact there was no sign of a forced entry led them to believe the murderer or murderers used a key to get in. That meant either 1) he or they knew Lynette, or 2) the murderers had contact with someone who knew Lynette and had a key. Remember, you women jurors were eliminated as suspects early on. None of you men knew Lynette personally, and as far as we can all tell, you had no access to a key. So you were eliminated soon thereafter.

"Now this all happened very quickly, within hours of discovering the body. As the investigation narrowed, it became necessary to examine more closely all the tall, powerful males who knew Lynette. It became necessary to ask two vital questions. Who of the remaining suspects had the opportunity to commit the murder? And who on that list had the motivation, or motive, to do it? Certainly some on the list had alibis, and as alibis go, some were probably better than others. So an investigation that started out as fair and open quickly became more subjective."

Leaving the vicinity of the jury box, he walked toward Jordan and took a position so that Jordan sat between him and the jurors.

"And there folks, is where the entire investigation went awry. What I mean by subjective has more to do with the opinions and notions detectives brought *in* with them from the get-go. For instance, if detectives for whatever reason thought a certain suspect was a grade-A jackass, it follows they might be less inclined to believe his alibi, regardless of its merit.

"But if they really dislike a suspect and they're not careful, there is a genuine danger they might impugn *false* motives and create or collect only the evidence that incriminates that suspect. At the same time, they might ignore or disregard evidence that points away from him, or at least to other possibilities. When two or more persons consciously work together in such a manner, I believe the proper way to label it is a *conspiracy*."

Patting Jordan's shoulder, he again walked toward the jury.

"Yes, a conspiracy. We wince at the word, because most of us don't really want to believe they go on, but they do, and they're especially treacherous when they're carried out by the men we trust to provide the facts.

"Folks, the whole problem with the prosecution's case is that they've put their blind trust in these guys. They've completely relied on what these police officers and detectives have testified to and written in their reports. I don't blame the other side for their Byronic innocence, but it would be unconscionable for any of you to fall into the same trap. There's just too much at stake.

"This is Jordan Alexander's life you're deciding on here. Let justice be blind, but you, the jury, have to go into these deliberations with your eyes wide open. So before we go over the evidence and testimony these detectives have put before you, you as wise jurors must consider the credibility of the sources you've seen, and that is the credibility and motives of the police themselves."

He walked to the defense table and took a document, a police record, from Lisa's hand, holding it out.

"First and foremost, let us consider the Police Commander, Dennis Webber. This is a man who came before you and told you he didn't particularly like the Alexander family. Others testified that over the years he had made many disparaging remarks about the family, and specifically, one witness swore under oath he heard the commander say he was going to *get Jordan one of these days*.

"Now if you remember back to the prosecution's case, remember? Webber is the one who threatened a patrolman with discipline if he didn't arrest Jordan during a visit to settle a domestic dispute. It was Webber who made sure Jordan was arrested and made sure Jordan spent the night in jail. The charges, by the way, were ultimately dismissed. While Jordan was at the station, an officer reported that Webber argued with Jordan. He said 'they were in each other's faces.' Does that sound like an animus to you? Think about it. After that, does anyone believe Webber could oversee a fair and unprejudiced investigation involving Jordan? No, and we actually see the proof a few years later."

He tossed the record aside.

"On August 17th, when the report went out that Lynette Alexander had been murdered, Webber and the police automatically believed Jordan was the killer. Now that's not entirely unnatural. The husband or boyfriend is always a logical suspect, but Webber went beyond that. Instead of sending his best detective over to the crime scene on Sacramento Street, he sent Inspector Osaka to Jordan's Loma Vista Way address to watch the residence.

"Inspector Osaka however, didn't go directly over to Loma Vista Way. First he stopped in the vicinity of the crime scene. He testified he was curious and just wanted to look. But taking into consideration he was acting under the orders of a man who hated Jordan, one has to ask, *Was there something more insidious going on?* Did Osaka have secret orders to carry evidence back with him over to Jordan's home? Did Osaka plant the blood evidence in Jordan's bedroom so the court would issue a permit to search the entire house? If you have to ask, folks, then I think the prosecution has a very big problem.

"But let's stop for awhile. Let's think about how Inspector Osaka got into the house in the first place. He told Stephanie Rodriguez he wanted to search the property because he was somehow worried Lynette's murderers might be calling on Jordan next. Now I don't know what he said exactly, but he must have been convincing, because she let him in. And then this trained detective, arguably one of the city's best according to Webber, then this detective, while searching the well-lit home in Stephanie's presence, somehow this crack detective failed to notice blood in four places downstairs. It's all in the record. Yet incredibly, hidden behind the screen in the bedroom, he managed to find a smear of blood in no more than one square inch of space in a dark area along the bottom corner. While conspiracy theories are the last things we criminal defense lawyers ever want to advance before a jury, in this case it would be criminal not to."

Right next to the rail, he was in the jurors' faces, his volume so low that Judge Morgan, along with the rest of the courtroom, strained and leaned forward to hear what he seemed to be confiding to the jurors.

"Why? Because a conspiracy theory, for its highly secretive and complicit nature alone, is hard to prove. It represents a high-stakes gamble in a criminal trial. I'm certain that, in her rebuttal, Ms. Mitchell will tell you a conspiracy in this case would have been impossible because too many individuals would have to be involved. Yet the facts disagree.

"Often a conspiracy can involve as few as two or three people who are the active participants, protected by the implicit silence of those who turn their heads to avoid being directly involved. It's the good ol boys' network, police style.

"If Inspector Osaka brought blood with him from the crime scene under orders from Webber, there's no question about a conspiracy. But let's just say, assuming the best about the commander, Osaka acted on his own. After he had planted the blood upstairs and the search warrant had been obtained, all it would have taken is for one of the other detectives, either Harris or Garner, each of whom had visited both crime scenes, to have smeared Lynette's blood in several strategic locations downstairs. The act could have taken less than one minute during a time in which Stephanie Rodriguez was distracted."

He backed to address the entire courtroom in a loud, confident voice.

"Now some of you might be thinking, 'this one-eyed fool of an attorney has just gone off the deep end.' Yeah, some of you are thinking, sure, Webber may have had it in for Jordan, but why would these detectives go through all this trouble to incriminate him? Why would they risk their careers and their reputations to fulfill Webber's agenda? Well, I can't exactly answer that question, but maybe you can, especially if you consider the fact that Webber is the Police Commander, a man with the power to influence careers, a man who may very well one day be chief."

He raised his hands, indicating symbolic forbearance.

"Then again, I could be wrong, but the important thing here is, the *facts* of this case don't make me wrong. The facts reflect that Webber sent Osaka to Jordan's Loma Vista Way address. The facts show Osaka visited the crime scene on Sacramento Street first, where he could have obtained blood evidence. The facts show he gained entry to Jordan's home under a questionable if not desperate premise. The facts show he searched the downstairs area of the home and found no blood. The facts show he discovered blood in a concealed area out of Stephanie Rodriguez's view. And the facts show that Inspectors Garner and Harris, two of the detectives who investigated the crime scene on Sacramento Street, were among the first to arrive at the Loma Vista Way crime scene. You have to ask, why did they want to get in that house so bad?"

"Can I prove they planted blood downstairs? No, I can't, but I've proven the opportunity existed, and that folks, is enough. With those facts, it isn't unreasonable for any of you to have serious doubts about how those blood smears came to be located in Jordan's home. With those facts, it isn't unreasonable for any of you to have serious doubts about the credibility and motives of the police in this case."

He nodded in the affirmative, his raised eyebrows causing his forehead to wrinkle.

"It's like I said in the beginning. No one in this room can prove what happened in Lynette's room on Sacramento Street August 17th last year, but we can get a sense of what didn't happen. The facts provide that at 11:30 p.m. on August 17th, Jordan made a call to the police department to report he was mugged and his car and keys were stolen. That report, as revealed in witness testimony, indicates Jordan said he was mugged and thrown in a garbage bin where he was unconscious until about 10:30. Contrary to the prosecution theory about Jordan receiving a scratch and bruises in a struggle with Lynette, Dr. Chinn testified his injuries were consistent with a beating sustained from a typical mugging.

"And Marcellus Taylor, the parking attendant, though he said he saw Jordan's Rolls Royce leave the parking lot, he said he couldn't see who was in it. So if Jordan, who suffered injuries consistent with a mugging, lay naked and unconscious at the bottom of a garbage bin until after 10:30, there is absolutely no way he could have committed a murder the medical examiner says happened between 10:00 and 10:15. He literally couldn't have."

Ironically, Barry was wearing his dark blue Hugo Boss suit as he delivered the closing. On the right sleeve, near the wrist/forehand, was his ubiquitous monogram: *BAD*. Though he was just a little better than average looking, he had an irrepressible charm and presence. Even Destiny, who fumed as she listened to his distractive arguments, couldn't help liking him on a personal level.

"He literally couldn't have. He simply wouldn't have. Yesterday, Ms. Mitchell suggested to you there had been some sort of history of abuse beginning in 1980, but the facts just don't support that claim. Sure, there were witnesses who came before you and said they remembered seeing her bruised from time to time, but not a one of them could tell you her injuries were a result of being beaten by Jordan. To the contrary, one witness, Mohammed Al-Azad, the motel owner, testified the minor injuries he observed Lynette having could have been from an accident or unintentionally inflicted by a person trying to defend himself.

"The prosecution has painted this picture of a maniacal, mean, insecure, psychopathic Jordan Alexander when all you have to do is look across the room to judge for yourself."

He walked over to Jordan, and stopped behind him, facing the jury. Waving his hand over the defendant's head, he continued.

"No matter how hard you look, you won't find a halo here, but Jordan Alexander is not a man would have murdered his wife and the mother of his children. His marriage to Lynette, like marriage for all of us, had its high and low moments, and we're not disputing the fact that at times, things got physical. Marriage, by its nature, is often very physical. Jordan loved Lynette, and as humans, we don't typically go out and brutalize and murder people we love.

"As for the psychologist who said Jordan only *thought* he loved her, that he was obsessed with her in some sick, tortured way? Maybe she should have been around during the time of Lynette's Valium addiction. I wonder if her opinion would have been so cynical and dismissive if she had watched Jordan take days off work to attend to Lynette, if she had heard his pleas to her mother and counselors to get her into a program, if she had witnessed the way he took great pains to keep the addiction from the girls in order to preserve their mother's dignity.

"Now I don't if or how many of you have ever had to deal with a loved one's addiction, but it's heart wrenching. It's not easy watching it, and it's not easy sticking around. You remember the counselor who came on and said 'Tough love is true love?' Well, it's true. Jordan's love for Lynette was put to the extreme test, and by being there for her, by sticking by her, he showed the world how much he loved her. No one can take that away from him."

Smiling, he walked over to the table and lifted a cardboard poster, putting it on an easel that Lisa had just placed in the jury's view. It was a picture the jurors had seen before.

"During the trial, you heard a lot about a supposed incident in 1984. You saw this unflattering and disturbing picture of Lynette with various bumps and bruises on her face and body. Her mother took the picture, and for all of us, especially for Jordan, it's not easy to look at.

"The prosecution would have you believe that Jordan, in some psychotic fit of rage, beat her up, causing those injuries. But folks, Dr. Wagner, the physician who examined Lynette right after the photo was taken, came before you last week and told you that then and now, he believed those injuries were the result of a car accident and had no reason to suspect otherwise.

"Beyond that, he told you Allegra Benson and Nora Drew, Lynette's own mother and aunt, indicated the injuries you're looking at were the result of a car accident. Now if Jordan failed to check the brakes or otherwise have the car properly maintained, on a stretch, you could blame him for the shocking injuries you're seeing, but beyond that, it was a car accident. They happen every day. It simply wasn't his fault."

In conversational tones, Barry continued his point-by-point examination of the facts and his rebuttal to Destiny's closing. Next, he argued motive, declaring Jordan was much too smart and much too popular to play the "if I can't have her, then nobody will" game. Barry offered,

"He's rich, he's good-looking, he's charming. He could have had just about any woman he wanted. The problem for a man like Jordan isn't getting stuck on one woman. By contrast it's the challenge of sticking to one woman."

Rather than criticizing psychiatrist Judith Wendt on damning statements made during the trial, he said that while she was very knowledgeable and capable, her errors in judgment occurred because she had never met Jordan and others close to him before rendering such a one-sided opinion.

Prosecution witness Patrick Kirby, Jordan's neighbor from across the street, presented a real problem. Patrick testified he remembered seeing lights come on and stay on in the downstairs portion of Jordan's home between 9:00 and 9:25. He testified that in his job as a software consultant, he always kept a careful log for client billing according to hours logged on each assignment. A page from his logbook with time entries and a photo of the view from his desk were introduced as evidence.

His testimony was particularly damaging because the defense hoped to maintain that during the time of Lynette's murder at roughly 10:00, Jordan was lying unconscious at the bottom of a garbage bin. A presence in the home rendered this defense unconvincing to most reasonable persons, unless of course, Barry could suggest a rational explanation for the apparent factual conflict.

While his earliest impulse involved subpoenaing all Kirby's client records and searching for inconsistencies, errors and corrections, he decided to suggest something less antagonistic, though he relied on the jury to understand the subtlety of what he was intimating. Thus even as he praised Kirby for his neighborly diligence, he pointed out that Kirby did not specifically recall whether or not the Rolls was in front of the house, wryly asking, "How do you miss a Rolls Royce?" He concluded that if the Rolls wasn't there, then Jordan couldn't have been there under any circumstances.

Yet even as he tried to go from this suggestion to a suggestion that someone else with a key, someone like Stephanie Rodriguez might have briefly stopped by, Destiny objected repeatedly on the grounds that Barry was misstating the evidence.

Even more difficult to explain was the failure to produce witness testimony by Stephanie Rodriguez, the only person who could corroborate important elements of Jordan's alibi and substantiate various allegations of police impropriety. This was the most vulnerable area of the defense case, and Barry did his best to gloss over it and leave little for Destiny to take up in rebuttal. When he tried to suggest however, that Stephanie's absence was a result of fearing the police, Destiny objected again. Raising his hands, Barry abandoned the subject.

As he began to discuss the physical evidence, Barry first took issue with the so-called tequila test, calling it little more than frat-house frolics performed by the nerdy coeds at CIT who couldn't get dates on Friday night. He ridiculed the whole idea as impossible and far-fetched, suggesting the test would probably work in some legal thriller or a movie, but not in real life.

While he praised criminologist Desmond Collins for his careful collection methods and Dr. Flessner for his ingenuity, he said the test itself was fraught with too many unknown variables and uncertainty, concluding,

"If we're uncertain about our starting point, then we absolutely cannot trust the results that come out on the other side, regardless of Doc Flessner's credentials. The so-called tequila test told us nothing!"

According to Barry, there was nothing remarkable about finding blood that matched Jordan's type in Jordan's home. "We all bleed at one time or another at home," he said, "we bleed when we shave, we bleed when we floss our teeth, we bleed in the kitchen, and sometimes we just get bloody noses and bleed on things."

The explanation for finding blood that matched Lynette's rare type in Jordan's house however, involved re-implicating Inspectors Osaka, Garner and Harris while alluding to Commander Dennis Webber's alleged animus. He called the jury to question Osaka's motive for trying to get in the home in the first place, he called them to question why a detective under orders to survey a specific subject property took it on his own to visit a crime scene blocks away.

He asked them to question why, after investigating the downstairs portion of Jordan's home, Osaka saw no blood. He asked them to question why Osaka checked behind the screen, himself out of Stephanie's view. He asked them to question how a man who missed four large blood smears in a well-lit room somehow found a tiny one on a dark background in a dimly-lit corner near the floor in a bedroom. And he asked them to question the motives and actions of Garner and Harris and to consider the possibility that they knowingly or unwittingly transferred blood from the crime scene to Jordan's home.

The blood found at Lynette's that matched Jordan's type, he asserted, could have come from any one of possibly 300,000 persons in the city with that particular blood type. The far more interesting fact, he indicated, was the existence of a *third* blood type in the room, a "somewhat distinct" type that matched neither Jordan's nor Lynette's.

"This would indicate the existence of *another* person in that room, a person who was somehow involved, or at least involved enough to leave blood. And not just blood, but a *trail* of blood that could be traced out the door and along the sidewalk past Gina Fasone's home. If you recall Gina's testimony, she said she was frightened by a strange, scary man who walked in a suspicious manner along that path at about 10:00 on the evening of August 17th, pretty close to the time of the murder. You might also remember that we showed you a police composite of the person Gina saw."

The placard he placed on the easel displayed a generic sketch of a clean-cut black man with glasses from the September investigation. Despite the suspect's well-kept appearance, it was obvious the police artist tried to portray him in the most menacing way possible.

"Is this the face of Lynette's murderer? We don't know that

for sure, but we do know this person was more than likely in the room. Beyond that, it's likely this person bled in the room. So what's the connection there? That's a question you'll have to ask yourselves as you deliberate in this matter. If nothing else, the existence of a third blood type in the room, and following from that, the existence of a third *person* in the room kind of ruins the prosecution's theory, if you think about it.

"That very detailed story Ms. Mitchell told you yesterday? How does this third person fit in? Maybe she can explain it to you in her final rebuttal, or maybe she can tell you an entirely *new* story to explain it. You have to realize though, if she doesn't, you'll be forced to answer that question yourselves."

Before beginning his conclusion, Barry took a little time to discuss the hair/fiber evidence. According to Barry, it wasn't unusual that Jordan's hair was found in Lynette's bedroom because he had shared that bedroom with her for the last six years of their marriage. It would have been impossible for anyone to remove every trace of him from that room.

Much the same held true for the fiber. The shred of material from the dark Hugo Boss suit, he added, held even less significance, "especially since we all heard from a buyer that Macy's San Francisco Men's store alone sells no less than 220 of the suits every year."

As he removed his jacket to begin his conclusion, several of the jurors' eyes locked in on the Hugo Boss emblem on its inside lining.

"All arguments aside, Ladies and Gentlemen, we're all here today and we've been here for the past ten weeks because of a horrible tragedy that happened last August 17th. On that otherwise peaceful Sunday night, some person or persons entered Lynette's home and viciously murdered her with a large knife. We were all shocked and appalled. We all wanted to see the murderer or murderers apprehended and punished. We trusted the investigative branch of our local law enforcement to do their job and bring us the person or persons responsible for that gruesome crime. We trusted them so we could do *our* jobs, so we could make that person or persons answer for the murder."

He closed on the jury box.

"Unfortunately, somewhere along the line, something went awfully wrong. The entire investigative process became tainted with resentment and with hate, with politics and with vendetta. Objectivity was lost and with it the best opportunity we would ever get to finding the real killers, and that's no doubt the greatest travesty of all.

"Instead we got Jordan Alexander, a man who wouldn't have killed Lynette for anything in the world, a man who couldn't have killed Lynette because tragically, he was himself a victim of violent crime on the night in question."

Barry motioned to a portrait of Jordan on the easel, his face bruised and swelling under the eye.

"Just as I reminded you in my opening statement, the burden of proof in this case and in any murder case, lies on the prosecution. It is the prosecution's job to come before you, offering physical evidence and witness testimony, and to prove its case beyond a reasonable doubt.

"If now, as we close this procedure, you are left with lingering doubts about whether or not it was in Jordan's character to commit such a gruesome murder, the law requires that you render a *not guilty* verdict. If you have reasons to doubt whether, despite the police report of Jordan's mugging and other police reports that detail a rash of recent muggings on the wharf, it was physically possible for Jordan to have been at Lynette's to commit the murder, the law requires that you render a *not guilty* verdict. If you have reason to doubt the credibility, motives, and reliability of the law enforcement representatives you had come before you to testify, justice requires that you render a *not guilty* verdict. It's very simple at this point. You have only to ask yourselves: did the prosecution prove its case beyond a reasonable doubt?"

He wagged his head.

"The answer to that question is No. No. No way. No how. Why? Because in their great haste to rush Jordan Alexander to judgment, the prosecution and the police never stopped to ask, do we have the right man? No, instead they all looked at Jordan and said, 'Hell, we all hate this arrogant asshole, of course he did it!' And completely self-satisfied, they did their best to customize the facts in order to make the crime fit the man. They'll admit it's a clumsy fit, but they'll say it's a fit nonetheless. It's a circumstantial case, so they, like tailors, have pieced together hundreds of little facts like tiny shards of fabric and have created an uncoordinated suit that they want to hang on Jordan.

"Ah, but fortunately for Jordan, and for you if you are ever in his position: there was a catch. There are controls within our system, controls built-in to protect the innocent. The first of those is the presumption that anyone accused of a crime must be considered as innocent until proven guilty beyond a reasonable doubt. This is true even if that person never takes the witness stand. And the second control is vested in the twelve of you as jurors. It is a sacred, time-honored, respectable duty that none of you took up lightly.

"You have a duty to look at the facts of this case, and based on what you've seen and heard, based on your sense of justice, based on the legal requirements the judge will provide for you shortly, based on the overall merit of the cases presented before you, you have a duty to look at this sloppy, sorry, ragtag suit the prosecution has tried to hang on Jordan. You have a duty to say 'the suit just don't fit,' and with that in mind, you must acquit Jordan of the charges the State has brought against him. Thank you very much."

"Earlier Mr. Divine came up here and said you were all very intelligent. In fact, he said it was the reason why you're here. But if you really listened to him, it should have become apparent that perhaps he doesn't believe you're intelligent at all, not if he expects you to accept half-truths in place of facts, speculation in place of corroboration and nonsense in place of common sense."

Systematically, Destiny began her rebuttal to Barry's closing statement, beginning with what she described as a litany of half-truths. She disputed the way the defense had characterized Commander Dennis Webber, pointing out that Mr. Divine used several supposed derogatory statements by him out-of-context to create the "so-called animus the defense desperately needs you to believe." Any resentment expressed on the night Jordan was arrested for spousal abuse, she maintained, originated with Jordan as corroborated by the testimony from arresting officers and sheriff personnel at the jail.

"Mr. Divine also told you that, as evidence of his great love, the defendant took days off work to take care of his wife during her Valium addiction. Well, the record showed that he took exactly one afternoon off work to pick her up from the treatment clinic. One whole afternoon!"

She also took issue with Barry's attempt to downplay the testimony of Patrick Kirby, Jordan's neighbor from across the street. Having no reason to lie, the man specifically said he saw the lights come on in the house. In response to, "how do you miss a Rolls Royce?" Destiny reminded jurors that, because that car was often parked in the driveway over the course of almost two years, it had lost any novelty a Rolls might normally generate.

She pointed out the defense was "counting on you to discount statements by Dr. Popinjay, a serologist who came on and testified the third blood type in the room and elsewhere was likely Lynette's blood in some degraded form."

And she reminded jurors that Osaka missed the four smears downstairs and noticed the one upstairs because the sample upstairs had a flag in it, a mass of blond hair, "something else the defense doesn't want you to consider."

She brought up the dark blue or black fabric found in Golden Gate Park on the bushes next to the Rolls. She said that while Macy's typically sells 220 Hugo Boss men suits every year, only 36 suits with that particular fabric pattern had been sold in the three years the fabric had been used, only 12 in that color, and a clerk had remembered selling one to Jordan.

Destiny continued, asserting that, while the prosecution realized from the beginning that the case was circumstantial, the defense tried to make the trial speculative in nature. She said Barry offered a fantastic conspiracy theory but had done nothing to corroborate any of what he offered.

While admitting the prosecution's burden of proof, she pointed out the State's onus didn't include disproving wild, irresponsible and groundless theories and innuendo from the defense. She said there was no demonstrated motive or animus on the parts of Osaka, Garner and Harris, who would have been risking their very careers and probable criminal prosecution for participating in some elaborate evidence-tampering scheme.

"Why would three of the city's finest detectives take such a huge risk? What was the benefit? During the trial, we went over their records and found nothing to indicate misconduct on any of their parts. On the contrary, they were praised for their dedication and honesty. We should be proud to have those three detectives working in our behalf."

Anxious for the trial to be over at last, Destiny pressed toward her conclusion.

"He said you were intelligent, but he wants you to believe nonsense in place of common sense. All of you, and many others in this courtroom have been involved in this case over the past few months, but if you can, just try to stand outside of yourselves for a moment. Let's try to look at this thing from a common sense point of view. I just want to make a few points, and I promise I'll move on."

She smiled.

"Number one, on the spousal abuse issue. It's nonsense to think that just because no one actually *witnessed* Jordan Alexander as he brutalized his wife on many occasions, it just somehow never happened. More than a few witnesses came on and described her injuries to you in telling detail. Now the defense would have you believe all the injuries could be attributed to accidents, but that's nonsense. No one's that clumsy or unlucky. Consider, for instance, a rape that was never witnessed, because as rapes go, there aren't usually witnesses. Because no one saw it, does it mean it never happened and the rapist should not have to answer for it?

"Number two, the idea that Lynette's murder was a random killing. That too is nonsense, unless we're expected to believe that some stranger somehow got a key to Lynette's house from Jordan, went in and just murdered her for no reason. Nothing was stolen, she didn't owe the mob, she wasn't involved in any controversy and she had no enemies. It makes no sense that a person, without a motive, without any purpose whatsoever, would track her down and murder her.

"And the mutilation, which Dr. Cipar said was a result of frustration and anger. Only a person who knew her well could be capable of that degree of anger, a person who was angry with her because he had lost the stranglehold he once held. That man right there—the man who murdered her, Jordan Alexander. Common sense declares Jordan Alexander is the only person who could have murdered her, the only person who would have murdered her in that way."

She nodded toward Brett, who began retrieving a large poster board from a zippered portfolio. Placard on the table, he awaited the next cue.

"And finally, we come to the greatest nonsense of all. Jordan Alexander's implausible *garbage* alibi as advanced by Mr. Divine. The defense wants you to believe that just coincidentally, on the same night that his wife was murdered, Jordan was beat up and thrown in a garbage bin where he was unconscious for two and one half hours. Garbage!

"And just coincidentally, he didn't wake up until after the murder was over and the car had been ditched in the park. And just coincidentally, one of the really big guys who beat him up scratched his face with a ring or something, despite the fact that Lynette had a sliver someone's flesh under one of her fingernails.

"And just coincidentally Stephanie Rodriguez, the only person who could verify many aspects of his alibi, Stephanie just up and left the country and never testified at a trial that could very well send her boyfriend to prison for life. And coincidentally, detectives found samples matching Lynette's rare blood type in Jordan's house and blood matching his type in hers."

She sighed.

"Just coincidence? Now Ladies and Gentlemen, if you really are as intelligent as Barry Divine said he believes you are, is it coincidence, is it common sense, or is it nonsense?"

She nodded toward Brett who rose and placed the display on the easel.

"Way back at the beginning of the trial, in my opening statement, I told you that because I was presenting a circumstantial case, it was going to be a lot like solving a jigsaw puzzle. In the end you would have a lot of little pieces which, by themselves, don't tell you everything, but when you put them all together, I said a distinctive picture would emerge."

She could tell the jurors were examining the display, especially the empty spaces.

"The fact that the defendant was abusive doesn't tell us everything. It's just a piece of the puzzle. The fact that he threatened her and various members on her staff by itself doesn't say it all either, neither do the separate facts that he had motive and opportunity. We've spent ten weeks doing this, carefully putting the facts before you, arguing them so that they could be clear and distinct for you. And now, it's up to you to put them all together. Take your time. Do a thorough job, and while you're at it, please don't forget what this trial is all about: justice in the murder of Lynette Benson Alexander.

"You know, somehow I think when you put all the pieces together, you'll arrive at the picture of a violent, insecure, jealous and angry man who robbed Caitlyn, Denver and Lyndsey of a mother, who robbed Allegra Benson of a daughter, who robbed us all of a precious life that enriched our city, all because he selfishly believed that if he couldn't have her, then none of us would."

She motioned to the display. It was a large jigsaw portrait of Jordan, caught in a malevolent glare. There were pieces missing in various places throughout. She withdrew two puzzle pieces from her suit pocket and held them out before the portrait, seeking to find where each fit as she continued.

"The picture you put together is going to look a lot like this one here. Sure, there will be pieces missing. The trial would have been over on the first day if we had all the pieces."

Two of the missing pieces in place, she backed.

"So it will be up to you to put it all together, step back a ways, and then take a long hard look. You'll see that Jordan Alexander *is* guilty of murdering his wife, Lynette. You'll realize that, as alleged in counts one and two of the Information filed with the court, Jordan Alexander willfully, unlawfully and with malice aforethought murdered Lynette, and upon that understanding, you'll return a guilty verdict of murder in the first degree. Thank you."

Judge Helen Morgan's face had begun to show the enormous stress she was under. In addition to the demands of such a high-profile trial, her husband's ongoing chemotherapy treatment was a stressful ordeal. She couldn't smile even when she wanted to, and understandably so. She had seen Bob go from a robust 195 pounds down to 120 pounds in a little over two months. His once-handsome face and fingers were skeletal, the life force draining from his body.

It was Friday, so she wanted to get the case to the jury as quickly as possible to take a flight down to Los Angeles where Bob was recently re-hospitalized. Thus although both lawyers requested a brief recess before jury instructions were read, Helen insisted on just getting it "the hell over with." She read fast, impatiently, omitting some of the lengthier and convoluted areas in a few of the instructions, concluding with the following,

"You shall now retire and select one of your number to act as foreperson. He or she will preside over your deliberations. In order to reach verdicts, all twelve jurors must agree to the decision and to any finding you have been instructed to include in your verdict. As soon as all of you have agreed upon verdicts, so that when polled, each may state truthfully that the verdicts express his or her vote, have them dated and signed by your foreperson and then return with them to this courtroom."

CHAPTER 41

After jury deliberations had gone on for eleven days, the conflict and discord among jurors became apparent. The jury had chosen the person in seat 4, a seasoned, older black man who had retired as an airplane mechanic, as foreman, but not without great division. The alternate, who the judge assigned to seat 10 after the dismissal of an original juror for misconduct, wanted the job.

Morning after morning the jurors went into the chamber, and they'd stay until early evening. Some seemed stressed-out and spent while others were worked-up and irritated. Still others agonized, their glazed-over, hopeless eyes and expressions, awaiting the day it would finally be over.

The first leaks happened during the second week. According to an inside source as reported in the *Examiner*, the initial vote had been 8-4 to convict, and arguments from both sides had been passionate and angry. The jury asked for trial transcripts including testimony from Marcellus Taylor, Patrick Kirby, Dr. Wendt, Inspectors Osaka and Garner, criminologist Desmond Collins, serologist Cy Addelberg, Gina Fasone, Aida Rodriguez and others. In addition, they asked to see photographs of the blood smears from Jordan's home, the photograph of the view from Patrick Kirby's window, the display showing results from the tequila test and Lynette's medical records.

According to the source, the foreman, along with five women, jurors 3, 5, 7, 9 and 12 were convinced of Jordan's guilt while the white male replacement, juror 10, along with jurors 2, 6, and 8 believed the prosecution hadn't proved its case beyond reasonable doubt. Jurors 1 and 11, while they sided with the foreman, weren't committed to either opinion. So along with the foreman, who was black, were the three black woman jurors along with two white women who pressed for a first-degree murder conviction.

Juror 10, the white male Destiny determined was a "definitely a Nazi," along with the Mexican woman juror, the Japanese male juror and the young black male juror, held steadfastly that Jordan should be acquitted. Juror 1, the young woman who graduated from Berkeley in May, and juror 11, a homemaker from Potrero, simply voted with the majority, hoping to help sway the standoff. After the fourteenth day of deliberation, the Japanese male decided to join the majority, leaving the deadlock at 9-3, in a position all indications suggested it was destined to remain in perpetuity.

On Tuesday, October 13, an impatient Judge Morgan spoke to the jurors, hoping to help them consider a compromise verdict, but the jurors held to their polarized positions. A week later, the frustrated judge declared the jury as hung. Jordan Alexander would walk.

Public reaction to the non-verdict was mixed-to-disappointed. Many people interviewed by reporters on the streets indicated they would have felt more settled if there had been a decision one way or the other. "You could react," some echoed, "to guilty or not-guilty, but how do you react to 'we just couldn't make up our damn minds after all these months?'"

Many blamed the jury, criticizing the twelve for not having the guts and good sense to do their job. Others called attention to the amount of money spent on the trial, referring to it as an incredible waste of taxpayers' money.

Private parties were suffering the same dilemma, wondering what policy to adopt when dealing with Jordan Alexander after his release. Harsh condemnation of Jordan by women's groups, the city's blacks and the city's Christian coalition made him a liability for all practical purposes, though many were beholden to Jordan and the Alexander family for decades of contributions, public support and various business relationships.

Thus a small group of social, political and industry leaders met with Dottie, hoping to dissuade her from forcing Jordan on them too soon. Instead, she insisted they all attend a grand gala she was throwing in celebration of Jordan's release from jail.

For others, like Mayor Tony Martini, who was engaged in a tough battle for re-election against Peter Granucci, the non-decision was the worst of all possible outcomes. If the jury had acquitted Jordan, the mayor would have welcomed him back in illustrious fashion. If they convicted him, Martini could have distanced himself by expressing regret even as he reminded the city that "no citizen in this country was above the law." But this jury stalemate left him vulnerable, trapped between his loyalty to the family and his desire to win the election.

Granucci, a shrewd operator, was quick to condemn Jordan, declaring a guilty man had gone free. He challenged the mayor to condemn Jordan as well, but Martini refused to respond in any way. Surveys and polls reflected Martini's growing disfavor with voters so that for the first time since the election began, Mayor Martini trailed Granucci.

Barry Divine was in shock. At various times throughout the trial, he thought the jury might hang, but not leaning 9-3 to convict. As he sat in the isolation of his pyramidal sanctuary high above the city, brooding, he came to the realization that he had been perhaps a juror or two away from losing the trial.

"It was a great trial," he thought, "fought hard on both sides." But he was certain it would have been the other way around—he was convinced the defense would have been a juror or two shy of an acquittal, especially after the Dennis Webber story broke. In the end, he realized that eleventh-hour *Chronicle* newspaper article had saved Jordan's ass.

Barry stared into a mirror, examining the lines in his face, the gray at his temples. At forty-five, he thought, maybe he was getting a little old for these big cases. Maybe he was losing the passion.

He smiled as he thought about Destiny, about her anger, about her natural flair for the dramatic, about an inward commitment she held that *required* her to speak in Lynette's behalf. He admired and envied her for it.

He was sitting in the cell next to Jordan when the clerk called to announce that the jury had hung. Though Jordan was elated, Barry warned against early exuberance, even as he phoned the judge. The DA, he cautioned, was likely to try the case again, depending on the jury split.

When Barry found out Jordan was almost convicted, he was certain of a retrial. His articulated concerns however, were only noise to Jordan, who pressed Barry and the guards for a prompt release from the jail. A hearing to plead for his freedom was scheduled for Thursday, October 22. If acting DA Janice Prescott wasn't planning on retrying him right away, it was a foregone conclusion that Jordan would be out in time to attend the gala Dottie was throwing on Saturday in his honor.

Peter Granucci was the first to congratulate Destiny, though she was in no mood for the champagne or the speeches. Election tracking on a poster, the entire district attorney's office celebrated the end of the trial and Peter's late surge in the polls. Barring unnatural events, Peter Granucci would become San Francisco's next mayor.

In a speech to his former employees, he promised a brighter, more inclusive city and praised Destiny for the formidable way she had handled the Alexander trial. He told the story about how several old-fashioned individuals in the office had doubts and reservations when he first appointed her lead prosecutor.

They believed she could never be competitive in such a high-profile case because she was a black woman. But given the opportunity to prove them wrong, she did. In prosecuting one of the city's favorite sons, she had gone up against one of the best lawyers in the criminal defense business and almost got a conviction. That alone, he commented, was "a major accomplishment that should make us all very proud."

Sounding mayoral, Peter went on to praise Brett, Gail and Janice for all their hard work on the case. When asked to respond to or comment on Peter's comments, Destiny made a terse declaration about the need to oppose Jordan's release and the need to re-try the case. Uncomfortable, the revelers paused a moment and then carried on as if she had never said anything at all.

Before the night was over, Destiny cornered Janice in her office and asked when the motion would be made for a re-trial, but the interim district attorney was evasive and vague. She seemed skeptical about the idea and said she wanted to talk the matter over with Peter. Sensing the matter had already been discussed between the two, Destiny went to Peter, pressing the re-trial issue.

"I'm no longer the district attorney, Destiny. It's Janice's call. Besides, I don't know if I think a retrial's necessarily a good idea right now."

"What are you saying, Peter? You think Jordan Alexander should walk?"

"No, I'm not saying that. I'm saying people are tired of this thing. Believe me, I talk to them every day, and that's what they're *telling* me. The trial was long. It was drawn-out. It was expensive, and nobody thinks they got their money's worth. The people of this city don't want this thing re-tried, not now, possibly not ever. They could give a shit if Jordan walks."

As Peter turned and headed for the door, Destiny stood in his path, her right hand clutching his left shoulder.

"What about *you*, Peter? We were both in her room that night. We both saw what that bastard did to her! Are you going to just stand by and let him get away with it?"

Peter removed his glasses and he slumped a little, at last

sloughing off his mayoral air. Frustrated, he sighed.

"Destiny, I don't know. It's not as simple as all that."

His fingers massaged his forehead.

"Yes, I was there, and I feel the same way you do, but there's not much we can do now. We gave it our best shot. You were incredible out there, but we didn't get the conviction. We all feel terrible about Jordan walking out of that jail, but the people are saying it's time to move on."

"Screw the people, Peter! What about Lynette? What about—"

He interrupted.

"You need to forget about Lynette! Or at least forget about your private vow or vendetta. She's dead, and nothing you do is going to bring her back. Jordan had his day in court and he wasn't convicted. It's that cut and dry. It's time to let it go."

She peered into his eyes, her gaze steady and intense.

"Maybe you can do that, Peter, but I can't. I'm not some public ass-kissing politician."

His face showed anger as he waived his hands, indicating resignation.

"Oh, I'm not going to listen to this! You keep this up, Destiny, and even people like me are going to start believing you're the psycho-bitch lawyer they're all saying you are!"

Peter's words cut into Destiny's heart for manifold reasons. For months, she had been reading and listening to rude comments and innuendoes. She even got a few threatening phone calls. For months, she blocked it all out, rationalizing that the remarks and mischaracterization were made by ignorant people reacting to the trial, made by people who didn't know her. In the end, however, she had the distinct impression that even a few people she considered friends seemed to be shunning her in public.

It was subtle. Virginia Cooper, a lawyer friend who had been a dinner and drinks partner at least once a month for years saw her at the courthouse and didn't bother to greet her or even acknowledge her. She saw another friend in a restaurant who either couldn't see her two tables away or purposely ignored her. But Destiny considered herself a rational woman and strove to rise above insecurity and paranoia. Certainly, her friends didn't buy into or believe the things being said and written about her. Not the friends who really knew her, not the friends who really knew what kind of person she was inside.

Peter's comment about her being a "psycho-bitch lawyer" however, shattered at last whatever confidence was left. The trial had cost her so much—Charles, marriage, happiness, her best friend, the respect of her colleagues, her love for the law profession, her faith in the legal system and finally, her own self-assurance.

She just stood there looking away from Peter, batting back the tears that swelled in her blurry eyes. Her arms were crossed in such a way that she held her own body in a desperate embrace, shivering, fighting to be strong.

Realizing how much he hurt her, Peter reached toward her, his voice was warm and caring.

"Destiny, I'm so, so sorry. I lost my temper. I didn't mean that. I really didn't mean that."

The damage was already done. She shrugged her shoulders, still looking away, still battling back the tears, still unable to speak.

Peter continued.

"On the contrary, Destiny. I'm so sorry. You've been just fantastic through this whole thing. You showed the world what a great lawyer you are. I'm proud of you."

He turned her toward him, holding her in place at the shoulders.

"I know you feel like you've lost, but you really haven't. You're a winner in my book and in the opinions of the people that really matter. Look at it this way. It was a hung jury. Jeopardy didn't attach. Who knows? Maybe you will be able to try this thing again a few years down the line and win it. Courts are bound to let the DNA stuff in eventually. Your case will be even *better* then."

He couldn't help himself. He had been living it, sleeping it, breathing it for two months.

"And as mayor, I'll do everything in my power to make sure we re-try this thing. I promise you that."

Janice's discreet knocking precluded any additional promises by the candidate. She apologized for interrupting and insisted on Peter's presence for a photo with a union leader who recently endorsed him. Eager for the press opportunity, Peter hugged Destiny, kissed her on the forehead and hurried from the room.

Locking the door, she settled into her chair at the desk where she cried for more than an hour and before clearing out her desk, boxing her law and case books, packing up all her personal belongings and going home.

CHAPTER 42

Dottie Alexander spared no expense for the gala she staged at the *Top of the Mark*, the art-deco style twentieth-floor penthouse bar situated atop the Mark Hopkins Hotel on Nob Hill.

A little over a century earlier, a fabulous palace-like home sat in the same location at 999 California Street. It was, according to various architects, a Norman château with Victorian overtones and Gothic towers. It also contained a picture gallery 90 feet long and 45 feet high, a medieval-style music room and thirty Louis XV and gothic guest bedrooms. Yet, spectacular as it was, it burned to the ground in the fires of 1906 resulting from the great earthquake.

Affects of the earthquake ravished all the mansions that sat on Nob Hill, had ravaged much of the city. Three thousand persons lost their lives and 250,000 lost their homes. In all, 514 blocks, 28,000 buildings and an estimated 500 million dollars in material losses went up in smoke. A conflagration burned for more than three days during rampant looting, dynamite explosions and martial law-style executions. As thousands fled by sea, the city resembled ancient Pompeii in the wake of Vesuvius.

It was a grievous time to be living in San Francisco, yet it was an unthinkable time to be born in the city. Silver king Thomas Alexander's first grandchild Dorothy, or Dottie as he called her, was born at 4:15 a.m. on April 8, 1906, in his Rincon Hill mansion near the bay, and he was as proud as he had ever been. He saw her birth as an omen. He saw his first grandchild as the symbol of a reborn and grander San Francisco. Ironically, one hour later came the shocking fulfillment of his bedside prophecy.

Though the earth under the city shook for only 48 seconds, it was one minute that would change San Francisco forever. The ground rolled like the sea with 8-foot breakers in earth and cement. Great fissures opened, gulping down streets, houses and terrified people. The electrical systems for the trolley cars ignited fires, which engulfed the city.

Frantic people scrambled about, like startled ants after some breech in the nest, and yet, as it so often happens in nature, plague followed upon plague. The earthquake ruptured the city's water lines, rendering them useless for containing fires that burned at temperatures as high as 2,700ºF.

Thomas Alexander got his family and some friends out of the city on the large boat he owned. Safely out on the bay, he cradled his new granddaughter as he, like Lot's wife, looked back on the once glorious Sodom that burned so brightly against the dark, smoke-filled sky. From that day on, he called his only grandchild Earthquake Dottie, a nickname that would persist for 80 years.

True to her grandfather's prediction, Dottie did come to symbolize the spirit of the rebuilt city. Though she was only 14 when women became eligible to vote, she was an early advocate for women's rights.

Her life was a reflection of 20th century America. She was a carefree flapper and college student in the 1920s. She learned the family business in the 30s. In 1938, she married a ship-builder and had George, her only son, and two daughters, Elizabeth and Victoria. Neither she nor any of the children kept her husband's last name after she was widowed shortly after the war in the 40s.

During the 50s, she had affairs with a famous German-born Hollywood director, a U.S. ambassador, a Swedish prince and a 20-something Brazilian heir to a huge fortune, though there were others. She was a progressive advocate of the excesses of expressed freedom in the 60s and once allowed her coiffeur to frizz her hair in something resembling an Afro.

Her son George died in 1969, a victim in a single engine aircraft accident, leaving Dottie worried about who would carry on the family business. Jordan was only 20 at the time, but Dottie decided then that she would groom him for the job. Bullying daughter-in-law Jayne, she moved Jordan into her home and began teaching him everything he would need to know about making the most of wealth and doing business in the world.

She had three other grandchildren, Barry by daughter Victoria, Cynthia by daughter Elizabeth and then there was Philip, daughter-in-law Jayne's other son.

"Philip," she told Jayne, "didn't look like an Alexander" and would probably never amount to anything. Cynthia was "a wuss" and "didn't have the balls for the job." And Barry, his father's family was Jewish, and the Jews, she often said, had plenty enough money without hers. Though Dottie blamed Barry for his failure to get an acquittal for Jordan, she was happy that her favorite grandson was finally free.

Thursday's hearing to free Jordan was short with no opposition from the State, though groups of angry protesters chanted and demonstrated in front of the courthouse. Instead of going home or to his mother's house, Jordan went to Dottie's, where he remained in seclusion until Saturday's gala.

The Mark Hopkins didn't usually rent out the *Top of the Mark* on Saturday nights, but Dottie always found ways for getting what she wanted. The turnout was all she expected. She had invited 160, and 154 showed. Not surprising, every one of the 18 board members were in attendance.

The glittering room was decorated in turn of the century themes as the city twinkled in the background through grand windows that offered a panoramic view of the area. Cocktails and appetizers were served at 7:00, followed by an announcement that Jordan was on his way.

When he arrived at 7:45, dressed in a stylish new tuxedo, a gift from his grandmother, he seemed the same Jordan Alexander the guests knew from 14 months earlier. His renewed confidence was apparent as he approached the microphone at the podium and directed the guests to find their seats. The two television news crews and the select newspaper reporters that Dottie invited were stationed at a table in front of the platform where Jordan stood, ready to speak.

Everyone in his or her pre-ordained place, the "man of the hour" began.

"Thank you. Thank you all for being here, thank you all for believing in my innocence. I can't begin to tell you how much that has meant to me."

Dottie began in applause, and the rest of the room reluctantly followed.

"I want to personally thank my family: my grandmother, *Earthquake Dottie*, for all her support, my mother, Jayne, for always being in my corner, my cousin, Barry, for the excellent job he did defending me and finally, I'd like to thank my younger brother, Philip, for holding things down the way he did while I was away."

Philip, sitting 20 feet away, did not smile. His repressed anger re-colored his complexion in shades of red. His wife, next to him, held her breath, hoping her husband wouldn't lose his temper.

Jordan continued.

"But I'm back now. It may take me a few weeks to get up to speed, but I assure you tonight that I'm firmly in control of Alexander Enterprises, and I will run things exactly as I have in the past. Nothing has changed."

Again Dottie began in applause, but this time many in the audience, perhaps a majority of the audience, refrained from joining her. Philip, seething, scanned the faces in the room, his glare toward his brother, malignant.

Sensing the audience's discomfort, Jordan didn't mince words. He spoke in a reassuring tone.

"Look, I know there are some of you out there who aren't quite sure how to handle me because the jury was hung, and that's all right. I tell you tonight: I will be exonerated. The big difference now is I'm out. I'm free to use all my resources and the favors I've earned over the years to single-mindedly pursue the murderers of my wife. And make no mistake, I'll find them, dead or alive. Not just to clear my name and any lingering suspicion some of you might have, but to see justice done for the loss to Lynette, to my own family and to Lynette's mother, Allegra Benson."

He glanced across the room toward the empty chair that had been reserved for Allegra and continued.

"Now contrary to reports in the newspapers and on television, I'm not normally a violent person, but I want to issue the following warning to Lynette's murderers if they're anywhere out there listening."

His expression stern, he stared at the cameras.

"Turn yourselves in, because if you don't, you just better hope the authorities find you before *I* do. You see, for me, this is a highly *personal* matter. I won't mind going to prison and doing time for avenging the murder of my wife, if I have to. It's worth that much to me."

He continued as he pulled a document from the inside pocket of his jacket.

"You know, talk is cheap, and I refuse to deal in idle bullshit, so I'm putting my money where my mouth is."

He held the document out.

"Here I have a pledge to every citizen of San Francisco and citizens in every other city and county in the Bay. Today I am offering a five million dollar reward to anyone who can help me find Lynette's killers. That's five million dollars. Surely *someone* out there knows something, and five million dollars buys a lot of fried chicken and black-eyed peas."

It was clear some in the audience were offended and uncomfortable with the ethnic reference Jordan made. Yet he continued over the murmur.

"Five million dollars for any information that leads to an arrest and conviction. All any of you have to do call our toll-free number and tell us what you know. We'll do the rest."

He looked toward his brother.

"Now because my time will be divided between pursuing Lynette's killers and my duties toward all of you, I'll be asking my brother Philip to take a larger responsibility in our business transactions. So the relationships many of you have built with him over the last year, they won't be lost. Between the two of us, we'll decide what's best. Once again, nothing has changed."

He flashed the patented Jordan Alexander smile.

"I said it earlier. It must have been hard for some of you to come out here tonight to show your support for me. San Francisco is a notoriously political and factional town. But this isn't about politics or special interest groups. It's about friendship and loyalty. It's about the Alexander family. I want to personally thank our present and next mayor, Tony Martini, for coming tonight. He's hands-down the best man we've had at city hall in decades. But beyond that, Tony has been my friend throughout the tragic ordeal of losing my dear wife and my liberty in one fell swoop. You should all have friends so loyal. I'll tell you, when I was sitting in that cell waiting to answer charges for a crime I did not and could not have committed, I found out who my real friends were. I'll never forget who was there for me..."

He glanced about the room, his nostrils flaring.

"And who wasn't."

He sighed, concluding as servers placed first entrées in front of guests.

"I look forward to sitting down and chatting with each of you in the next few weeks to re-evaluate your respective working relationships with Alexander Enterprises. Thank you."

Dinner was quiet with little action except for the woman who crashed the party, shouting obscenities toward Jordan and calling him a murderer. The reporters, careful not to upset Dottie, never raised a pen, a camera or an eyebrow.

After dinner and dessert, Dottie stood at the podium to thank her guests who were gracious enough to show support for her grandson, the appointed heir to the family empire. Dottie was typically a forceful speaker, so while her speech that night was not up to her usual aptitude, it was adequate nonetheless. On two occasions, she lost her place and seemed disoriented, but she recovered and finished with her dream for Alexander Enterprises with "a steady Jordan at the helm." No one stayed for cognac or conversation after dinner. By 10:00, the room was empty.

Unfortunately for former district attorney Peter Granucci, a *completely natural unnatural event* occurred that night. At 11:15 that same night, Saturday October 24, the woman that reborn San Francisco affectionately knew as *Earthquake Dottie* suffered a massive stroke and was rushed by ambulance to the hospital. Frantic doctors worked for almost an hour, but Dottie was old and her body was weak and tired. She was pronounced dead at 11:59.

The entire city and many others in the Bay Area mourned her death. Flags over the city flew at half-mast the next morning, and story after story about Dorothy Alexander ran on the radio and television news stations. Sunday morning's papers featured photographs of Dottie at various stages of her life. Church bells all over the city tolled in her honor. Her funeral was planned for Thursday, October 27, five days before the election.

Because Mayor Tony Martini was such a close family friend, he was involved in much of the public display of mourning for Dottie. In fact, he led the city as it dealt with the impact and implications of her death. Only after she died did many people in San Francisco realize what a remarkable life she had lived and how her history was so intertwined with the history of the reborn city.

Stories of her benevolence, her business acumen and her progressive ideas came in from all quarters, including one from the Prime Minister of Japan. According to one prominent religious minister, she was "the closest thing San Francisco had to a home-grown saint."

Mayor Martini, who agreed to deliver the eulogy, benefited by a remarkable change in the polls as a Wednesday morning survey reported he had surged almost fifteen points. His association with suddenly iconic Dottie wasn't hurting his election hopes.

Peter, stuck outside all the pomp and ritual, helplessly watched his 6-point lead decay and yield to Martini's regained support and popularity. Even worse, Jordan spoke out against Granucci at every opportunity, insinuating that all the pain and humiliation Granucci put the family through caused Dottie to weaken and succumb. Peter's campaign manager, a man who had handled over 40 campaigns in California and across the country, could only laugh in the last days, wryly remarking,

"Why, I'd kill that old bitch if she wasn't already dead!"

CHAPTER 43

Throughout two weeks of mourning for Dottie and for two weeks after, the public ignored critics with concerns about Jordan. By Thanksgiving however, a series of events unfolded that brought much of the former suspicion back to the minds and lips of the community.

First, on November 20, lawyers for Allegra Benson announced their intention to sue Jordan in civil court on wrongful death charges, raising the specter of another long, ugly trial, ripe with all the unflattering details of Jordan's life. In such a civil trial, Jordan would not be able to avoid testifying, which meant he would have to answer direct questions and discuss details about August 17 under oath.

Barry recommended two of the best civil law strategists. The lawyers made generous settlement offers to Allegra, but Lynette's mother wanted to see Jordan testify more than she wanted the money. The trial was set to begin in January.

And then in December, the young black male juror, a man who in September rigidly held that the prosecution hadn't convinced him of Jordan's guilt, told reporters he was wrong. He said that, upon greater reflection, he believed "Jordan was the only person who could've killed his wife. He did it."

Jordan's publicist was quick to point out the young man was just responding to the criticism leveled at him by the black community, but days later, the Mexican woman juror who supported an acquittal reversed her position as well.

Though Dottie had officially retired in 1981, her death affected Alexander Enterprises in several unexpected ways. Free of her overwhelming influence, the board members became more vocal on concerns about Jordan being an effective CEO. It was Dottie's will, but Dottie was dead. And though no one conducted an official vote, there were rumors that Philip had enough of the board's support to take over outright.

Since the beginning of the criminal trial in July, Philip courted key members to establish a small support base, insuring he wouldn't lose much position when or if Jordan returned. To his surprise, this growing support base, in the wake of Dottie's death, seemed likely to be the majority.

Jordan, shrewd as his grandmother, could see changes coming before anyone else and went to Philip's supporters with a deal, rather than risk losing his seat in an outright vote. Thus on December 14, Philip became CEO and Jordan retained limited executive privileges as he and lawyers planned their defense for the upcoming civil trial.

Friday, January 8, the day before opening statements in the civil trial, didn't portend well for Jordan. Philip called before court began to tell his brother the company had "lost their asses" on the big board that morning. In fact, it turned out to be the third highest one-day fall in history, with the Dow Jones average down 140.58 on the day.

Kevin Simmons, attorney for the plaintiff, laid out a case that resembled, in many ways, the case Destiny put on, only he asked the jury to pay particular attention to the testimony Jordan would give.

Defense attorney Peter Jensen seemed representative of the establishment white business community. His opening statement focused on Jordan's accomplishments, his contributions to the city and his character. He played what some would later call "the race card." It was no secret many of the city's blacks disliked Jordan, owing to several public remarks he made, and it was no secret the defense took great pains to exclude blacks from the jury. A *Chronicle* editorial questioned the strategy, since the legal community saw blacks as typically "pro-defense."

From a pool that was 40% black, only two sat in the jury box, both young males, one mulatto. And when Jensen suggested the impetus for the civil trial, despite generous offers to settle, originated with "a bitter and disillusioned segment of our society bent on personal vengeance and resentment rather than true justice," it was no secret he was referring to the city's black population.

Analysts predicted that if the defense could effectively pit the city's whites against its blacks, Jordan's lawyers would have the better advantage with the jury.

Compared to the criminal trial, civil proceedings moved at breakneck speed. Witnesses came on, testified and left the stand one after another. By the second week, plaintiff attorneys called their final witness, Jordan Alexander.

Despite intensive rehearsing, Jordan still seemed nervous going on, and Simmons began with the most difficult questions.

"Mr. Alexander, didn't murder your wife?"

"No."

"Weren't at her house at sometime between 9:45 and 10:15 on the night of August 17th, 1986?"

"No, I was not."

"Are you aware of the fact that a neighbor testified under oath she saw your Rolls Royce parked in front of her house during that time?"

"Yes, I'm aware of that."

"Didn't you drive it there?"

Jordan sat back, crossing his arms. He was becoming more comfortable.

"No, no I didn't."

"And are you aware of the fact that samples of blood matching your blood type were found in Lynette's bedroom and elsewhere on the way out the house as well as in the Rolls?"

Jordan shrugged, feinting confusion.

"Well, that's what some of them are saying."

Kevin directed jury and witness attention to a photo of Jordan's face, taken on the afternoon of August 18.

"Is this what your face looked like the day after the murder?"

Jordan studied the display.

"I, I guess so. If that's the picture they took at the station."

"And as for the scratch that runs from your temple to a place under your right eye there. Didn't your wife inflict that scratch on your face as she desperately fought for her life?"

Jordan looked toward Peter Jensen and answered.

"No, that didn't happen."

"Are you aware of the fact that she had flesh under one of her nails?"

"Yes."

"And are you aware that the medical examiner testified the flesh found there 'most likely came from a Caucasian person'?"

Peter Jensen sighed aloud, disgusted.

"Objection, your Honor. Counsel's asking the witness to answer questions in an area where the witness obviously has no expertise."

Kevin Simmons interrupted.

"Your Honor, I'm just asking the witness if he's aware of that aspect of the medical examiner's testimony."

Judge LaBrada lowered his glasses and winced before turning toward Jordan.

"Objection's overruled. You can answer the question."

Jordan smiled at the jury.

"Yes, I've been briefed on the medical examiner's testimony."

Portly Kevin nodded as he approached the photograph, pointing toward the eye.

"And the swelling and bruising under your left eye here, didn't you sustain that injury in the struggle with Lynette before you murdered her?"

Jensen called out.

"Objection. Compound question."

"Sustained."

Simmons sighed and reworded the interrogatory.

"Weren't your scratches and bruises the result of a struggle with Lynette on the night of August 17th?"

"No."

"No? Well, if the scratch and bruises weren't the result of a struggle with Lynette, can you in any way substantiate any other possible explanation offered for the injuries? Do you have any proof or any person who could corroborate an alibi?"

Jordan started an explanation, but Kevin cut him off, pressing for a simple yes or no.

"No."

"Can you offer anything in the way of evidence or a witness to substantiate you were anyplace else other than in Lynette's room between 9:45 to 10:15 on August 17th, 1986?"

Jordan answered.

"No, I'll let my lawyers do that."

"Can you offer evidence that anyone else other than Lynette scratched your face and bruised your eye?"

"No."

Kevin stood before the jury, asking a final question from a position in which Jordan was forced to face the jurors.

"Mr. Alexander, can you offer us any shred of credible, corroboratory evidence that on August 17th, 1986, the man who viciously and brutally murdered your wife could have been anyone other than you?"

Hesitating, Jordan answered.

"No."

"Thank you. I have nothing further."

Peter Jensen stood, removing his glasses. He was in his sixties and comfortable in the adversarial courtroom environment as he approached the witness.

"Jordan, did you kill your wife?"

"No."

"Do you remember the night she was murdered?"

Jordan closed his eyes, pursing his lips as he nodded.

"Yes."

"Where you anywhere near her house?"

"No."

"Would you mind telling us where you were?"

Jordan's eyes watered as he reflected.

"I was unconscious at the bottom of a garbage bin. I didn't know if I was dead or alive."

"A garbage bin? And how did you come to end up there?"

Jordan took a deep breath, answering in the jury's direction.

"Well, as I was leaving Alioto's that night at about 8:15, two very large black men accosted me and mugged me in the lot where I parked my car. They beat me up, stole my wallet, my keys and my clothes. Then they threw me naked headfirst in a garbage bin, leaving me for dead."

Peter continued in a concerned voice.

"Do you remember how long you were unconscious in that trash bin?"

Jordan squinted, wagging his head.

"It's hard to say. I don't remember, but by the time I crawled out and called someone to pick me up, it was at least 10:30."

"So you were unconscious for about two hours until about, say 10:20?"

"Yes, I think, I think that's pretty much it. Yes."

"So you're saying it would have been impossible for you to have murdered Lynette because at 10:00 to 10:15 when she was killed, you were unconscious, is that right?"

Kevin's voice interrupted Peter's rhythm.

"Objection. Counsel's leading the witness."

"Overruled."

"Were you unconscious during the time the medical examiner indicated she was killed?"

Jordan nodded, his face struggling to maintain composure.

"Yes."

At the desk, Peter returned the glasses to his nose as he

selected a document from a 3-inch thick pile of papers.

"And the hoodlums who accosted and mugged you, the two very large black men, is there anything specific you remember about either or both?"

"No, not really. They were just big and black and obviously full of bitterness."

Peter approached the witness.

"Bitterness? Why would you say they were 'full of bitterness?'"

Jordan answered toward the jury.

"Because one of them, as he was beating on me, said he was the kind of black person—*Nigger* was the word he used. He said he was the kind of nigger who would just as soon kill a 'fucking peckerwood white boy' than look at him."

As many in the jury box cringed in reaction to the statement, Peter Jensen, seeking to play on the power of the words, was quick to pursue a subtle defense-based insinuation.

"So these very large black men, they had your car for transportation, they had Lynette's address from the driver's license in your wallet and they had your key to her house. Is that correct?"

"Yes."

"Sounds a lot like opportunity. And one of these men had already indicated an extreme malice or bitterness toward white people, is that right?"

"Yes."

"So do you believe these two black men, after leaving the wharf, went over and murdered your wife?

Kevin was on his feet.

"Objection, your Honor! There are absolutely zero facts to support any of what counsel's suggesting, and even it there were, he's inviting the witness to engage in speculation."

Judge LaBrada nodded.

"Objection's sustained. Mr. Jensen, it seems you've pretty much exhausted this area of questioning. Move on."

Suggestion already in the ears of the jury, Jensen asked several questions on police decorum during Jordan's arrest and interrogation and sat down.

In re-direct, Kevin Simmons asked questions about the so-called assailants from the wharf. He asked Jordan if he made the alibi up to play on the public's fears and prejudice. He asked for a description of either attacker. He asked about complexion, hair length and style, body type and facial features, but Jordan was unable to provide specific information.

Kevin also asked pointed questions about Stephanie Rodriguez. He asked why "someone you've described as your girlfriend has so far been unwilling to corroborate your alibi?"

Through pointed questions, he characterized Stephanie as the one person who could settle the most salient issues involving the case.

In re-cross, Peter Jensen sought to put up an explanation. for the lack of an exculpatory witness or exculpatory evidence for the defense.

"The men who beat you up? Do you think they'll ever come forward and admit their part in this?"

Jordan sat back, sighing.

"It's been almost two years. They're long gone or dead."

"And when they threw you in the garbage bin, they didn't throw someone else in who would be able to substantiate that you were unconscious for more than two hours, did they?"

"No."

"Do you believe they chose you as a victim specifically because you were alone and there was no one around to witness the mugging?"

"Yes. Now I do."

"Did they wear gloves?"

"Yes."

"Do you think they wore them so there wouldn't be any fingerprints left behind?"

"Yes, that's why criminals wear gloves."

"And the bruises and scratches on your face in the display? Were they the result of the beating you suffered in that lot on the wharf?"

"Yes."

"Thank you. Nothing further."

In a brief re-re-direct, Kevin asked about the scratch on Jordan's face. At one time, the underlying suggestion was that he was scratched by a ring on one of the assailant's fingers, but the testimony about gloved attackers undermined any such explanation. Thus when asked about how his face had been scratched, Jordan was forced to answer, "I don't know."

The defense case Peter Jensen put on was short and to the point. He put on a police lieutenant who testified about the frequency of muggings around the wharf area during that time-period and the make-up and race of the typical assailant. The lieutenant described how the mugging Jordan testified about could have been accomplished. Jensen also put on two other victims who testified about how they were mugged by large black attackers in the area.

Simmons, in his cross-examinations, sought to make a distinction between muggers and murderers, which he tried to define as "two completely different animals."

Jensen had also put on Aida Rodriguez who testified that Stephanie left the country because she was "frightened of the corrupt police." While Jensen never attacked the police and police methods as directly as Barry had, he made oblique references to impropriety on the parts of Inspectors Osaka and Garner.

Jensen made a specific reference to the possibility of Garner planting evidence, hoping to play up news of a criminal investigation involving Garner relating to the Tasha Taylor case being re-tried in another courtroom.

His last witness was Jordan, who came on and answered that his face probably was scratched by something in the garbage bin after being thrown in headfirst. The defendant on the stand, the last witness testimony the jury heard was Jordan's flat denial of any involvement in his wife's murder.

Plaintiff attorney Kevin Simmons' closing argument contained a gripping description of the circumstances surrounding the murder and the murder itself, though not with the detail and emotion Destiny brought to her closing. A capable lawyer, he encouraged the jurors to consider the tough questions and he reminded them to remember what they *hadn't* seen,

"...any evidence that corroborated Jordan Alexander's suspicious alibi, Stephanie Rodriguez and any shred of physical evidence."

Then in hard-hitting sequence, he detailed all the central facts of the case "which prove *beyond a reasonable doubt* that Jordan was Lynette's killer, facts that go way beyond the threshold for the twelve of you, which is a mere *preponderance of the evidence*."

Defense attorney Peter Jensen countered that Jordan's alibi was already established, insisting plaintiff attorneys were blind to facts that contradicted their weak and circumstantial case. The physical injuries to Jordan's face and body, he said, were the proof that he was mugged.

Relating to the lack of physical evidence, he said,

"Only in a perfect world would we find muggers who leave a calling card behind or muggers who might have politely thrown in a witness who could testify in court."

He said that while both he and Jordan Alexander "wish like hell there was more in the way of evidence to establish the truth of what happened," there simply was not.

"If Jordan had known on August 17th as he walked to his car that he'd soon be mugged and that his wife would be murdered, that he would somehow be accused of the murder, he might have brought along a camera and a tape recorder."

As he concluded, Peter asserted that the real murderers of Lynette were still at-large, that "the same two large, black hoodlums who attacked Jordan near the wharf were the same angry, bitter, hateful killers who then read the address from Jordan's driver's license, drove over to the house on Sacramento Street, went into that house and murdered Lynette Alexander."

A week later, the foreperson called Judge Michael LaBrada to announce the jury had reached a verdict. When the judge reconvened the court the next morning, the city's latent interest in the case was exposed as flocks of reporters, seas of cameras and hordes from various special interest groups converged on the courtroom. Even Mayor Martini was in attendance, seated behind Jordan.

As soon as she heard news of the pending verdict, Allegra Benson phoned Destiny. She asked the former prosecutor to sit beside her as the verdict was read. Thus as the crowd in the courtroom awaited the arrival of the judge, Destiny held Allegra's cold and clammy hand, her own stomach in knots as she looked at Jordan sitting across the room.

Minutes later, the jury returned and not long after that came the judge, who called the court to order, asking for the jury's finding. After glancing at the decision, Judge LaBrada handed it back to the foreperson, a middle-aged woman, who read,

"In the matter of Benson versus Alexander, we the jury, by an 11 to 1 margin, do find for the plaintiff, Allegra Benson, who is suing on behalf of herself and on behalf of Caitlyn Alexander, Denver Alexander and Lyndsey Alexander, and do find Jordan Alexander *responsible* for the death of Lynette Alexander."

During the next week, the jury awarded damages to the plaintiffs in the unprecedented amount of $35 million, an action that thrilled many in the city who had felt no resolution from the unsettled criminal trial. Allegra, in a rare interview with a CNN reporter who covered the story, said that while she felt there was finally some degree of atonement,

"No amount of money in the world could lessen the void and the wretched sense of loss I will feel until the day I die."

While Jordan's $21 million in liquid assets had been frozen from the beginning of the civil trial, he had scores of other assets, which for various reasons were shielded, exempted and excluded from the civil judgment. Thus even after $21 million was paid to Allegra, to a trust fund for the girls and to attorneys, Jordan still had a $14 million judgment hanging over his head.

Naturally, his predicament didn't sit well with the Alexander Enterprises board of directors, so the odds of him ever running the company again were miles long. Even the limited executive privileges he had preserved for himself when Philip took over were curtailed. Socially, his name became anathema. He became a liability for anyone who associated with him. After a few months, even the mayor was inaccessible to him.

Desperate, he hired press agents and public relations firms who, though they tried many strategies, were unable to rescue his ruined reputation. Because the criminal trial ended in a stalemate, Jordan Alexander retained his precious freedom, but he had lost something he realized was far more valuable, his once good name.

Unless he could find some way to resolve Lynette's murder in the minds of the public, unless he could find some way to solve the murder, his name would continue in disgrace for all time in the history of San Francisco.

CHAPTER 44

Twelve years later

Bryan Osaka turned the key and pushed the door open as he steadied the swaying woman on her feet. Suzi's reception at *Tommy Toy's* had been a disaster for him.

He and fiancée Destiny were sitting in his car outside the restaurant when he told her about a woman had come forward in the Jordan Alexander matter. He said the woman was claiming she could somehow prove Jordan Alexander's innocence. Destiny was so overwhelmed by the news that she feinted. Minutes later, she recovered and insisted on attending the reception to avoid insulting or disappointing Suziko and the family.

Inside the restaurant, she was too nervous to eat, but she had at least four vodka martinis, according to Bryan's count. The affect of alcohol on her empty stomach led to extreme depression and despair. Sadako, Bryan's mother, went into the restroom to check on Destiny after she was conspicuously absent for thirty minutes, and she came out to tell Bryan his fiancée was disoriented, crying and embarrassed.

Bowing and making discreet apologies for his early exit, Bryan and Sadako practically carried Destiny to the parking lot where she threw up a clear green liquid before getting into the car. She cried and apologized as he drove, mumbling about Jordan Alexander and various details involving the murder. She cried about Lynette. She cried about the persecution she endured. She even cried about Charles.

Finally at home, she stumbled through the door, swaggered down the hall, bumping against the wall on each side, tottered toward the couch and fell onto it, weeping.

"Bryan! Stay with me, please!"

Sagging to a place on the couch beside her, he sat, worried. In the six years they had dated, he had never seen her drunk before.

He met her for the first time thirteen years earlier in 1986 at a little restaurant in Japantown. Back then, he was an inspector working for the San Francisco Police Department and she was an impassioned county prosecutor working on the biggest and most controversial murder case in the city's recent history.

During his testimony at the trial, he didn't comprehend the forces at work around him. Naïve, he had no idea his own involvement and actions were part of a high-stakes power play being waged by county district attorney Peter Granucci and police commander Dennis Webber. Being young and idealistic, he didn't understood the politics until his world came crashing down around him.

The Granucci-Webber takeover was well-planned and would have worked if Dottie Alexander's death hadn't influenced the outcome of the '87 election. When Granucci lost his bid to become mayor, Webber lost local political support and the support of many on the police force who were once loyal to him.

Then came the purge, a politically-motivated, orchestrated action by Mayor Tony Martini, police chief Bill McGuire and other key political players to destroy all resistance and internal opposition throughout the city. Webber was attacked from all quarters, especially in light of the Tasha Taylor story. The press castigated him, state and local law enforcement agencies condemned him and the public spurned him. He escaped by taking an early retirement in June '88.

With Webber gone, the faction of detectives and officers who were once loyal to him scrambled for cover. McGuire welcomed many back into the fold, but he went after detectives Garner, Harris and Osaka. Garner he got. After an Internal Affairs panel recommended dismissal for *a pattern of probable evidence tampering*, the city fired Garner.

Osaka, who McGuire called a liar, a betrayer and the worst of the three, was demoted and put back out on the street in the most troublesome areas of the city. For six months, supervisors targeted him and wrote him up for petty infractions, interposed him in dangerous situations with less-than-adequate back up and ostracized him.

Trained by his father to interpret persecution as an opportunity to display character, he struggled to distinguish himself as an honest, loyal and capable police officer. It was all for naught. After systematic documentation for violations through write-ups and testimony from fellow officers, Bryan was forced to either resign or be fired by Internal Affairs. He resigned in August '88.

Ashamed about losing his job, Bryan returned to his mother and father's home at Tiburon where unemployed, he lived with them and Suziko for 11 months. As he looked back, they were the most wonderful and relaxing 11 months of his life. His parents were understanding and supportive of their only son. As for Suziko, she was just a tiny baby when he left for college. He really got to know her during that year.

He spent most of his stay there helping his father Ichiro put in gardens and the large koi pond. Neither of the two would ever forget the hours they spent together that year *making new from old*. Sons and fathers needed such experiences, he thought, but sons should also go out to seek their fortunes in the world, so he decided to look for work as a detective in the private sector.

After two months and more than fifteen interviews, the only job offer he got was from *Sears* as a store detective. Though he was disappointed, he had accepted the job when another offer came from a small agency he never knew existed. Bryan had no idea how the man who called him got his resume and knew so much about him.

The man, who said his name was Vic Ehlers, didn't reveal much, but he invited Bryan for an interview that same day.

"You know Osaka, I've been watchin you for about four years now, and you're pretty good, but ya got a lot ta learn, kid. Somehow I think ya *know* that."

Bryan sighed and glanced away, sidelong.

"I don't know everything, but I think I was a good detective."

"You were okay, but ya got in trouble cuz ya didn't know shit about the politics! Ya were a real idiot about the politics that's part of the big picture. Ya ended up bein the fuckin patsy!"

Bryan stood, ready to walk out the door, but he stopped.

"Look! I told the truth."

"No one was payin ya good enough for ta tell the truth. If ya wanted your job, ya shoulda lied, ya shoulda played the game. You were way green, kid! Ya were a fuckin idiot! It's the truth and ya know it!"

Vic stood, mashing his cigarette in an already over-full ashtray.

"Aw, sit down, kid."

Bryan remained standing until Vic grabbed his shoulder and pushed him down into the chair.

"Hey, I didn't call ya over here ta tell you how stupid ya are. I called ya ta give ya a chance ta dummy-up, ta get cha some smarts."

For all his life, Vic prided himself on working alone, but at seventy-six years old, he tired out too easily to do much of the legwork required in his day-to-day schedule. Explaining as much, he proposed a deal to Bryan that, in exchange "for 60 hours a week as my errand-boy, I'll teach you the real detective business." Only after the young detective agreed to work without pay did Vic offer a salary double what Bryan made with the San Francisco Police.

A rare relationship developed over time, and the secrets Bryan learned about city and state officials, about high-profile business executives and about federal agencies were mind-boggling. He learned about accidents that were hardly accidents, about political assassinations disguised as suicides, about blackmail plots and quid pro quo deals on the international scope.

And cynical Vic, even when discussing the most extravagant scandal, never raised an eyebrow or batted an eye. "Selfish bastards, all of em!" he would say. "Everyone's goin ta hell, and it'll be one hellava party!"

Over time, Bryan also learned detectives Garner and Harris really *did* plant the blood in the downstairs portion of Jordan's home during the morning after the murder. It was something he wondered about during the trial, but Vic had proof.

Vic had proof for everything and had something on everybody. He was amazing. And the black book he sometimes carried around in his pocket—rumor had it the book contained the real truth about the JFK assassination. When asked about it, Vic would always laugh and answer, grinning, "Well, *someone's* gotta have the fuckin proof."

After the trial and his resignation, Bryan didn't see Destiny again until the third Sunday of May 1993, at the Bay to Breakers annual 7½ mile race from the bay to the ocean. Both were participants. He recognized her, but she didn't remember him until he told her his name.

Though she was standoffish and reserved even after she had given him her phone number, she warmed over time and they began dating. In the early going, it was clear his feelings were much more intense than hers, though she enjoyed spending time with him and considered him a less-than-serious boyfriend.

After the second year of dating however, her feelings deepened. She was first to use the "L" word. It wasn't until after they were together for three years that Bryan realized she was familiar with the Japanese language and culture, and that was only because he overheard an extended conversation between her and Kiyomi on Destiny's answering machine.

Yet even though she admitted to understanding a limited

amount of Japanese, she was reluctant to reveal how much. It was something that made him nervous whenever she was around his Japanese-speaking relatives.

While parents Ichiro and Sadako were disappointed Bryan hadn't found a nice Japanese girl, his mother appreciated Destiny's intelligence and passion as a lawyer and the director of a big foundation, while his father appreciated her *gaman* and her physical attractiveness.

After quitting the district attorney's office, Destiny accepted a job teaching *Criminal Procedure* and *Torts* at Loyola Law School in southern California. She had always dreamed of moving to Los Angeles, and yet her dream bore no resemblance to the reality of the LA traffic and smog problems. The dream bore no resemblance to the harshness and egocentrism that afflicted the populations of mega-metropolises. It bore no resemblance to the extreme racial tensions that culminated in 58 deaths during the riots and looting after the Rodney King verdict in late April '92. By the time the smoke cleared from the riots, she was ready to leave LA.

Allegra had been begging her for years to come back to San Francisco to serve on the board of the *Aegis Foundation*, so Destiny saw the opportunity as an escape and took it. Only after she moved back did she learn to appreciate San Francisco for what it was, the most cosmopolitan city in America.

Allegra donated all the money she won from the civil case to the foundation, expanding its reach to cities across the country. She also created a branch of the foundation designed to go after corporate donations and to provide education.

Over time, the job of running *Aegis* became too big and too involved for Allegra. The foundation, she believed, needed a director who had both fervor and intelligence, someone who was both realistic and disciplined, someone who would care more for the women in need and Nettie's dream than the bullshit politics and head games of running a multi-million dollar enterprise. She handpicked Destiny for the job, and Destiny began directing the foundation that year.

Destiny was awakened the next morning by a phone call from Allegra, who wanted to know if she had heard the news. Head pounding and hands still quivering from the toxicity of the vodka, she sat up on the couch, wiping the thin line of saliva that trailed from the left corner of her mouth to her chin.

"Yes, I heard, and I'm not doing so well either."

Roused by her voice, Bryan stood, horrified by the number of wrinkles he saw in the brand new silk suit he had slept in. He headed for the bathroom as Destiny continued on the phone.

"Well, I hadn't really thought about it, but I guess I'll have to go in my capacity as director, if for no other reason. Are you going?"

She listened through the response and nodded.

"Good, then we'll go together. Wait a minute! What time is it?"

She checked her watch.

"No, it's just that I wanted to make the Sunday morning service over at the foundation. You going?"

Wireless phone cradled between her shoulder and ear, she checked her face in the mirror, grimacing.

"You are? Great. Just have to get a shower and I'll be right over."

She sank back onto the chocolate brown leather couch, deep in thought, reflecting on all the emotion of the trial, all the anger and frustration. Nothing good had come from it. So what now? And more importantly, *who the fuck was this Karen Epps woman?*

When Bryan re-entered the living room minutes later, his hair was wet and combed straight back, fresh out of the shower. He stood behind the sofa in a pair of comfortable black wool slacks with a black button-up silk shirt, staring down at Destiny.

"You going to be okay?"

She closed her eyes, her head throbbing.

"Dozen aspirin and I'll be fine. I'm sorry about last night."

He came around the sofa and sat next to her, pretending not to notice the fact that her beautiful red silk kimono-style Halston outfit was ruined.

"Vic tells me this Karen Epps character has a father living down in San Diego. Says if I want *real* answers, he's the guy I've got to talk to."

"So, are you going down there now?"

"Yes, but I'll be back late tonight. The press conference is at eleven, tomorrow morning. If you want me to go with you, I will."

She leaned close and kissed his lips.

"You really are a special guy. I love you."

She stood, swaggering.

"Actually, Allegra and I are going together. Believe it or not, she probably needs me more than I need you. I'll be all right."

He rose, taking her in his arms.

"Well, I'll be there just in case, and hopefully I'll have the low-down on this Karen Epps woman by then."

Her face showed concern.

"You really think you'll be able to find out something?"

He laughed.

"Well, Vic has spoken, and if Vic thinks there'll be an answer down there, believe me, there will be."

While Karen Epps chose the prestigious law firm of Chase, Walthrop & Kinney to handle the legal aspects of the conference, Leslie Wilke, from the PR firm of Reed and Wilke, was the person who dispersed information and answered questions.

Uncomfortable in the new designer outfit she'd been instructed to wear and the complete makeover, timid Karen stood off to the left, her light brown hair up, whispering to lawyers, as Leslie gave last minute instructions to the many reporters crowded around the platform in the amphitheater at Yerba Buena Gardens.

Spring was in full bloom on that second Monday in May, as the bright sun warmed the morning air. A gentle breeze tinged with the subtle scent of the ocean animated a sea of multi-colored flowers next to the staged event. Yet Nature's annual May exhibition was lost on the crowd of reporters assembled there, maneuvering for position in front of the stage.

Farther back, one hundred or so chairs were arranged across the grass, so the more reserved observers, Destiny and Allegra included, studied the awkward and somewhat unpolished subject of the press conference from front row seats. Both wore sunglasses and slacks, though Destiny had on a blazer.

Seeing Leslie on stage, Destiny reflected on former police spokesperson Rikki Thomas. Leslie looked nothing like Rikki, but the two had the similar mannerisms. Leslie's short hair shone red in the sun, but because she was in her early to mid-fifties, Destiny was certain the hair was dyed. She remembered it being *brown* last summer. Both Destiny and Allegra knew Leslie from receptions and fund-raisers around town, and although Leslie's firm made annual contributions to the foundation, neither Destiny nor Allegra liked her.

Allegra had to lean to one side to see the stage because CNN, CourtTV, MSNBC and other national news agencies had managed to get front-and-center footing for their reporters and equipment. The coordinating producer had already cued an on-stage director on the ready status of the press. Deeming the moment appropriate, Leslie blew into the microphone to estimate volume and began.

"Ladies and Gentlemen, thank you for coming. Let me say up front that all you're going to get today is merely an *opportunity* to know the truth of what happened on August 17th, 1986, an opportunity to know whether or not Jordan Alexander is a murderer. That's not to say any of you will walk away knowing any more than you did when you came. No, hopefully you'll get the full story at our *next* press event, and we hope that'll come within the week."

As Leslie studied the eager faces in the crowd, she was certain she had piqued great interest. Karen Epps stood next to her, and behind both was a phalanx of bodyguards, lawyers and Reed and Wilke staffers.

"In 1987 right after the trial—in fact it was at a party the night Dottie Alexander died. Jordan Alexander issued a pledge on television to the city of San Francisco and beyond. He said he would pay a $5 million reward to anyone who could provide information that would lead to the arrest and conviction of the person or persons responsible for his wife's murder. As we know, Mr. Alexander suffered a major financial setback as a result of the civil trial. Because he owes a $14 million judgment and he's no longer running the family business, it's questionable whether or not he could actually *pay* the reward he offered. The very purpose of the press conference today is to settle that question."

Leslie paused a moment and backed, allowing Karen to move forward as they had rehearsed. In that instant, the sound of cameras clicking was audible even above the din of the crowd's wary mumbling.

"Ms. Epps may very well be the only person in the world who can provide answers to the questions we all have about the Lynette Alexander murder case, but she's indicated she will refrain from making any statement or comment on the matter until the reward issue is settled. She's hoping that, if Jordan can't pay the reward, perhaps the Alexander family or any other interested party might be willing to step forward to honor his commitment. After all, at the time he offered the reward, he was speaking as president and CEO of Alexander Enterprises."

She paused to indicate a change in direction.

"Ms. Epps has also indicated she is very uncomfortable with publicity, the press and the unethical tactics of many of you reporters. When this is all over, she wants to return to a life of privacy. She is also uncomfortable about having come forward in the first place. With that in mind, she is giving interested parties one week to settle the issue of the reward in formal writing. If it doesn't happen within a week, she'll go back to a life of anonymity and she'll probably carry the information she has and her unsettled suspicions to her grave."

The essential points of the message out, Leslie smiled.

"So that's all. Hopefully, we'll all be getting together again within the week. Thank you. No questions, please."

Leslie stood aside as bodyguards surrounded Karen Epps, escorted her to a car and whisked her away. The reaction from observers who watched Karen disappear was one of uniform astonishment, followed by a sense of anger for having been led on.

The crowd of reporters, family members, friends, foes, court personnel, business interests and inquiring San Franciscans had assembled in Yerba Buena Park that morning because they all expected an answer to the question, "Did he or didn't he?" Instead, this Karen Epps and her lawyers had baited and blackmailed them into urging a $5 million payment in exchange for the answer to that question.

Yet even as the disappointed crowd worked its way out the park, few objected to Karen Epps insistence on the reward Jordan offered, if she could solve San Francisco's crime of the century.

CHAPTER 45

The initial news stories indicated Alexander Enterprises CEO Philip Alexander was not likely to yield to the blackmail terms of a woman he publicly called a criminal and a charlatan. The stories ranged from a rehashing and analysis of the criminal trial to backgrounds on Lynette, Jordan, Destiny, Barry, Dottie and various trial judges. They ranged from the civil trial to an assessment of Jordan's wealth, his losses and the overall solvency of Alexander Enterprises.

While CourtTV's *Trial Story* informed the country and the world on the intricacies and enigmas related to the 1987 trial, guests on CNN were invited to compare it to a similar high-profile criminal trial from the 1990s, with its implications on the civil judgment. Commentators on another program wondered if Alexander Enterprises was legally liable for paying the reward regardless of any other circumstance.

Many stories credited Destiny for having the perspicacity to carefully preserve all the DNA fingerprinting and for the meticulous records she insisted on obtaining and documenting. She was praised as a visionary. In 1991, the California courts began allowing DNA testing results to be used in criminal cases.

There was a story in the newspaper about Jordan Alexander and his fall from grace and one about Allegra Benson and her quest to keep Lynette's memory alive. There were stories about Jordan's daughters. Caitlyn was a high fashion model working in Italy and France. Denver was the married mother of one child. And then there was unsettled Lyndsey, who had dropped out of college, chopped off all her beautiful brown hair and died it black. She worked in San Francisco booking bands for the local nightclubs along the South of Market strip.

Finally, there were stories about Karen Epps and details from her four arrests, mostly petty offenses. There was one for welfare fraud, two for DUI, one for shoplifting and a cocaine possession arrest. The man she was married to for eight years told reporters she was an honest person, with a few problems.

On the official record, the majority of the board urged Alexander Enterprises to commit to paying the reward. The prevailing argument focused on Jordan's possible innocence. If Karen Epps was going to indicate that another person murdered Lynette, then Jordan had been falsely accused and therefore wronged.

It would be an abomination of justice if it turned out he was innocent, especially after losing all the money paid for his defense in the criminal and civil trials, after losing the $21 million paid out for the civil judgment, after losing his $950,000 annual salary plus healthy bonuses as CEO of Alexander Enterprises over 12 years.

Thus in a little over 48 hours, Jordan became a sympathetic figure to the public while his brother Philip was depicted as a greedy schemer and ruthless usurper.

Philip however, was unfazed by the fickleness of the public and refused to yield to the elaborate blackmail scheme, even hinting that Karen Epps, her story and the press conference were all part of Jordan's Machiavellian takeover bid.

The press conference and the excitement it generated angered Allegra. First, she was suspicious of Leslie Wilke, and she denounced the press conference as "criminal and cruel to a victim's mother and daughters." She distrusted any new information Karen Epps might provide and wondered why it had taken her almost 14 years to come forward with it. She was even more angry with the Alexander family, and more specifically, with Philip for balking rather than committing to pay the reward.

"We've only got three days left. If Philip isn't going to pay, *we're* going to have to find some way to do it."

Destiny was reviewing the foundation's financial statement from a seat across the table.

"Allegra, we *can't*, not with donations. And we're already well into this year's budget. We just don't have five million dollars to give away."

Allegra sighed, disgusted.

"There just *has* to be some other way! We can raise the money. I know we can raise the money!"

Destiny extended her hand.

"Look Allegra, I know you're anxious, but I have a strong feeling Philip's going to commit to paying the money. He can't afford not to. He's just bluffing, waiting till the last possible moment, hoping he'll get some new information or a break. He probably has investigators working around the clock to find out what she knows so he won't have to pay her. If they can't find anything, he's going to pay, believe it."

Allegra closed her eyes.
"You really think so?"
Destiny smiled.
"Bet my life on it."

Bryan never made it back for the Monday morning press conference. Though Vic told him Karen's father was the key to the whole matter, all records indicated that she had no father, or at least no father on file. According to Bryan's research, Karen was born at San Francisco General Hospital on Potrero Avenue in February 1958. Her mother, a clerk with city planning, listed the father as "unknown" on the birth certificate, and she never married. Christine Epps died of brain cancer in 1995.

Karen's school records reflected that her young life was typical, that as a girl she wanted to be "an astronaut and a writer." She graduated sixth in a class of a little over 150 students and attended San Francisco City College for one year before becoming pregnant. From there, her life took a downward turn.

At twenty years old, with aid from the county and welfare, she moved into her own apartment in the Western Addition with her 8-month-old son. Eleven months later, she had a daughter by a 19 year-old who sold *weed* and *coke* to pay for his fully-restored 1966 Mustang and a special edition Harley-Davidson motorcycle. He occasionally stayed the night at her apartment, especially right after *Mother's Day*. On the first and fifteenth, money flowed in the neighborhood, as all the young single "mothers" had cash in hand to buy booze and drugs, money to give to men who exploited them.

Karen believed she loved Glennie, though she knew his other girlfriends. For two months while he was in jail, she had sex with older men to pay his legal expenses and to put money on his book. She even agreed to participate in one of his illicit schemes that involved collecting food stamps on phony names and social security numbers and trading them for cash at 50% to 75% value.

It was a profitable little racket for about 10 months until county investigators closed in and Glennie disappeared, leaving Karen and six other women arrested for fraud. Karen cut a deal with the district attorney, promising to get clerical work in order to pay back the money, which she eventually did.

When she got pregnant by a supervisor at work, she decided it was time to get married and accepted his proposal, though she knew he was an alcoholic. Her first DUI came two months after she married him, while she was seven months pregnant. Her indulgence led to more misfortune, when the new baby was three months old.

Karen, husband Dennis and the three children lived in squalor in a small run-down apartment complex off Mission at the time. They had no furniture, so they slept on a makeshift bed composed of two twin mattresses and queen box springs. The box springs rested on the floor, and the mattresses were placed side by side on top. The whole family slept on that bed, elevated six inches from a floor covered with grime and dirt, a floor that crawled with insects and tiny rodents. They had gone to Dennis' brother's house for Thanksgiving dinner, and naturally both he and Karen were drunk when they arrived home, so drunk that they placed the baby, a little girl, in the spot where the two mattresses came together.

Over the course of the night, the mattresses moved apart, and the baby fell between them, where its desperate crying was muffled and ignored. When Karen awoke at noon, the baby lay there dead, stiff as a board, its eyes open and its mouth twisted from the slow torture of suffocation. She called 911 and the ambulance came and took the baby away. Distraught, Karen never knew what became of her little girl's body after that, and she was afraid to ask. There was no funeral. Not surprising, CPS came in and removed the other two children from the home.

Eventually, she divorced Dennis and got a clerical job with the county where she worked five years before dropping out of sight. In all his research, Bryan found nothing about any father in her life, and the San Diego investigation hadn't provided any real clues.

It wasn't until Destiny made a comment during Friday morning breakfast that he understood why Vic suggested checking San Diego in the first place. The Friday morning *Chronicle* featured Karen's picture on the front page along with the story of her tragic life.

Studying the photo, Destiny said in passing,

"If I didn't know any better, I'd swear she's got some black in her somewhere, especially around the mouth and nose."

That's when it hit him. That's when he hustled over to Bryant Street to look over all the displays from the trial again. He knew what he was looking for. It was a sketch, a composite of a man described by defense witness Gina Fasone. The sketch seemed familiar to him from the moment he saw it, but the pressures of the trial and the Internal Affairs investigation kept him from acting on his intuition. It was a long shot, it was a desperate long shot, and yet it was a possibility.

After getting a copy of the sketch, he rushed down to city hall where he searched for a face and a name he couldn't quite remember. An hour later, he had a name, Walter Monroe. He searched for an hour, but he couldn't find a good picture, so he called Kiyomi over at the *Chronicle* and asked her to pull a few articles written about the man, especially the ones with pictures.

Because Kiyomi had been promoted to editor, they were able to meet in her private office.

"I'm sorry Bryan, but I just don't think that sketch looks anything *like* him."

She laughed.

"I know you want to figure this thing out, but don't you think your whole theory's a bit of a stretch? It's just too fantastic."

He shrugged.

"Not really. Especially since I know he moved down south, and I'm just about sure it was to San Diego. Vic said my answer's down there. It's worth at least a second look."

She sighed.

"Well, if you find anything out, I *will* be the first to know, won't I?"

She winced, closing her eyes.

"I mean second. After Destee, of course."

Glancing at his watch, he laughed to himself.

"Of course. That is, if you don't break the story without checking with me first."

She laughed and winked.

"Oh I'm completely trustworthy. Just ask your fiancée."

CHAPTER 46

"That's right. For 14 years I've lived in the shadow of suspicion. Despite the fact that I was never convicted of any wrongdoing in any criminal court, I have been criminalized by the press, ostracized by people I believed were my friends and forced to renege on a solemn promise I made to my grandmother, Dottie."

As dozens of cameras flashed after the statement, the tears filling his sensitive eyes were obvious.

"The night she died, right before dinner, my grandmother called me into her room. She said she had been awakened by a dream that deeply disturbed her. It was one of her "Bible dreams" as she called them, a story about two brothers. Both were competing for the family business or their inheritance or whatever they did back then. In it, she said, the one destined to head the family was exiled for 14 years before returning to assume his proper place as leader and rightful heir. She made me promise that, no matter what happened, I would never relinquish my rightful position as president and CEO of Alexander Enterprises."

He looked toward his mother and aunts sitting with other board members convened for the emergency meeting.

"To my great regret, it is a promise I broke soon thereafter as I scrambled to protect myself from excessive civil liability. Almost 14 years ago, I was accused of committing a murder I did not commit. When I was unjustly arrested and imprisoned, I was forced to transfer many of my powers and duties to my brother Philip, who did an exceptional job in my absence. And then after the civil trial, through our mutual agreement and your unanimous consent, Philip became president and CEO of the company."

He glanced in his brother's direction.

"Once again, Philip has done a great job, and I don't mean to take anything away from him as I speak, but just as this company is the culmination of Dottie Alexander's dream, you must realize it was her will for *me* to lead it into the 21st century."

He stopped.

"But that isn't why we're here, is it? We're not here to debate leadership. No, we're here about justice. We're here about exoneration. Now, when I told you I was innocent 14 years ago, I think most of you believed me initially, but as the years went by, you somehow stopped believing so much. I'm certain some of you even convinced yourselves that I really *was* guilty."

He half-laughed.

"Oh come on. Don't look so circumspect. You all know who you are. You're the ones who took the stairs rather than riding with me on the elevator, the ones who stopped asking my opinion on anything, who stopped inviting me to celebrations and events, who whispered to news reporters, registering your suspicions and divulging lurid little details about my personal life. My grandmother and I have called many of you our friends for years, and if she were here today, looking back she'd say, shame on you! Shame on you for being so weak and disloyal!"

He paused as he watched uncomfortable board members shifting in their seats.

"But that's how Dottie was. At her age, all she could really do was look back, and she knew it. That's why, in the early eighties, she changed the company logo to what you see now, the image of the Roman god *Janus*, with her face looking into the past and mine toward the future."

He smiled.

"As I look to the future, I see us all working together. I envision forgiveness and strengthened bonds between us. I see the company moving boldly into the global market of the 21st century stronger than ever because, looking back, we have learned from what has passed."

The smile fading, he began.

"We're here tonight to consider whether the company should stipulate to pay Ms. Karen Epps $5 million for revealing information that could put the murderer or murderers of my wife behind bars at last. The question is a simple one: Do we or do we not make the commitment? Now there's been a lot of debate about the character and trustworthiness of this woman Karen Epps. I guess she's had some problems, but we have to realize that her character is not the issue here. You see, according to the original offer, the reward is paid only in the event of a conviction."

He nodded in the affirmative.

"So if the woman is lying or running some scam and there's no conviction, we're under no obligation to pay her anything, not one red cent. We pay only after the murderer of my wife is locked away in some prison, hopefully with zero possibility of ever being paroled. Would I pay five million dollars to see whoever murdered Lynette brought to justice? I'd pay three or four times that much if I had it, but I don't. As you know, all my money was taken in the civil judgment where I was punished a second time for a murder I had nothing to do with. It's a wrong I'd eventually like to set right, but for now, I'm in no position to make a five million dollar commitment."

He scanned the room, making eye contact with key board members.

"But as a company, *we* are. As a company, we should. As a company, we must. Why? Because right now, the city of San Francisco and the entire world is watching us, waiting to see if we value truth and justice over mere dollars. It's an opportunity for us to show the cynics and critics alike just who we are and what we're about. The truth is, Ladies and Gentlemen, we can't afford *not* to make the commitment in this no-lose proposition we have before us. I urge for your aye vote."

He turned toward the vice-chairman who was acting in Philip's stead for the emergency board meeting.

"I move that the vote be taken by *Yeas and Nays*."

Jordan sat, the vote on *Yeas and Nays* carried and the chair called for any last comment before the vote on the prevailing question. In that moment, all eyes in the room shifted to Philip, awaiting his official position and his response. He stood.

"Ladies and Gentlemen, friends, family. I've been president and CEO of Alexander Enterprises for the past 12 years, so while Jordan has gone out of his way to commend me on the job I'm doing, his disingenuous approval is wasted on you. It's unnecessary. My record speaks for itself. We came here to discuss one issue and one issue only: should we as a diversified, multi-national company involve ourselves in a sensational localized murder trial and strike up some kind of deal with a woman who's already been convicted of fraud? A woman's whose drunkenness, drug abuse and negligence cost the life of her own child? Is anything this felon might tell us worth five million dollars? Is anything she might tell us worth the potential liability and negative publicity the company might face? I have to say no."

He scanned the expressions on faces in the room.

"Look, I realize it was advertised as the trial of the century, so we want the truth, but it just seems unlikely at this late date that anyone could provide anything new. You have to remember, that trial alone cost the city almost two million. Every stone was overturned, every lead was exploited, and we got what we got. And now this Karen Epps character, this common criminal, in her press event made a direct appeal to Alexander Enterprises saying, 'you want the truth? It's got a five million dollar price tag. Otherwise you get nothing.' Well, I say it sounds like solicitation of a bribe with no guarantees, an offhand blackmail attempt and a scam by a person who has already been convicted of running scams."

He paused for effect.

"I say that woman is a liar and has nothing to tell us as a company. It's not our business. If Jordan believes her and he wants to hear what she has to say, let him do what he legally has to do to free up his shares and sell them off to raise the money himself. If she tells him something that'll clear his name, it'll be worth the five million to him. Most of you don't know this, but after her little press conference, we had her investigated to see if she had information that might pose a liability to the company."

He raised a document into the air.

"All the reports came back saying there's *nothing* she could possibly know, and we've made plenty of copies for all of you to examine at your leisure. As a company, we benefit in no way by succumbing to this woman's blackmail attempt. On the contrary, any compliance with her demands would make us look exploitable and weak, and we simply cannot afford to look vulnerable. Not now, not ever."

Philip's smile was rare, yet it was reassuring.

"Far from being harsh and insensitive, I've come before you tonight because I'm looking to the company's best interests just as all of you should. And you should all recognize that looking to the company's best interests tonight means a nay vote on this matter."

Philip sat, and the interim chairman began calling names as the board began the *Yeas and Nays* voting ritual.

As Bryan hurried toward terminals in the San Diego International Airport at 5:30, brushing by bumping into travelers in his haste, he only hoped he wasn't too late. It had been a hectic day.

He arrived in San Diego at 8:00 a.m. and had run himself ragged in and out of dead-end leads. He visited the police station and the water, gas and electric companies. He went to the phone company, all to no avail. His subject didn't exist in the city.

Then he remembered a trade secret Vic always recommended and tried it. In a last ditch effort, he visited the public library, befriended a clerk and asked if Walter Monroe had a card on file within the system. It turned out that Walter had no active card on file, but there was a note in the computer about a book he checked out in February 1991 and never returned. From there, Bryan persuaded another clerk to allow him access to library card records from 1990 through 1992 and found Walter's application, complete with an address and phone number.

The phone was disconnected, so Bryan hurried to his car and rushed over to the Cedar Street address listed on file only to find the home was occupied by Ron and Louise Chadwick and their two children. He canvassed the immediate neighborhood for 45 minutes until he found an old woman who remembered a former resident of that house, a man who fit Walter Monroe's general description.

"He was a very nice man, very quiet, very polite. He loved children, but his name wasn't Walter Monroe. It was Nat, Nathaniel Adams, I believe. Sometimes he'd go out caroling with the neighborhood kids during Christmas. And he could sing that *Chestnuts* song just like Nat King Cole. He really could!"

"Did he live by himself? Did he have a wife or any kids?"

She thought for a moment, her face perplexed.

"He wasn't very old, in his early fifties, maybe. But I think he was a widower. Hardly anyone ever went by to see him."

She stopped, remembering something initially forgotten.

"Oh, it seems I remember there was a white gal and some odd-looking kids who stayed with him for a week or so a couple of times, but aside from that, he was just by himself."

Though Bryan was eager to get back to a name and address database, he lingered to ask a few additional questions.

Records indicated Walter had lived on Cedar Street as Nat Adams from early 1989 through July 1994. His wife Eliza had died November 1988. From Cedar Street, Nat Adams moved to an apartment in August 1994, before purchasing a condominium in Coronado under his assumed name.

Neighbors in both places described him as taciturn, as a man hiding some dark secret. Just the day before, the neighbor in the condominium next to him watched as he loaded his car with three or four suitcases, something out of character for a man who seldom went anywhere.

Bryan figured Walter was heading south by car. According to chits and receipts found ripped in two and discarded in a trash bag, Nathaniel Adams withdrew $21,000 in cash from his bank account, ordered a counter check in the amount of $90,000 and took the balance of $2,600 in travelers checks.

Based on the quantity of cash Walter withdrew, Bryan guessed he was headed out of the country by air, probably to a warm place where he could disappear into some native population without a trace. Calls to the airlines resulted in information about a Nate Adams traveling to Barbados on a 6:01 flight out.

Bryan arrived at the gate at 5:35, just as the call went out to board first-class passengers. Still gasping for breath, he paced the area, his eyes darting to the inconspicuous seats in the corners, around open newspapers, along the long line waiting for boarding passes and seat assignments. One man resembled Monroe, but when he stood, he was far too short. Instinct caused Bryan to turn and to examine passengers waiting at the gate across the aisle, and bingo!

There was his man, in dark glasses and casual wear, briefcase in his hand. He was watching and waiting to board the plane at the last possible moment. Bryan knew who he was, but Walter Monroe had no idea the detective had come for him. Bryan's oblique approach went unnoticed until he presented a card.

"Walter Monroe, my name's Bryan Osaka. I'm a private detective. I'm going to need to ask you a few questions."

The man ignored the card and never looked at Bryan.

"Look, I don't know *who* the hell you are, but my name's not Monroe, so it you'll excuse me, I've got a plane to catch."

He tried to walk past Bryan toward the gate, but Bryan grabbed his arm.

"Mr. Monroe, I'm sorry, but you're not going anywhere. We can do things the hard way or the easy way. It's up to you, but I hope you don't think I came out here without the means to keep you in this terminal and in this state."

The shivering man closed his eyes, bowed his head and drew in a quiescent breath.

"Who are you working for? Karen?"

Bryan steadied his gaze, relieved that Monroe hadn't called his bluff.

"No. In this case, I suppose you could say I'm working for the *Aegis Foundation*. I'm not the enemy, but make no mistake about it, they'll be coming after you in full force."

The old man batted his watery eyes, shoulders slumping as he cocked his head and looked to Bryan for mercy and compassion.

"Hey, have a heart. I'm just a tired old man who wants to just go away and die in peace. Please Sir, please just let me get on that plane."

Bryan looked back over his shoulder as passengers boarded the plane, finding it difficult to deny the man's pitiful plea. Monroe was much different than Bryan imagined. He was thinner and seemed older than 62. He seemed distinguished.

"I'm sorry, Mr. Monroe. If it were just up to me, I'd help you onto the plane, but I'm certain you're aware of how much is at stake here. I can't let you run out on this. Somewhere along the line, we're going to have to get to the truth."

Monroe sighed, shaking his head.

"Well, I guess we are, but I'll tell you today, young man, none of you are ever going to hear it from me."

On the third Monday in May, exactly one week after the first press event to the minute, Karen, Leslie, lawyers and advisors sat at a long table before rows of cameras and reporters.

After a week of stories, re-enactments, prognosticating and endless blathering, the Karen Epps press conference had become a major media event. Across the country, there was renewed interest in the infamous Jordan Alexander murder case.

On late Saturday night, Philip Alexander phoned Leslie to inform her that the Alexander Enterprises board voted to honor Jordan's reward promise, paving the way for Monday's session before the media.

Leslie, true to form, took great pains to choreograph the event, from seating arrangements for reporters to the lighting above the stage, from color coordination for herself, Karen and whoever else was on stage to the tenor and pace of Karen's reading, from the message the world would hear to various medium considerations such as camera angles, shots and editing. Thus, the stage was set as the world awaited Karen's dramatic revelation.

"My name is Karen Epps and this is my story."

She looked toward the cameras and then back down at her script. Her voice trembled as she spoke.

"I was born and raised here in this city. My mother Christine worked for the city of San Francisco for 33 years before she died of cancer. For all my life up until months before my mom's death, I never knew who my father was. I got Christmas gifts she said *came* from my father, but I always thought she was just being a good mom, making me feel I had a father out there who cared about me. For all my life she never said anything about him, just that he had always been there for me in the important ways, that he loved me, and that I should be good because I might never know when he's out there watching me."

Once again, she looked up from the script, her lip shaking.

"About six months before she died, my mother told me who my father was. She said his name was Nathaniel Adams and that he lived in San Diego. After she died, I used part of the insurance money to take a trip down there to find him. When I found him, he denied ever knowing my mother and said he wanted nothing to do with me. But I had already come all the way down there, so I wasn't about to go away without some answers. We went back and forth for a while until I mentioned that my son looked a lot like him. He asked to see a picture, which I was all too happy to show him.

"From that point on, he accepted me. He told me he was the one who sent the gifts and the money and paid for my school. He said that sometimes, when I was younger, he would drive all the way up to San Francisco to watch me sleeping. He said he'd cry as he stood there, wanting so much to hug me just once."

As she looked up, her eyes were filled with tears.

"He met his two grandsons and he helped them out a lot until one went to prison and the other was the victim of a drive-by shooting. He saw a picture of my daughter."

She flipped the page without losing continuity.

"Three summers ago, I learned my father was keeping a secret from me, I learned his name really *wasn't* Nathaniel Adams. Instead, it was a name some people in San Francisco knew well. The father my mother didn't dare tell me about was former City Councilman Walter Monroe."

She stopped on cue as a wave of camera flashes flowed back and forth across the room. The din of amazed reporters, mumbling among themselves, filled the room, reaching an objectionable level, and Leslie stood to quell the interference. Getting a nod from Leslie, Karen continued.

"I discovered his true identity on medical documents he asked me to take from his home the hospital. When I confronted him about the discrepancy, he admitted the truth and asked me never to reveal his real name, and I kept my promise to him until today."

She withdrew a handkerchief from her pocket.

"I really didn't want to come here today. In fact, if I could have had it any other way, I wouldn't be here before you now. I've only had a father for the last five years, a man who's been nothing but good and generous to me and my sons, and today, I come before the world to betray that man."

She blotted her eyes.

"In February this year, my father became very ill. I think it was pneumonia, but no one was sure if he'd pull through. I got a call from him, he was wheezing, he said he was desperate, that he needed to talk to me about something important. I flew down and went to him. He seemed delirious at first, but then he began to talk about Lynette Alexander. They were obviously close friends at some time, and though it surprised me, there was nothing strange about it. My father was friendly with many women."

She closed her eyes, struggling to go on.

"But he told me he was in Lynette's room on August 17th, 1986, and the blood sample no one had been able to identify—it was his."

She looked up, staring into the cameras.

"Jordan Alexander didn't murder his wife, Lynette. I repeat, Jordan Alexander isn't and never was responsible for her death. My father, Walter Monroe, my father killed Lynette Alexander. God help me!"

Pushing the script aside, a teary-eyed Karen stood, knocked her over chair and rushed from the room, followed by a bevy of bewildered lawyers and bodyguards.

CHAPTER 47

"Mr. Monroe, did you murder Lynette Alexander?"

Walter stared at the television that depicted the scene outside the front door of his condominium.

There were news vans, police cars and a great horde of people. Inside, he and Bryan could hear the sound of a helicopter hovering over the house even as they watched it on television. Thirty minutes earlier, Walter and Bryan watched a re-broadcast of Karen's press conference.

"Mr. Monroe?"

It was the fifth or sixth time Bryan asked the question with no response from the older man. Finally Walter wagged his head, his eyes fixed on the television.

"No. To answer your question, Bryan, I didn't kill Lynette. I would have never killed Lynette. Lynette was one of the nicest persons I have ever met."

"Were you in her room that night?"

Walter nodded.

"Briefly. More precisely, I was at her house. She was my friend. She was a fellow artist and I visited her from time to time. She did her artwork in a corner of her bedroom. I went up there briefly to look at a new piece she was working on."

Bryan squinted as he sought to remember details from 14 years earlier.

"Was it your blood in the room and on some of the stairs?"

Walter nodded, never looking away from the television.

"Yes. The third blood sample, it was mine."

Shrugging his shoulders, Bryan stared at the mysterious man.

"What happened?"

Finally, Walter turned toward the detective.

"Look, I meant what I said back at the airport. I'm not going to help anybody out here. I've watched them over the years, all those reporters, all those television lawyers and talk show hosts. I hate the whole lot of them. No one's going hear anything from me. Not even you."

Bryan scratched his head, still baffled.

"Mr. Monroe, You're a lawyer. I'm sure you know that if you *don't* say anything, Jordan Alexander and the State might be able to pin the murder on you—especially after what your daughter said today."

Walter turned back to the television, responding as he watched a suited man, escorted by two police officers, approach his front door.

"If the Alexanders and the system are so unjust that they can convict an innocent old man for murder, then let them do it."

Allegra sat on her couch, flipping from one news story to another. In the span of one minute, she watched Karen Epps implicate her father on six different stations. Destiny returned from the kitchen with a serving tray that held a large silver teapot and two fancy teacups. Her eyes were fixed on the television as she placed the tray on the table.

"Wait Allegra, stop right there!"

Both women squinted as they stared at the screen.

"Isn't that *Bryan*?"

Allegra stood, approaching the set.

"Yes, I believe that *is* him. You talked to him today?"

"We've been playing phone tag. I haven't been home since Friday."

Destiny sat, her eyes never averting from the television.

"Looks like he was right about Monroe."

Allegra had returned to the couch and was pouring tea into the cups.

"I met him once, a long time ago. This whole thing is unreal. I don't know *what* to believe anymore."

As she handed Destiny a steaming cup, Destiny bowed her head without thinking. Tea, it always seemed, made her revert to many of the Japanese customs she practiced over the years.

"Thank you. You know Allegra, I said it before. The story Karen Epps told doesn't add up. I mean, there's no motive. Why would Councilman Monroe just one day up and kill your daughter? It makes no sense."

She stopped as she watched Walter Monroe, Bryan and the uniformed men at the car, just before the doors opened. Reporters shouted questions at Walter who covered his face and bowed his head. When Walter was inside the vehicle, Bryan stopped and turned, facing the reporters.

"Mr. Monroe has asked me to inform you that he won't be answering any of your questions at anytime. He maintains he's innocent and that he doesn't feel obliged to prove anything to anyone. That's all."

Before Bryan could turn, reporters pressed him against the car with a new onslaught of questions. Shoving one man aside, he snapped angrily.

"I said that's all!"

"Waitaminute!" yelled one woman. At the moment Bryan hesitated, she grabbed his arm, turning him toward the cameras, "Who are you?"

He looked at the cameras as he climbed into the car.

"I'm a friend."

Within minutes, the news station had identified him and began a story on his involvement in the original murder investigation and the ensuing trial. Another station followed the segment with a story on the history of DNA fingerprinting and suggestions that from as early as 1987, some of the samples found in the room were identified as having come "from a male subject of African American ancestry."

Walter Monroe was black, but among blacks, he was considered light-skinned. For that reason, his brown-haired daughter Karen, though she was a mulatto, seemed Caucasian.

After the conference, Karen went into hiding. She begged the world, through Leslie, to leave her alone, to give her time to deal with what she had done, to give her time to one day make amends with her father.

Turning off the set, Destiny turned toward her friend.

"Why would a daughter, for any reason, come out publicly against her father like that?"

Allegra sighed.

"That's easy. She's doing it for the money. It's five million dollars."

"Yes, but that's the easy answer. If it were *you*, Allegra, what could possibly make you turn your own father in?"

Allegra sat back, shaking her head.

"Destiny, I loved my father. There's nothing in this world that could have ever made me betray him. It wouldn't have mattered what he had done."

Destiny's eyes were closed as she bowed, blowing across the rippled surface of the steaming tea in the cup.

"Don't be so sure about that. I have an answer. We see it all the time at the foundation, and in almost every case where a child turns against the father, it's for the same rationale."

Allegra set down her teacup, turning toward her younger friend.

"Really Destiny? And what rationale is that?"

Destiny sipped the tea and spoke, looking straight ahead.

"The most natural one. Crimes against the mother."

A production assistant came out, blotted Jordan's forehead and applied more rouge to his cheeks. The direct lighting made him hot, sticky and uncomfortable. Nationally syndicated news commentator Titus Coffee sat across from him, directing Jordan's attention to the cameras as the producer ended the silent countdown.

After a brief introduction and reference to a cut away segment, Titus turned toward Jordan to begin the interview.

"Jordan, of all the bizarre stories! Yours is a riches to rags and back to riches one. Tell me, in light of the arrest this week of former San Francisco City Councilman Walter Monroe, how do you feel?"

Jordan evinced a tight-lipped smile and shrugged.

"Well Titus, I don't know. I feel a lot of things. On one hand, I feel vindicated. I mean, losing Lynette was a blow, but being arrested and accused of her murder was just so painful and so wrong that whatever happens now, I can only hope to get over it."

"You were never convicted?"

"That's right, I was never convicted, but the stigma was still there. Unfortunately, in the court of public opinion, a mere accusation is the equivalent of a conviction. It didn't *matter* to anyone that I wasn't convicted. They all believed what they wanted to believe about me."

Jordan smiled toward the host.

"I mean, I watched *your* show. You were one of the loudest voices out there proclaiming me guilty."

Titus laughed.

"I was! And due to recent developments, I guess I might have to eat that crow and say maybe I was wrong, but this thing isn't over yet. I think we should all wait to see if there is a conviction before I start apologizing for things I've said. Fair enough?"

"Yes, that's fair."

Glancing toward the producer, Titus' transition was smooth.

"A far more interesting issue though, Jordan, is that of the *civil* trial. You *lost* that, didn't you?"

"Yes."

"And you had to pay? Millions of dollars?"

Jordan finished the sentence.

"The judgment was for thirty-five million dollars, and I've already paid out a little over twenty-one million."

"Meaning you still *owe* fourteen million?"

"Yes."

Titus turned toward his camera.

"So what happens if Walter Monroe is found guilty? What if he confesses or the State provides evidence that he is the *only* person who could have murdered your wife? What happens then? Do you still owe the money?"

Jordan nodded.

"That's what my lawyers are telling me."

Titus smirked.

"Now that seems a little idiotic. After all, what is the premise for this civil judgment? What, what was the money awarded for?"

Jordan sighed and began.

"The civil trial jury somehow found me 'responsible' for Lynette's death, and thirty-five million dollars is what they awarded in damages to the plaintiffs."

"So even if we all find out you had absolutely *nothing* to do with your wife's murder, if we find there's no way at all you could be responsible, they're saying you'd still owe the money?"

"Yes I would."

Titus sighed, playing to the camera.

"What's that legal axiom? *If the law's against you, argue the facts, but if the facts are against you, argue the law?* I'll say this much, Jordan. I've spent the past 14 years calling you a murderer and a slime ball. I've pretty much done my best to denigrate you. But I'll also be the first to say that if Walter Monroe is the murderer, it's *wrong* for the government to make you pay anyone thirty-five million for a crime you didn't commit. If it's the law, let me be the first to say we need to change that law."

Jordan smiled.

"Thank you."

Titus continued.

"Now if anyone had the juice to change those type laws, it seems you're in a pretty good position. Aren't you pretty close to Mayor Towne and some of those other movers and shakers in San Francisco who are in with state and federal legislatures?"

Jordan shrugged.

"I, I don't know about Mayor Towne, but I know a few people. My lawyers are working on it."

Once again, Titus changed direction.

"Speaking of juice, I heard the board voted, and now you're once again president and CEO of Alexander Enterprises?"

Jordan smiled.

"Yes."

"And I've also heard about some ill will between you and your brother, Philip. Philip had been in that position for the past 12 years?"

Jordan turned toward his camera as he answered the question.

"Yes. When I, when I was arrested initially, I asked Philip to take over, and he was great for the company. Did a great job."

"So the rumors about power struggles and ill will? Unfounded?"

"Absolutely unfounded. I love my brother, and he will continue to be a major voice and resource for the company. There's never been a power struggle. The situation now is exactly as my grandmother Dottie meant to be."

The two just stared at each other in silence before she asked the guard to wait outside. Though the guard balked and began reciting policy, Allegra insisted until the resentful man was on the other side of the door. Clearing her throat, she turned toward the prisoner seated on a cot in the small enclosure and began.

"Mr. Monroe, I've spent the last 14 years agonizing about what happened the night my daughter was killed. If what they're saying about the DNA is true, there's no question you were in her room that night."

The guard's warning on her mind, she approached the man.

"Mr. Monroe, I swear whatever you say to me will stay locked in my heart forever. I just have to know the truth. Did you murder my daughter?"

Tears swelling in his eyes, Walter stood and answered, shaking his head, his voice low.

"No. No, Mrs. Benson. I didn't murder your daughter. She and I were friends. You know that. I adored Lynette. I was devastated when I heard the news."

Batting back tears in her own eyes, she nodded.

"I believe you. So you have to tell me. Do you know who *did* murder my daughter?"

Walter turned away, silent.

"Mr. Monroe?"

He answered, his back to Allegra.

"Mrs. Benson. I can't. I'm sorry. It's nothing personal. I've already said I'm not going to talk about it. Not now."

"But you have to talk about it! The DA seems to think he's already got enough on you to convince a jury. You'll be convicted for Lynette's murder if you don't stand up and defend yourself."

He stood there for a few seconds and turned toward Allegra.

"Let's be realistic here, Mrs. Benson. If they want to pin her murder on me, nothing I can tell anyone will make a difference. I came to that conclusion early on."

Again, he turned away.

"But I owe this much to Lynette. You're her mother. When this is all over, I'll tell you everything. You, and only you. Other than that, I have nothing to say."

She sighed.

"I don't understand you! So that's it? You're not going to tell me anything else?"

He answered.

"I'm sorry, but I've said as much as I'm going to say."

Disappointed, Allegra turned to go, hot tears on her cheeks.

"Mrs. Benson?"

She turned as he began.

"I know I'm in no position to ask you for a favor, but I need you to do something for me."

Although she gave no verbal response, Walter continued.

"At the arraignment, the judge advised me to get a lawyer, and I was hoping you could somehow make Destiny Mitchell take my case. Tell her I can pay her."

Allegra stood, bewildered.

"Excuse me? *Make* her take your case?"

"She does work for you, doesn't she?"

"Not really. She runs the foundation."

Walter seemed tired, almost out of breath as he sat, sighing.

"Look, we both know what time it is. The bottom line is she works for you and she's not going to volunteer to take up my defense on her own. If anyone could make, or if you want to say *persuade* her to do it, it'd be you."

Allegra nodded.

"I'll talk to her about it, but I can't make you any promises."

Walter's eyes were closed, his head bowed.

"Mrs. Benson, somehow I think all you'll have to do is ask her. None of our lives will ever be right until we finish this thing."

CHAPTER 48

"I told her the whole idea was ludicrous. I mean, first of all, I have no desire to go through another ugly trial, much less one on a subject so close to me. And second, I'm not a *defense* lawyer, never was. They're all sleazes, every last one of them."

Kiyomi finished breaking open the red-orange shell, extracted the flesh from a pincer, dipped it in butter and chewed, moaning aloud before responding.

"But you're perfect for the job, Destiko. You know that case better than anyone."

After almost a year and a half of not speaking with each other, Destiny and Kiyomi found themselves embracing, grieving together at the funeral of Hanako Yamakita, Kiyomi's mother. From the beginning of the ceremony at "mom's" Buddhist temple, it was as if all former angst and anger had dissolved. Spoken regrets and apologies gushed from each, along with a shared oath to never become so angry again.

"Who *cares* if you've never done a defense case before. You're a natural. And the idea of this whole thing coming back to you! The *universe* is saying you really need to do this."

Kiyomi married Cedric Mitchell, Destiny's first cousin, 10 years earlier and the two bought a nice home in Mill Valley shortly thereafter. Although both were busy in their careers, they went out of their way to have Destiny and her fiancé over for dinner twice a month.

Their seven year-old daughter, Natsumi, was a beautiful little girl who resembled her famous second cousin, though her complexion was much lighter. Across from Natsumi sat Bryan, who took the task of decapodal dismemberment seriously. Never looking up, he echoed Kiyomi's opinion.

"That's exactly what *I've* been telling her. We all thought the thing was lost in '87, but now it's come back to you. It's providence."

Cedric, four years older than Destiny, had always been protective of his younger cousin.

"I don't know, Kiyo. You remember what she went through during that last trial, what you both went through. You didn't speak to each other for over a year! Besides, I'm not so sure if Monroe *didn't* commit that murder."

Bryan looked up from the meal.

"Oh you're wrong there, Cedric. Monroe didn't kill Lynette.

Jordan did. Monroe knows it but he figures he can't prove it."

Interest piqued, Destiny cut in.

"And how do you know that?"

"I've been investigating. I know that in 1980 when Lyndsey was born, Jordan for some reason thought he wasn't the father, and that's why the incidents of violence rose after that year. He thought his youngest daughter looked like she was part black, and I think that's eventually what drove him to murder Lynette."

Kiyomi interrupted.

"And how does Monroe fit in?"

"Well, he was one of Lynette's friends and he was black, so he was a natural suspect. I understand he and Jordan went at it a few times, but he's denied being anything other than Lynette's friend."

Destiny squinted as she considered his words.

"Anyone ever do a paternity test?"

"No. Jordan never wanted to. You've got to figure he thought if news of a paternity test ever got leaked, he'd have been humiliated."

Cedric, wiping sticky hands, spoke from his own memory.

"Waitaminute. Wasn't Monroe *married*?"

"Yes he was, but his wife couldn't have any kids. He had Karen Epps as the result of a long-term affair, and there are people who say he pursued the affair from the beginning to get himself a son. He really wanted a son. When his wife found out about his daughter by Christine Epps, the affair ended."

After a long pause, Kiyomi sighed.

"So what do you think happened, Bryan?"

"Not sure. This whole thing's pretty weird. Monroe's not talking, Karen Epps has disappeared, Jordan's back on top of the world. I don't know what's going on, but I'm pretty certain Monroe didn't kill Lynette."

He sighed, a little frustrated.

"But then, Monroe was definitely there. I don't think he would collude with Jordan because they hated each other. So there's the mystery. He was in the room, Jordan was in the room and Lynette was murdered in that room. Somewhere along the line, we're going to have to hear his story."

Kiyomi finished the thought.

"And that's why I think you should defend him, Destiko. He asked for you. He specifically wants *you* to defend him, and he has some reason for that. If nothing else, you have to go over to the jail to talk with him."

She grasped Destiny hand and continued.

"Girlfriend, you've said it yourself: This thing being unresolved has left you incomplete. It might be the only chance you'll get to finish it and move past it. At least go on over there and *talk* to him."

Further urging was unnecessary. Even as Kiyomi spoke, Destiny was already formulating the questions she would ask of the one person who could bring the most torturous, frustrating and painful chapter of her life to an unequivocal and dramatic close.

A legal debate raged across the country relating to what remedies Jordan should or could be able to pursue in the event Walter Monroe was found guilty of murdering Lynette. Most scholars held that civil judgments, once the period for appeals had run out, were unalterable by the principle of *res judicata*.

One Yale Law School professor went on CNN and said, "Even if there were some newly-revealed videotape showing Monroe committing the murder and Jordan completely out of the picture, it would change nothing. Unlike criminal judgments, in which corrections can be and are often made, civil judgments have always been final."

Throughout the week, it became clear to America in the hypothetical that the rules on civil judgments, as written, granted no legal remedy for a person who had paid out twenty-one million for a crime he didn't commit. According to civil law, all the money Jordan had already paid out was unrecoverable.

A separate issue however, was the fourteen million he still owed. While the law provided he would owe the money regardless of the outcome of any subsequent trial, many in the legal community were proposing various remedies to allow Jordan some relief. These solutions ranged from motions to set aside the judgment in a manner similar to remedies utilized in criminal cases, to proposed changes in the law through state and federal legislatures.

The public saw the potential travesty to Jordan Alexander as an abomination of justice and expressed support for changes in the law, much of this resulting from Jordan's public appearances and pleas for relief.

To stem the growing backlash toward the foundation resulting from Jordan's campaign, Allegra and Destiny made a series of public appearances, getting out the message that *Aegis* was Lynette's dream and that all the money Allegra received from Jordan had been donated to the foundation.

Destiny, in an appearance on *The Titus Coffee Show*, thought it was important to let the public know that the majority of the money Jordan had paid out and owed was going to the estates of his daughters. The remainder had gone to a foundation that had, over the years, helped thousands of women escape or manage violent domestic situations. Thus Jordan's money had gone to worthy causes.

It was only after the weeklong PR campaign that Destiny was finally able to go over to the jail. When the door to the cell opened and she entered, Walter stood, extending his right hand.

"Ms. Mitchell? Destiny, it's so wonderful to meet you."

All business, Destiny perused the small enclosure askance. Eyes darting toward the conspicuous metal toilet and about the Spartan setting, she walked toward and sat on the rickety cot. He took a seat on his thin mattress of a bed as he watched her open a folder.

"Why me, Mr. Monroe?"

"Walter."

"Okay. Why me, Walter?"

"Because I followed you through that other trial. I like your style."

She sighed.

"I'm not a defense lawyer. I don't even *practice* law anymore, though I'm still an active member with the State Bar."

"Defense or prosecution, you know this case better than anyone."

She laughed to herself.

"Oh really? Then why didn't I know about you?"

His face grew serious.

"Because I was, because I was really a non-factor."

"Were you romantically involved with Lynette?"

He sighed, exasperated.

"No. Now why would you ask me that?"

"Because you were involved with Christine Epps. It just kind of seemed like a pattern."

"What? A black man is involved with one white woman and

all of a sudden that means he's into some kind of a pattern?"

She ignored the sarcasm.

"Are you Lyndsey's father?"

"No, Destiny. I've told you. Lynette and I were friends. We were both artists."

Pausing, she looked up from the document she was examining.

"You went to Hastings Law School?"

"Yeah, long time ago. Worked my way through doing janitorial work and other odd jobs."

"Never practiced law?"

"Briefly, till I got involved in city politics."

She closed the folder and tucked it back into the briefcase.

"What are you up to, Mr. Monroe?"

He seemed confused.

"I, I don't know what you're talking about."

"Look, if I'm going to defend you, you can't play games with me. I know there's a lot more to this than I realized before. You were in that room, Jordan was in that room. Now all of a sudden, you're here, Jordan's at the top of his game, and somehow you don't want to talk about things. Do you two have some kind of a secret *deal* going on?"

"What?"

"Is he paying you to take the fall for him or something?"

"No, it isn't like that. I detest that man, and he doesn't like me. Anyone will tell you that."

She seemed baffled. Withdrawing a small notebook and pen, she began to write notes as she continued the questioning.

"Well, why would your daughter, Karen Epps, why would she tell the world you told her you murdered Lynette? Why would she *lie* on you?"

He shifted in the seat, extending first one leg and then the other.

"Now *that* I don't know, but the way it all went down, I think that five million dollar reward had something to do with it."

She didn't look up.

"Does she know Jordan?"

"Wouldn't know."

Destiny paused, thinking.

"Did you witness the murder?"

"No, I did not witness the murder."

"Well, is there anyone who can verify your whereabouts

during the time she was killed?"

"No. For all intents and purposes, I was alone that night. I was with my wife who was medicated, and she's dead now. Didn't talk to anyone else."

Tucking the notebook into a pocket, she closed the briefcase and stood.

"I'll be honest with you, Mr. Monroe. Your evasiveness isn't making this easy for me."

He stood, his expression hopeful.

"I take it that means that you *will* represent me?"

She nodded, extending a hand.

"I will, but you're going to have to meet me halfway. I don't know what you're up to, but somewhere along the line, you're going to have to let me in."

He smiled.

"Well, I don't know how this is going to end up, but when or if the time comes, believe me. I'll let you in. I'll let the whole world in."

Fourteen years earlier, Barry Divine seemed larger and more arrogant, but time and conscience, like cancerous tumors, had begun to sap all signs of his youth and exuberance. Barry was still charming and smooth, still one of the most sought after lecturers and analysts in the country.

Notwithstanding, during the weeks after Walter Monroe was arrested, Barry remained conspicuously quiet about offering predictions and opinions. In fact, he avoided the subject.

At almost sixty, he had closed his practice at the urging of his new wife who was just barely twenty-five. She loved traveling, with or without her husband. So on one of the many occasions he was left alone, he invited Jordan out to eat, beginning a tradition of Tuesday night dinners at *Masa's* on Bush Street. Because cousin Barry was one of Jordan's closest allies at Alexander Enterprises, the two, over French champagne and *fois gras*, typically discussed strategies for dealing with Philip and minions in attempts to regain former power.

If Barry had been uneasy during Karen Epps's initial appearance and revelation, he was unnerved when Monroe was arrested, and he was confounded by Jordan's high-profile attempts to clear his name and recover the money he paid out to Allegra and the girls.

Despite the legal impropriety of Jordan's campaign, it seemed a majority of the public supported him. In fact, a group calling itself *Citizens Against Double Jeopardy* circulated a statewide petition to put an initiative on the ballot that would altogether expunge civil claims in the event of an acquittal. The measure would limit these claims in the event of a hung jury. Analysts predicted California voters would see the proposed amendment to the state constitution on the November ballot.

Reluctant to broach the subject for over three weeks, Barry finally found occasion to discuss recent developments with Jordan as they sipped cognac after dinner one Tuesday evening.

"Somehow I think you really should keep a lower profile on Monroe and the money and everything. I think it's a major gamble. There's just too much out there."

"For instance?"

Barry couldn't believe he was having to explain the risks to his cousin. It should have been obvious.

"For instance, there're the DNA tests Destiny Mitchell ran during that first trial. Now, I'm not suggesting anything, but unless you know what the findings were then, and more importantly, what they'll find now with the better technology, I think it's best to let sleeping dogs lie."

Jordan sipped the XO and responded.

"I'm not on trial here, Barry. Monroe is. What else?"

Barry sighed, almost resigning.

"Well, there's Monroe himself. I don't trust him. He's not a stupid man, Jordie. He's cagey. He's up to something. This could all be part of a big set-up."

Jordan hardly considered the concern.

"Look, Monroe did it. He's not putting on a defense. He's going to jail for it. Open-shut case."

Barry leaned closer toward his cousin.

"Jordie, I'm not one to give credence to rumor, but I understand he *will* be putting up a defense, and just guess who they're saying he's hired for his defense?"

Jordan was caught off-guard by the seriousness of Barry's tone.

"Who?"

"Destiny Mitchell, so believe me, Jordie, if you're hiding anything, between that woman and Monroe, it's going come out."

As he watched Jordan's expression erode, Barry decided to ask the one question he hadn't dared to ask during the trial fourteen years earlier.

"So tell me, Jordie. I never asked before because I didn't want to know. But I swear, it will stay right here. *Do* you have anything to hide? Were you in any way involved in Lynette's murder?"

Jordan looked his cousin straight in the eyes, his expression unwavering.

"No Barry, I swear. I had nothing to do with the murder. I swear I knew nothing until the police came by at 5:00 that morning to tell me about it."

Eyes equally intense, Barry countered.

"Then why did they find *your* blood in the room?"

"It wasn't my blood."

"And you never wanted to kill her?"

"Never. I loved that woman."

Barry sat back, sighing.

"You know, during the trial, I was never sure about whether or not you were involved, but my job was to defend you. Since that time though, I've had serious questions, serious doubts."

Ironically, Jordan was engaged in a similar conversation with oldest daughter Caitlyn a few nights earlier. Back in the United States to honor her mother's legacy on Memorial Day, the twenty-four-year-old model asked her father about her mother, about the abuse she remembered, about her mother's death and his possible involvement.

After thanking her for being honest enough with him to announce her doubts and concerns, for being honest enough to ask difficult and painful questions, Jordan took her into his arms and hugged her long and hard, crying. Staring into Caitlyn's eyes, he swore to God that he had nothing to do with her mother's murder.

"Hopefully after Monroe's convicted, people will finally believe me."

Despite Jordan's resolute denial, Barry still expressed concerns about the degree of press coverage the resurrected murder investigation was getting, especially after Jordan confirmed a rumor that CourtTV was negotiating for rights and permission to broadcast the trial live.

"You can do whatever you want, Jordie, but I wouldn't trust Karen Epps or Monroe and I sure as hell wouldn't trust the press.

They're the worst. Just because they're feasting on Monroe for dinner tonight, don't think if they get hungry they won't be carving up your ass for breakfast in the morning."

"Karen, why do you think your father would lie?"

Her attorney, Nathaniel Simms, nodded, indicating it was okay to answer the question.

"I don't, I don't know."

Destiny was seated at the table next to Karen, gently posing the questions.

"Well, if he told you he killed Lynette and he told us he didn't, would you agree he can't be telling the truth in both cases?"

She seemed confused.

"I guess not. Look, I only said what he told me."

Destiny nodded, smiling.

"That's fine, Karen, but do you remember exactly *how* he said it? Do you remember what words he used?"

"Not really."

"Well, did he say *I killed Lynette* or *I murdered Lynette* or anything close to that?"

Tortured by the thought of what she was doing, she closed her eyes, bowing her head.

"I said I don't remember exactly."

Destiny touched her shoulder.

"Karen, look at me."

Karen raised her head, mascara running, as Destiny continued.

"Look Karen, I know this is difficult, but we're trying to work things out here. Take this."

Karen took the handkerchief and blotted her eyes as the lawyer pressed on.

"Karen, do you think it's possible that you *misunderstood* your father? Do you think he could have been trying to tell you something *else* about the murder? Maybe that he knew who the real murderer was?"

She closed her eyes in thought and opened them after a few seconds.

"No, I don't think I misunderstood him. I think he did it."

Destiny pursed her lips, nodding.

"Okay, so if you think he did it, why did you go public with it? Was it for the money?"

"No! It wasn't the money. I, I was just thinking of her family, the mother and the girls. I thought they should know the truth. I mean, everyone believed Jordan Alexander did it."

"So why the play for the money?"

"That wasn't me. That was Leslie. When she told me I could get five million dollars, I just said 'why not?' and went along with it. I mean, who wouldn't?"

There was a tap on the door, and the door opened even before Destiny's assistant could rise and turn toward it. Bryan's expression was anxious as he slid around the door, pushing it shut behind him.

"I'm sorry for the interruption."

He motioned toward the tape recorder.

"You might want to turn that thing off."

Destiny was standing, annoyed.

"What's going on, Bryan?"

He took a seat at the opposite side of the table.

"That's what I want to know?"

She sighed, growing perturbed.

"Bryan, what's going on?"

Eyes fixed on Karen, he began.

"Karen Epps here hasn't been telling us the truth, Walter Monroe hasn't been telling the truth and Jordan hasn't told the truth. I wouldn't be surprised if they weren't all in on it together."

Karen's face showed confusion while Destiny's interest was piqued.

"In on what, Bryan?"

He looked toward his fiancée.

"Ask Karen how long she's known her father is terminally ill with prostate cancer? Ask her if she knows how long he's expected to live?"

Bryan continued.

"Shakespeare couldn't have conceived a better denouement. Walter Monroe, the chivalrous father, takes the fall, but he won't live long enough to do time. Karen, the distraught and hapless daughter, gets a five million dollar inheritance and an opportunity to have a good life. While Jordan, the actual murderer, gets a clean name and a clean record, complete exoneration, bought and paid for by the company. It's a perfect ending, and Destiny, you, me, along with the rest of the San Francisco, have been played."

CHAPTER 49

Walter Monroe denied involvement in any plot that would transfer the stain, suspicion and bloodguilt from Jordan's name to his own. He insisted that while he had not led a perfect life, his public record demonstrated he was a man of principle. Jordan Alexander, he declared, was his avowed enemy, and he added that any suggestion of collusion was the result of overworked, cynical imaginations.

However, he did not dismiss the suggestion that *daughter* might have somehow accepted a deal offered by Jordan. It was a remarkable coincidence, he opined, that Leslie Wilke, the same woman who handled Karen's press conference, had also been involved in the publicity campaign that led to Jordan's return to power at Alexander Enterprises.

Walter said his prostate cancer was a private matter, and his failure to reveal the condition irrelevant and immaterial, yet he confirmed Bryan's suggestion he'd probably be dead within the year.

A week earlier, Bryan had lost friend and mentor, Vic Ehlers, to throat cancer. It was ironic. Vic was one of the most intelligent people Bryan had ever met, and yet he ignored warnings by doctors and friends that cigarettes would kill him. His death was sad, painful and ignoble after radical tissue removal, radiation and chemotherapy.

In the end, Vic sat in a bed, emaciated, disfigured, his irregular breathing amplified through a respirator. He seemed hardly alive, like a shadow or shell of something that had once been alive. Though his mind was sharp, his heart, his liver and his kidneys were slowing to an inevitable conclusion. Bryan was the only person there for him in the last days, indicative of the virtual life of solitude Vic lived.

Days before the end, Vic motioned for Bryan to come the bedside and he handed him a large envelope. Though Vic was not capable of speech, Bryan understood to open it. The envelope contained Vic's notorious black book, a lighter and a note.

"See ya in hell, kid. It'll be one helluva party!"

Bryan opened the book and began to read, but he stopped, looking up at Vic.

"You're joking. Is this really what I think this is? Are you the *only* one who knew?"

Vic forced a pained smile, nodding. Bryan looked back

down, reading with great interest. After he reached the end of the selection, he sighed aloud, astonished.

He sat in a daze for minutes before Vic, through gestures, insisted on the book burning. First, he had Bryan rip out all the pages, tearing each individual page into four pieces. These fragments were then placed on a platter in front of the old man, doused with fluid and ignited with the lighter. Vic nodded as the secrets burned, but the smoke made him wheeze and cough phlegm into the tracheal suction tube attached to the opening just above his clavicle.

An excited nurse came in and tried to snuff out the growing flames, but Bryan held her back until the better part of Vic's black book had decayed in the fire. The charred remnants of pages were then deposited in the toilet and flushed. Vic slipped into a coma that very night and died two days later.

The trial was set for Monday, July 26, a date that was a month or so earlier than Destiny hoped for and a month or so later than Walter Monroe's preferred timeframe. Destiny's former colleague, Ted Waters, though he had been district attorney for the last twelve years, opted to prosecute the case himself, and news agencies played up the evident animosity between the two.

Early on, Ted predicted Monroe, "in light of the overwhelming evidence against him, would submit a full confession before the trial was over," ridiculing suggestions by some that he would pursue a plea of insanity resulting from work-related stress during the period prior to the murder.

According to reports, Walter Monroe left the city council in 1984 because of finançial difficulties brought on by his wife's exorbitant medical expenses for treatments not scheduled or covered by insurance. The city charter disallowed him to seek outside work in order to supplement his income in any way. So after being denied a stipulation to moonlight with a company that conducted less than 2% of its business in San Francisco, Monroe quit the council to work in the private sector.

By all accounts, incredible anguish, turmoil and despair marked that period of his life. While the black community suggested Monroe's involvement was related to personal trials, Ted, against Jordan's wishes, insisted the murder was the result of a tragic love affair gone wrong.

Jordan implied that Monroe had revealed hidden desires for Lynette and that she rebuffed him, sending him over the edge on that Sunday night. Irreverent local radio and television hosts discussed everything from Jordan's new wife, Stephanie Rodriguez Alexander, whom he married on the day she returned to the United States, to questions about Jordan's own fidelity and sexuality.

One newspaper suggested Monroe fathered Lynette's youngest daughter, Lyndsey, while another cast Jordan and Monroe as lovers and Monroe murdering Lynette in a jealous rage upon discovering the couple was considering reconciliation.

Destiny, frustrated as she worked to defend a man who offered little assistance, refused to speak with the press. Unable to extract any new information from the stubborn old man, she was forced to consider other possible sources.

The loud, discordant music that blared inarticulately from the stage seemed every bit as nervous and wired as the pasty-skinned, androgynous twenty-something artists who created it, their tattooed, skinny bodies pierced with rings and studs.

There were no available seats at the bar of the dilapidated nightclub along the South of Market strip. There was hardly room to stand in one place. Yet standing there, Destiny felt she was drifting in a vast sea of detached bodies and faces, all clones from perhaps three or four original prototypes.

A young, short-haired woman behind her sat at a barstool, her legs open as another woman stood between them. The seated woman was crying as she described being fired from her job that day. Her friend comforted her with gentle kisses. Another woman stood in front of Destiny, seeking eye contact, but the lawyer avoided looking in her direction.

Anxious, Destiny checked her watch at one-minute intervals. She sighed, relieved that she had changed from her business suit into the black slacks and sweater before coming out. She felt old, out of place, but no one seemed to notice it. A person grabbed her shoulder from behind, asking her if she knew anyone who had *E*. She shook her head to indicate she did not. She closed her eyes, rubbing her temple as she could feel a headache coming on.

"Hi Destee!"

The face, despite the context, seemed different as the two embraced.

"Hi. Lyndsey?"

The young woman laughed.

"What? You don't recognize me?"

Destiny held the young woman at arm's length as she shouted, trying to speak over the music.

"Of course I do. It's just that, it's just that I haven't seen you since Christmas! Your hair was *blue* then. You've changed!"

Lyndsey laughed and smiled in a way that made Destiny remember a special ten year old girl from many years before, a sensitive girl she who became her surrogate daughter when she moved back to San Francisco. During Lyndsey's high school years, she lived with Destiny, but she remained close to her grandmother, Allegra.

Lyndsey was the only one of Lynette's daughters who was ever close to Allegra. She was the only daughter Dottie and Jordan ever allowed to visit Lynette's mother. In fact, Lyndsey was sent regularly over to Allegra's during formal family functions and gatherings. She was sent there during summers and during the holidays, and she was sent there permanently when Jordan remarried.

Dottie, until the day she died, made it no secret that she despised the little girl and often referred to her as the tramp's little mongrel daughter. Lyndsey was the prettiest of all the girls, but she was darker and had fuller facial features.

Her hair, before she chopped it off and dyed it black, was wavy and dark brown. Caitlyn and Denver, like their mother, were blonde. Lyndsey also had larger breasts and a more athletic build than her sisters did, with a *butt* that stood out in tight clothing.

Her butt was still noticeable as she led Destiny down the long hallway and into the private office.

"So, what is she going to need from me?"

Destiny closed the door, glad that the annoying music was no longer audible.

"Just blood, I think. And she might want a little hair."

"I just dyed it."

"Shouldn't matter. They use the roots. It'll take a couple of weeks before the results are in."

Lyndsey lit a cigarette and inhaled, the silver stud in her tongue evident as she slowly blew out the smoke.

"Destee? Are you *sure* this'll be confidential? No one's going to know?"

"Don't *you* want to know?"

The cigarette trembled between her thin fingers.

"Not really. I don't see it as something I really need to know."

Destiny sighed.

"Well, I think it's important. It'll answer questions that have bothered both of us for a long time, and your grandmother too."

After a pause, Lyndsey began.

"Who's uh, who's going to do this?"

"Hope, my sister at a lab in Emeryville. You *remember* her. The test is called PCR. You won't feel a thing."

Lyndsey laughed, her voice sarcastic.

"Well, we won't know that until the *results* come back, will we?"

❖❖❖❖❖❖❖❖❖❖

"Don't be afraid to come over and give me a hug. I swear I'm not mad at you."

Walter extended his arms, motioning with his hands.

"Come on. Come on."

She approached timidly before rushing into the embrace.

"Oh Daddy! I'm sorry! I'm so, so sorry. I didn't realize—"

He patted the back of her shoulder as she sobbed.

"No, no. Don't do that. Don't torture yourself. It's all going to work out. We're going to make it all work out. I promise."

"I've missed you so much! I love you!"

"I've missed you too, Angel, and I love you. Everything's going to be all right. We're going to be just fine. Don't worry."

Karen clenched her wilted father, determined never to let go.

"I thought Leslie was my friend, so I told her everything, and next thing I knew, I was on TV, reading from a script *she* wrote. I was so stupid! She used me! And now you're in jail! I'm so sorry."

He stared into her eyes.

"Look, I said everything's going to be all right, so stop your worrying, okay?"

She wiped her cheeks with her palms, smearing tears and mascara down her face.

"But this is serious. I've been talking to lawyers. They say I'll have to go to court and testify against you."

"Of course you will."

"But what do you want me to say?"

He embraced her a final time before backing. He led her to the lone bench in the cell and sat her down. Kneeling beside her, he spoke.

"You have to listen to me, Karen, because what I'm about to say is extremely important."

She held her breath, listening as he spoke.

"No matter what happens in that courtroom, no matter what they ask you, you have to tell the *truth*. You have to be honest. You have to tell the truth as best you know it. Do you understand that?"

"But—"

"No buts! I need you to promise me you're going to tell the truth. You promise?"

She was crying again as she nodded.

"I promise."

He stroked her face to wipe away a tear.

"There's my girl. I love you so much."

Rocking Karen, Walter began humming to himself and singing, sounding, as his neighbor from San Diego suggested, very much like Nat King Cole.

Smile, though your heart is aching,
Smile, even though it's breaking
When there are clouds in the sky, you'll get by—
If you smile through your fears and sorrow,
Smile and maybe tomorrow
You'll see the sun come shining through, for you—
Light up your face with gladness,
Hide every trace of sadness,
Although a tear may be ever so near—
That's the time you must keep on tryin,
Smile— what's the use in cryin—
You'll find that life is still worthwhile...
If you just, smile.

When the song was over, Walter Monroe had at last managed to elicit from his daughter something he considered more and more valuable as he neared the end of his journey on earth: his daughter's timid, imperfect, self-conscious and trembling smile.

CHAPTER 50

The magistrate's finding from the preliminary hearing back in late May had been, from its onset, a foregone conclusion. There had never been any doubt that the Walter Monroe matter would result in a high-profile criminal trial. District attorney-turned-prosecutor Ted Waters, in a straightforward manner, simply sought to establish that Monroe was present at the crime scene at or about the time Lynette was murdered.

After the original medical examiner came on and established the murder most likely occurred between 9:45 and 10:15, Gina Fasone testified she remembered seeing Walter Monroe, sweaty and bleeding, walk by her house between 9:30 and 10:00 on Sunday night, August 17, 1986. Ted's fifth witness was a criminologist who came on and showed photos as he described the trail of blood droplets which led back from the sidewalk in front of Gina Fasone's home to Lynette's home and into the bedroom where she was found murdered.

A little later, a former FBI crime lab director came on and told how former prosecutor Destiny Mitchell and criminologist Desmond Collins carefully collected, preserved and prepared samples of blood evidence for DNA analysis and sent them out to various labs, the FBI lab included. He described the nature of the testing and the various expectations of researchers and prosecutors alike. He detailed the degree of effort put forth and controls in place to mitigate improper conclusions and false inferences that might be drawn from test results. Above all, he stressed the integrity of the process and the reliability of end results.

Weeks earlier, the magistrate ordered Monroe to provide samples of his blood and hair for PCR testing at the FBI's Washington DC crime lab. According to the former lab director, both PCR and RFLP tests were performed, though the results from the longer RFLP test were still pending.

Thus Ted's final witness was one of the FBI's top DNA analysis experts who testified that the trail of blood drops that led out Lynette's room, out the house and past Gina Fasone's home could have "come from only one person in the known universe."

"And who might that be?"

"The man sitting right there. Your defendant, Mr. Walter Monroe."

Because Destiny conceded de facto that Walter Monroe was at the crime scene on the night of the murder, her cross-examination of the FBI witnesses centered on the other unidentified blood sample in the room, not the blood that proved to be Lynette's, but the other unidentified sample.

Neither FBI agent had an answer. In closing, Destiny alleged that the unidentified sample had come from the real murderer of Lynette Alexander, that the sample, which had been carefully preserved, "would fit the real murderer's DNA fingerprint like the glass slipper lost at the ball." Beyond physical evidence, she argued that Walter Monroe and Lynette Alexander were friends.

"Walter had no motive to murder Lynette, especially in the angry, vengeful and brutal way she was murdered."

The biggest surprise for Destiny during the course of the preliminary hearing was the presence of Bryan's Aunt Harumi from Tokyo in the front row of seating for observers. When Bryan told her his aunt wanted to attend the hearing and the trial, Destiny was astonished. She was, after all, the relative Destiny offended at Suziko's tea ceremony by telling her she needed to get off her fat ass an realize there's a world outside Japan. Though skeptical, Destiny arranged for Harumi to have a good seat during the upcoming trial.

The protocols Judge Gerald Garcia intended to impose on everyone involved in the trial concerned limits on the media ranging from proposed camera angles to the determination of which display or evidentiary items could or couldn't appear in the video feed.

If the presence of cameras and the implication of viewership weren't enough of an intimidation and distraction, the computerization of many aspects of the trial process and other technological advances in the courtroom were bewildering.

For instance, Judge Garcia was experimenting with a technology called voice recognition, wherein the accuracy of computer-generated court transcripts was being compared to the efficacy of an actual human court recorder.

As he played to the viewing world, Ted Waters' prosecution promised to be dynamic and seamless in an engaging application of state-of-the-arts technology. Keeping pace for Destiny and Walter Monroe would be both expensive and time-consuming. But in early July, three weeks before the trial was set to begin, Destiny hadn't been able to put together much of a defense, something Walter was quick to criticize her for in spite of his reluctance to help her.

She had the defendant's *lack of motive to commit murder*

and little else other than an old black man who admitted to being at the scene of a gristly murder, the murder of a young white woman.

Hope Jefferson looked up, glancing toward the door before adjusting her glasses and resuming an intense conversation with the young couple. Nervous, Lyndsey peeked around the corner through the narrow opening and, following Destiny's lead, tipped toward the chairs in the hallway. She sat, fidgeting folded hands in her lap.

Listening, Destiny and Lyndsey could hear Hope's low modulated voice speaking in a reassuring tone. The woman inside was emotional while the man seemed angry. Both emerged from the room 15 minutes later, lips drawn and eyes fixed straight ahead.

Lyndsey was picking at the black fingernail polish on her right index finger when Hope's face appeared at the door.

"You ready, Lyndsey?"

Lyndsey took a deep breath, stood and marched into the office, followed by Destiny. Door pulled shut behind her, Hope went around the desk and took a seat, retrieving a file from the drawer at bottom left. Lyndsey stared at Hope, intrigued by how much she resembled Destiny and had similar mannerisms.

"Who's older?"

Both women responded, pointing, inculpating each other, voices in unison.

"She is!"

Hope laughed.

"No, actually I am, by eighteen months. But she *looks* older."

In fact, Hope looked older. She was fuller-figured and her long tresses revealed more grays than Destiny's shorter haircut. Sliding a pair of wire-rimmed glasses up the bridge of her nose, she opened the file and began.

"Lyndsey, I asked Destiny to bring you over here because the PCR results came back."

Lyndsey's voice quivered as she responded.

"Okay?"

"Let's just cut to the chase. You want the long version of the short version?"

"The short version."

Hope closed the file.

"All right. According to the tests, which were pretty conclusive, your father, Jordan Alexander, has been your father all along. Genetically, you're his daughter."

Lyndsey's face showed confusion.

"I, I don't understand."

"The tests prove conclusively that Jordan Alexander is your natural father."

"Oh my God!"

Burying her face in her palms, Lyndsey began sobbing.

"Oh my God, that bastard!"

She looked up, her eyes showing both pain and anger.

"That bastard! I knew it! I knew my mother was never like that!"

As she continued, her words were an unintelligible muddle of sobs and slurred speech. Yet through it all, there was a definite sense of outrage, a sense of simmering anger.

"And for that, they treated me like shit!"

She looked over, appealing to her mother's greatest advocate.

"*You* remember, Destee? They treated me like shit, not like family! They never wanted me around. They were always sending me away! And everyone knew what that was about. It was all because they thought my mother was out screwing around. They thought I was part-black."

Destiny and Hope exchanged a tentative glance and allowed her to continue.

"And my great grandmother, Dottie! That bitch! I hope she's burning in hell right now for the way she treated me! She used to call me *the whore's nigger child* right to my face! All because she and my father thought I was part-black!"

She sighed as she wiped the tears from her eyes with her fingers, gesturing emphatically.

"Fuck them! Fuck them all for what they did to me! After the way they treated me, I'd rather *be* part-black than have anything to do with that family!"

Hope cleared her throat matter-of-factly, indicating a necessary interruption. She reached across the table, placing her brown hand atop the trembling white one.

"Listen Lyndsey, before we let you go too far with this. The truth of the matter is, you *are* part-black."

"What?"

More confused than angry, Lyndsey looked toward Destiny for clarification.

"What's she saying?"

Lyndsey looked back toward Hope.

"What're you talking about? You just said Jordan Alexander's my father."

Destiny cut in, uncomfortable about how to begin.

"Lyndsey, when Hope called me about five days ago and told me that genetically, you were Jordan's daughter, it just made me wonder."

She bowed her head and sighed.

"I mean you, you really *do* have features that kind of made me wonder."

She glanced over at Hope who nodded in agreement.

"So I asked Bryan if he would check it out for me."

Engrossed thus far, Lyndsey sought the conclusion.

"And?"

"Well, Bryan said he got the story from a man named Vic who he worked with, and it wasn't easy. In fact some of the records had been lost, altered or mysteriously destroyed, but he was able to confirm it all this week."

She turned toward Lyndsey.

"Vic said he found proof about your great, great grandfather Thomas Alexander's first wife, Maria, Dottie's real mother. Maria was a mulatto who passed herself off as Italian. Her mother was African. Maria died when Dottie was about five years old, so Dottie was raised by Thomas' second wife, Sarah, a woman who resented blacks."

Eyes wide, Lyndsey half-laughed to herself.

"So you're saying my grandmother *Dottie* was part-black?"

Hope answered.

"She was a quadroon, one-quarter black. So while there's no telling how much other mixing went on in your family, we know your father Jordan's at least a sixteenth black."

Lyndsey, eyes glazed, shook her head as she spoke.

"All these years! I've felt, I've felt this incredible guilt about my mother. In the back of my mind, I guess I really believed maybe she had, maybe she had... made a mistake."

Once again, tears spilled down her cheeks.

"I felt *I* was the result of that mistake, and when she,"

Lyndsey looked toward Destiny.

"On the night my mother was murdered, there was just a part of me..."

She closed her eyes, agonizing.

"I loved my mother, but there was just a part of me that blamed her for it, blamed her for the way they treated me."

She sat up, trying to re-compose herself.

"There was a part of me that didn't feel sorry she was gone. There was a part of me that was *glad* she was dead."

She smeared the tears into her cheeks.

"I'm sorry now, though. My mother was a good person. She was innocent"

Destiny stood behind Lyndsey, a firm hand on her shoulder.

"She was. She was a victim who didn't deserve to be murdered. And Lyndsey, all those stories about Walter Monroe and her, they weren't true. They were friends, that's all. He didn't kill your mother."

"I know. And that bitch, Dottie! That hypocrite! I can't believe she went so far out of her way to make me feel bad about looking different. She called me a *nigger* when she knew all along she was the biggest *nigger* in the whole family!"

"As our first witness, the State calls Mrs. Gina Fasone, your Honor."

The Gina Fasone who took the stand this time seemed very much different than the woman who had testified almost 15 years earlier. While the woman from the 1987 trial had been sophisticated and pretty, this older woman was slow about moving and speaking.

Instead of counting on her to recall specifics of the night in question, Ted went over her testimony from 1987, asking her if she remembered making specific statements under oath relating to the suspicious black man she saw in front of her house back then. Gina affirmed those previous statements, adding that the man she saw had blood dripping from his hands. When asked if she could identify the person, she confirmed the man she saw was the defendant, Walter Monroe.

In her cross-examination, Destiny asked Gina why, when testifying in 1987, she failed to mention the "blood dripping from his hands." Gina answered that she remembered telling *someone* about the blood, but she said she didn't remember if she did it while testifying. Prepared to question this witness, Destiny produced a transcript from the trial where Gina said "the man's face was sweaty" and that she didn't remember whether or not he was bleeding.

"So how would you advise the jury, Mrs. Fasone? We have inconsistent statements here. In the one right after the murder, you said you didn't recall seeing any blood, but now, almost 15 years later, this even after the mild stroke you suffered three years ago, you say you saw it. Which statement would you have the jury believe?"

Next, Ted put on former city council members who served with Monroe during the time prior to his resignation. One colleague, Pat Lahey, remembered Monroe as "a troubled soul on the brink." He remembered nothing of Walter's friendship with Lynette Alexander, but he said he wouldn't have been surprised if the two were involved in some kind of an affair.

"We all found out about Christine Epps, but Walt was very secretive. He didn't volunteer the information and he denied the affair even after we all knew."

A former secretary remembered transferring a few calls from Lynette to Walter's private line and described the relationship she observed as "chummy, but somewhat formal."

Then came a doctor who had treated Christine Epps for a minor injury to her face. He said the injury apparently came from "a domestic altercation" with Monroe in which he was held by police, but never charged.

Just before the end of the first day, a real estate agent testified about how anxious Monroe was to leave San Francisco in the month right after the murder. To the agent's surprise, Walter accepted an offer that was at least $20,000 under the market value and closed "from wherever he was living down there in San Diego."

The next day featured witnesses who knew Walter under his alias, Nathaniel Adams. One early neighbor described him as "polite and educated," but the man remembered "Nat seemed pretty much preoccupied with that 1987 trial." While the neighbor was surprised at how much Nathaniel knew about all the parties involved in the Jordan Alexander trial, he really hadn't considered it unusual at the time.

Ted's arrogance grew as he laid out the State's case, especially since Destiny challenged few of his witnesses and the statements they made before the jury. At almost 65 years old, Ted became a television novelty for being the most senior active prosecutor in the country.

The pundits adored him and credited him with almost single-handedly solving the crime of the century. The senior citizens loved him for the "inspiration he provided for other old-timers," and his straight-forwardness, his clarity and style captivated the public.

Destiny on the other hand, was portrayed on television as a lawyer out of her element, as out of touch with the defense side and as "a lawyer who will have to hit a grand slam homerun when she presents her side." Some commentators suggested Walter Monroe would have been better off getting himself an advocate who had more skill and experience and blamed Destiny for not having a clear defense strategy.

Once again, the nation's blacks and whites were divided along racial lines with blacks rallying behind Destiny and whites convinced that Walter Monroe was guilty of murdering Lynette Alexander.

During the next week of the trial, Ted called on his DNA expert analysts from the FBI's Washington D.C. crime lab and from Cellmark Diagnostics who, using numbers with exponents ten digits long, assured the jury that the blood in Lynette's bedroom and along the blood trail outside the house had come from Walter Monroe.

When Destiny asked about the unidentified blood samples found in the room, all three experts testified that tests performed on those particular samples were inconclusive. Destiny asked each why the results were called inconclusive and got each to admit they were described as such because the blood in question was a match to neither Lynette's nor Walter's DNA patterns.

"And the DNA extracted from those samples? Did you perform any tests to see whether it matched any other profile you had on record?"

The answer was no in all three cases because,

"No one felt any necessity to compare it with the hundreds of thousands of profiles we have in various DNA databases. We consider our client's requests very specific and don't typically run our own investigations. We're simply not in that business."

Bryan Osaka was called toward the end of the prosecution's case, and knowing he was Destiny's fiancé, Ted was careful and specific in his questioning.

"When you finally located him in the week after Ms. Epps'

announcement in May, where was he?"

"At the San Diego International Airport."

"And were you able to determine if he was there to pick someone up?"

Bryan sighed, glancing toward Harumi and then toward Destiny before responding.

"No, he was headed out. He had uh, purchased a one-way ticket to Barbados."

The witness right before Bryan was a bank manager who told the jury about Walter's abrupt withdrawal of over $110,000 in cash, checks and money orders. Thus Ted sought to use Monroe's involved plan to flee the country as an indicator of his guilt.

"You brought him back from the airport, didn't you?"

"Yes."

"And how did you discern he was leaving town?"

Bryan paused, considering how much detail he wanted to give.

"Well, I knew about the bank withdrawals, and I knew the assumed name he'd been using. I also knew after questioning neighbors and the bank clerk that he'd go to some warm place with a substantial black population where he'd blend in, so I checked the various airline databases for the name and I guess I got lucky."

Ted smiled, studying faces in the jury box.

"Okay, and did you confront him about the murder?"

Bryan shook his head in the negative.

"No. I just told him I wasn't going to let him leave."

"And what did he do?"

"He stayed."

Ted put an item up on the easel.

"Mr. Osaka, did this drawing have anything to do with you eventually tracking down Walter Monroe?"

"Yes, it did."

"Well, can you explain to the jury where it came from and how it helped you find Monroe?"

Once again, Bryan paused before answering.

"It's the sketch a police artist did based on the description of the man Gina Fasone saw walk past her house between 9:30 and 10:00 on August 17th, 1986. It didn't really look like him, but there were some features I thought were similar, so I matched it to one of Mr. Monroe's old photos in a newspaper and followed his trail down south."

Destiny, in cross-examination, focused on one area.

"Mr. Osaka?"

She smirked on hearing her own words.

"Mr. Osaka, when you went to the airport and you found Mr. Monroe, did you bring the police with you?"

"No, I doubt I could have gotten anyone from the San Diego Police Department to have come. There was nothing they could have done."

"So when you said you couldn't let him leave, what did you mean? Where you suggesting that you would have physically held him there?"

"No, I wasn't saying that. It was a figure of speech meaning I felt really strongly that he should stay."

"If he had walked past you and gotten on that plane, would you have done anything to hold him back?"

"No. He knew that and I knew that. I mean, the man studied law."

"So, he could have left if he wanted to, and he would have never been arrested, correct?"

Bryan nodded.

"Yes. He could have gotten on the plane and this trial would have never happened. He'd have been in Barbados soaking in the sun."

Destiny smiled.

"Thank you, and as a trained detective who investigated the details of Lynette Alexander's murder in 1986 as well as other details about the murder this year, have you in either investigation uncovered any evidence that would make you believe Walter Monroe murdered Lynette Alexander?"

Bryan's eyes fell to the jury box.

"Nothing. Nothing at all."

Ted's last witness was Karen Epps who, teary-eyed, told jurors about her relationship with her father over the past five or so years. She told about his connection with her mother, about the money and the gifts, about finally getting a name, Nathaniel Adams. Then she told about how she went to find him, about how he denied knowing her mother and about finally gaining acceptance.

"He never wanted to talk about his past and he tensed up whenever I brought up San Francisco."

They grew closer as they tried to reclaim his grandsons from the street and they attended the funeral for youngest together.

As Walter's health deteriorated, she said, he came to depend on her more for transportation to and from the hospital when doctors advised him not to drive.

Though she still lived in San Francisco, Karen said she flew down to San Diego at least twice a month to visit him and to do things around the house. When Ted asked how she discovered her father's true identity, she repeated, almost verbatim, what she told the world at the press conference. She had encountered his real name on medical records and promised never to reveal him.

She also testified that the first time her father ever mentioned Lynette Alexander was in February when he was very sick with pneumonia. That's when he told her he was there, in the room, that the murder of Lynette Alexander was the big secret he'd been hiding, that he felt guilty about it, that the murder was the reason he had changed his identity and gone into seclusion.

"I guess he thought he was going to die, so he was making the big confession to make his peace with God. I don't know."

Ted handed her his handkerchief, telling her how brave she was. Then he tried to get her to repeat suggestions he made about Monroe saying he *was* guilty as opposed to *felt* guilty, but the *spontaneous declaration* exception Judge Garcia granted to the *hearsay rule* did not extend to such a distinction. Thus finally out of new ways of phrasing the same question, Ted sighed and returned to his seat.

"Your witness, Ms. Mitchell."

Destiny did not stand right away. To everyone in the courtroom, it seemed she and Walter Monroe were in some sort of a disagreement about how to proceed. She started to rise once, only to be tugged back down by the defendant. Motioning to the judge for his patience, she listened to Monroe's spirited whispering, patted his shoulder and finally stood.

"Ms. Epps, just to make sure we're all clear here. You told us your father said he *felt* guilty, is that correct?"

"Yes."

"And would you agree that people sometime feel guilty for things they *don't* actually do?"

Karen looked from Destiny to the judge.

"I'm sorry. I don't understand."

"Well, let's say for example you're at a park and you see a little girl playing, when all of a sudden a sexual predator comes up and befriends her. Now if you didn't intervene and something happened to that girl, could you see yourself feeling a little guilty about what happened to her?"

Karen thought and answered.

"Yeah, I *would* be guilty."

"But you didn't in any way harm the little girl yourself, did you?"

"No."

"But you'd still feel guilty?"

"Yes."

As she made the transition to the next area of questioning, Destiny could see the cameras following her up to the mark on the floor that television producers asked her not to cross. Resentful about the way the press was treating her, she smiled as she crossed the line.

"Do you love your father?"

Karen looked over toward Walter, who sat with his head bowed.

"Yes."

"Then why did you betray him?"

All at once, Karen seemed betrayed.

"I didn't betray him! He told me to tell the truth, and that's what I did!"

"Didn't you turn him in? Didn't you destroy his reputation? Didn't you tell the world he was a murderer?"

The questions hit Karen like physical blows. Stunned, her shoulders hunched, she began to cry.

"No! I mean yes! But I told the truth! That's what he wanted me to do."

"Didn't you sell your father out for five million bucks?"

Ted interrupted on the grounds of "badgering," but the judge overruled the objection.

"Didn't you sell your father out for the money?"

Karen looked over to her father for help, for a reaction, for something!

"No, no, I didn't!"

"Well, aren't you the person who's responsible for him being here? Don't you know that, in the end, you'll be the person responsible for sending your father to prison?"

"He's not going to prison!"

Destiny paused, returning to a place where cameras could resume taping her.

"Ms. Epps, are you telling us you don't realize he'll go to

prison if he's convicted of this murder?"

Closing her eyes, Karen gritted her teeth to build resolve.

"No, he won't go to prison!"

"Ms. Epps, are you telling us that if your father is convicted of murder he won't go to prison? Why do you believe that?"

"Because he won't *live* that long!"

The courtroom erupted in mixture of moans and murmuring. Even Judge Garcia seemed confused as he pounded the gavel. After the judge advised all in the audience about spontaneous comments and reaction, Destiny was allowed to continue.

"He won't live that long? Can you explain?"

Karen sighed.

"Why are you acting like you don't know? You already know my father has prostate cancer. His doctors say he'll be dead within four to six months. He's not headed for prison."

She lowered her voice, glancing over at her father.

"He's headed for the hospital and the grave!"

Unable to handle the stress of testifying against her father any longer, Karen broke down, sobbing. She couldn't even respond to the judge's gentle questions. Thus after being unable to assuage this final witness for the prosecution, Judge Gerry Garcia was forced to release the jury and adjourn court for the day.

Prosecutor Ted Waters opted not to re-direct the next morning when court reconvened and rested the State's case on that Thursday, with the defense set to begin on Monday morning.

Ted sought sanctions against Destiny for failing to disclose discovery she had on Walter Monroe's terminal illness, but the judge ruled the illness was immaterial and bore little relevance on the question that was most central to the case: did he or didn't he murder Lynette Alexander?

The media, once again running well ahead of prudence, responsibility or corroboration, flooded the newsstands and news stations with theories about a secret deal between Jordan Alexander and Walter Monroe.

One nationally circulated newspaper ran a bold headline over a story about the trial entitled, THE FIX IS IN! while other newspapers echoed similar suspicions. On many of the news-format cable television shows, pundits predicted a quick conviction and wondered who had approached whom with the deal.

Then historians came on, describing other famous alleged *quid pro quo* deals made in the past, but this one, they all agreed, if actually true, was by far the biggest. CourtTV and other stations with the video feed, as a result of gavel to gavel trial coverage, pulled in a combined record 40% of the morning and mid-afternoon viewing audience for five days going into the final week of the trial, and it didn't appear that public interest was waning.

It was the biggest television trial of the decade, if not the century. Every witness who came on became an instant celebrity, the judge and lawyers became icons and trendsetters while the trial was spawning dozens of books and launching media careers.

Yet in the eye of the storm sat Destiny and Walter, motionless, as the world waited for the defense to begin. In the months since she decided to take the case, Destiny insisted that Walter had no chance of winning unless he took the stand and told what he knew. Walter criticized the strategy as hopeless because he had no one who could corroborate his story, so as they discussed the Monday morning beginning of the defense case-in-chief, Destiny suggested considering a deal with the State.

"It's like my father used to tell us all the time, Walter. 'There comes a time when you hafta shit or get up off the pot.' Monday's two days away. You have to do something, because if you don't, it's already over."

Just then, rattling keys indicated that the door was about to open. Both Destiny and Walter stood and waited for the guard. They could hear his voice, speaking to someone.

"You can just go on in. It's all right. I'll be back to get you in five minutes."

The man who entered seemed familiar to Destiny, and then she recognized him.

"You're Destiny Mitchell. What an honor. It seems neither I nor the guard knew you were here. Would you, would you mind excusing us for a moment? I've got a private matter to discuss with Mr. Monroe here. I'll call the guard."

Walter interrupted.

"She's my lawyer. Anything you want to discuss with me, you have to discuss with her. We're in this together."

The man thought for a moment before conceding.

"Okay. Well then, I don't think we've ever formally met. Allow me to introduce myself, Ms. Mitchell. My name is Philip Alexander."

CHAPTER 51

Jordan awoke with a jolt, covered in sweat and out of breath. Stephanie, lying next to him in the bed, reached over and patted his shoulder, never even opening her eyes. Over the years, she had grown accustomed to the night terrors, to watching him startle himself up in the middle of the night, to watching him sit there, in the dark, reluctant to return to whatever torture he'd escaped by wresting himself from sleep.

She tired long ago of asking him what he dreamed about because she knew, as always, he'd say he couldn't remember. Maybe he couldn't remember. Way back when she was a girl, her *Abuela* used to say, "great men have great secrets." He could keep his secrets, she thought, because she had Jordan Alexander. It was four in the mourning!

When Jordan and Stephanie were at *Ernie's* with Barry and his young wife during the previous evening, Barry seemed worried about Jordan. He wanted to talk about Lynette's murder, but Jordan became angry and walked out on dinner. When they were alone at the table, Barry told Stephanie he wasn't comfortable with the way the trial was going.

"There's going to be a bombshell somewhere. I can feel it."

Barry's concern made Stephanie realize that she too had secrets. She wanted to tell Barry she picked Jordan up at the *park* instead of at the wharf, but she held her tongue. She wanted to tell him about the package she threw off the Golden Gate, but she stopped herself. She was so naïve back then! And so young!

When she married Jordan, he was as low as she'd ever seen him. His friends were gone, people avoided him and his finances were shot to hell. No one would hire him and he was living with his mother. Though Stephanie was nearing the end of her modeling career, she managed to get a few good contracts so that she and Jordan had a comfortable life.

Then when Karen Epps came along, things really got better. Stephanie had the man of her dreams at the top of his form. Once again, he was dynamic, charming and a brilliant businessman. He was the good captain, the champion of personal responsibility, the skilled orator, the generous grantor, the loyal husband and father and the true friend.

After the Karen Epps press conference, Stephanie was at last convinced that Jordan had been on the level all along, that political enemies in the city and state's criminal justice machine had wronged him.

Turning over in the bed, she raised herself to an elbow and stroked his back as he sat there.

"What did you dream about?"

She was shocked when he turned and answered.

"Lynette," he said without emotion, "I just had a dream about Lynette."

Destiny took a deep breath before she stood in the courtroom, sporting a conservative navy pinstripe suit.

"The defense calls Walter Monroe."

She watched the near panic in Ted's eyes as Walter stood, walked around the table and ambled toward the witness stand. This, she thought, had to be the highest point of the trial. She located the four cameras in the room as Walter was being sworn-in. It was an unforgettable moment, being broadcast to millions of viewers all over the world.

No one expected Walter to testify. No one, including Destiny, had any idea about what he might say. So clearing her throat in order to project her voice, she approached the witness.

"Mr. Monroe, do you understand why you're here?"

"Of course I do, I'm here to defend myself against murder charges brought by the State."

"Did you murder Lynette Alexander?"

"No, I did not."

Uncertain about how he would answer, Destiny asked simple, careful questions.

"Were you in any way *involved* in the murder?"

He answered.

"No, I wasn't."

"Did you know Lynette Alexander?"

He smiled.

"Yes I did, and I say that proudly."

Destiny glanced toward the jury.

"Proudly? Why do you say proudly?"

"Because she was a good person, a wonderful person. I was proud to have been her friend."

Warming up, Destiny delved deeper.

"Mr. Monroe, would you mind describing for us the nature

of the relationship you had with Lynette? What was it?"

He nodded.

"It was a close friendship. I met Lynette in 1979 on the same day the students seized the U.S. embassy in Iran. I remember that because in her first words to me, she was asking if I heard the news. She was at city hall putting in some art pieces. She was an artist and I do art, so we talked. Over time, we became friends."

"So it was just a friendship, based on art, and nothing more?"

He corrected her.

"No, it was a close friendship, based on mutual respect and the fact that I think we really cared about each other."

"You were married and she was married?"

"Yes."

"Was there an affair? Were you two romantically involved?"

Walter sighed.

"No, never. It was a friendship, Ms. Mitchell. There was never anything else."

Satisfied with having established the lack of an affair, Destiny changed direction.

"Were you aware of the problems Lynette Alexander was having in her marriage?"

Walter sat back in the seat and answered.

"I knew about the problems she had in the early 1980s. She told me about the abuse. I saw the black eyes and the bruises. A lot of people knew, but by '85, I think the marriage was pretty much over."

"But they were still legally married?"

"Yes, I think she stayed married to him out of respect for him and for the girls, because after all that had happened, I think she still loved him, really. She was just tired of the abuse and wasn't going to put up with it any longer."

Destiny glanced toward the jurors who seemed impressed by the well-spoken, poised witness.

"Mr. Monroe, in the course of your friendship with Lynette, did you ever meet her husband, Jordan Alexander?"

"Yes."

"Did you know him?"

"Yes."

"Well, can you describe the nature of the relationship you had with him?"

Walter looked toward the jury box.

"Unfriendly. It was kind of a mutual disrelish, a general dislike. It went both ways."

"Why?"

Walter shrugged.

"Well, I can't speak for Jordan, but my problem with him had to do with what I perceived as an animus he had against black people."

"Did he ever accuse you of having an affair with Lynette?"

Walter nodded.

"Yes, and when I told him we were only friends, he told me the friendship was an embarrassment to him and demanded I keep my distance."

"And did you keep your distance?"

"Well yes. I thought about what he said, and I'm a man. I know how it is. I didn't want to embarrass him. So for a few years, I kind of shied away from her. But after she opened her clinic, she asked me to help with art concerns, and we just... became close again."

Destiny went back to the defense table to retrieve her notes before beginning her final area of questioning. She scanned the notes as she approached the witness.

"Mr. Monroe, were you at Lynette's Sacramento Street home on the evening of August 17th, 1986?"

"Yes."

"Were you in her bedroom?"

"Well, yes. She had a little art studio in the corner up there."

"And if there was blood in the room that DNA experts attest is your blood, would that be consistent with the facts as you remember them that night?"

"Yes."

"And if these same experts say samples of blood coming down the stairs and in the hallway are yours, would that be consistent with the facts as you remember them that night?"

"Yes."

"And if the experts say the blood trail out the front door and along the sidewalk in front of Gina Fasone's house is your blood, would that be consistent with the facts as you remember them that night?"

"Yes."

She nodded, pausing to build the suspense.

"Your blood was in that room, obviously Lynette's blood was in that room, but there were unidentified samples in that room that belonged to a third person. Do you have any idea how that could be, Mr. Monroe?"

Monroe took a breath, showing an uncharacteristic tinge of nervousness.

"Yes. There was a third person in the room."

"A third person? Can you tell us who the third person was?"

"Yes."

"Then we're waiting. Tell us who it was?"

Walter's eyes scanned the courtroom, from the judge to the jury, from the reporters who anxiously held their collective breath to Jordan's daughters Caitlyn and Denver, whose lawyers were assiduously preparing a wrongful death civil suit against him, from Ted, who sat at the desk, biting the end of his pen to Destiny whose face beckoned the truth that would set her free.

"Jordan. It was Jordan Alexander."

The whispering and unrest throughout the courtroom were sprung from the revelation. Walter paused a moment and, turning toward the jury, he began to tell his story.

"Lynette called me that morning. She said she felt uneasy, like she knew something bad was going to happen. She said whatever it was had her moping over two or three days. She didn't make it to the service at the foundation that day, so I called her that afternoon. I got no answer. I wasn't able to reach her until about 8:15 or 8:20, but she was happy to hear from me and asked me to stop by at about 9:00."

"So you went by at 9:00? 9:00 p.m.?"

"A little after 9:00, maybe 5 minutes after. Anyway, the girls were asleep when I got there. They'd been playing at the beach all day, so Lynette and I kind of sat downstairs in the living room for 15, 20 minutes talking about things. I brought a bottle of *pinot noir* and opened it for us. I tried to cheer her up, told her not to worry, that things would be okay. Then we started talking about art..."

He smiled.

"Now *that* always got her going."

From the corner of his right eye, he could see Allegra sitting in the front row, dabbing her eyes with a handkerchief.

"She had just finished an eight-by-ten foot oil canvas she was planning to display at the foundation and wanted me to come up and look at it. I followed her upstairs, and we were going over this painting when Jordan just showed up at the bedroom door."

Destiny closed her eyes, remembering the room that night and the blood smeared on that door.

"And then what happened?"

"Well, Jordan was drunk, or least he seemed drunk. He was just... um, in a state. So he came in the room and started accusing Lynette and me of, you know, having an affair. He made threats toward me. He told me to get out and to take my *bastard nigger kid* with me."

"Did you leave?"

"Not at first. I tried to calm him down, to appeal to reason, but he wouldn't hear me. I told Lynette I'd wait for her if she wanted to get the girls and leave, but that just made him more angry."

Reliving the moment was agonizing for Walter.

"He came at me and before I knew it, he cold-cocked me, punched me right in the nose, so hard that I got dizzy. I thought for sure my nose was broken. The blood of mine they found in that room, it came from my nose."

"So he hit you in the nose. And then what happened?"

"Well, I was at a disadvantage, but I was ready to fight him when Lynette begged me not to. In fact, she asked me to leave. She said she'd be all right."

"So you left?"

"Well yes, I didn't know what else to do. I asked if she was sure, and she insisted she'd be all right, so I left and went to my car, which was parked down the street."

"And that's all you remember about that night?"

"Well, what I remember most now was the look in her eyes right before I turned to leave. It was such a pleading, desperate look. It's haunted me ever since. I think she knew at that moment she was going to die. She knew she was going to die and no one in the world could save her. It was up to God at that point."

Walter's watery eyes caused Destiny to bat back her own tears before continuing.

"Did you call the police?"

"I thought about it, but what was I going to tell them? That I *thought* Jordan Alexander was about to murder his wife? No, at the time I guess I just fooled myself into believing Lynette when she said everything was going to be all right. I went home to my wife and ended up reading about the murder in the paper the next morning."

"And why didn't you come forward at that time?"

"Because I didn't think I *needed* to. I figured once the detectives started looking, they'd wind up getting Jordan. I figured he'd confess once he was arrested. I mean, who else but a jealous husband would have wanted to kill Lynette? Who else?"

"Okay, so why didn't you come forward at any other time?"

"Well, by the time the trial happened and the jury was hung, I didn't think it'd be possible for me to *prove* my story. Besides that, my wife was dying. It might seem selfish, but I chose to be with her in her last days instead of in some courtroom with a wild story I couldn't possibly corroborate. After my wife died, I just withdrew myself from everything. I didn't even do art anymore for a long time."

"Are you guilty for Lynette's murder?"

"Legally no, but in terms of being derelict on a moral/social responsibility, I always felt like I was."

"You didn't murder her, did you?"

"No."

"So when you told your daughter you felt guilty, you were referring to this moral/ social responsibility, weren't you?"

"That's correct."

Destiny sighed and went back to the defense table, ready to sit, but she stopped.

"Oh, one last question, Mr. Monroe. Have you at any time made a deal with Jordan Alexander?"

"No."

"Have you, knowing that you are dying, agreed to take the fall for Jordan in order to benefit your daughter?"

"No, and that should be obvious by the fact that I've taken the stand today."

"Thank you. No further questions."

Because Ted Waters asked for a half day to prepare his cross-examination, the judge adjourned the afternoon court session. Ted and Walter would be on first thing the next morning.

Outside the courtroom, the lurid nature of Walter's direct testimony had driven the media into frenzy with no discernible bounds.

Walter, promptly returned to his cell, was spared passing through the gauntlet of reporters who were intent on getting exclusives and inside scoops. Destiny on the other hand, was prodded, grabbed, snatched at and outright blocked as she tried to exit the court building.

The television news ran stories on issues relating from *The Disintegration of the Alexander-Monroe Deal* to the details of a civil suit against Walter Monroe and his estate being filed by Jordan's daughters, Caitlyn and Denver.

On the latter issue, legal experts debated about whether or not *two* separate individuals in two separate legal actions in conflicting scenarios could be held liable for the same wrongful death. The girls' lawyers, notwithstanding, were intent on pursuing the suit to its end.

Like a salmon that had endured barriers, predators and perils on a journey against the odds, like the spent male, clinging tenaciously to life for the sole purpose of ensuring its genetic line, Walter Monroe struggled against pain and fatigue to free his conscience of the oppressive burden he carried inside and protected for almost fifteen years.

Instead of succumbing to the current, he had struggled forward. He returned to protect his legacy, for himself, for his daughter, Karen, and for his grandson. But like the fish that had arrived and accomplished its purpose, Walter seemed worn-out, battered and mortally afflicted.

Anemic and emaciated, he collapsed upon returning to his cell and was immediately hospitalized. Despite a suggestion by Destiny and an offer from Ted to postpone the cross-examination, Walter was determined to finish the next morning. So many were surprised the doctor-in-charge dismissed Walter so he could go to court the next morning.

Ted smiled, placing his gentle right hand on the table before Walter.

"Mr. Monroe, I realize you've been having problems with your health, so I'll try to make this as brief and painless as possible."

Walter smiled.

"Thank you, Mr. Waters."

Ted looked over at the jurors, beaming.

"Good morning, ladies and gentlemen."

The jurors responded, and Ted began.

"Now Mr. Monroe, you said yesterday that you and Lynette Alexander were just friends, correct?"

"Yes."

"And how would you characterize the relationship between you and Christine Epps? Just friends?"

Walter sat up in the seat.

"Yes, we were friends, but—"

"Didn't you in fact insist to several of your co-workers that you and Christine were 'just friends'?"

"Yes."

"And you had a daughter by her? You and Christine begat Karen Epps? Right?"

"Yes."

"Did you and Lynette have a similar 'just friends' relationship, Mr. Monroe?"

"No."

"Are you the father of Lynette's youngest daughter, Lyndsey?"

"*Hell* no. I mean I'm sure she's a nice little girl, but Lynette and I were never like that!"

Ted sighed, nodding his head.

"You went to law school, didn't you? Wasn't it Hastings here in town?"

"Yes."

"Mr. Monroe, are you, like another famous lawyer in this country's recent political history, are you playing lawyers' games with words? What is *'is?'* What is 'friendship?' What are 'sexual relations?' Are you insulting our intelligence by playing games with definitions, Mr. Monroe?"

"No, not at all?"

Ted's voice, gentle at first, had grown louder and more antagonistic.

"So what is it? You and Christine Epps were friends, and you had a baby by her. I ask again, were you and Lynette Alexander sexually/intimately involved?"

Walter answered, defiant.

"No."

"And you and Christine Epps?"

Walter paused, sighing to himself before answering.

"Now I think that's pretty obvious, don't you?"

Ted pursued the line of inquiry, suggesting to jurors through his questions that Walter had a history of lying about his indiscretions. When he had gone too far and too long, Judge Garcia insisted that he move on.

The next area of questioning involved the pressures of

Walter's job and his wife's illnesses.

"You remember Pat Lahey, don't you? He served with you on the city council?"

"Yes."

"Well, he described you as a troubled soul on the brink. And the troubles you were having with the city refusing to help cover your wife's medical expenses. Didn't that big dispute, which ultimately led to your resignation, coincide with the murder of Lynette Alexander?"

Walter thought for a moment before nodding.

"Roughly. Yes, roughly."

"Those were desperate times for you, weren't they, Walter?"

"No. Not really. I remember it more as a *sad* time in my life."

Ted had returned to the prosecutor's table. Turning back toward the witness, he continued.

"Okay, now about the evening of August 17th. You said you went over to Lynette's at about five after nine with a bottle of wine, correct?"

"Yes."

"You also said you parked down the street. Why was that?"

Walter was unprepared for the question.

"Well I, I didn't like to park in front of the house. I knew Jordan drove by regularly to check to see if Lynette had company."

He looked pleadingly toward the jurors.

"I just didn't want to add to the problems she was already having with him."

Ted's tone was sarcastic.

"So because you didn't want to add to the problem, you park down the street and sneak over to her house when the girls are asleep with a bottle of wine?"

Walter answered.

"The wine was an afterthought. I went over there to be her friend."

Ted was unable to push the idea of impropriety any further because of Destiny's frequent objections to the argumentative way he put the questions. Moving along, he came to the alleged confrontation.

"You told us all that Jordan somehow appeared at the bedroom door at about 9:30. Now at the time you say he showed up, what were you and Lynette doing?"

"We were... looking at her art."

"Okay, but what were you doing? Were you doing it on the bed? Were you behind her, looking over her shoulder? What?"

"We were standing in front of the painting."

"And in this so-called memory of yours, what was Jordan wearing?"

Walter wagged his head, thinking.

"I don't know for sure, but I think it was dark. Blue or black."

"Did he have a knife?"

"I don't know. I didn't see one."

"Was he angry with you? You said he accused you and Lynette of an affair?"

"Yes."

"You said he was in a state. Now if he had had a knife, don't you think he would have attacked you with it?"

Walter thought a moment.

"Well, for some reason, he didn't."

"So you're telling us that Jordan, a man you already said suspected you of sleeping with his wife, you're saying this man went into her house and found the two of you in her bedroom drinking wine and doing whatever. He had a knife, but he only slugged you in the nose and asked you to leave?"

"Yes."

Ted held his head back, illustrating a typical reaction to a nosebleed.

"And instead of pinching you nose like most of us do, you just walked around and bled all over the place?"

"Yes."

"Mr. Monroe, didn't *you* have the knife that night?"

"No."

"Didn't you accidentally cut yourself in the act of murdering Lynette?"

Insulted by the suggestion, Walter sighed.

"No."

"Wouldn't that explain your blood all over her house?"

"That isn't what happened."

"Didn't you plan on murdering her all along? Isn't that the reason you parked down the street?"

Walter drew a calming breath, maintaining his gentle poise.

"No, that's ridiculous."

"Isn't it true Jordan Alexander was never in the house that

night?"

"He was there, he was definitely there."

"Isn't it true that you, as your neighbor from San Diego said, you followed the 1987 Jordan Alexander murder trial closely to the point of obsession?"

"I followed the trial, yes, but I wasn't obsessed."

"Didn't you fabricate this whole story about what he wore, about the jealousy, about the abusive nature and about his being drunk based on the facts you discerned from that '87 trial you were so obsessed with?"

"No, I *lived* it."

"Was yesterday the first time you ever told that story?"

"Yes."

"So for all any of us know, you could be making it up, right?"

"I'm not making it up. It's the truth."

"Well, can you offer us anything corroborative? Did you save something for insurance in case the police came looking for you?"

"No."

"Did you keep a journal? Did you take a picture of your nose?"

"No."

"Did you tell anyone any part or parcel of the story you told us yesterday?"

"No."

"Well, then Mr. Monroe, you're obviously an intelligent man. You're a lawyer! How do you expect any of us to believe you?"

Walter was apparently tiring, his stamina giving out, his voice almost resigning.

"Because it's the truth."

"Mr. Monroe, we all know this is arguably the biggest, most-observed, most-sensationalized murder case in this century so far. Are you telling us that in lieu of any offer of proof on your part, we're all somehow supposed to just take your word on it?"

"I told you what happened, and God knows, that's *exactly* how it happened!"

CHAPTER 52

In order to spare her client further stress, Destiny opted not to re-direct, satisfied that Walter Monroe had finally put his story before the world. Before resting the defense's case however, she briefly questioned the current mayor, Billy Towne, about Walter Monroe's character.

Like Monroe, Towne was African American. In fact, city councilman Monroe had been one of Towne's earliest inspirations and role models. While shying away from the racially charged aspects of the case, Towne commented on Monroe's character.

"One of the most honest, devoted, most caring human beings I know, period. The thought of him murdering another person, and murdering a person in the fashion Lynette Alexander was murdered, would be unthinkable."

Ted had one question in cross-examination.

"Mayor Towne, do you personally have any exculpatory information about Monroe's involvement in this case you might want to share with us?"

"Mr. Waters, I came here as a character witness, so what you're asking is not part of my function here. Even a dinosaur like you should've learned *that* in law school."

As the nation prepared for closing arguments, all the individual factions of San Francisco staked out various positions on the issue of Walter Monroe's involvement in the killing, the possibility of an inside deal and the re-implication of Jordan as the murderer.

Without a doubt, Jordan was the biggest loser. In an unofficial confidence vote taken by the Alexander Enterprises board, it was clear his support began eroding the moment Walter took the stand. Despite vehement denials by Jordan and a hastily launched media campaign purposed to impeach Walter Monroe and his testimony, Jordan's business future was questionable.

The dynamics of the case had changed dramatically since *voir dire*, or jury selection. Many of Destiny's questions were designed to exclude potential jurors who would be more inclined to infer guilt on the basis of a defendant's refusal to testify.

Yet Ted, better practiced because of his experience, ultimately dominated the process and got the jury he wanted despite the fact that Destiny managed to include two blacks.

The jury *was* San Francisco. With the two young black males sat six whites, four women aged from 28 to 64 and two older men. There was a Korean woman, an older Japanese man, a middle-aged Mexican man and a young Brazilian woman of mixed heritage. Seven of the jurors had attended some college, while only three had earned degrees.

Throughout the trial, the jurors had been attentive and compassionate, at times given to smiles and laughter. While their careful attention to Destiny's questions and inferences indicated their respect for her serious demeanor, it seemed they liked Ted better for the droll style and confidence he had acquired over the years.

Ted's summation, delivered over a period of 90 minutes, seemed especially persuasive to the jury. In it he described Walter Monroe as a troubled, desperate man who, losing his wife to illness, was deathly afraid of also losing Lynette, his lover of 6 years and possibly the mother of his child.

He characterized Monroe as "a man who can't realize when he's lying to the rest of us because first and foremost, he's lying to himself." He detailed the affair Walter had with Christine Epps and pointed to his denial of the affair, a denial despite the fact that he had fathered a daughter by Christine, as proof of the assertion.

He portrayed Walter's reluctance to come forward as *indicative of guilt* and declared that Walter's fleeing San Francisco in the month after the murder suggested,

"...guilt beyond any reasonable doubt. An innocent man would have stayed. A true friend to Lynette would have come forward."

He called Walter's story a fabrication vainly purposed to save the legacy and reputation of a dying man.

"Because of his deteriorating heath, your guilty verdict won't be sending Walter Monroe to prison. He'll live out the rest of his life in a hospital. But your guilty verdict will be sending a message, a message that none can escape the law. You'll be sending a message that eventually, in one way or another, murderers must pay the price for their misdeeds."

Ted spent 40 minutes of his summation going over evidentiary items, mainly the significance of the blood trail and the DNA findings, which placed Walter in Lynette's bedroom on August 17, 1986. In closing, Ted detailed his theory about how and why Walter murdered Lynette. In irony, he borrowed from Destiny's closing from 14 years earlier. In closing Ted asserted that Walter, insecure and maniacal,

"...not unlike Othello, *threw away a pearl richer than all the tribe*. Tragically, in his deeply-troubled mind, he murdered her so he wouldn't lose her."

Thus calling again for a guilty verdict, Ted thanked the jury and sat.

Destiny's closing argument focused on motive, and more specifically the lack thereof. She quoted the mayor in describing Walt as an honest, devoted and caring human being. She said he was Lynette's friend, that any insinuation about anything between them other than friendship was completely unfounded, that Lynette, by all accounts, was a woman of integrity, that the State's attempt to besmirch and adulterate a dead victim's reputation was cruel and unconscionable.

She said the prosecution invented the affair in order to establish a motive.

"Simply put: no affair, no motive, no motive, no case."

She said the trail had in effect proved Walter Monroe right for not coming forward.

"He had no proof other than his word. If you don't believe him now in spite of the fact that he really has nothing to gain by telling the story, what makes you think anyone would have believed him then? It's like he answered Mr. Waters during the cross-examination. He did not want his wife to die alone while he sat in a jail hoping someone would believe his story."

Yet she said he had finally come forward at the end of his life and had done the right thing. He told the truth, a truth completely consistent with the facts of the case.

"He's finally given us the last few pieces to a puzzle that has baffled and bewildered us all for almost 15 years. The murder of Lynette Alexander has been a mystery for all this time. Justice was never served. It's only now, after Walter Monroe's painful testimony, that we know for certain who killed Lynette, and it wasn't Walter Monroe."

Finally, she reminded the jurors of an instruction, which indicated that, in the event of two possible conclusions that can be reached on the evidence—one that points toward guilt, and the other that points toward innocence—the defendant, in this case Walter Monroe, should be presumed innocent, entitling him to a verdict of not guilty.

In his rebuttal, Ted reiterated that 1) Walter murdered Lynette; 2) He fled San Francisco, assumed an alias and went into hiding; 3) He sought to leave the country to escape justice when he was implicated by his daughter; 4) He fabricated the story about Jordan suddenly appearing at the bedroom door to mitigate the fact that DNA experts positively concluded that it was his blood in the bedroom, in the hallway, on the stairs and along the trail outside the house; and 5) Despite his physical condition, it was the jury's duty to convict Walter Monroe for the first-degree murder of Lynette Alexander.

After Ted concluded, Judge Gerry Garcia went over detailed jury instructions, taking the time to be thorough. He commended the jurors for their patience with delays, forbearance with the cameras and sequestration and thanked them for their service. Finally, he instructed them to retire to the chamber to elect a foreperson and begin deliberations.

A guard from the jail went to CNN with the information, and within 24 hours, the story was on the front page of every major paper and the first news story on every station. The guard indicated that on the night before Walter Monroe agreed to testify, Philip Alexander, the brother who Jordan ousted from the top spot at Alexander Enterprises, secretly went to the jail seeking to cut a deal to induce the former city councilman to testify.

Editors speculated that Philip probably assured Walter that if he testified, and his testimony led to Jordan's conviction, which would be a conviction nonetheless, the company would be obligated to pay the reward to his daughter. In short, it was a no-lose proposition for the former city councilman.

If Walter testified and the world believed him, Jordan would ultimately be prosecuted and convicted, and Karen would get the five million dollars. If Walter testified and no one believed him, then he himself would be convicted and Karen would get the five million dollars, based on the information she had already provided.

According to the company's offer, the reward would be paid to anyone who provided information that led to the arrest and conviction of Lynette's murderer or murderers. Thus by testifying, Walter gained the opportunity to clear his name, make his daughter five million dollars and, if his testimony was believed, the opportunity to bring Lynette's murderer to justice. To the delight of the media the world over, the story just kept turning, kept twisting and growing more convoluted.

After five days of deliberation, the jury foreperson, one of the older men, called Judge Garcia to inform him that the jury had reached a unanimous verdict. Reacting quickly, the judge called the defendant and lawyers back, though he decided to convene the court on the following day in order to accommodate media requests for the necessary delay.

Thus at 10 a.m. on the last Friday of August, those around the country who had followed the Lynette Alexander saga sat fixed before television sets. In offices, many others watched the proceedings on computer monitors through a live feed on the Internet. All the early morning shows featured lawyers and legal analysts who discussed everything from the judge's name to jury tampering.

The courtroom that morning was awash with excitement. The spectators and reporters arrived first, so the earliest stories detailed who was on hand to witness the verdict in person. Allegra was there, Caitlyn and Denver were there, and a much older-looking Peter Granucci was there. Cameras panned on various others, including Karen Epps, retired judge Helen Morgan, Federal Judge Brett McPherson, Titus Coffee, Jayne Alexander, Bryan Osaka, Roscoe DuBois, Barry Divine and other recognizable personages.

Ted Waters and Chester Douglas arrived next, smiling for their audience, poised and confident about the upcoming verdict. Destiny came next, accompanied by a guard who handled Walter Monroe's wheelchair. Stern and serious, she sat at her table and began writing. Then came Judge Gerald Garcia, somber for the cameras, though throughout the trial he always loosened up when they weren't running.

Taking up the mallet, he tapped the gavel.

"This court will come to order."

Upon his instructions, a bailiff went out to get the jury who walked into an eerily silent, though crowded room. Nervous about all the suspense and attention, the jurors scrambled for their assigned places and sat. When the twelve were settled, Judge Garcia spoke in their direction.

"On the matter of *The People of the State of California verses Walter Monroe*, has the jury reached a verdict?"

The older man stood.

"We have, your Honor."

"Wait!"

The female voice startled everyone in the courtroom. She shouted again.

"Wait! I can't let this happen! I've got something to *say*!"

Judge Garcia tapped the gavel to still the murmurs and whispering. He slid his glasses up his nose to examine the young woman standing in the gallery.

"Young lady, the jury's already reached a verdict in this matter. The trial's over."

"But don't you want the truth? Isn't that what all this is supposed to be about? What I have to say is very relevant to this case."

Judge Garcia paused, uncertain about how to proceed. From the corner of his left eye, he could see the camera moving to get a close up.

"Who are you? What is your name?"

"My name's Lyndsey Alexander. Lynette Alexander was my mother."

Angry, Ted interrupted.

"I'm sorry, your Honor. But I'm going to have to object here. The trial is *over*. This isn't Perry Mason or some John Grisham movie. It's a public trial, so whatever she has to say, she can say it later in the proper forum and at the proper time. The jury has already reached a verdict in this matter."

Judge Garcia looked from Ted to Lyndsey and then toward Walter Monroe in the wheelchair.

"This court will be in recess until I have taken the opportunity to privately hear what Ms. Alexander has to say. After that, I'll make a decision on whether or not the jury will hear any of the information she discloses to me. If the jury has to reconsider the entire matter, so be it."

Sighing, Ted spoke up.

"Once again, I really have to object here, your Honor. This is completely irregular and out of order. We don't want to do it, but we're going to have to move for a mistrial if you allow this to alter the verdict."

Insulted by the challenge, the judge became angry.

"Your objection is noted and your motion is denied, Mr. Waters. This court stands in recess."

CHAPTER 53

"Ladies and Gentlemen of the jury, on very rare occasions in the course of a trial, an independent witness comes forward with information so vital to the question at issue that it would be improper, indeed it would be a travesty not to admit it."

Judge Garcia looked up from his notes, panning the jurors' faces.

"I realize you've already come to a verdict, but now I'm asking you to set that verdict aside. I'm asking you to hear the testimony of Ms. Alexander and to reconsider your decisions after weighing in whatever relevant new evidence you believe she's provided for you."

His eyes dropped again to his notes.

"My decision to proceed in this manner was not an easy one. Obviously, Mr. Monroe's health was a major factor in my mind. The court could, as Mr. Waters suggested, simply not consider her testimony and let her say her piece 'in a later forum at a later time.' But the fact of the matter is Walter Monroe wouldn't be around for that. For him, this is the moment of truth."

He directed the bailiff to bring the witness in.

"What's going to happen here is this. Ms. Alexander will sit, I'll question her on the matter and then Mr. Waters and Ms. Mitchell will have the opportunity to cross-examine her and re-close if either side so decides."

Lyndsey wouldn't look at anyone as she entered the courtroom and approached the stand. Her eyes were fixed straight ahead. She didn't dare look at her sisters, her Uncle Barry or Grandmother Jayne, afraid she might lose resolve. As she sat, she glanced toward Destiny and half-smiled. Eyes held low, she drew a troubled breath as she prepared for the questions.

"My first question to you, Ms. Alexander, is why have you waited so *long* to come forward with this information?"

She blinked back the tears in her eyes.

"Because I, because I've been confused about this thing."

"Can you explain that?"

She sighed, trying to be strong.

"All my life, I've felt guilty. I've felt guilty for everything. My sisters are blonde and look alike, but I've always looked different, and the family always made me feel I *was* different. They blamed my mother. There was always the suggestion that she had gone out and cheated on my father, that I was the result of an affair of some kind, they've all made me feel guilty about it."

"And you don't feel guilty any longer?"

"No. For a long time I hated my mother. Deep inside, I felt that when she was murdered, she got what she deserved. I believed she was the person who had made my life so miserable."

"And you don't feel that way anymore?"

"No, not after I discovered the truth."

"What truth, Ms. Alexander?"

She glanced toward her sisters and began.

"Well, a big part of the problem my family had with me was that they thought I looked part-black. They thought I had black features. I heard it so much I even started believing it. I believed my mother had gone out and slept with a black man and I was the result."

"And is that the truth?"

"No."

"How do you know that?"

"Because recently I had some testing done. Destiny, I mean Ms. Mitchell, helped me. We had a lab perform DNA testing on me. I showed it to you."

"Yes. And what did you find out?"

Lyndsey, who had been clutching a file folder of documents in her right hand, held it up briefly.

"Well, Ms. Mitchell had a copy of my father's DNA sequence from some testing her team did in 1986, and the lab compared them."

"So what were the results?"

"The genetic tests confirmed that Jordan Alexander is my father. My mother was never unfaithful to him. The reason I look part-black is because my *father* is part-black. *All* the Alexanders are part black, even my blonde haired sisters. My grandmother Dottie—her grandmother was a black woman, an African. Dottie's mother passed herself off as white in the late 1800s. I've got the proof right here."

She was crying. While Caitlyn and Denver seemed in shock, Barry nodded, smiling.

"And my poor mother! She was innocent. She was murdered for something that wasn't her fault."

Judge Garcia handed Lyndsey a tissue and gently posed another question.

"What do you know about the night of August 17th, 1986,

Ms. Alexander?"

Lyndsey found Destiny's face and spoke toward to her friend.

"My sisters were sleeping. We were all sleeping, but I woke up. I thought I heard my mother's voice screaming, so I got up and sat by the door, peeking out the crack. I could hear some commotion in the room. I heard a man's voice."

"And then what happened?"

"He came out. He had a big knife in his hand. He was wet. He was red—all covered with blood."

"Who? Who was it?"

"I was only five years old. I didn't make the connection. I didn't know why he was covered with blood. I thought he was hurt. I thought he was bleeding, so I opened the door."

She daubed her eyes with the already-soaked tissue, and swallowed.

"I remember it so vividly now, the look in his eyes when he saw me standing there."

She seemed to be gazing at a horrible specter directly before her through glazed-over, tear-filled eyes.

"I remember I smiled and said, 'Daddy, what are you doing?'"

Suddenly, she stopped crying and became calm, her face blank.

"And he, he said, 'This is all *your* fault, Lyndsey! Get back to bed!"

Judge Garcia, a little choked up himself, looked around the room and saw that Allegra, Jayne, Destiny, Caitlyn and Denver as well as many others in the courtroom were also crying.

"And what did you do?'

Lyndsey sat back in the seat, re-composing herself.

"I went back to bed, and until today I've never said anything about it."

Judge Garcia, moved, looked over toward Ted Waters and Chester Douglas, as if to dare a response.

"Your witness, Mr. Waters."

Ted looked at Lyndsey, at the other pained faces in the room and then at the jury.

"We have no questions, your Honor."

"Ms. Mitchell."

Destiny was sobbing, her face buried in her palms.

"Nothing."

CHAPTER 54

Jordan drove slowly along the northbound 101, still haunted by the sound of her strained, broken voice. His cell phone began ringing for the fourth time since he left, and once again, he didn't answer. Rolling down the window, listless, he tossed the phone out onto the highway. Steadying the steering wheel with his left hand, his right hand fumbled to uncork the half-full cognac bottle he held between his legs. Already drunk, he took a big mouthful of the 40 year-old *eau de vie*, too numb to savor the flavor.

He and Stephanie watched the trial on television, watched Lyndsey come on and tell the world her father, Jordan Alexander, had murdered her mother, Lynette. And he noticed immediate changes in Stephanie's behavior after Lyndsey's testimony. He heard the nervousness in Stephanie's voice. He knew she was at last convinced of what she suspected all along. Things would never be the same between them.

He watched daughters Caitlyn and Denver crying on television. Both seemed devastated. He could never face either again. And Lyndsey, the thought that she was his flesh and blood all along! He had been so cruel to her! And grandmother Dottie was one-quarter black!

Finally, he thought of Lynette. He thought about how many times she swore to him that she'd been faithful, about how many times she pleaded with him to trust her, to believe her. He thought about the anger, the accusations, and the violence.

Then the gruesome scene flashed before him, an episode he had blocked from his memory for over 14 years. His mind had found a way to do it, had found a way to reconcile the horror of the night with a part of his consciousness that was still in denial, a part of his soul he left behind when he went to her house that night.

The memory had become surreal. It never happened; it was nothing more than a disturbing movie he remembered from many years before. As he pictured Lynette's face, his guts turned watery and his heart sank, aching with regret.

He stopped at what he figured was the mid-point and, turning off the engine, he pounded his head on the steering wheel, crying.

"Oh God! Nettie, I'm sorry!"

Bottle still in his hand, he took another mouthful and emerged from the car, looking out into the blue sky. He saw the sun, he saw the ethereal, wispy clouds hanging on nothing, he saw birds rising and falling on billows of air. Their lives were short and simple, but those birds were free. Crying, he took another swig. He remembered the ten months he spent in the jail cell. It was the darkest period of his life, and the thought of ever going back was too terrible to imagine.

Taking a deep breath to relish the briny air, he walked toward the afternoon sun, climbed over the barrier and then onto the ledge. By this time, other cars had stopped, causing a minor traffic jam. Some honked their horns to get his attention, but he didn't hear them. He only heard the breeze, the birds and the sound of his name the way Lynette said it.

"I'm sorry, Nettie."

Loosening his fingers, he let the neck of the bottle slip from his grasp and watched the crystal flask tumble three times and disappear on its way down. Then, closing his eyes, he took a deep breath to achieve a state of calm before leaning forward. He didn't struggle as he fell toward the buzzing hypnotic blue and he wasn't afraid. In fact, he was thinking of Lynette at the very moment the side of his head smacked the water. His skull exploded, tainting the ocean with blood and particles of brain matter. When the coast guard arrived five minutes later, the gulls had already descended on the body and were fighting over scraps of tissue they had ripped from his corpse.

The news of Jordan's suicide fall from the Golden Gate Bridge saddened many in the city, including some of the people who had been his most vocal and severe critics.

Roscoe DuBois wept before news cameras, describing Jordan as a "lost soul who had sinned, but he was worth savin." He called on blacks in the city to begin the healing process by extending sympathy to those saddened family members who Jordan left behind. Destiny and Allegra found Lyndsey, and the three cried together.

Even Walter Monroe, hospitalized, his health deteriorating, felt touched by Jordan's death. His head was bowed in prayer when Philip arrived unannounced and settled himself in the chair next to the bed.

"How's it going, Walt?"

"I've been better. Sorry about your brother."

Philip smiled.

"Thank you. Well, we're all sorry about that. It's a tragedy."

Terminal illness had taught Walter to be direct.

"So why are you here? You must want something."

Philip sighed.

"No, Walter. I'm actually here because I've got some bad news for you."

"What is it?"

Philip hesitated before continuing.

"It's about the reward. Now, this is going to sound like a technicality, but according to the offer, the company agreed to pay only in the event of a *conviction*. With Jordan dead, that doesn't seem likely. I'm sorry, but five million dollars is a lot of money. The company's not about to just give it away, especially where the family name and reputation are involved. And then there's the reputation of the business. Five million dollars has got to buy us *something*."

Walter had risen up in the bed.

"You're a bastard! You're a no good bastard."

"I'm sorry you feel that way, Walter, but our lawyers think we have pretty good grounds to challenge your daughter if she makes it an issue."

He stood to leave, winking.

"So tell her to be smart. Tell her to save her money, because we can afford to spend a lot more on lawyers than she can."

The court stood in recess for seven days in order to allow grieving friends and family members the time to attend the funeral. When the court was reconvened, Judge Garcia offered both the prosecution and the defense an opportunity to re-close before the jury in light of the new testimony provided by Lyndsey Alexander. Ted, at length conceding, declined the offer, asserting the State stood by "everything argued prior to Ms. Alexander's testimony on her version of the evening."

"Fuck you, Ted."

Walter Monroe's loud declaration caught the entire courtroom off-guard. The CourtTV personnel on hand were at a loss about how to handle the outburst. Judge Garcia, removing his glasses, addressed the defendant.

"Now Mr. Monroe, I realize you're ailing, but this court isn't going to tolerate—"

Walter interrupted.

"Fuck you too, Judge! I'm dyin. I've had it with *all* of you!"

By this time, Destiny was standing, trying to calm the older man.

"Let me go, Destiny. I've had it with all of these folks and their bullshit attitudes! I *knew* it would be like this!"

He stared toward the jurors with contempt.

"What're you looking at? I did it! All right. I swear I'm going to kill somebody up in here! Let me go!"

Destiny got in his face, speaking sternly.

"Stop it, Walter! Just stop it! You're blowing everything we've worked so hard to achieve. Stop! Just close your mouth! Okay!"

Tears streaming down his eyes, Walter slumped in the chair, silent and shattered, while the entire courtroom of spectators, media personnel, Karen Epps, Ted, Chester, Destiny, Judge Garcia and the jury stared at him in confusion and disbelief.

Three days later, the jury informed the judge that it had reached a verdict, and the court was set to reconvene the next morning.

Few news commentators knew what to make of Walter's outburst in court, though some were quick to speculate that perhaps "the Walter we all saw that morning may have been the same Walter Lynette saw on the night of August 17th, 1986."

In the aftermath of Jordan's suicide, no one knew what to make of his rationale. Miserable, had Jordan taken his own life as a result of the ugly story his youngest daughter told about him? Was it true? At five years old, was her recall reliable? Did he kill himself because he discovered he was part black? Were he and Walter still both in on it? With Jordan dead, many questions would never be answered. So at 10 o'clock that morning, the twelve arrived. After days of deliberation, the jury had come to render their amended verdict.

"Has the jury reached a decision?"

The foreman stood.

"We have, your Honor."

"Very well."

A bailiff walked the written decision to the judge who read it, winced and handed it back. When the form was returned to the foreman, the judge nodded.

"What say you?"

"In the matter of the *State of California verses Walter Monroe*, on the crime of murder in the first degree, we the jury find the defendant guilty, in violation of Penal Code Section 187, as charged in count one of the Information."

The courtroom erupted in equal parts of exhilaration and disappointment. The prosecution and its supporters stood excited, embracing, while defenders of Walter Monroe remained seated. Right after the decision was read, many of the reporters made beelines for the door to set up first-hand descriptions of the verdict and reactions throughout the room for viewing audiences at home.

Yet through all the noise came the sound of Judge Garcia's gavel, purposed to restore order to the courtroom. Destiny could not look at Ted or Walter. She only leered in disgust at the ignorant jury that had just convicted an innocent man of murder in the first degree. What a bunch of idiots! Tears in her eyes, she turned toward her client.

"I'm so sorry, Walter."

He smiled weakly.

"You did an outstanding job, Destiny. It wasn't your fault. It's all right."

Several of the jurors participated in press conferences soon after the decision was read. The foreman, an older white man, insisted the jury made the right decision, referring to California jury instruction 2.81, which addressed credibility, *You are not required to accept such an opinion but should give it the weight, if any, to which you find it entitled.*"

Lyndsey's testimony, to him and several colleagues, was highly suspect. He said she didn't impress him as a believable person. Other jurors admitted that the decisive factor for them had been Walter's angry outburst in court. Some legal pundits argued the prosecution had gotten its jury and the cards had been stacked all along. Yet others believed the sequestration failed and the trial was tainted by publicity from fourteen years earlier. They believed the jury acted on information that had never been presented in the courtroom.

Later that night, as Destiny sat next to Walter's hospital bed, filling in for Karen who had flown down to San Diego to retrieve some of her father's personal belongings, there was a knock on the door. Waking up, Walter called out.

"Come in."

The door opened and Philip Alexander walked in. He seemed uncomfortable on seeing Destiny sitting there. Still, he approached the bed and extended his hand toward Walter, smiling.

"Well Walter, they *warned* me to be careful with you. They said you were smarter than the rest of us, but I didn't believe them."

He reached inside his jacket pocket and pulled out a legal-sized envelope, extending it toward the older man.

"Here you are."

Unable to resist the suspense, Destiny interrupted.

"What is it?"

Philip placed the sealed envelope in Walter's hands.

"It's a draft for five million dollars. Seems there *was* a conviction in the Lynette Alexander murder case after all. Congratulations Monroe. In losing, you and your daughter won, but somehow I think this the way you *planned* it all along. Good luck."

CHAPTER 55

The teacup before each guest had been placed no more than an inch and a half over the front edge of the adjoining tatami straw mat. In a line before Destiny and Bryan knelt Suziko and Shizuo Yokohama, his sister and brother-in-law. Next to his sister was Destiny's best friend Kiyomi, then Bryan's parents Ichiro and Sadako Osaka, Aunt Harumi from Toyoko and Harumi's daughter and her daughter-in-law. The ceremony was irregular for American-born Japanese, and this time even Sadako resisted in her way, but Ichiro insisted on the ritual following the wedding of his only son.

On that warm afternoon there seemed to be a content and appeased spirit in the gazebo. There was the peaceful scent of jasmine incense in the air as streaks of warm sunlight filtered through the ceiling and slanted diagonally toward the floor. The soulful and hallowed sound of the bamboo flute played by the older man who squatted near the door lent completion to the ceremony.

Bryan wore a traditional black suit, not unlike the one Ichiro wore 49 years earlier on the day he married Sadako in Japan. Destiny wore a special-made silk red kimono that Sadako ordered from a friend in Yokohama, and Suziko made up her face in the traditional fashion. Nervous about the custom and rites that accompanied such a ritual, Destiny's hands were unsteady as she poured the first cup of steaming ceremonial tea.

After the trial was over, Destiny resumed her position of director of the *Aegis* foundation. The publicity about the trial proved beneficial to the foundation and its cause, resulting in larger donations and expansion into other cities.

Walter Monroe was never taken into custody. Instead, he was taken to a hospital, where he would live out his last days, his daughter, grandson and Destiny beside him.

An hour after the jury's decision, Destiny received a telephone call from U.S. Army General Charles Covington, who congratulated her for doing "an impressive job." After so many years, her ex-fiancé wanted to make peace with her.

She was flattered by the gesture, until he mentioned he might be asked to run on the Republican ticket as a vice-presidential candidate. Knowing Charles, he sought peace only to eliminate the possibility of Destiny making unfavorable statements about him to the press. Unwilling to give him the peace of mind, she insisted that, if asked, she'd tell the truth, but she also told him he should be more worried about his association with Rikki Thomas.

"Now *she's* a political liability, but rumor has it that your wife doesn't want to give her up."

When Lyndsey's other grandmother and sisters began making her feel guilty about her father's suicide, Destiny suggested therapy. Over time, Lyndsey began to understand the shortcomings of her family and to forgive them. She took Destiny as a surrogate mother and embraced her recently-discovered mixed heritage with great pride.

Because Kiyomi was eight months pregnant, Lyndsey was Destiny's maid-of-honor at the September wedding, but Destiny insisted she remove the stud from her tongue during the service. Allegra, who finally had the truth about what happened to her daughter, retired from the foundation, seeking a relationship with her other two granddaughters, Caitlyn and Denver, and her great grandchildren.

The first cup was poured for Suziko, who bowed and presented a chocolate-brown felt pouch that Destiny opened excitedly. Bowing, she thanked her new sister-in-law, whispering under her breath.

"*Arigato*"

Destiny held the thick herringbone 24-carat gold chain high for all to see before putting it on. Shizuo presented an envelope to the couple, which contained valuable stock in his family's company. Kiyomi, true to her prankish nature, gave her best friend two 24-carat gold diaper pins. Ichiro and Sadako Osaka presented the couple with a deed to the property adjoining theirs and matching gold tennis bracelets. Harumi's daughter and daughter-in-law bestowed a gold pen set to Destiny and gave Bryan a jade ring.

And then Destiny finally came to Aunt Harumi. As their eyes met, both remembered their first encounter with a degree of embarrassment. Through their manner and body language, both Destiny and Harumi indicated profound regret for past offenses.

Filling the teacup, Destiny bowed low.

"*Doomo Sumimasen.*"

Harumi smiled, speaking in English as she bowed.

"No. I judged you without knowing you. Please forgive *me*."

She presented a red silk pouch to her favorite nephew's new wife, who emptied it into her shaking hand. It was a pendant in the form of intricate, stylized Japanese characters, glinting there in one of the rays of sunlight. Tears in her eyes, the new bride held it up.

"*Unmei!*" she exclaimed, reading the characters, and then she translated, smiling.

"Destiny!"

OTHER TITLES
AVAILABLE BY MARCUS MCGEE

FOUR STORIES
(Short Stories, 210 pages paperback)
Humorous collection of short stories

SYNCHRONICITY
(Short Stories, 245 pages paperback)
"The Club," "Anthropophagi" and other stories

SHADOW IN THE SKY
(Suspense thriller, 265 pages paperback)
Asteroid threatens Earth, Last year of life

THE SILK NOOSE
(Short Stories and essays, 217 pages paperback)
"Denouément," "On Niggers and Squirrels," and others

MURDER FROM THE GRAVE
(Suspense thriller, 421 pages paperback)
Berkeley professor-turned-SF police detective matches wits with a killer who wants to commit seven murders after he is already dead

Coming Soon:

SANITY SLIPPING
(Short Stories, @ 275 pages)
VIRAL VECTOR
(Suspense @ 375 pages)
Sequel to Legal Thriller

www.ingramcontent.com/pod-product-compliance
Lightning Source LLC
LaVergne TN
LVHW050914080826
845145LV00001B/83

* 9 7 8 0 9 6 7 3 1 2 3 8 5 *